1/20

Coming Back

Also by Jessi Zabarsky
Witchlight

Coming Back

Jessi Zabarsky

RH
GRAPHIC

NEW YORK

Coming Back was drawn on smooth Bristol board, with a
3H pencil and Kuretake disposable brush pens.
It was lettered in Procreate and colored in Photoshop.

Text, cover art, and interior illustrations copyright © 2021 by Jessi Zabarsky

All rights reserved. Published in the United States by RH Graphic, an imprint of Random House Children's Books, a division of Penguin Random House LLC, New York.

RH Graphic with the book design is a trademark of Penguin Random House LLC.

Visit us on the web! RHKidsGraphic.com • @RHKidsGraphic

Educators and librarians, for a variety of teaching tools, visit us at RHTeachersLibrarians.com

Library of Congress Cataloging-in-Publication Data is available upon request.
ISBN 978-0-593-12543-4 (hardcover) — ISBN 978-0-593-12002-6 (paperback)
ISBN 978-0-593-12004-0 (ebook)

Designed by Patrick Crotty

MANUFACTURED IN CHINA
10 9 8 7 6 5 4 3 2 1
First Edition

A comic on every bookshelf.

To everyone who has had to find a
truer story to tell about themselves

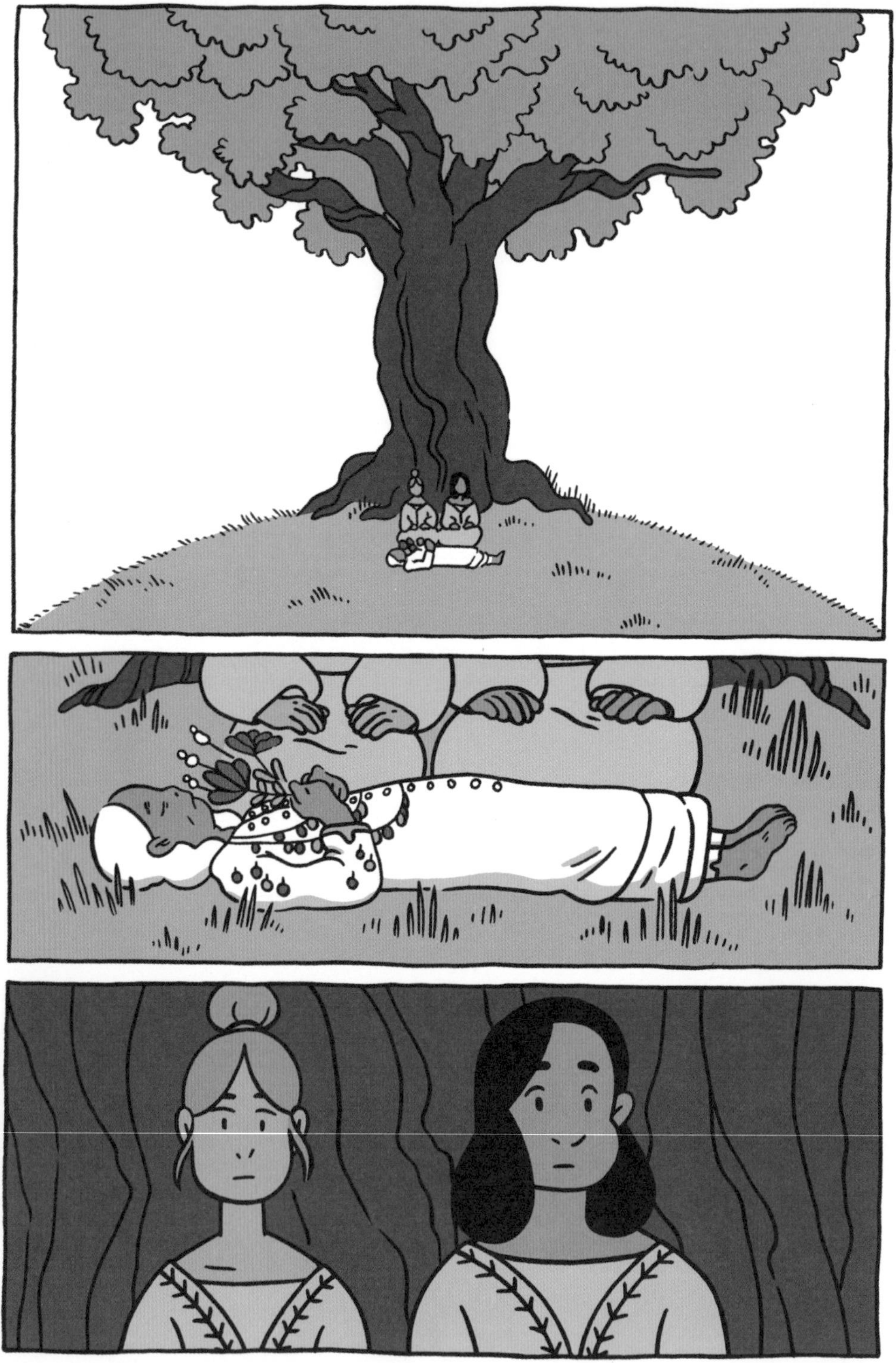

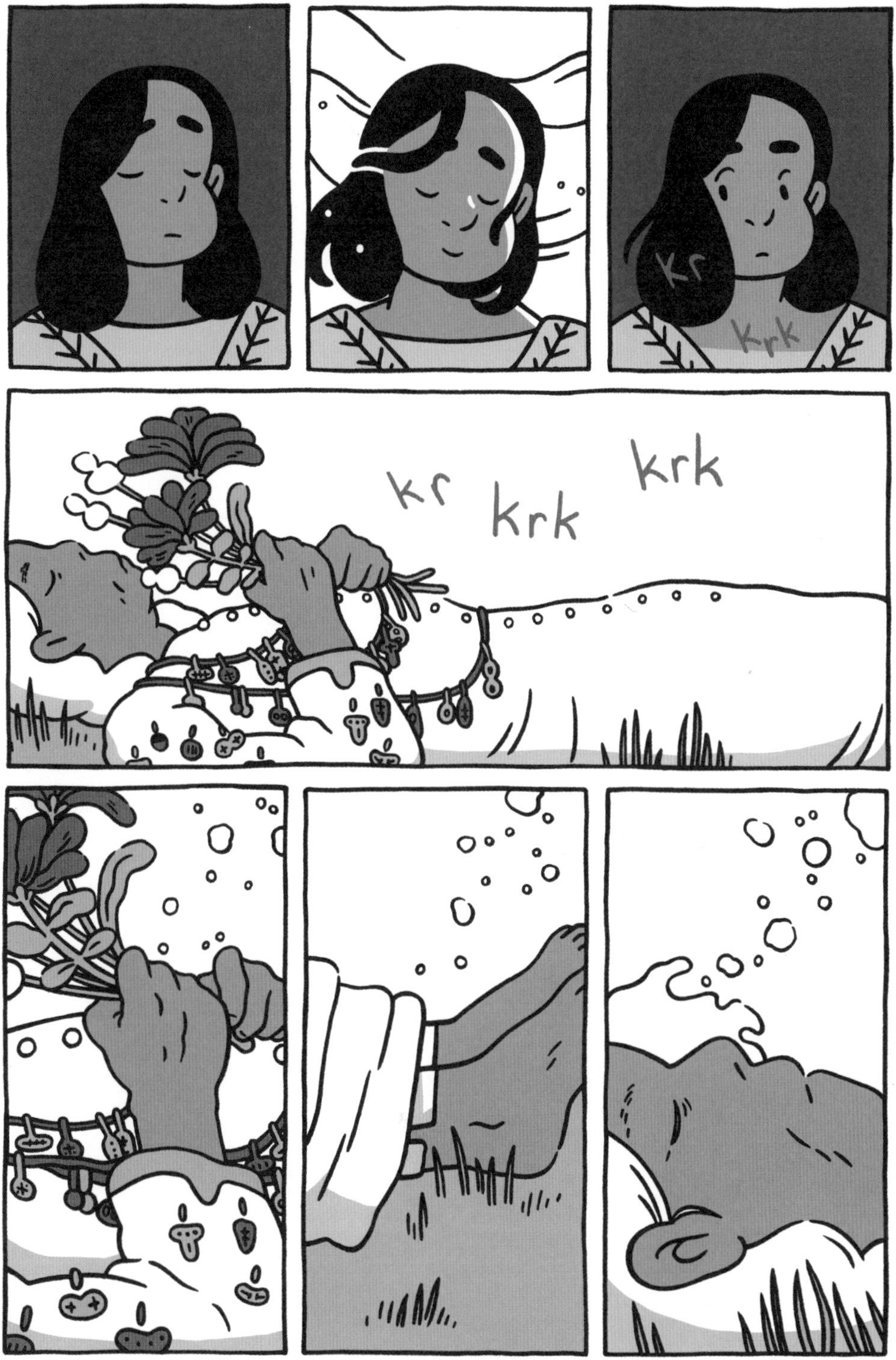
kr
krk
kr
krk
krk

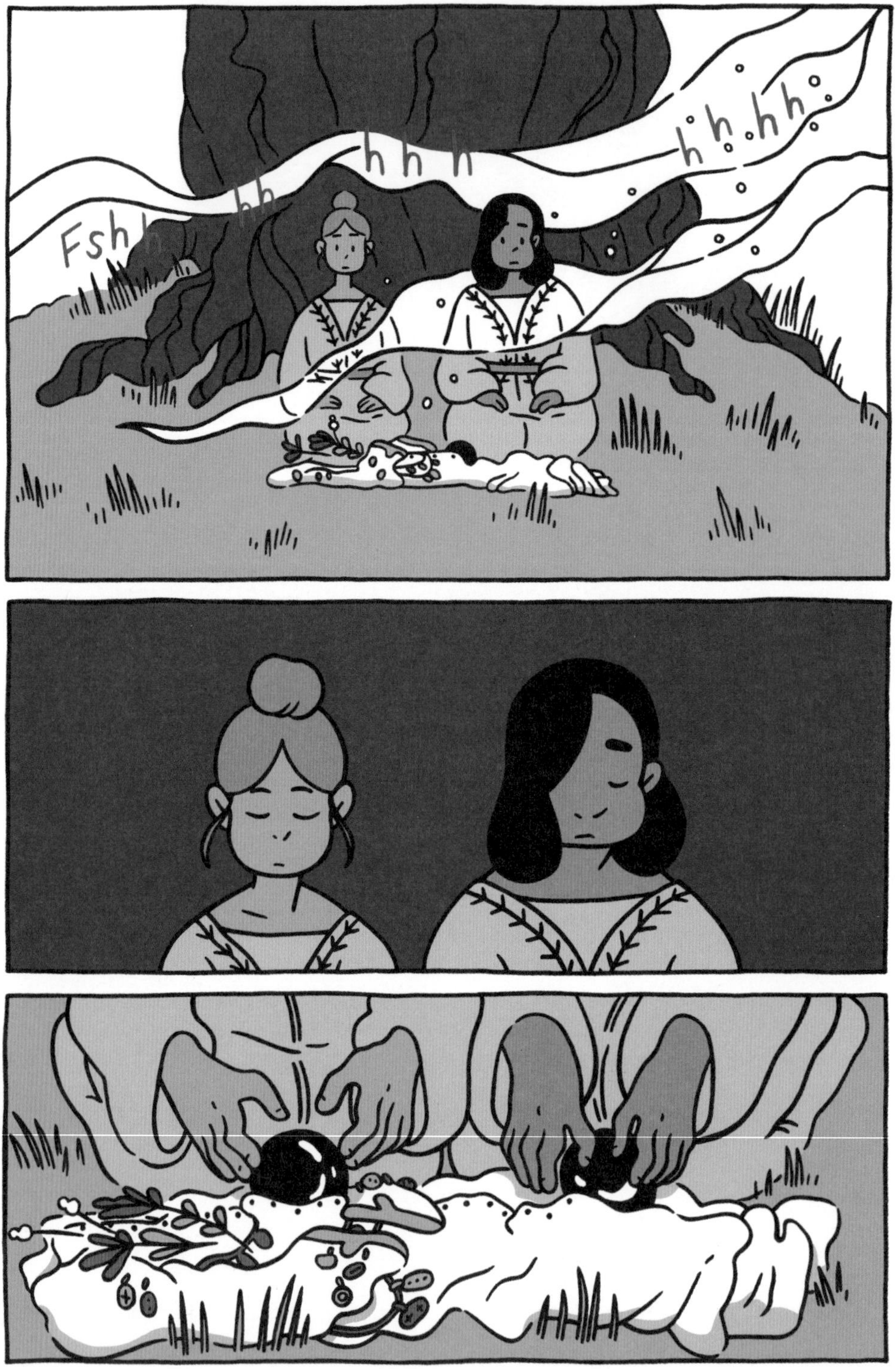
Fshhhhhhhhh.hhh

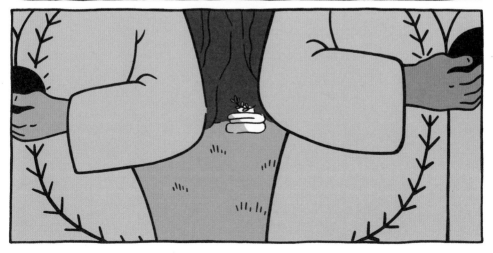

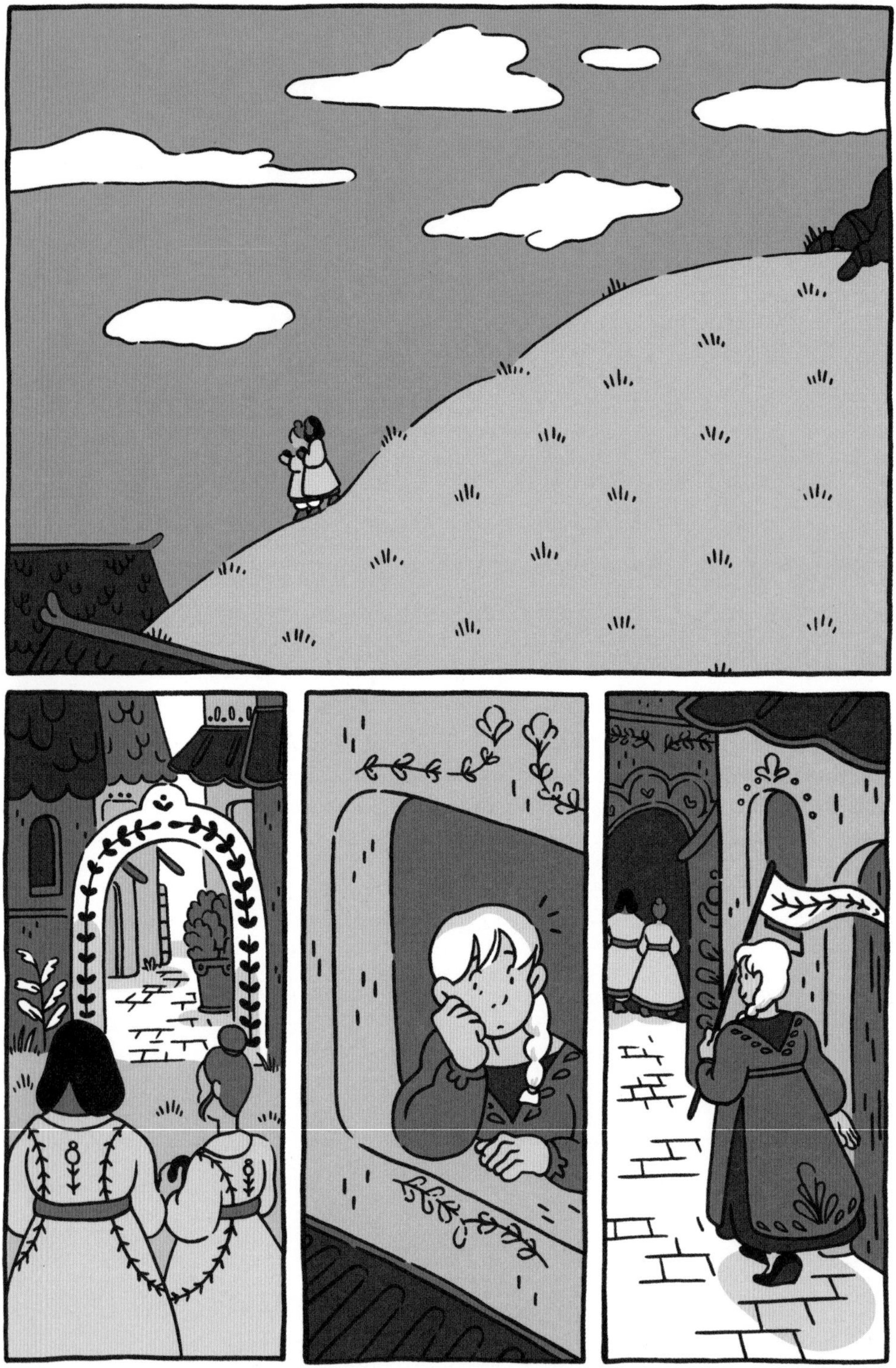

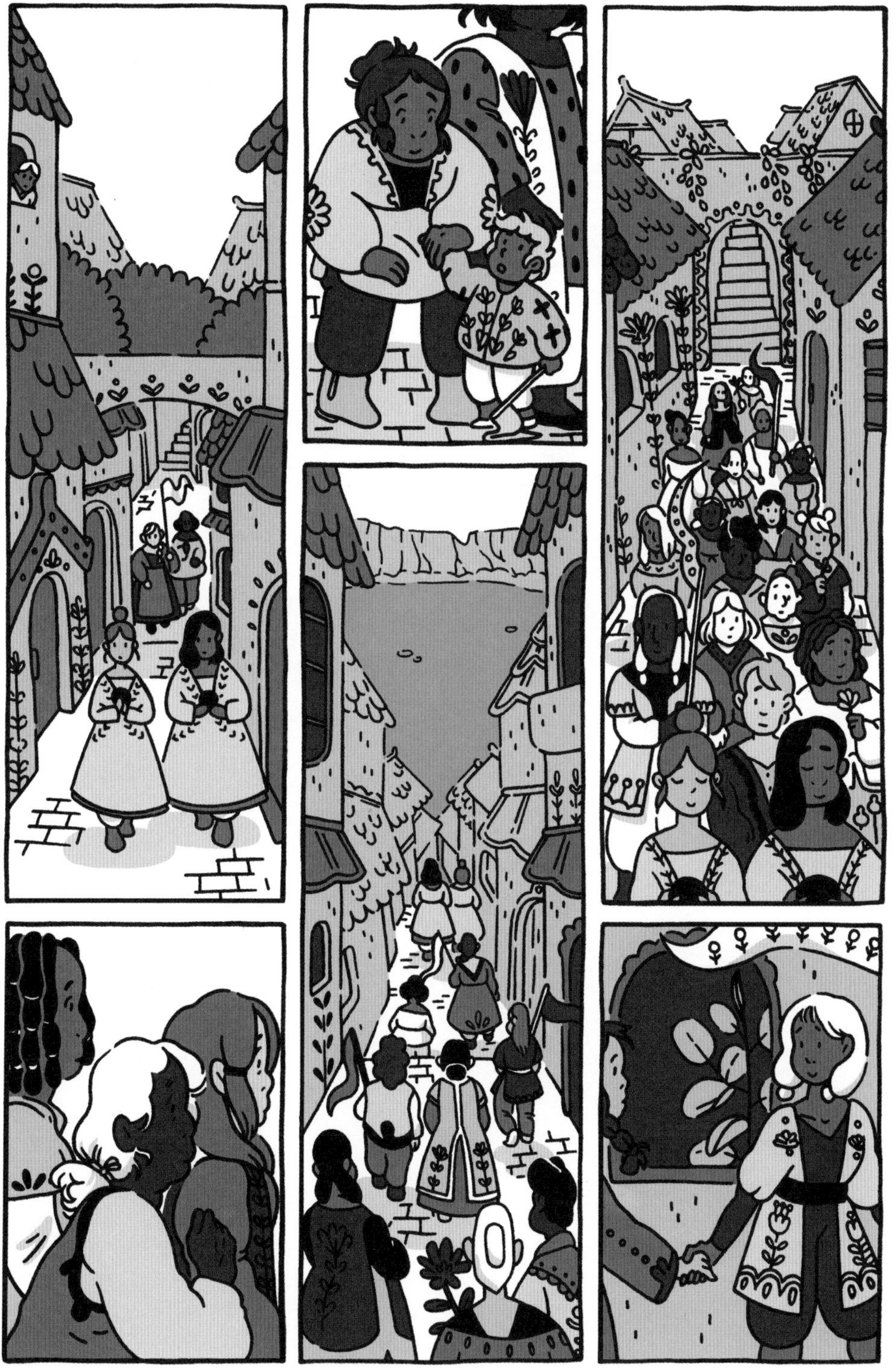

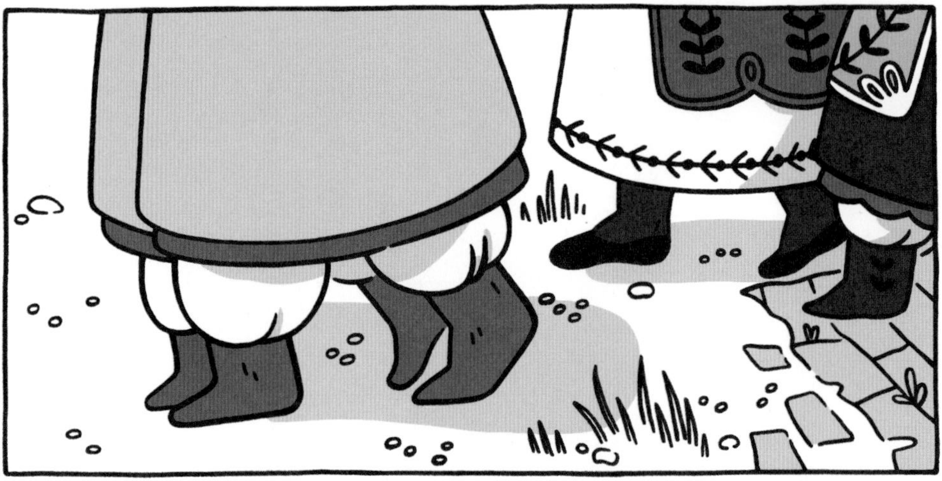

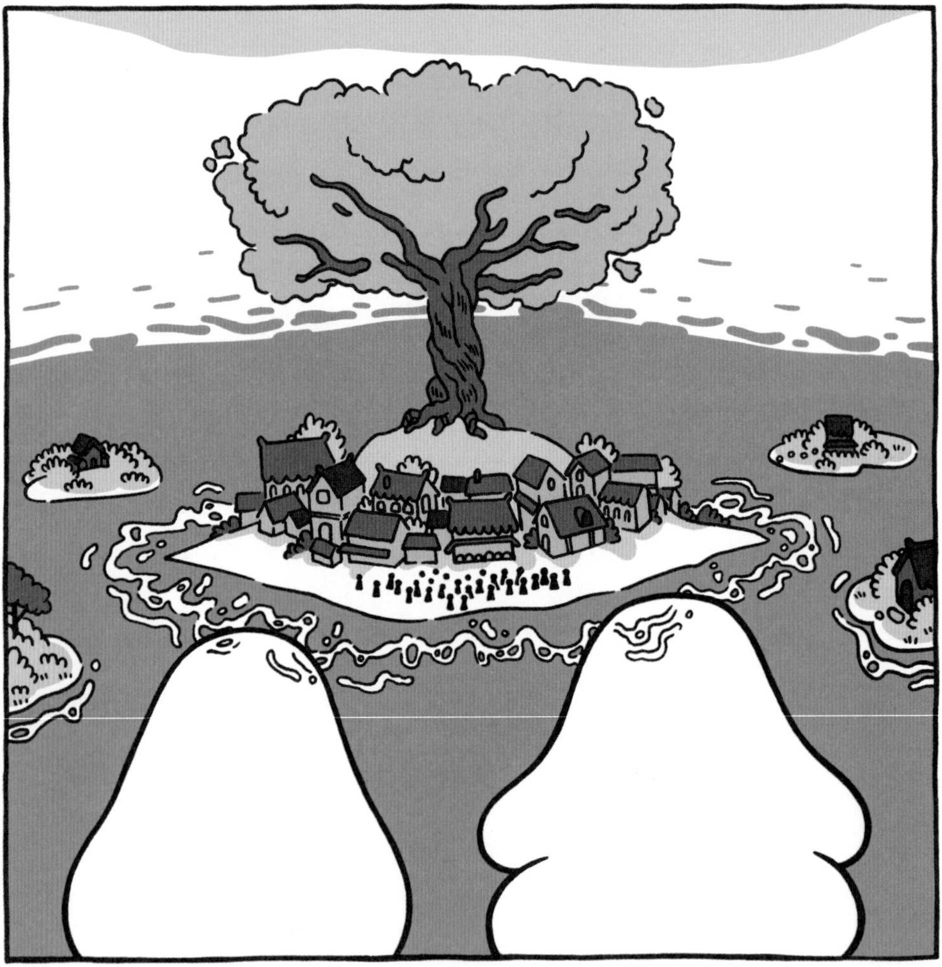

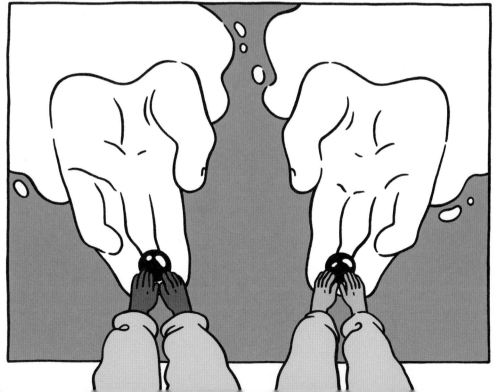

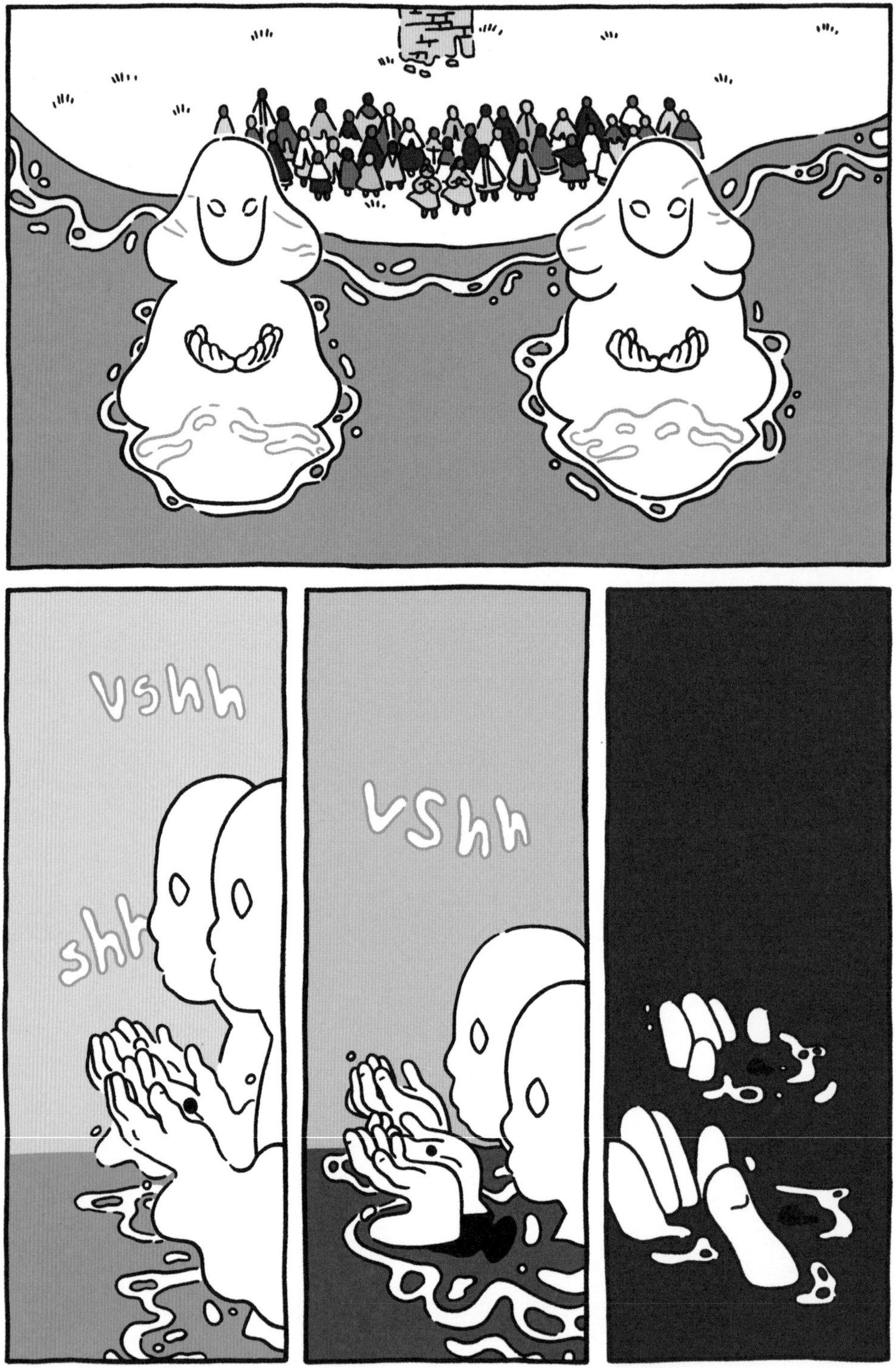
vshh
shh
vshh

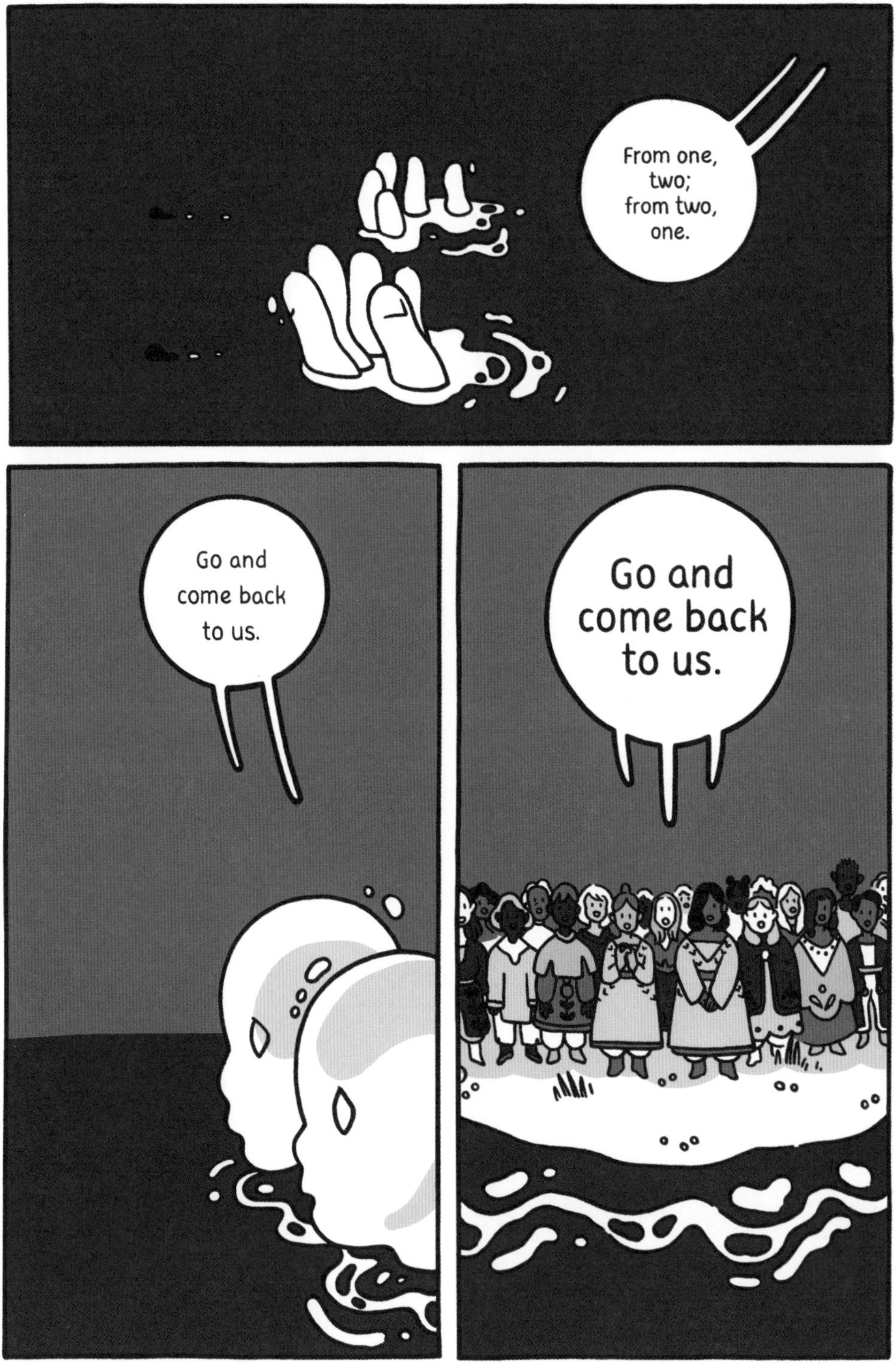
From one, two; from two, one.
Go and come back to us.
Go and come back to us.

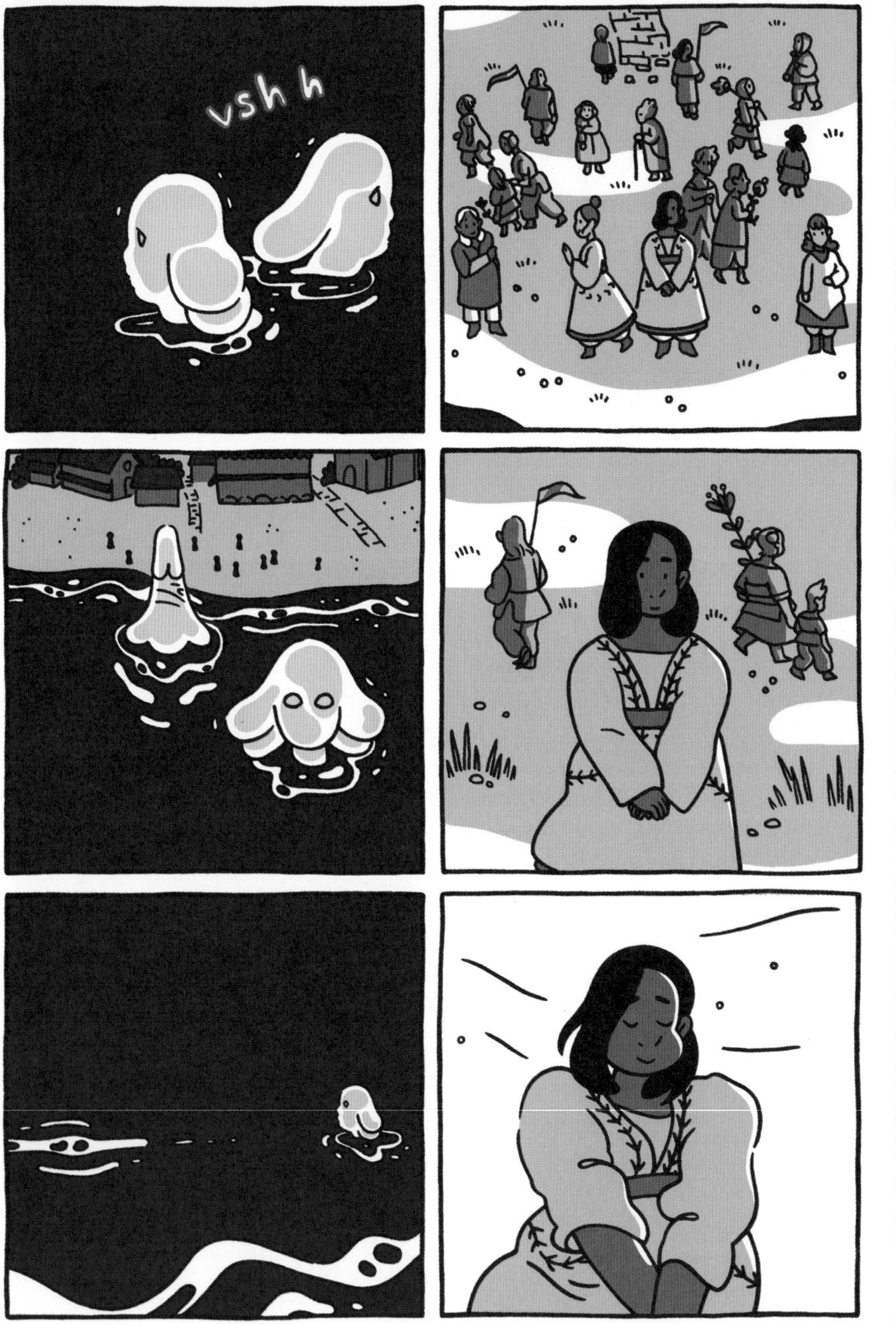
vsh h

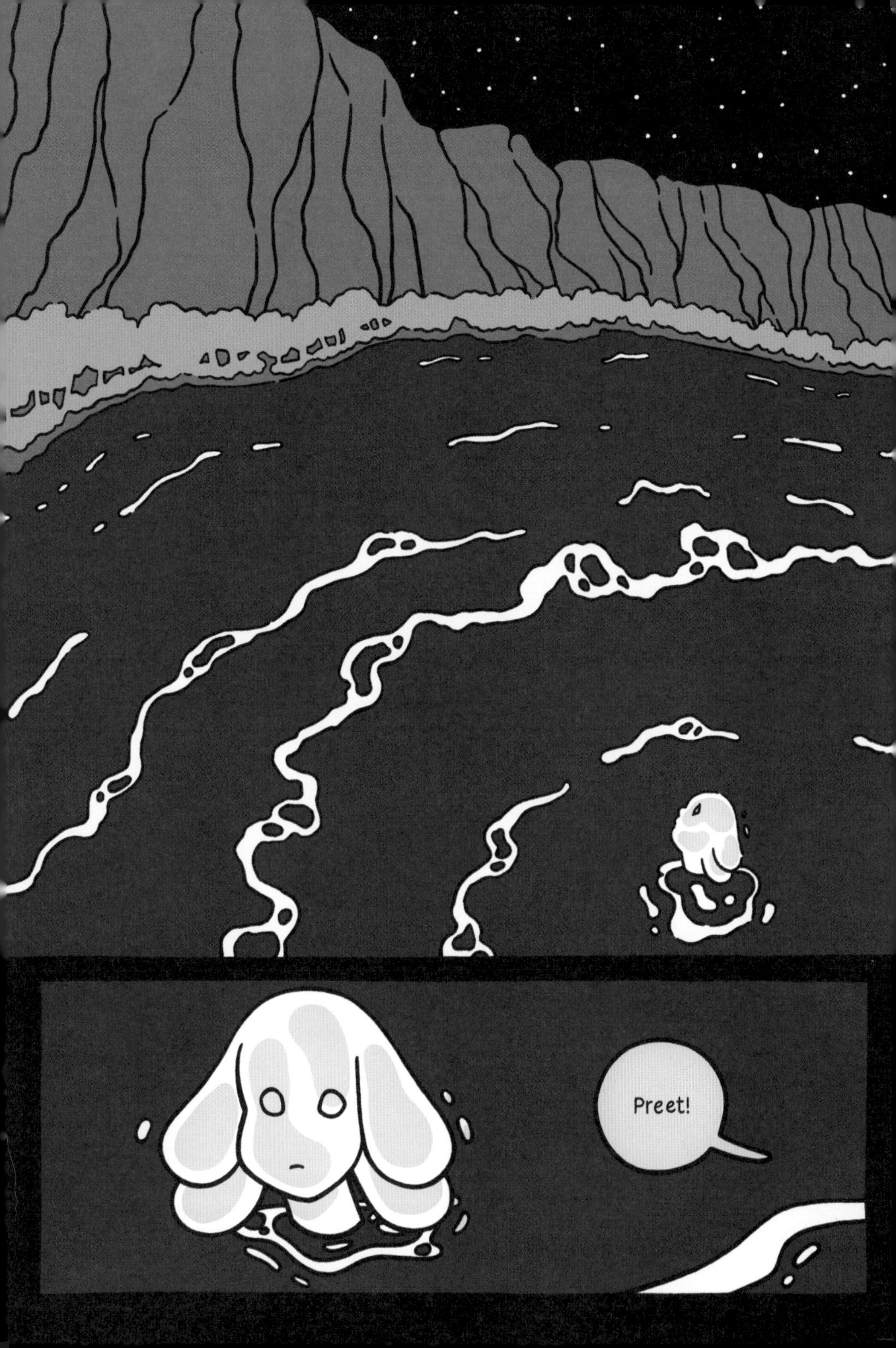
Preet!

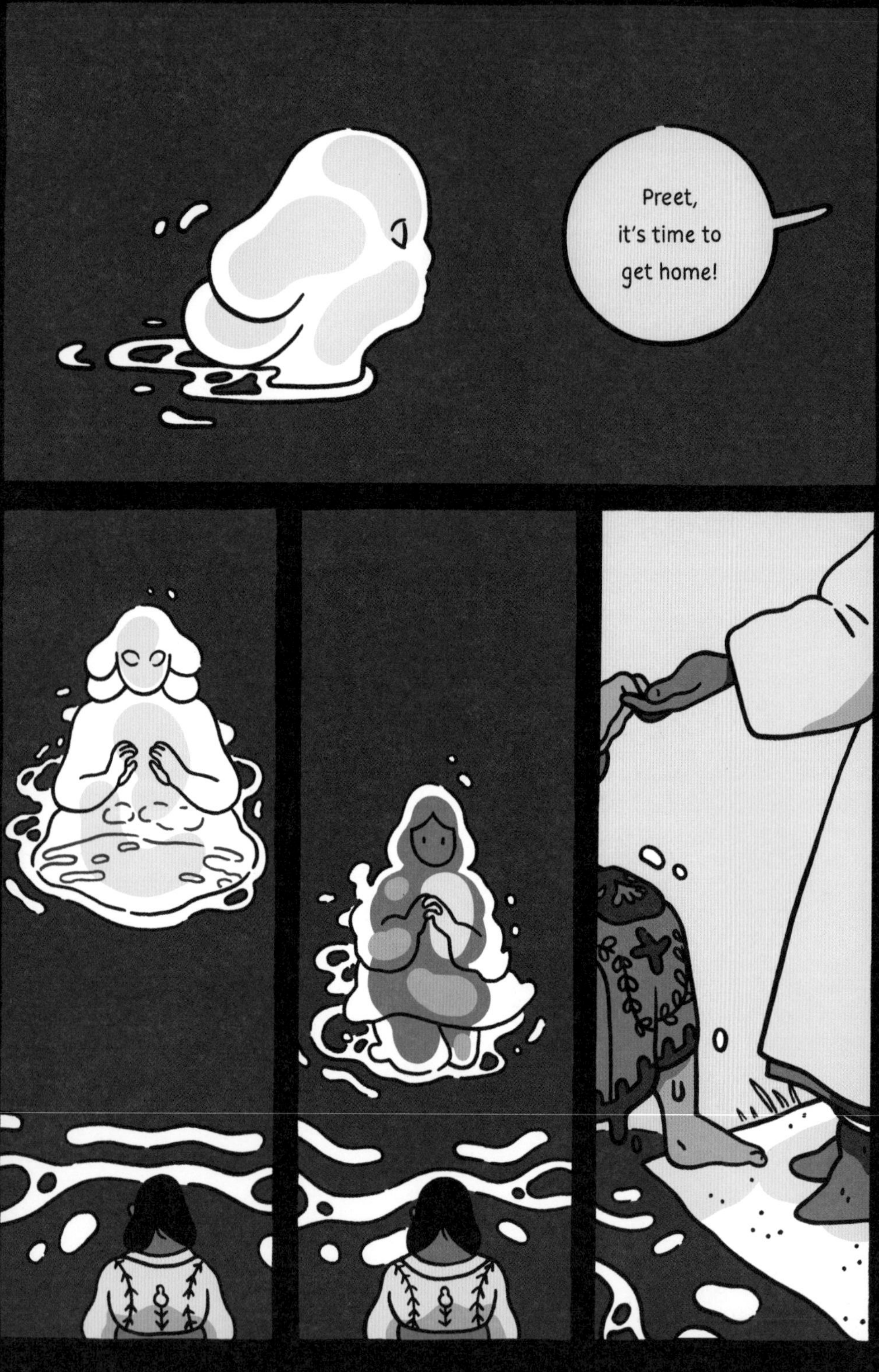
Preet,
it's time to
get home!

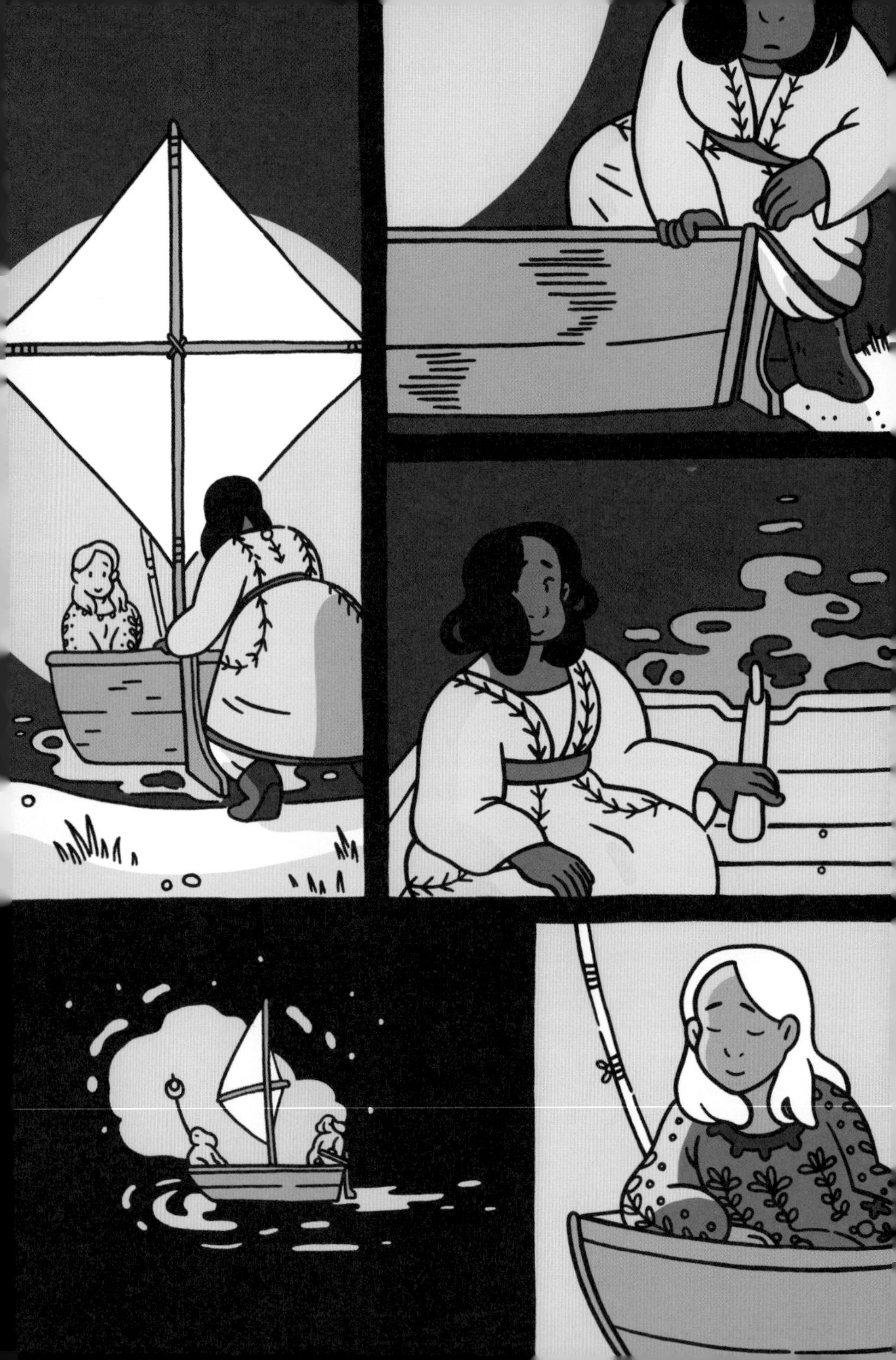

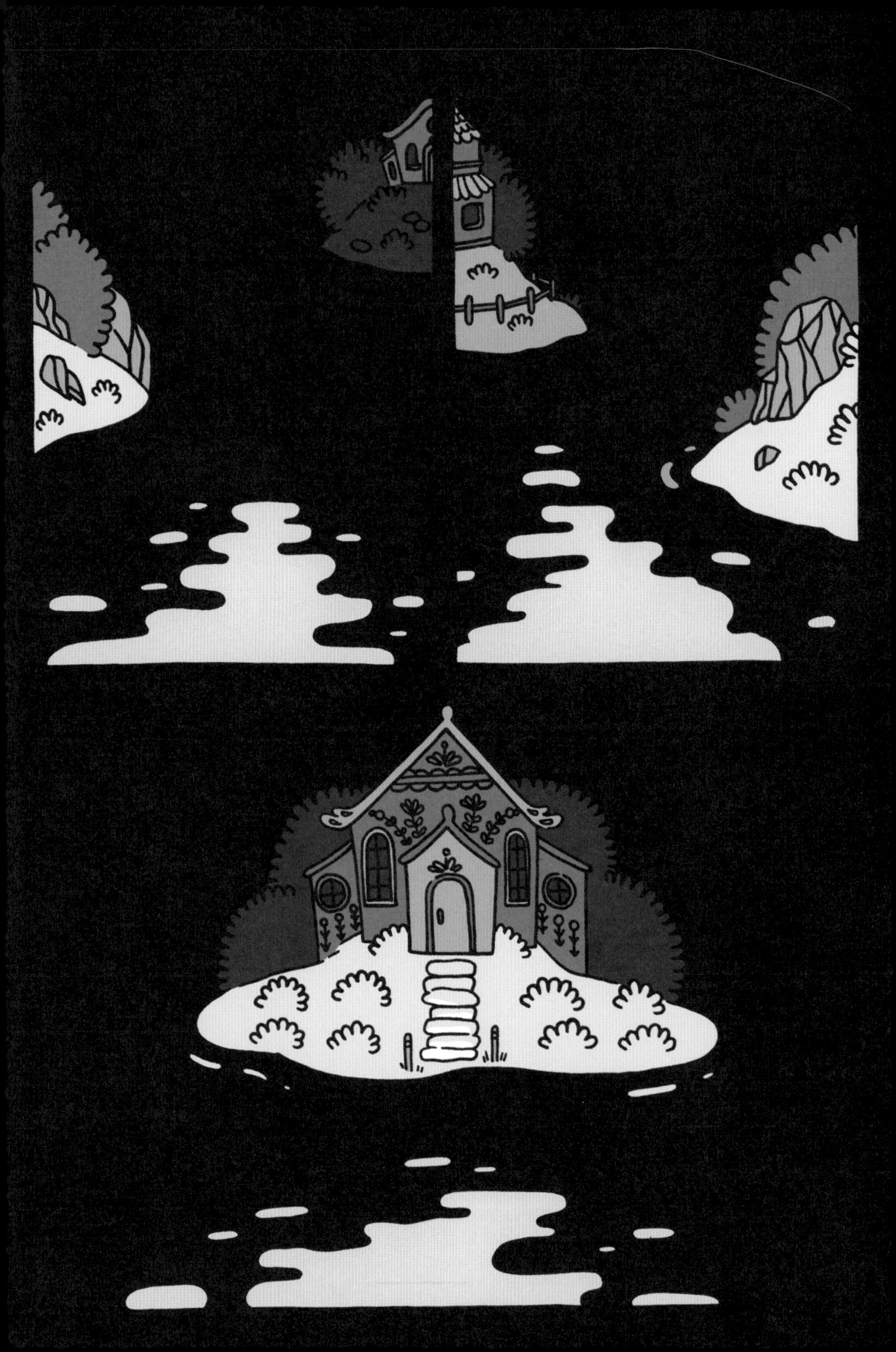

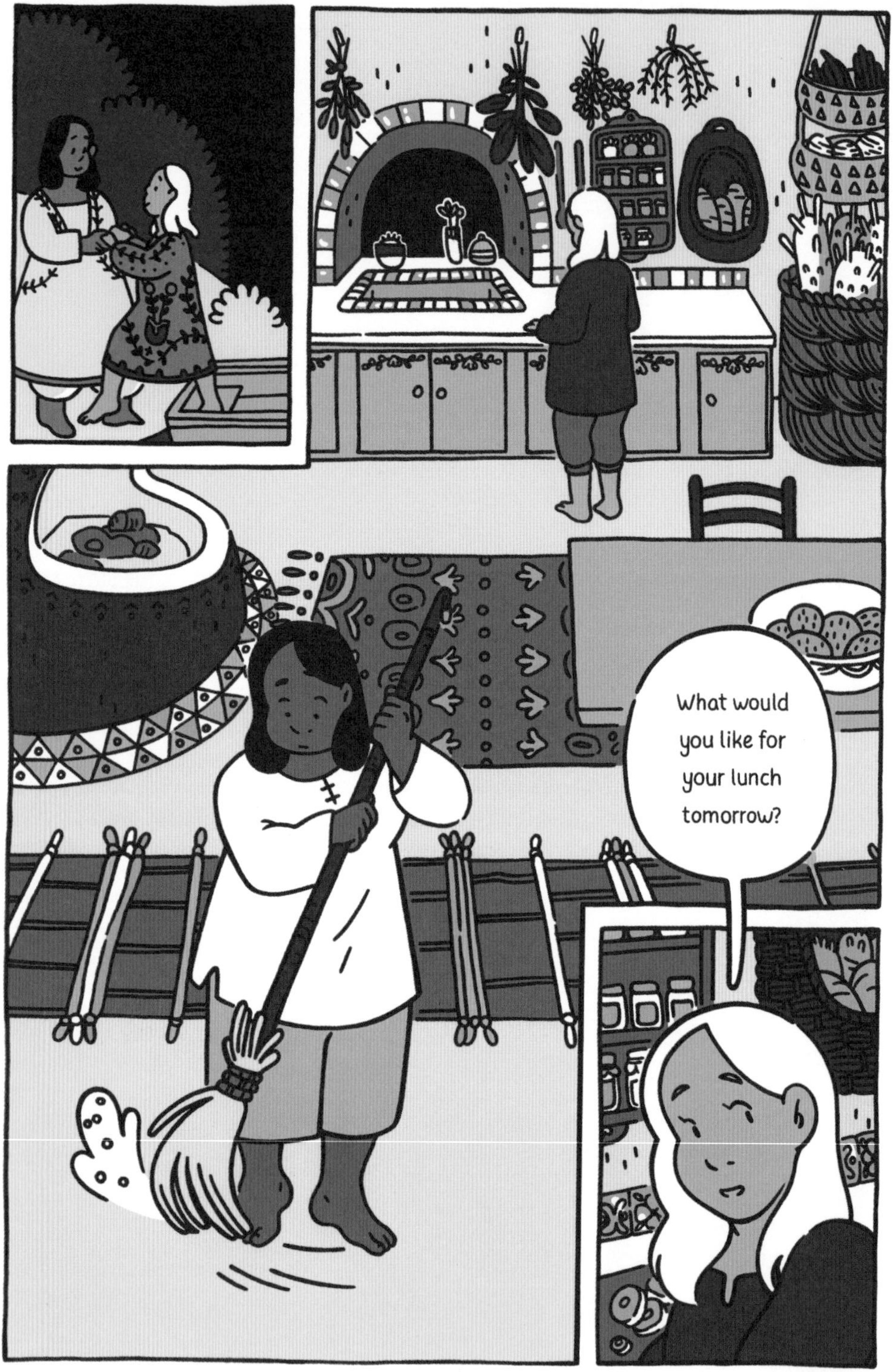
What would you like for your lunch tomorrow?

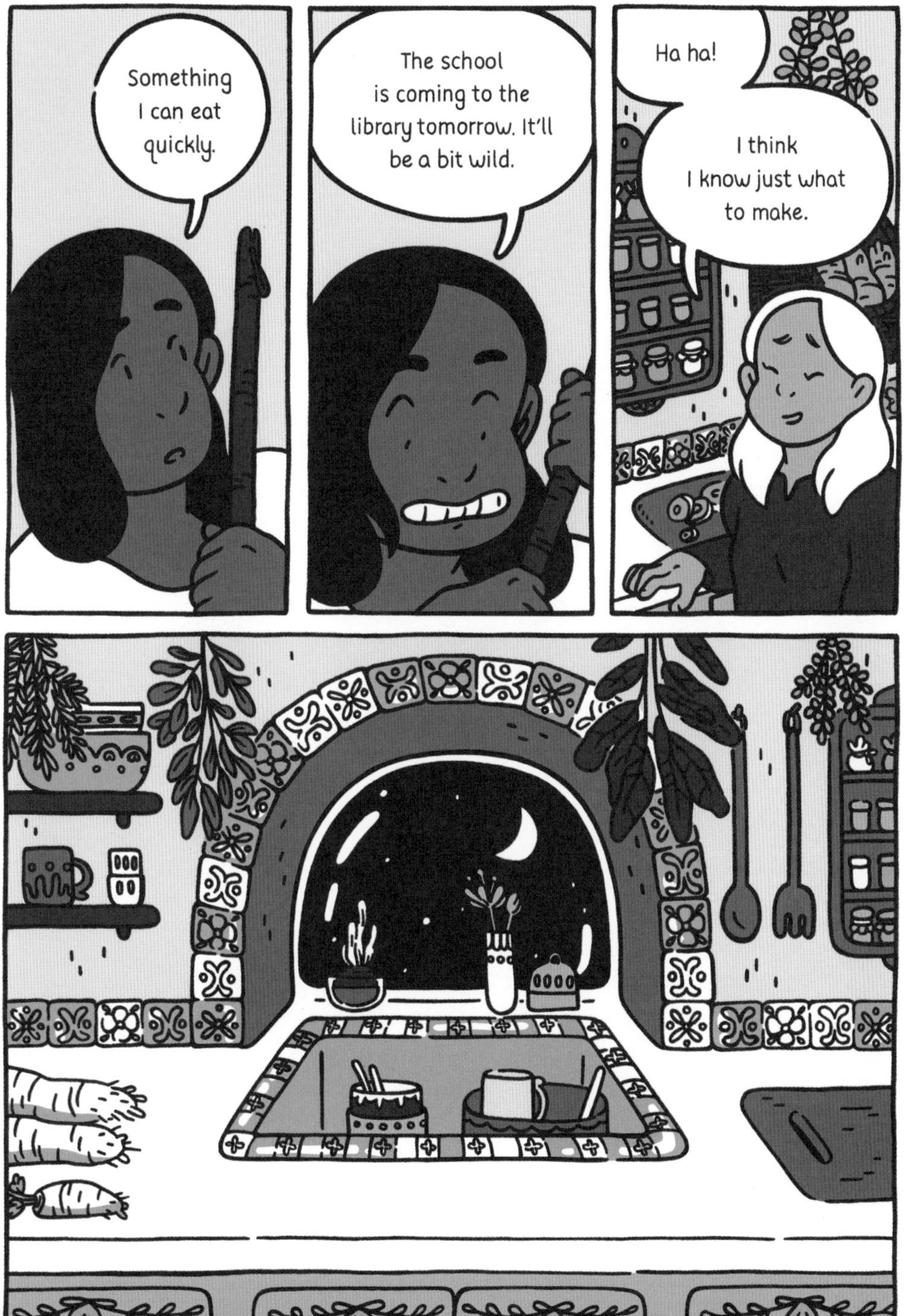
Something I can eat quickly.
The school is coming to the library tomorrow. It'll be a bit wild.
Ha ha!
I think I know just what to make.

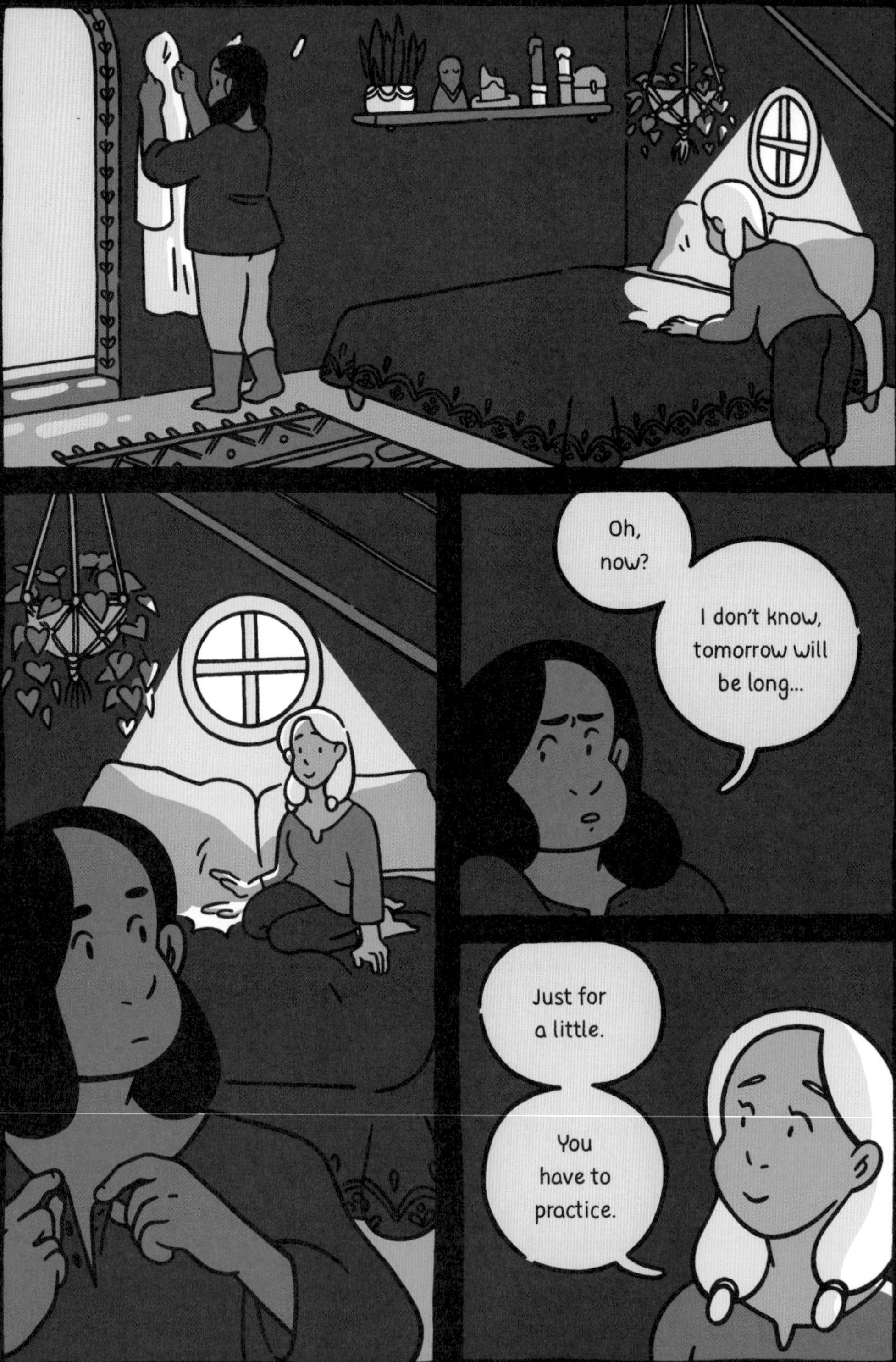
Oh, now?
I don't know, tomorrow will be long...
Just for a little.
You have to practice.

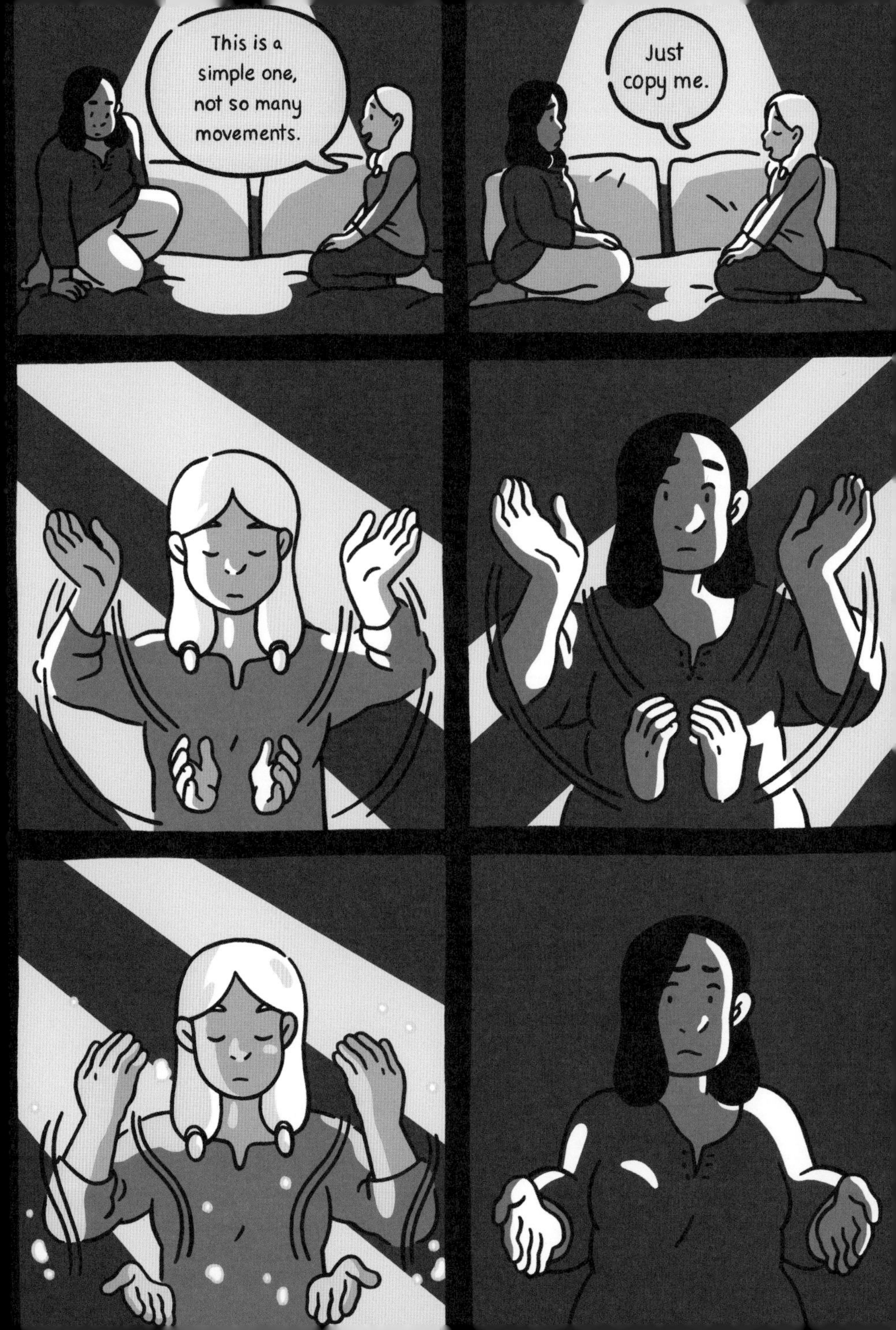
This is a simple one, not so many movements.
Just copy me.

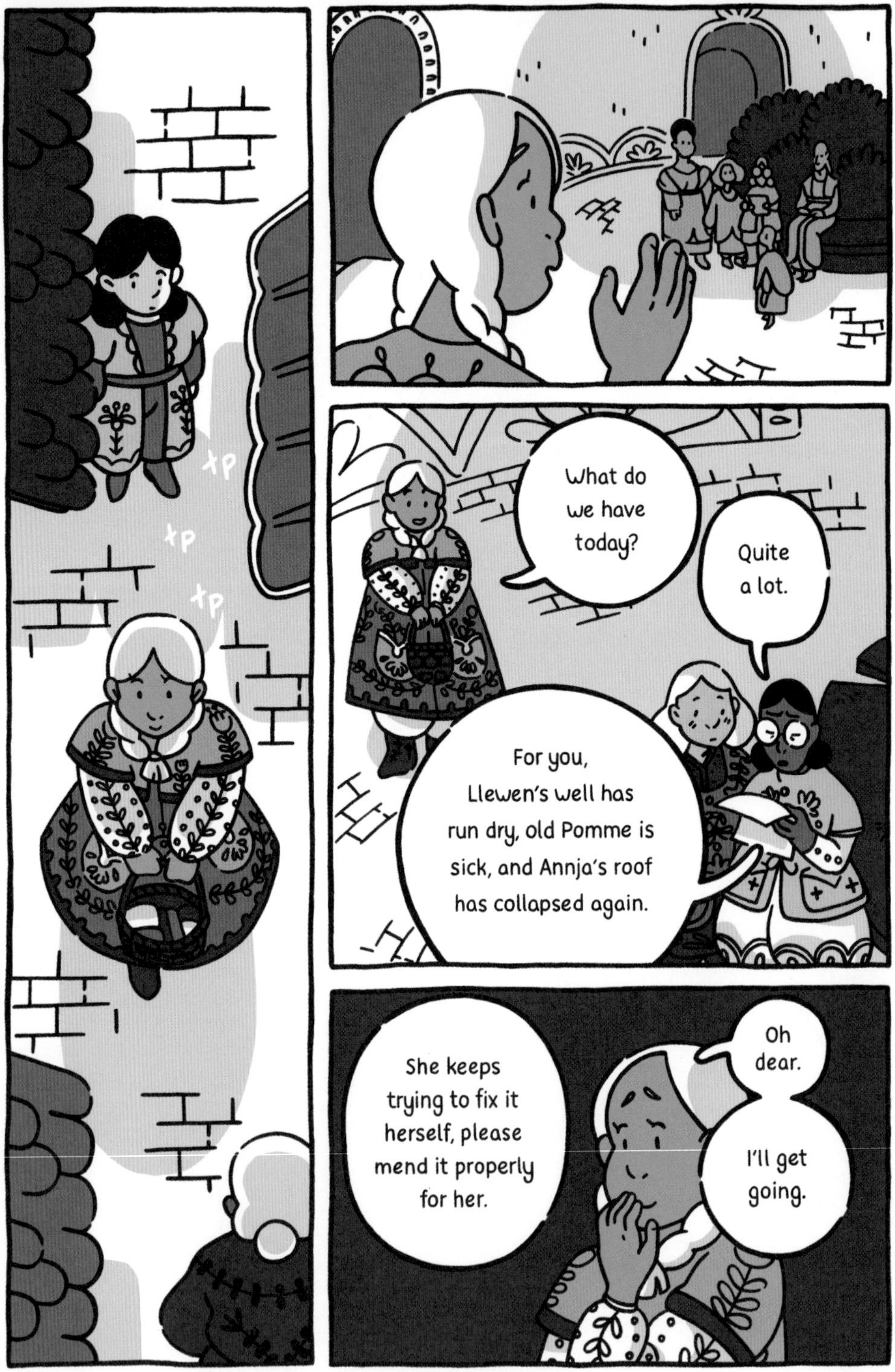

tp
tp
tp
What do we have today?
Quite a lot.
For you, Llewen's well has run dry, old Pomme is sick, and Annja's roof has collapsed again.
She keeps trying to fix it herself, please mend it properly for her.
Oh dear.
I'll get going.

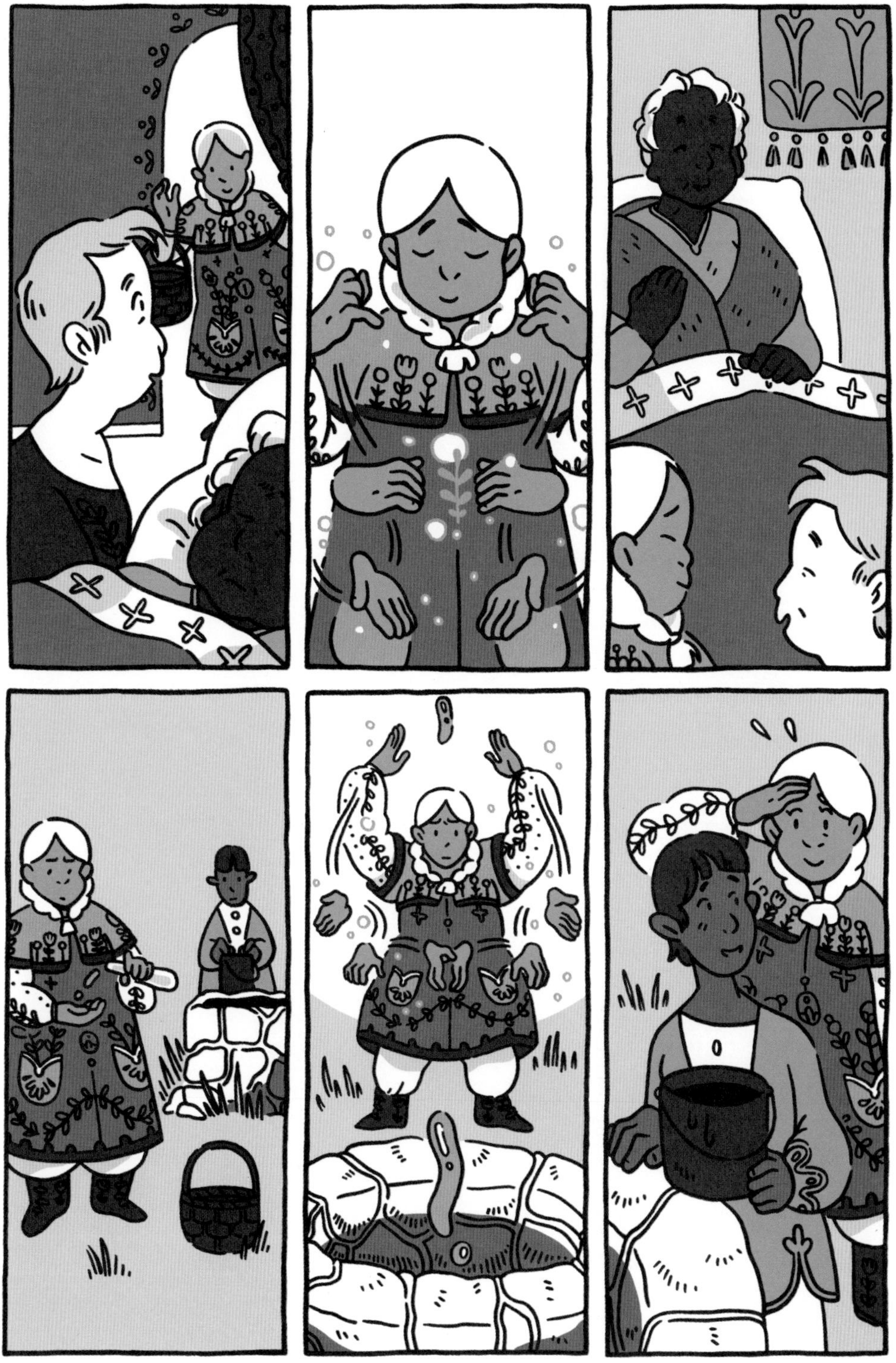

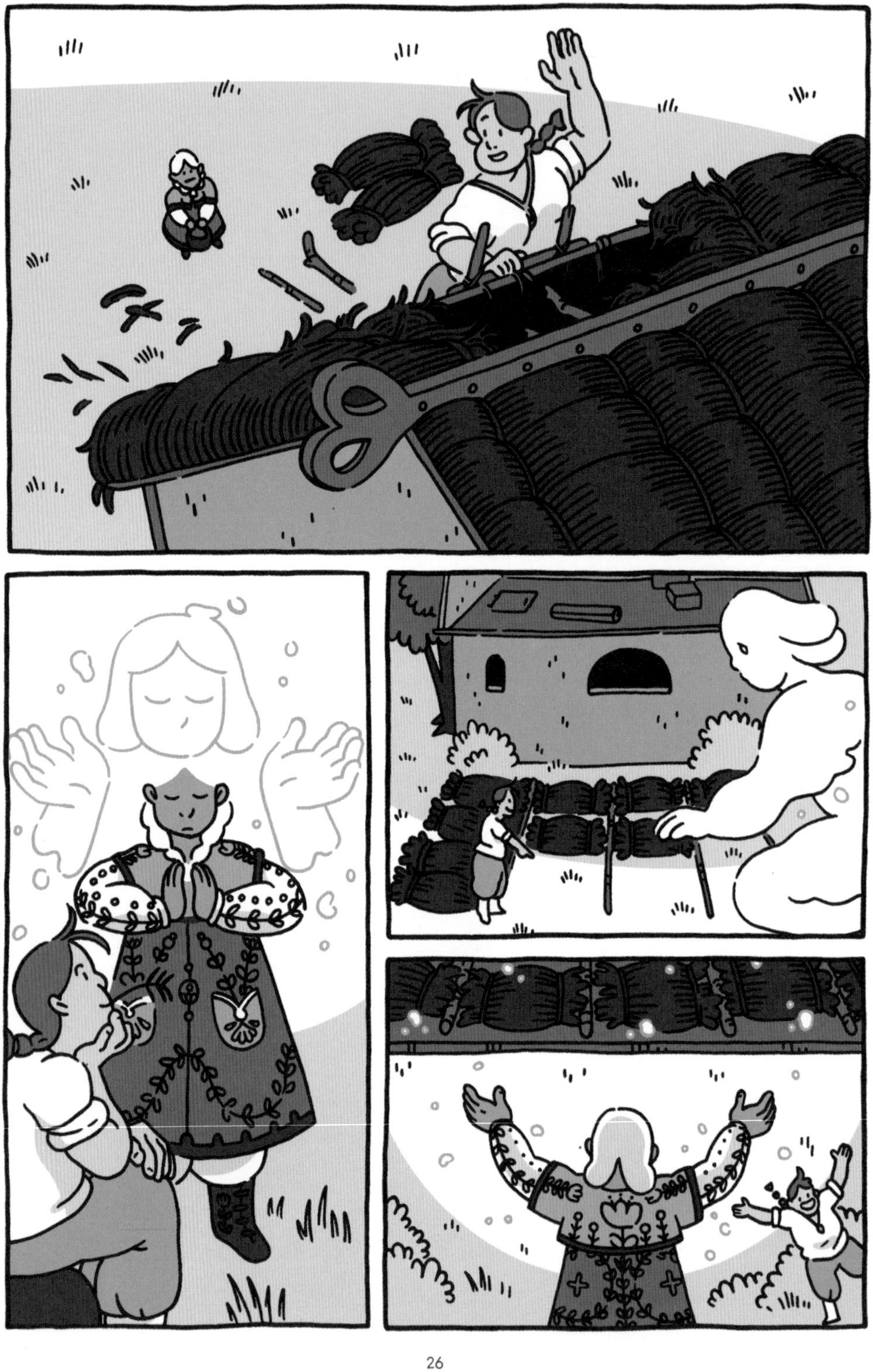

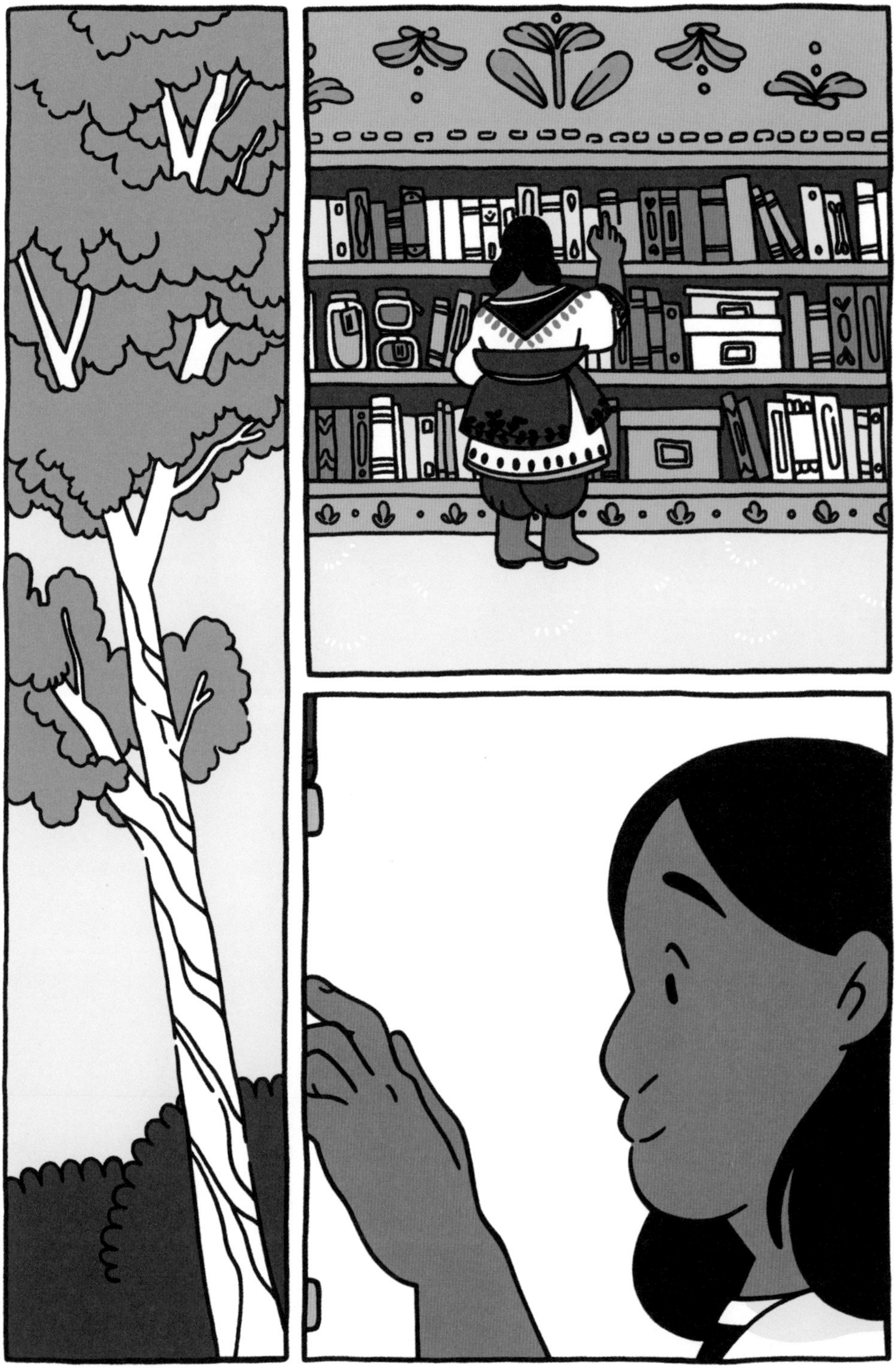

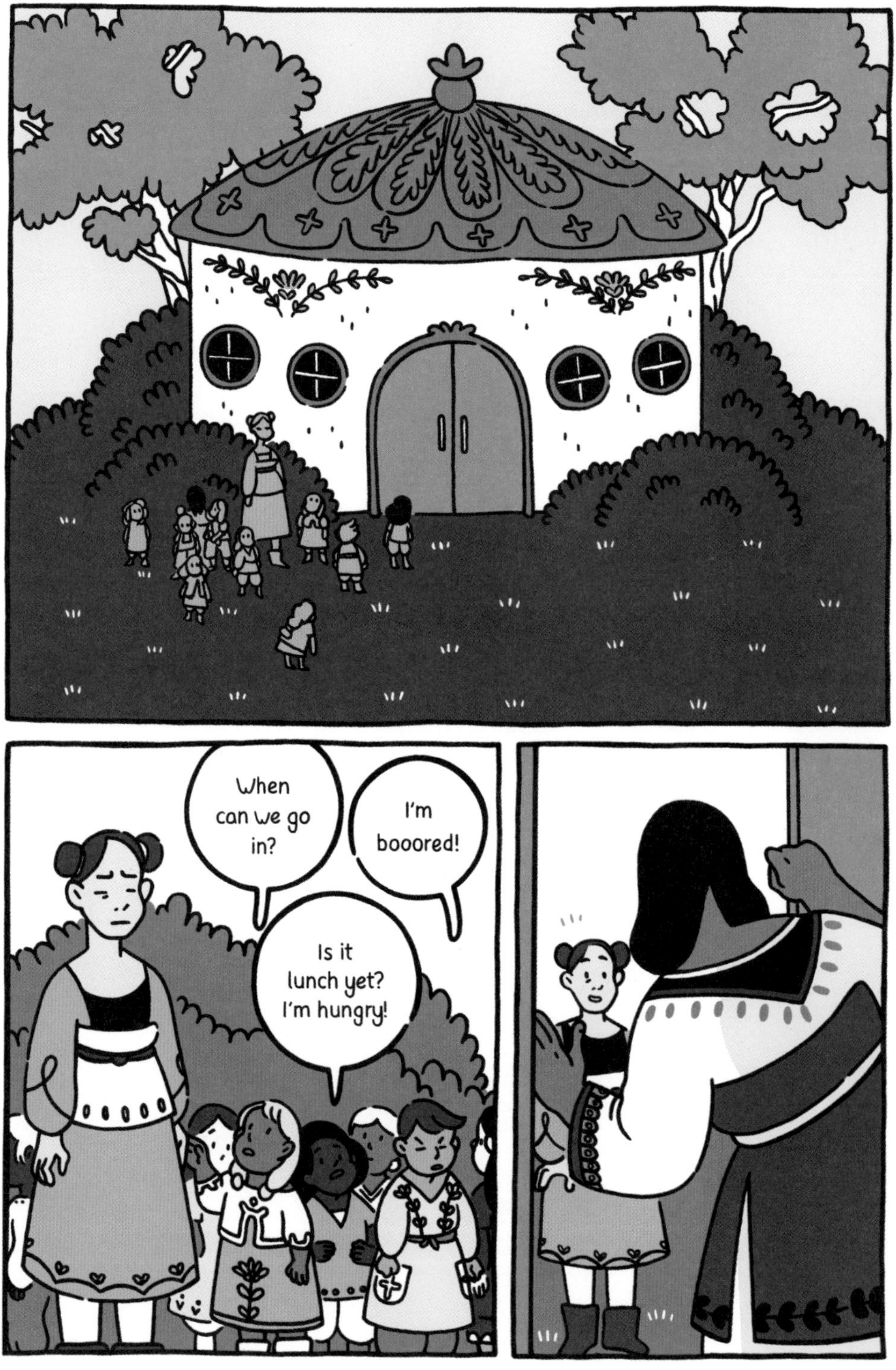
When can we go in?
I'm booored!
Is it lunch yet? I'm hungry!

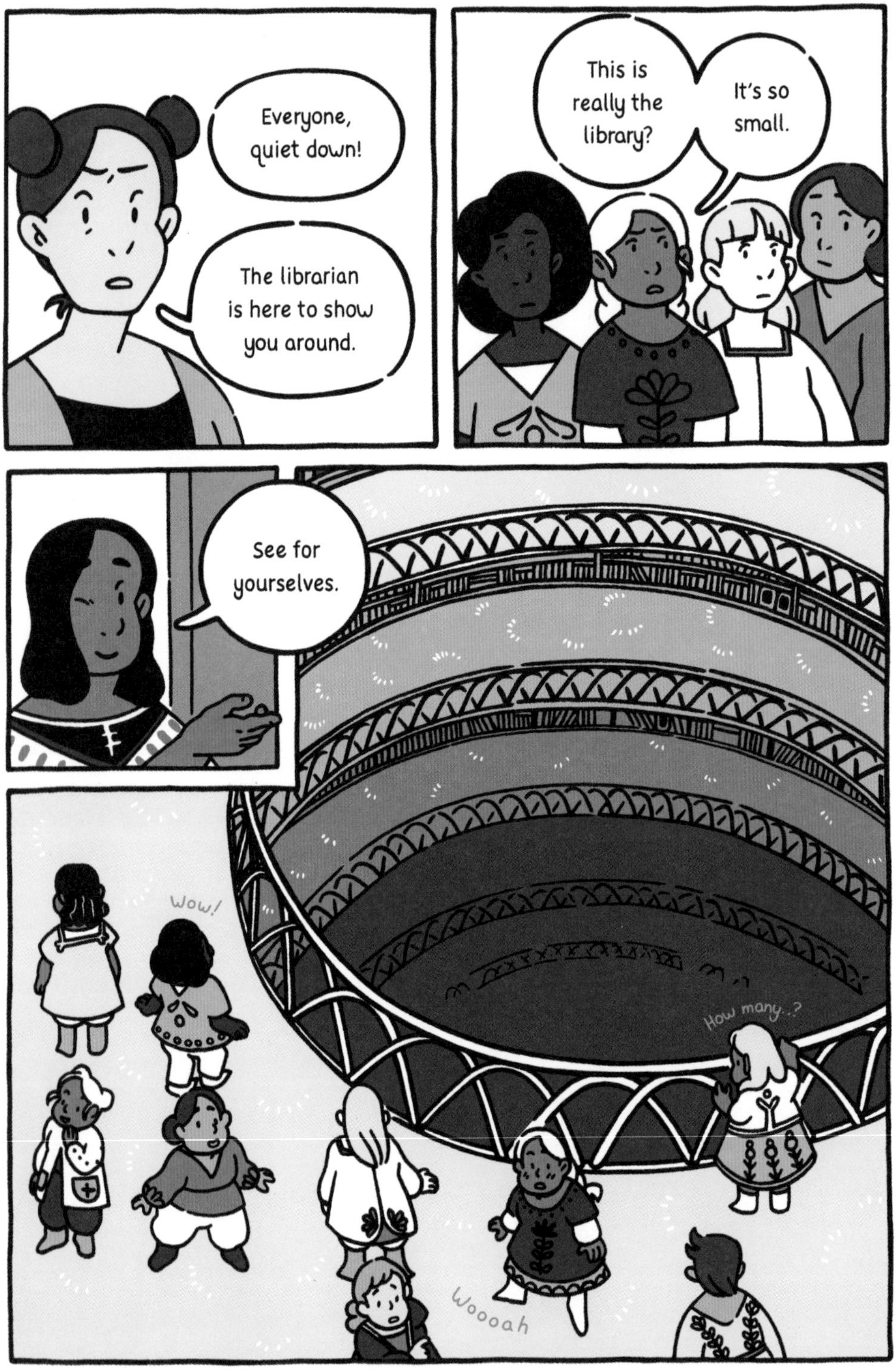
Everyone, quiet down!
The librarian is here to show you around.
This is really the library?
It's so small.
See for yourselves.
Wow!
How many...?
Woooah

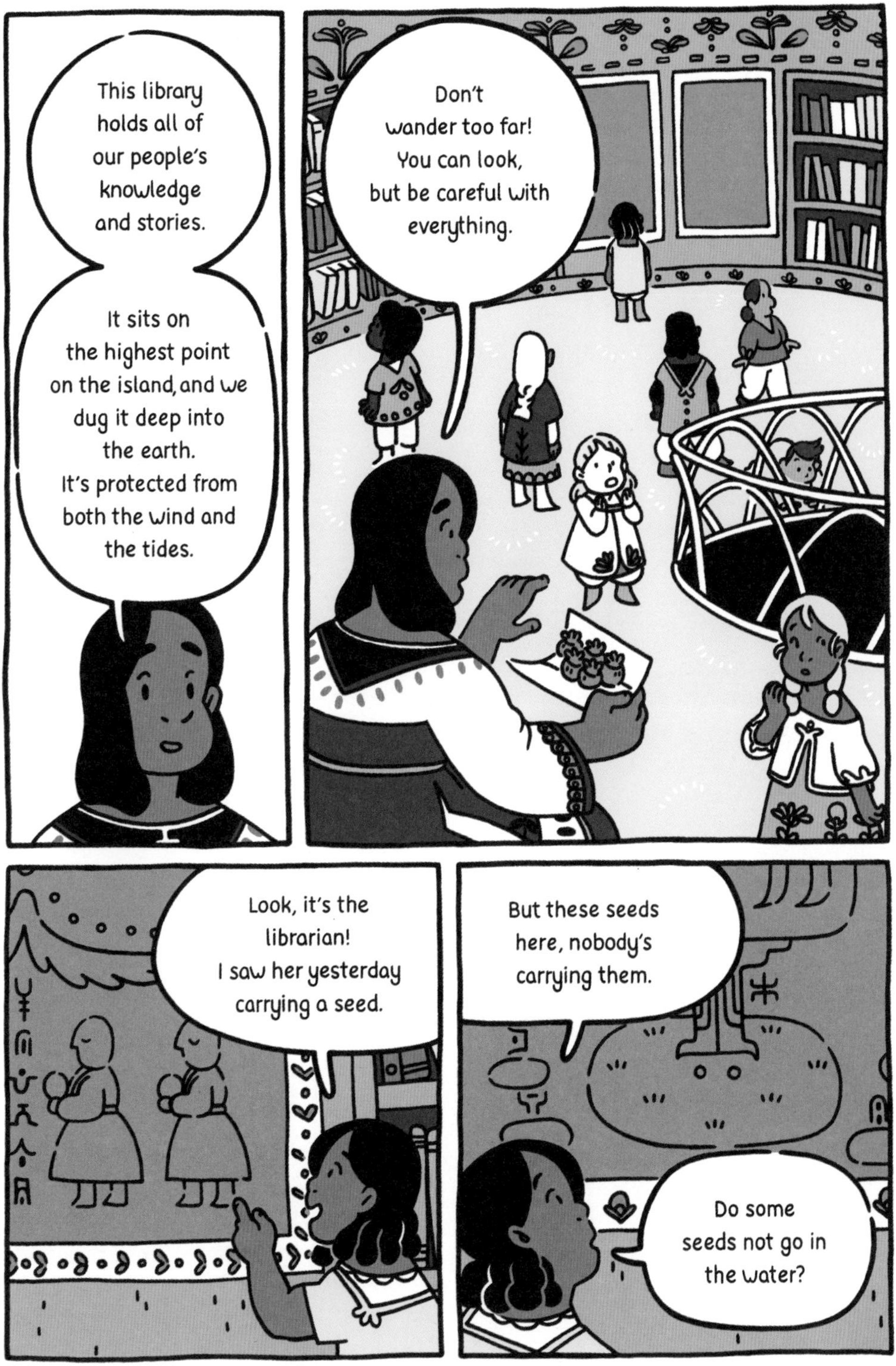
This library holds all of our people's knowledge and stories.
It sits on the highest point on the island, and we dug it deep into the earth. It's protected from both the wind and the tides.
Don't wander too far! You can look, but be careful with everything.
Look, it's the librarian! I saw her yesterday carrying a seed.
But these seeds here, nobody's carrying them.
Do some seeds not go in the water?

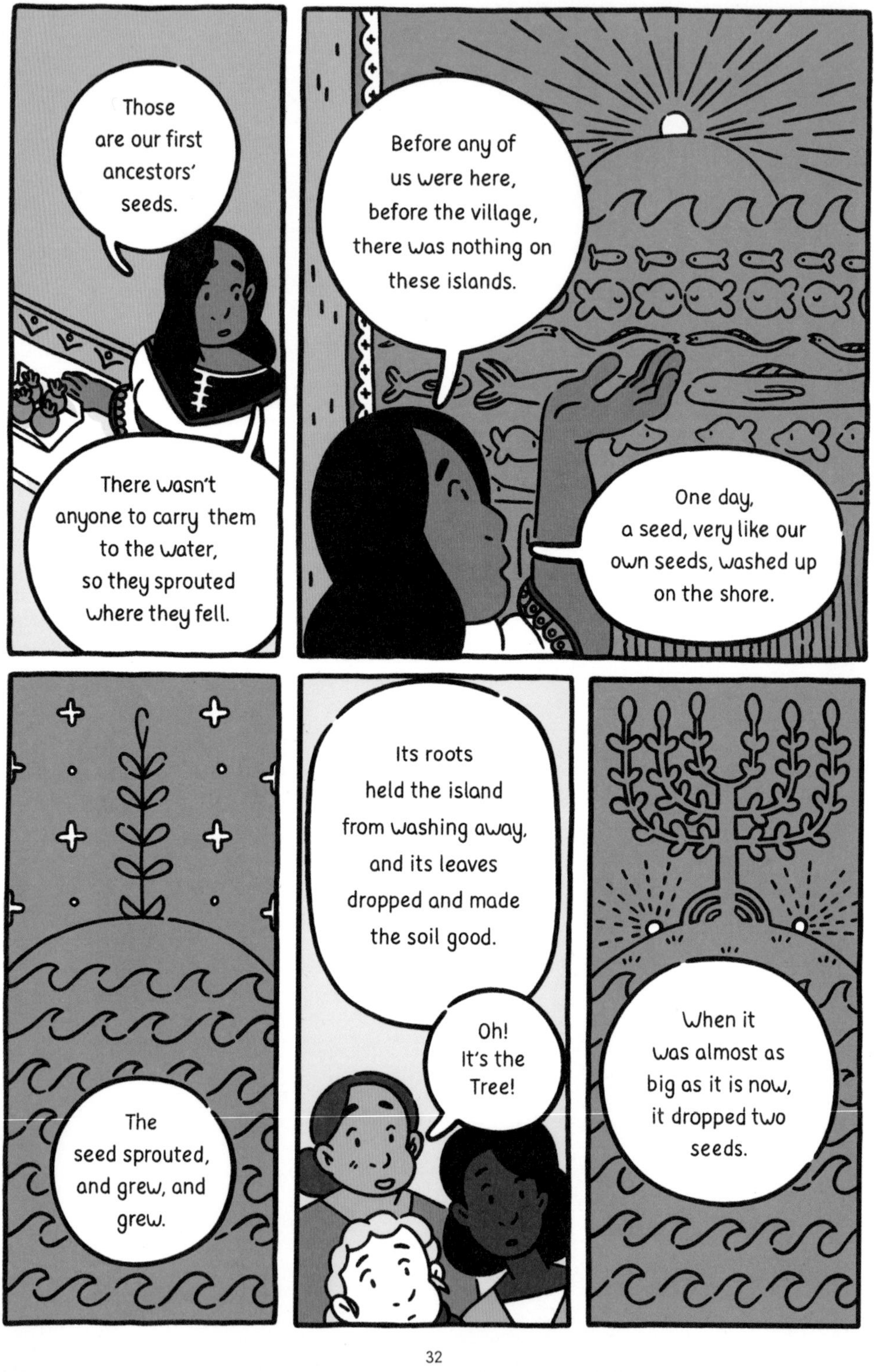
Those are our first ancestors' seeds.
There wasn't anyone to carry them to the water, so they sprouted where they fell.
Before any of us were here, before the village, there was nothing on these islands.
One day, a seed, very like our own seeds, washed up on the shore.
The seed sprouted, and grew, and grew.
Its roots held the island from washing away, and its leaves dropped and made the soil good.
Oh! It's the Tree!
When it was almost as big as it is now, it dropped two seeds.

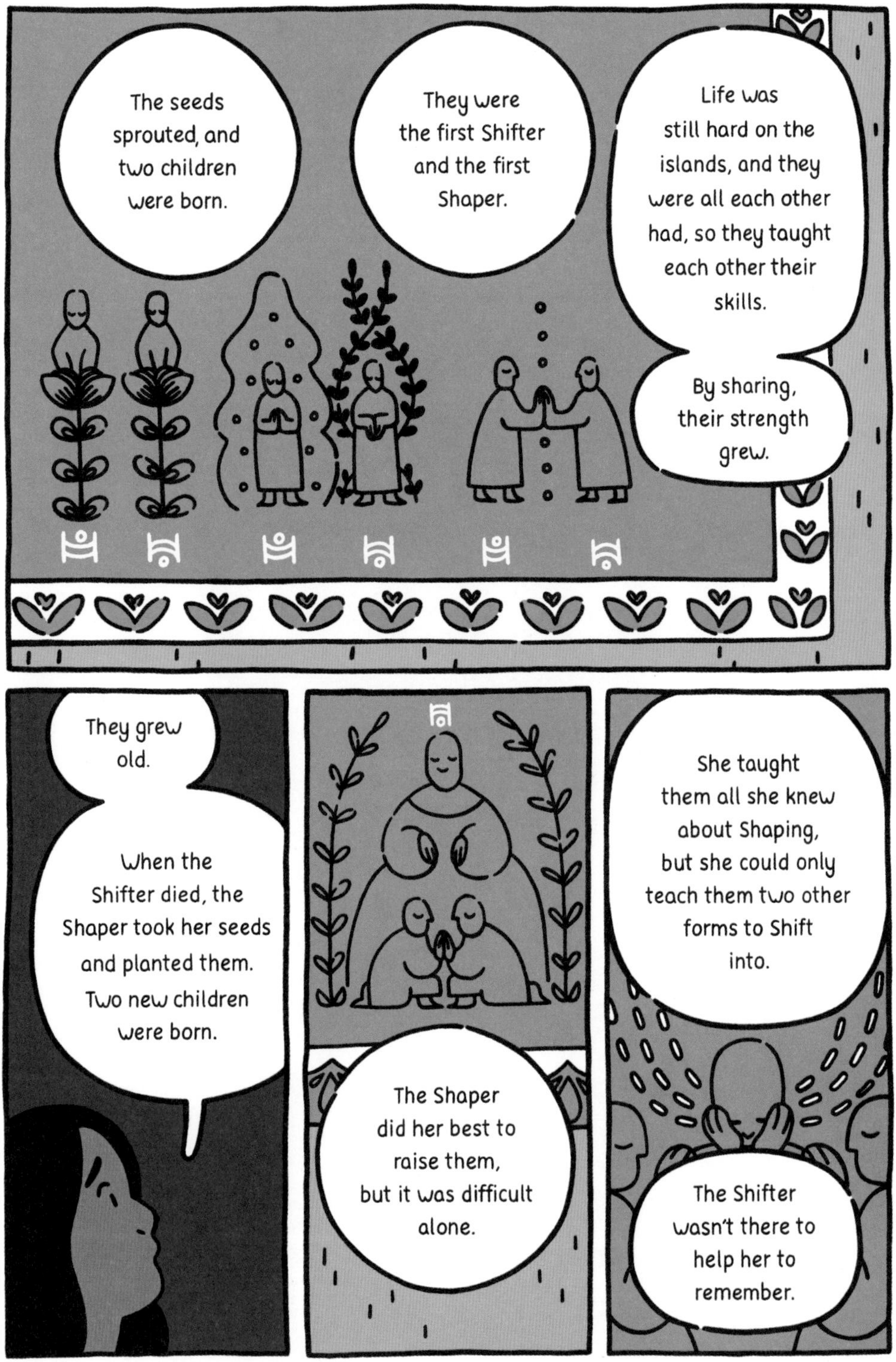

The seeds sprouted, and two children were born.
They were the first Shifter and the first Shaper.
Life was still hard on the islands, and they were all each other had, so they taught each other their skills.
By sharing, their strength grew.
They grew old.
When the Shifter died, the Shaper took her seeds and planted them. Two new children were born.
The Shaper did her best to raise them, but it was difficult alone.
She taught them all she knew about Shaping, but she could only teach them two other forms to Shift into.
The Shifter wasn't there to help her to remember.

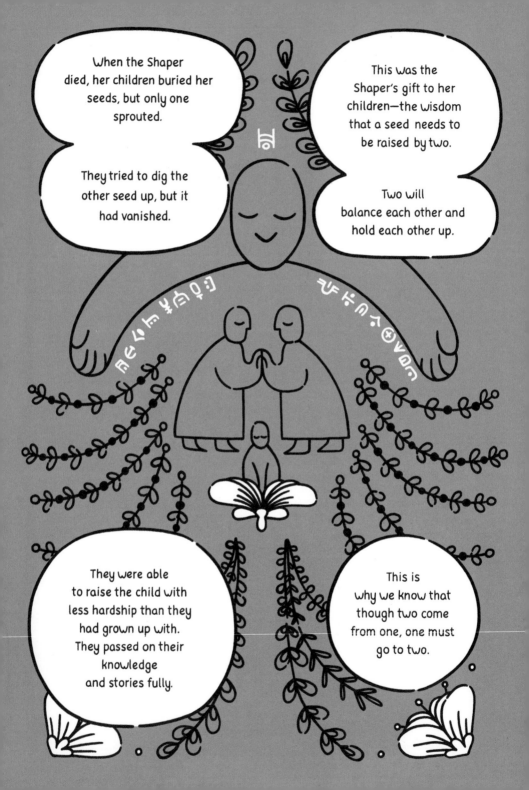

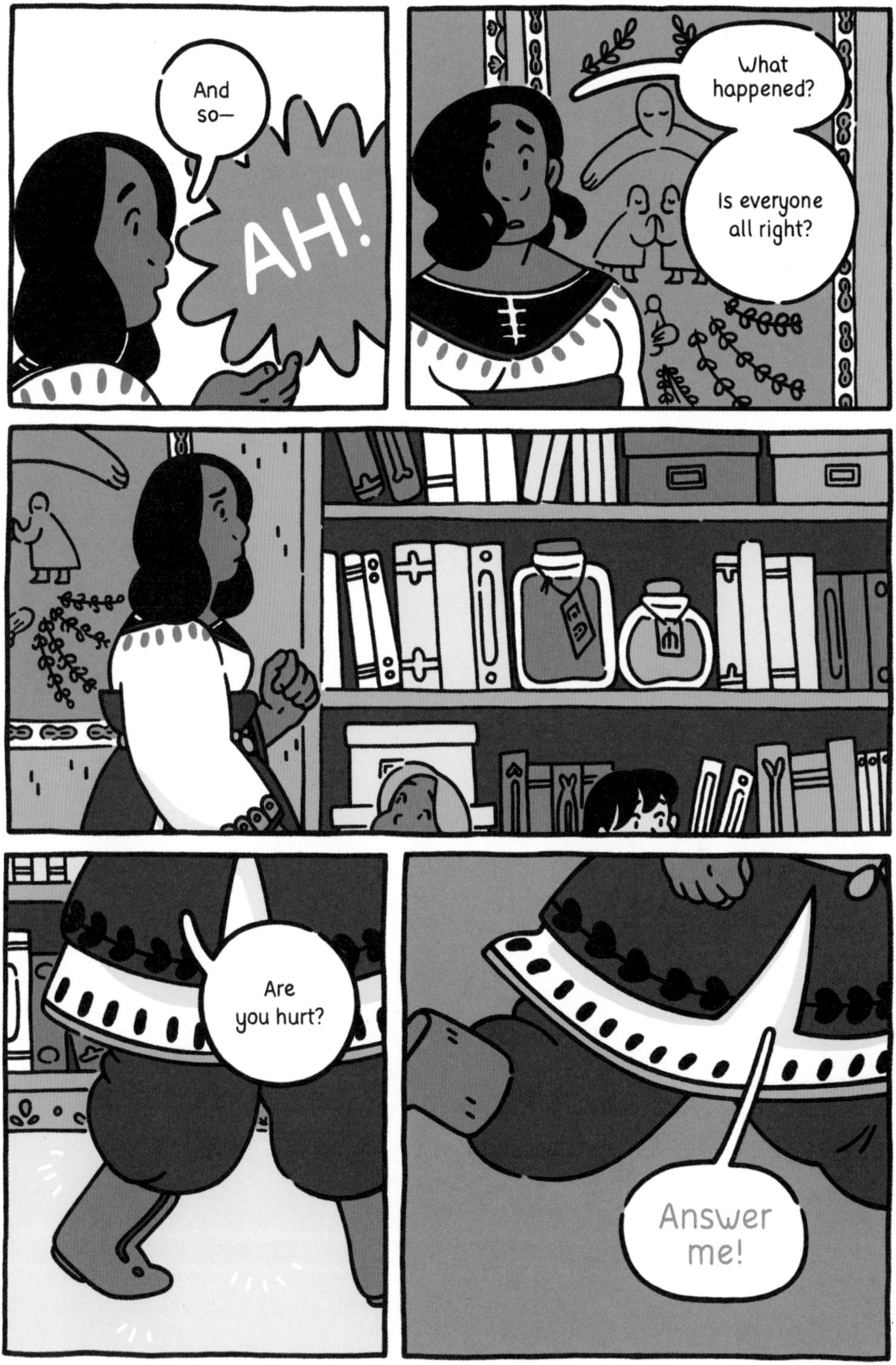
And so—
AH!
What happened?
Is everyone all right?
Are you hurt?
Answer me!

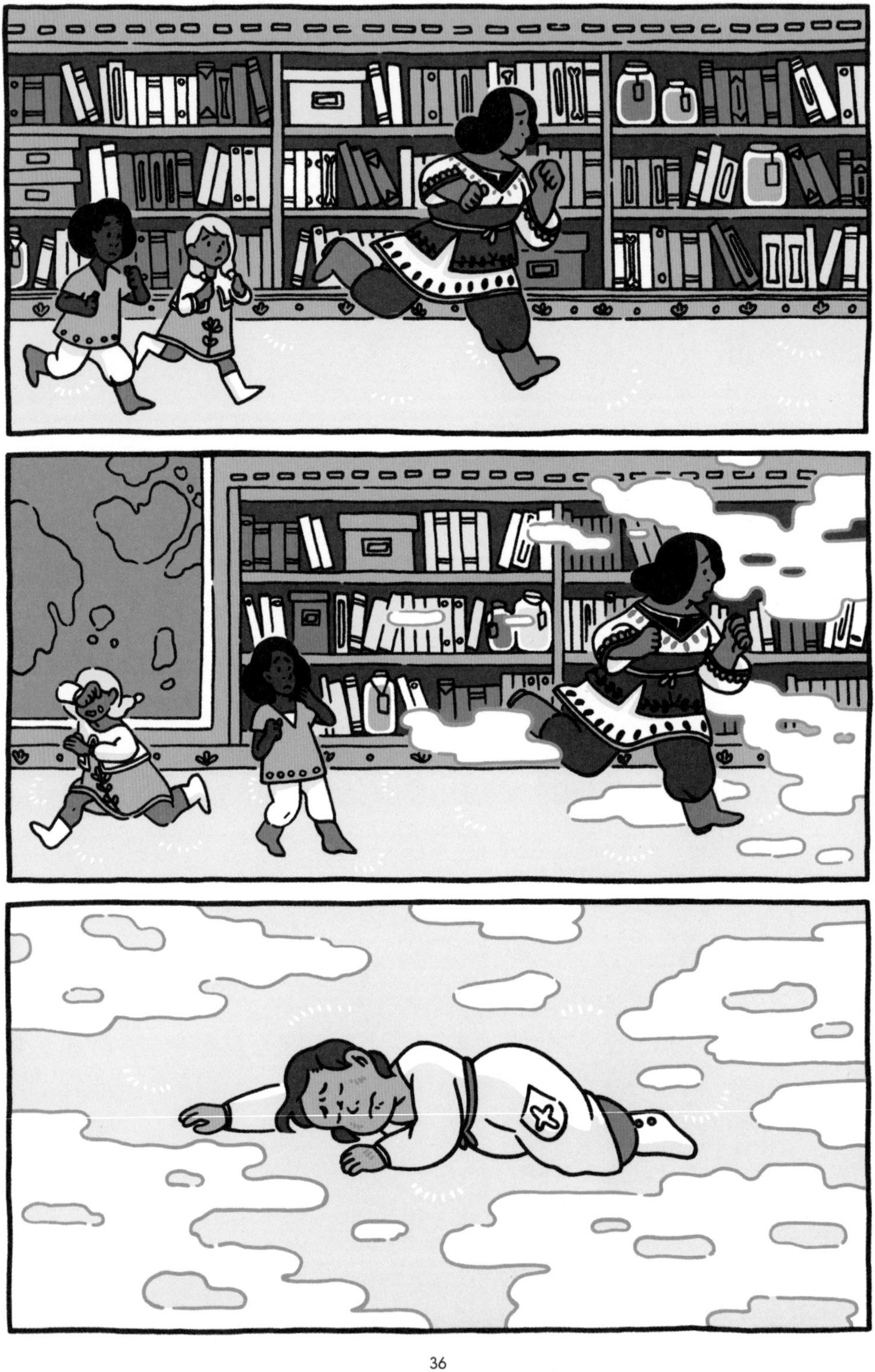

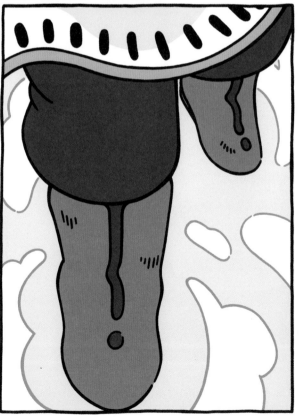

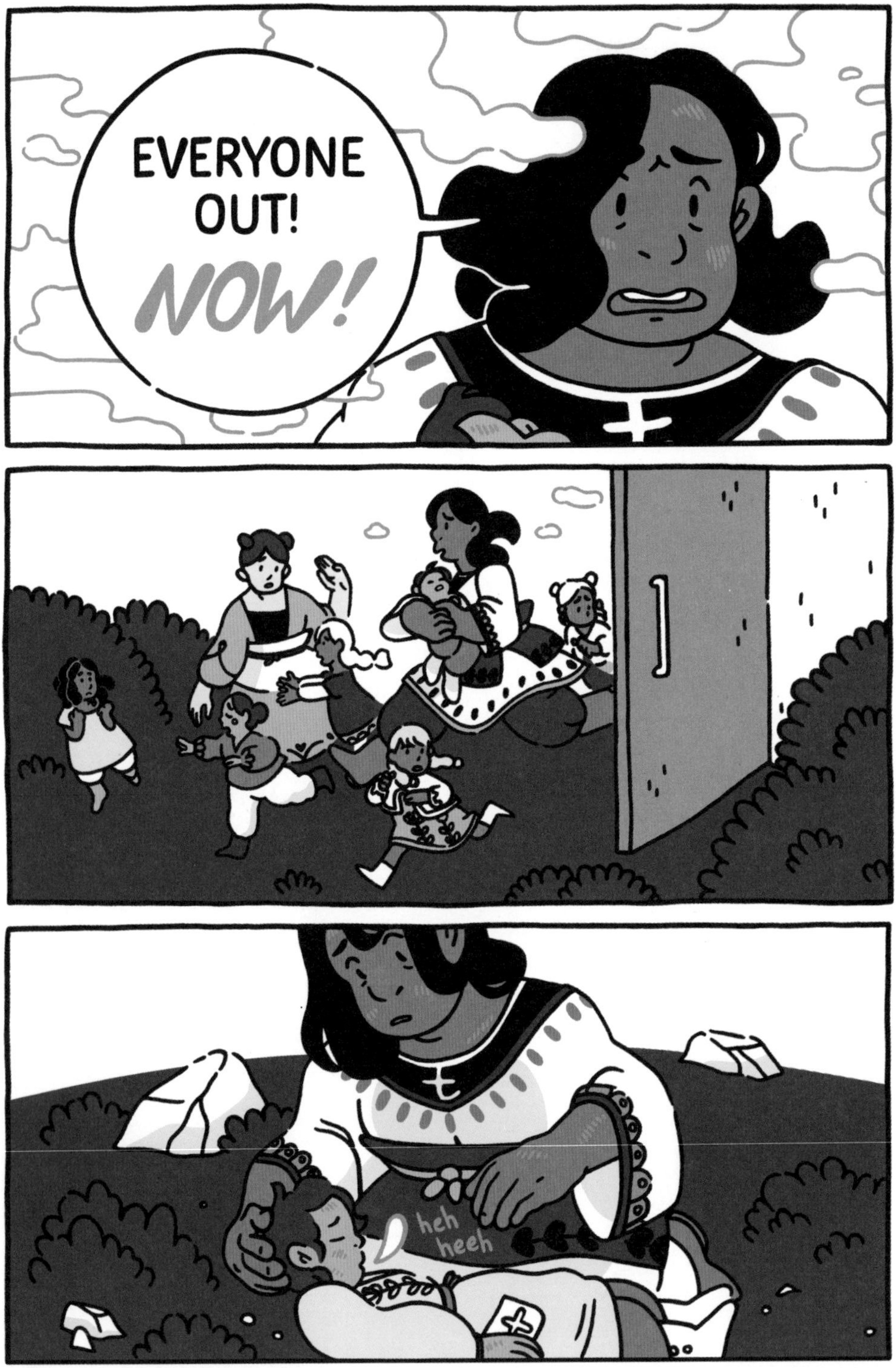
EVERYONE OUT! NOW!
heh heeh

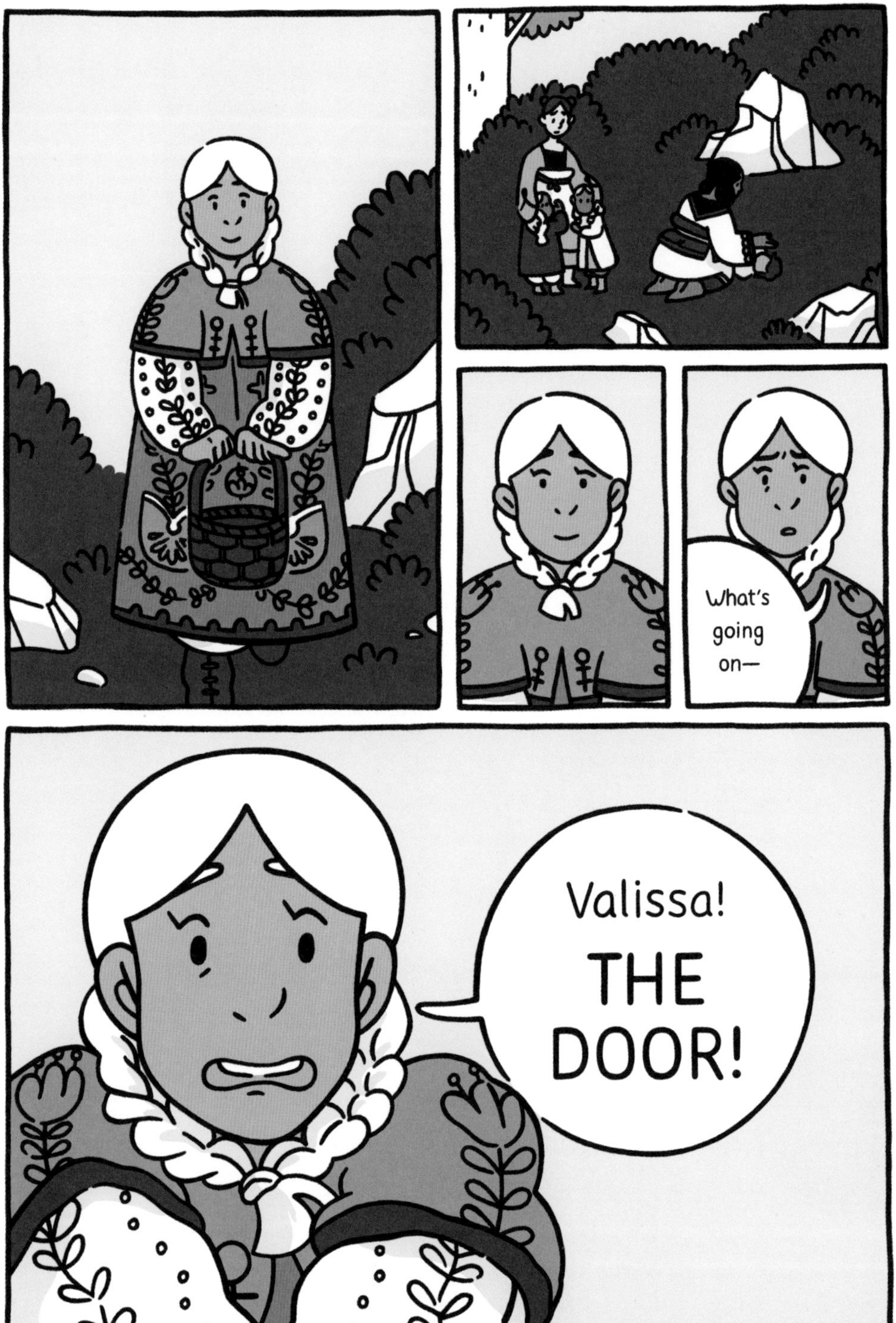
What's going on—
Valissa! THE DOOR!

vshhh
ssshh
SLAM

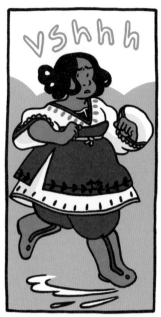

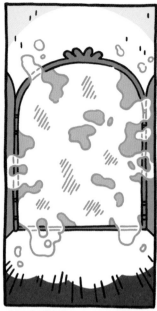

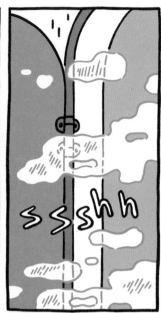

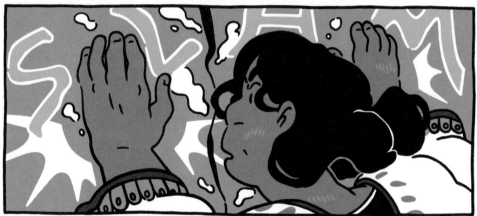

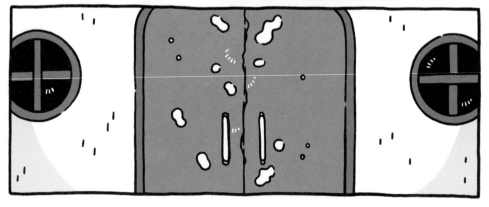

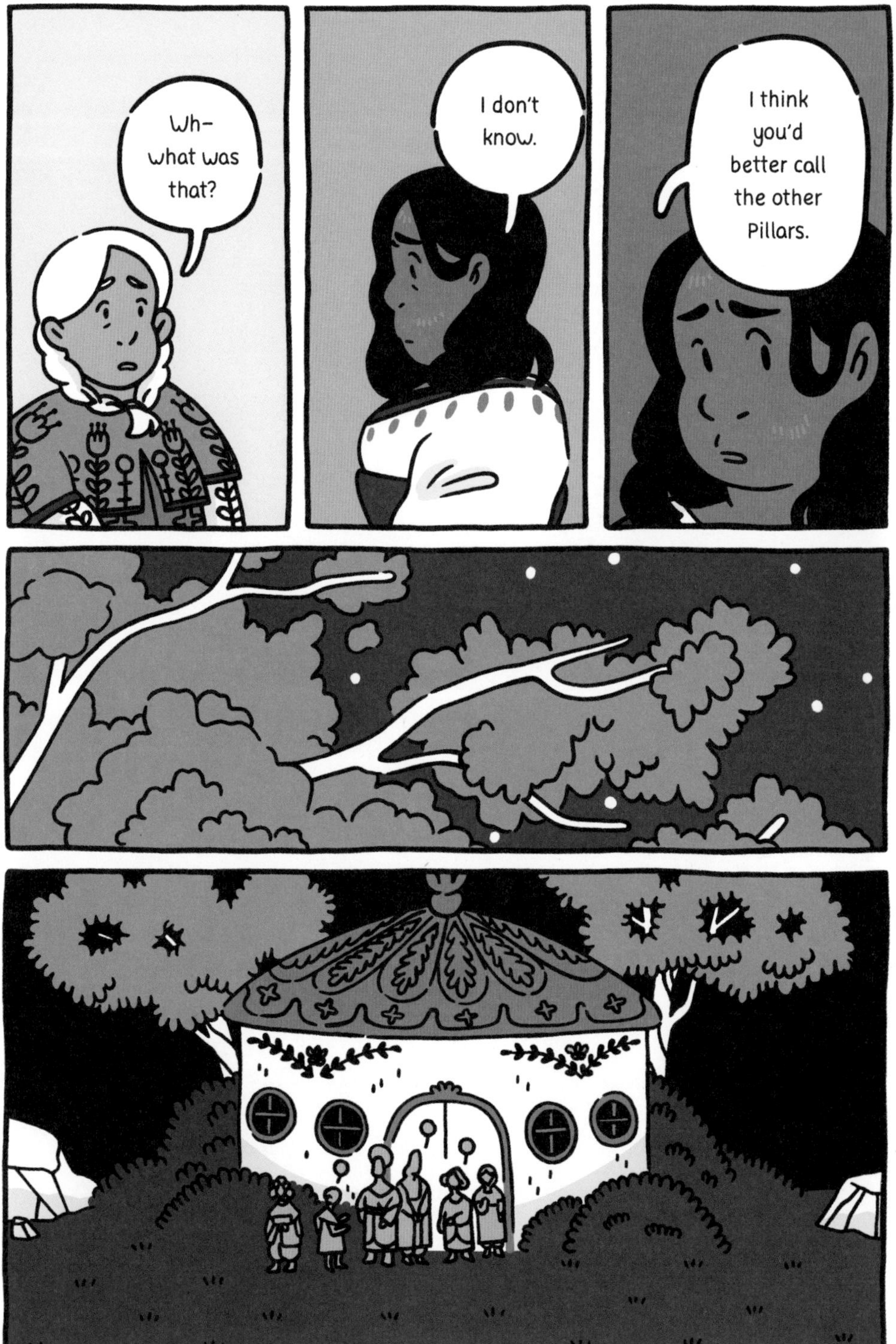
Wh-
what was
that?
I don't
know.
I think
you'd
better call
the other
Pillars.

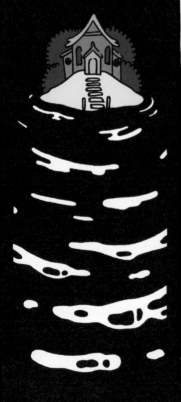

krr

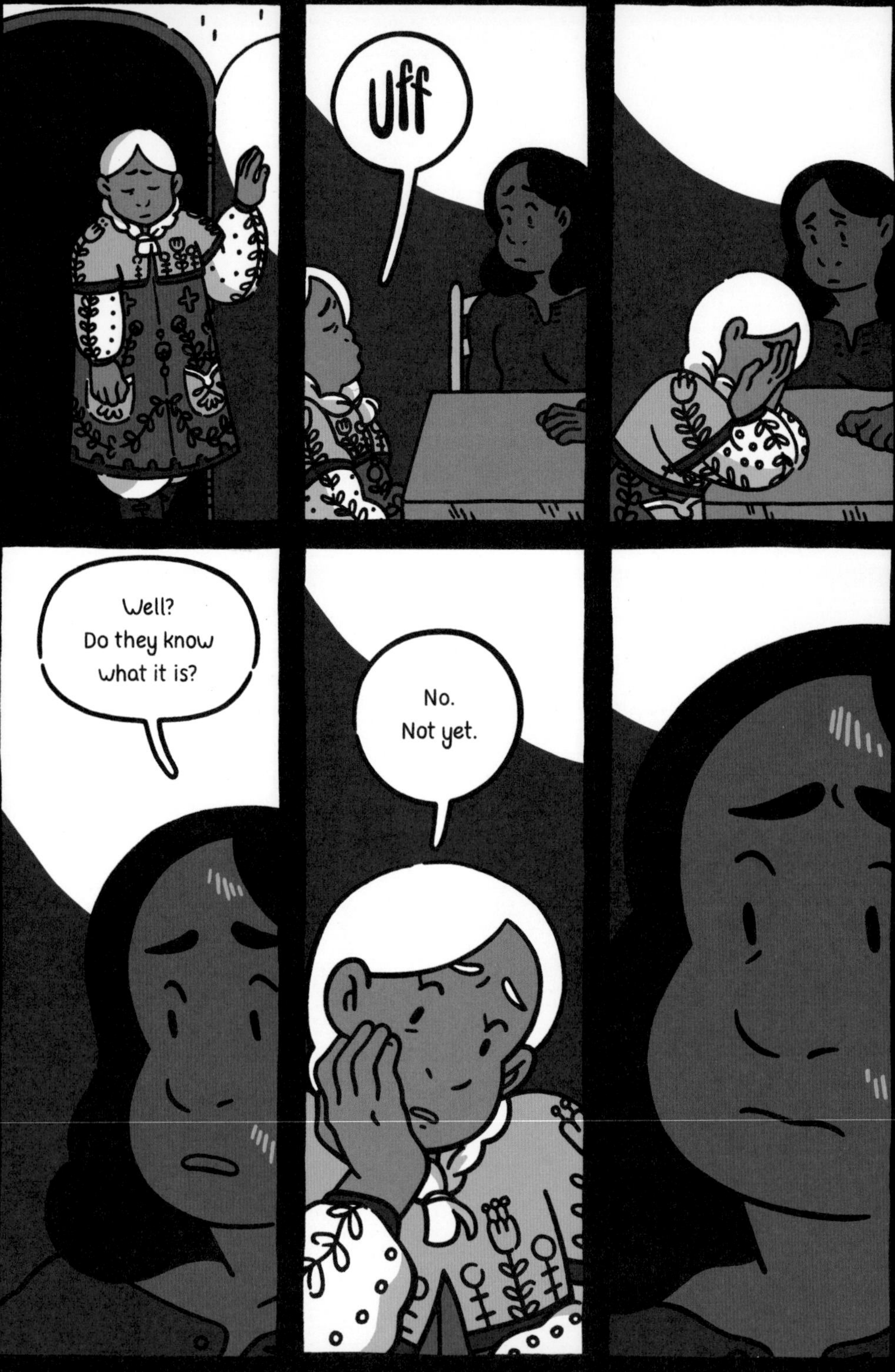
Uff
Well? Do they know what it is?
No. Not yet.

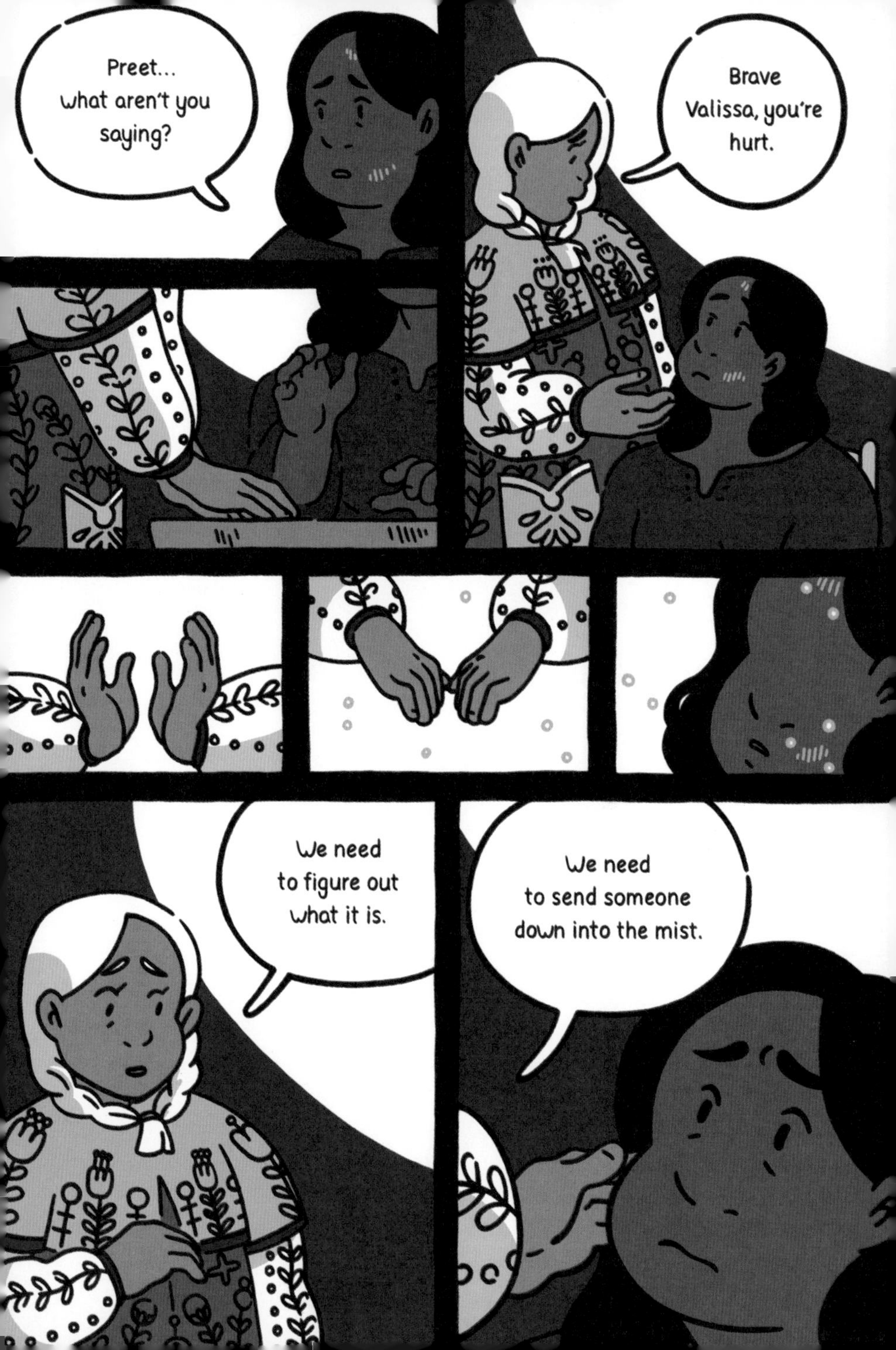
Preet... what aren't you saying?
Brave Valissa, you're hurt.
We need to figure out what it is.
We need to send someone down into the mist.

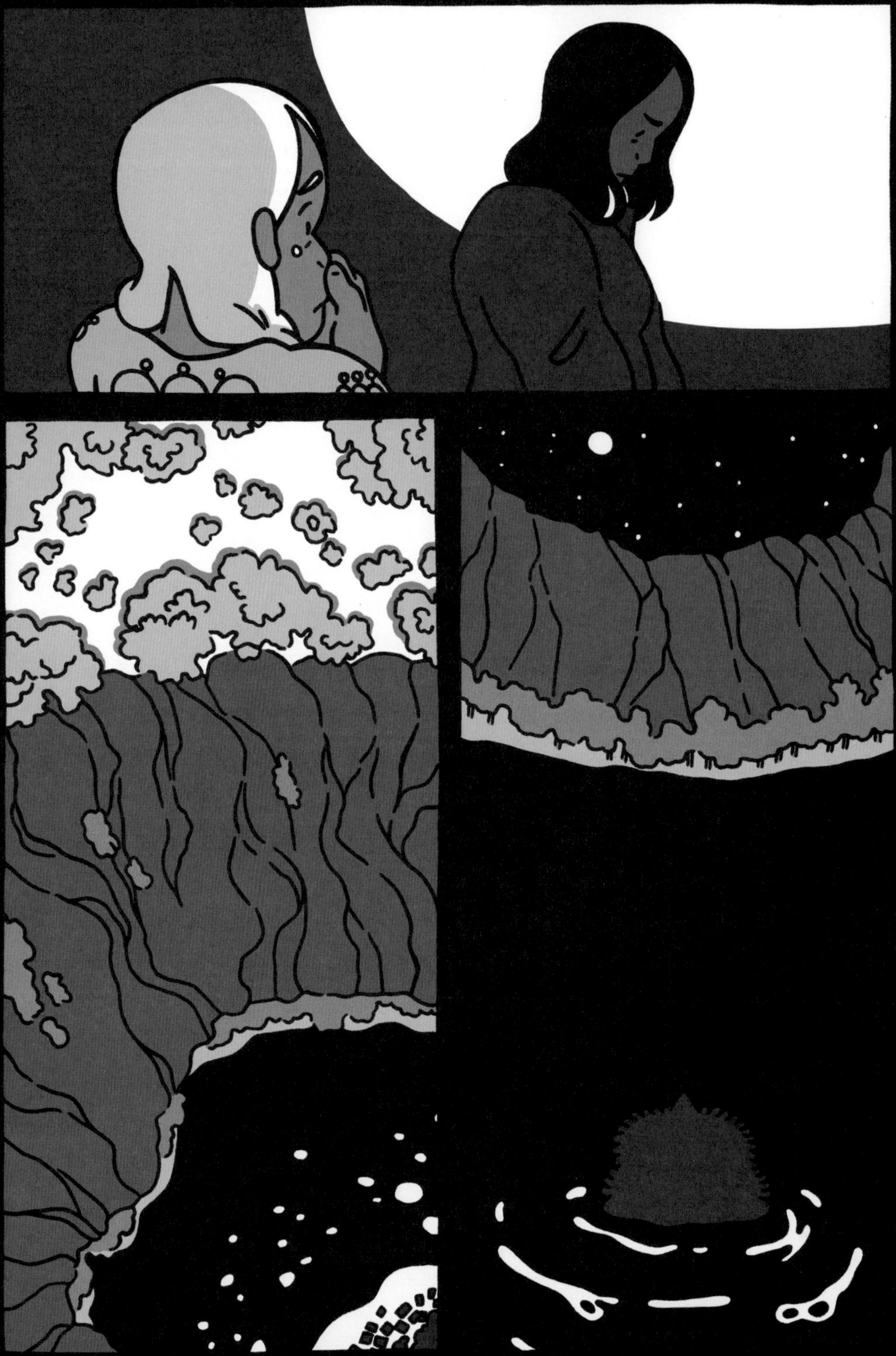

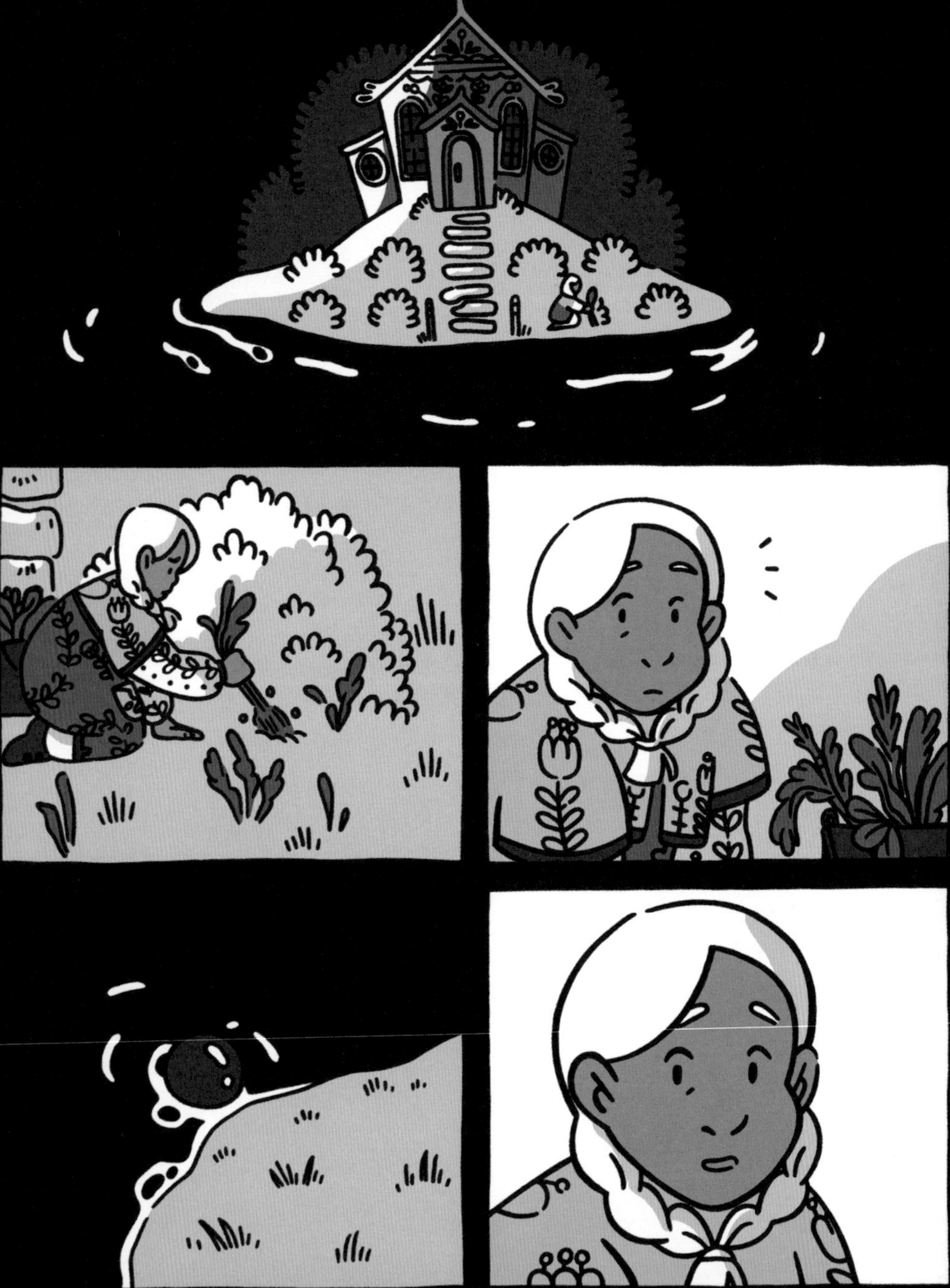

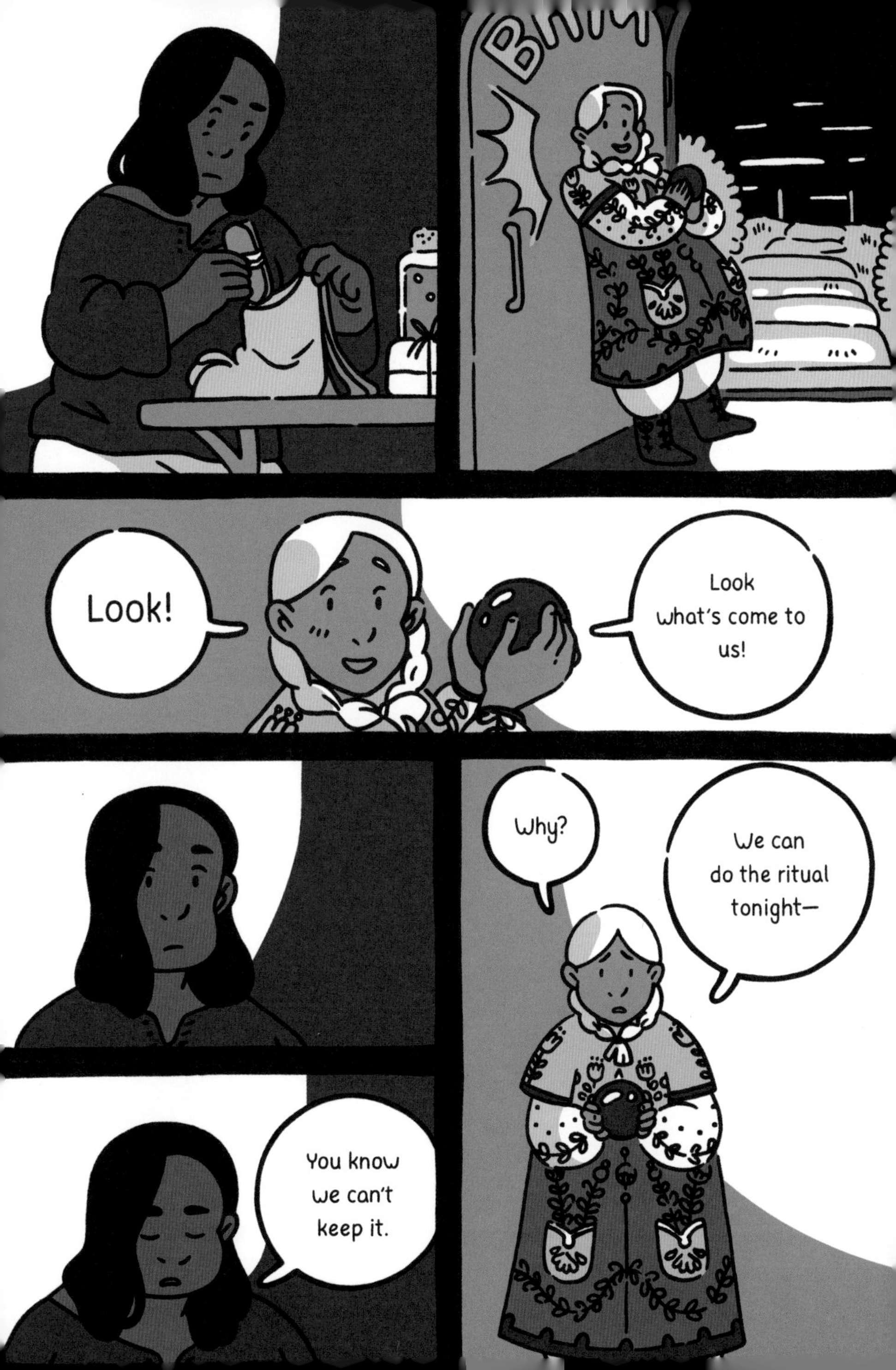
Look!
Look what's come to us!
Why?
We can do the ritual tonight—
You know we can't keep it.

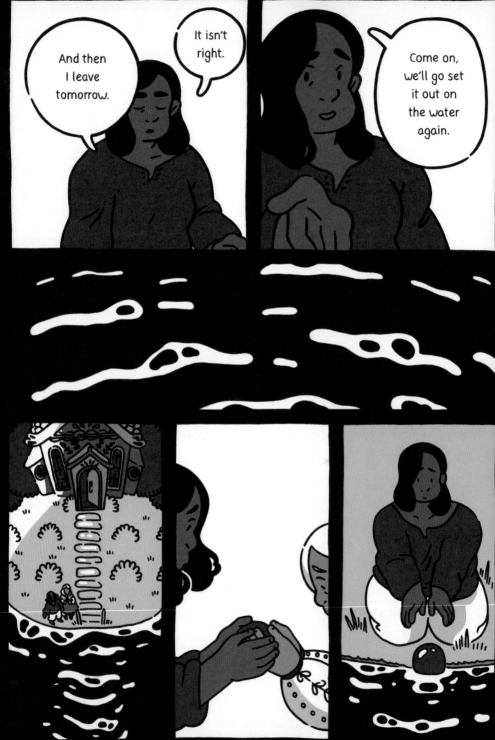

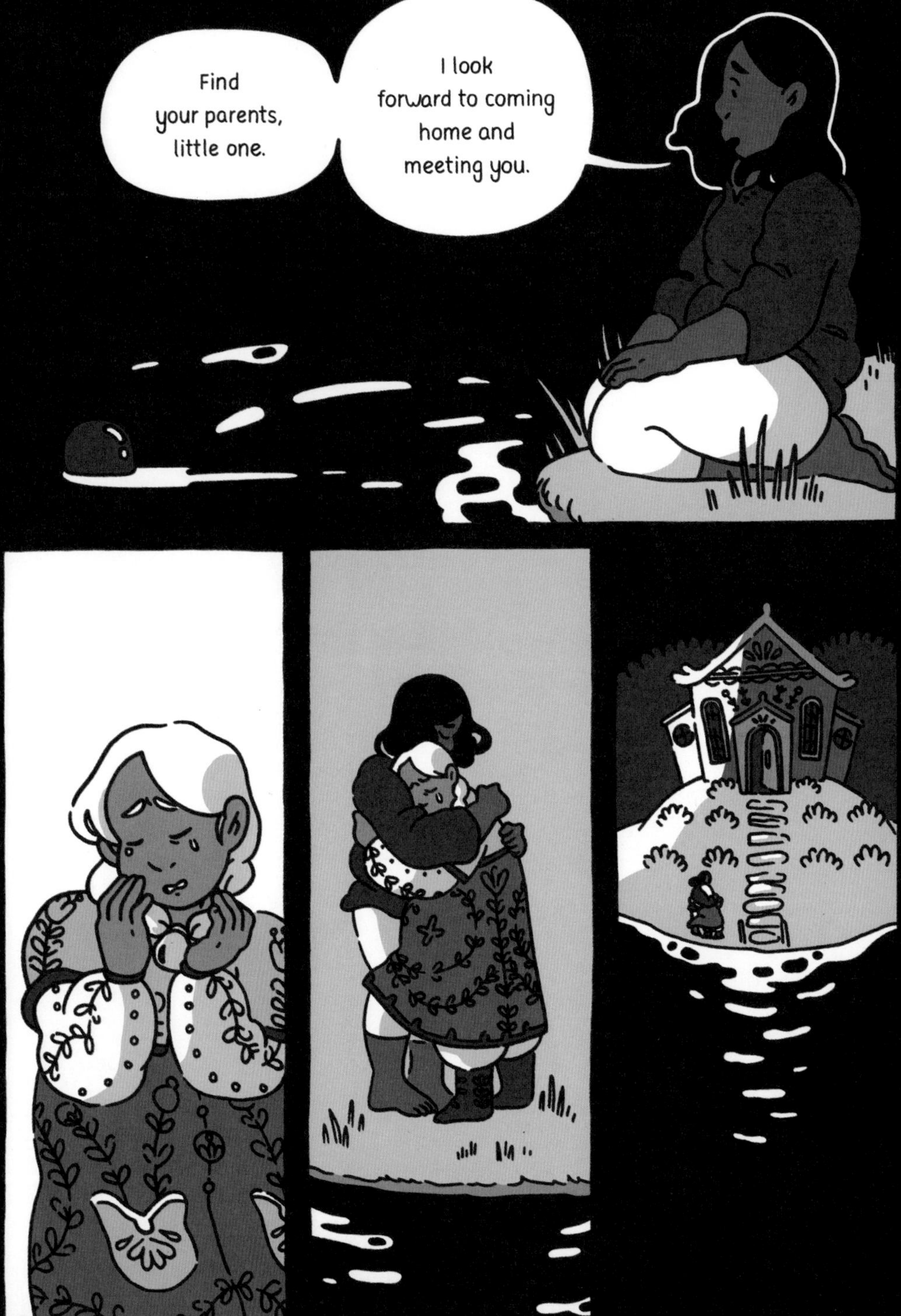
Find your parents, little one.
I look forward to coming home and meeting you.

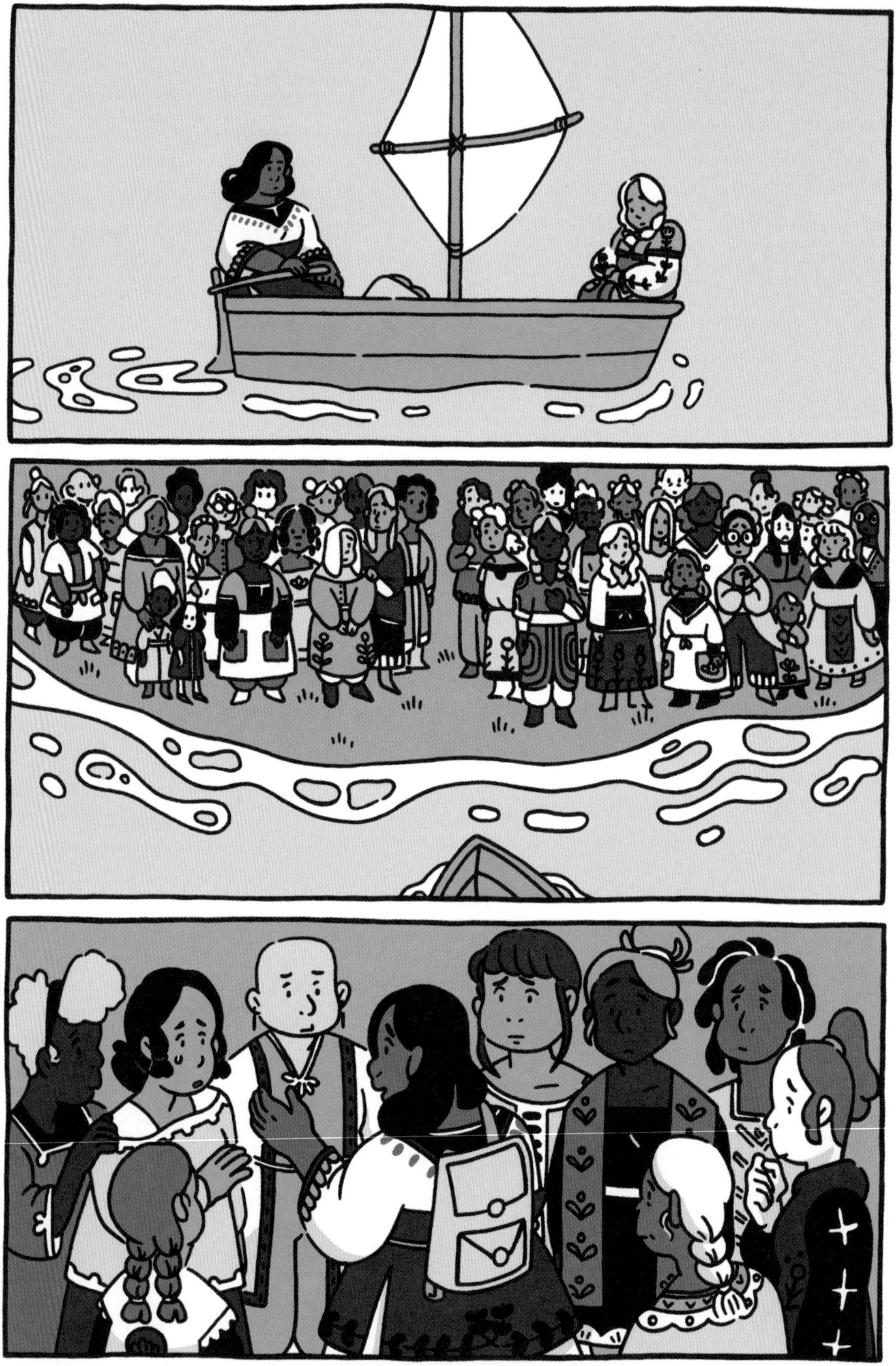

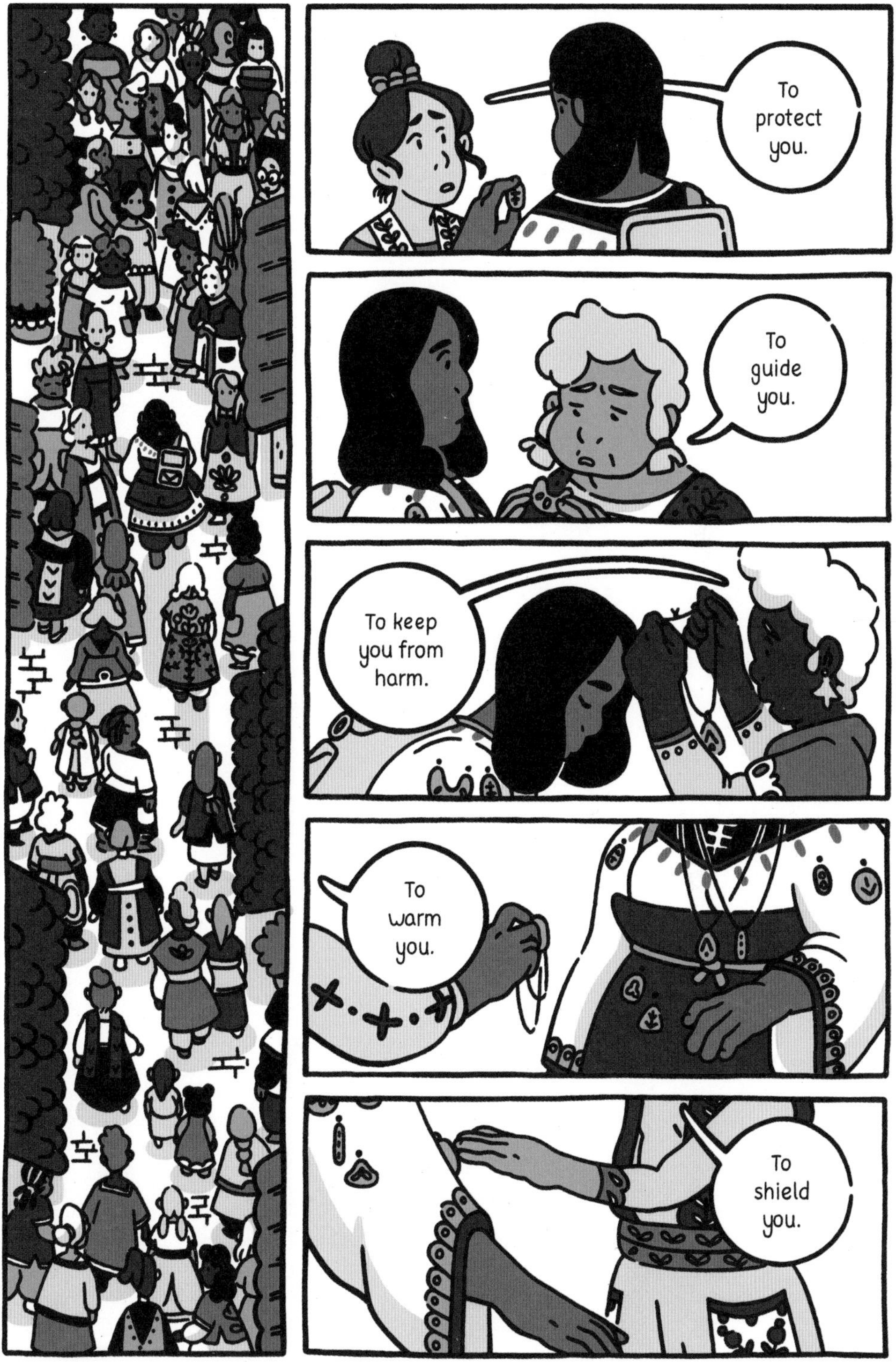
To protect you.
To guide you.
To keep you from harm.
To warm you.
To shield you.

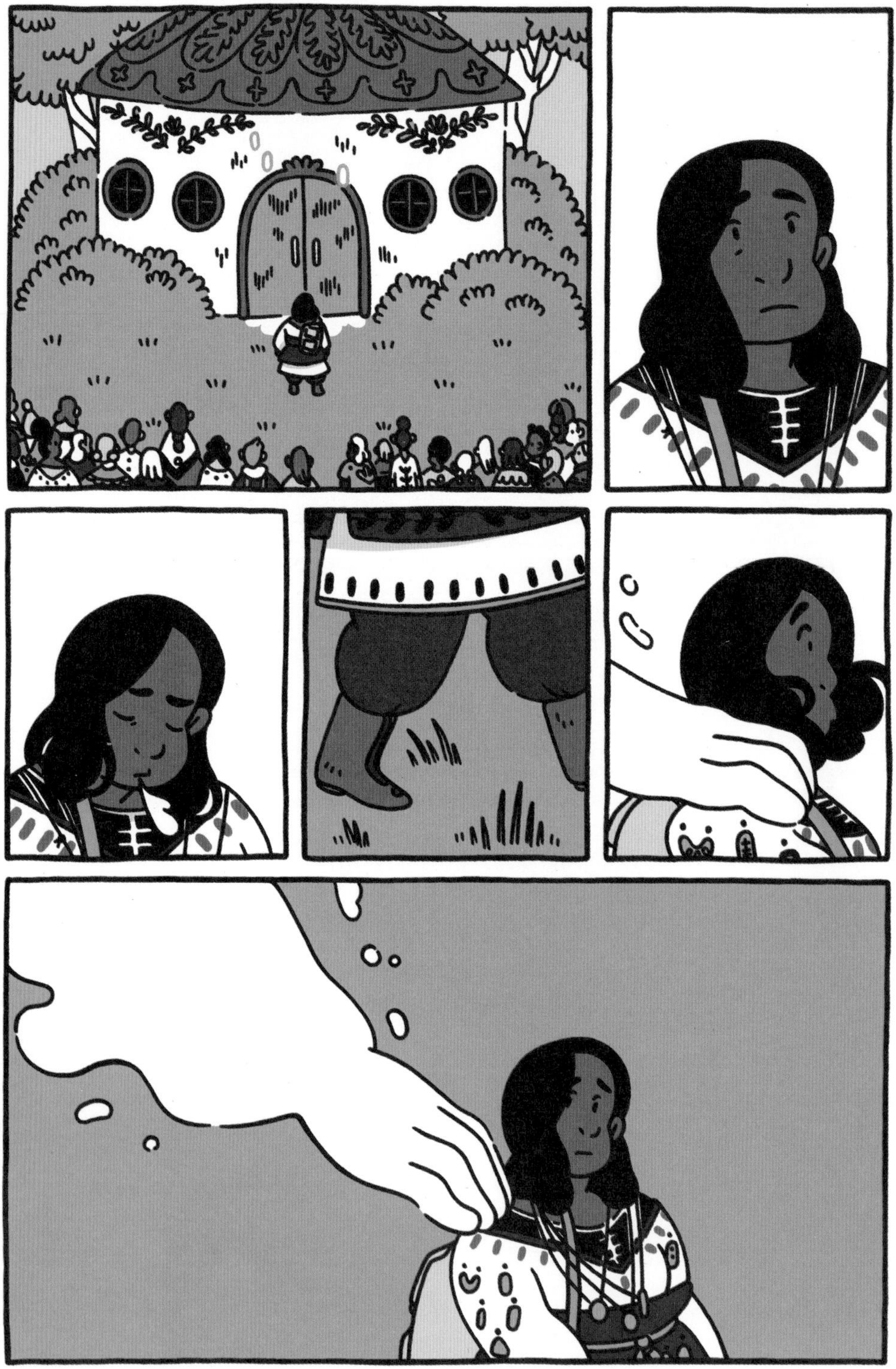

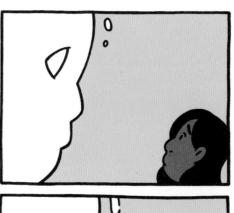

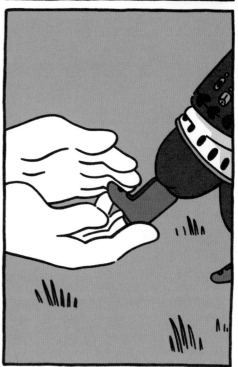

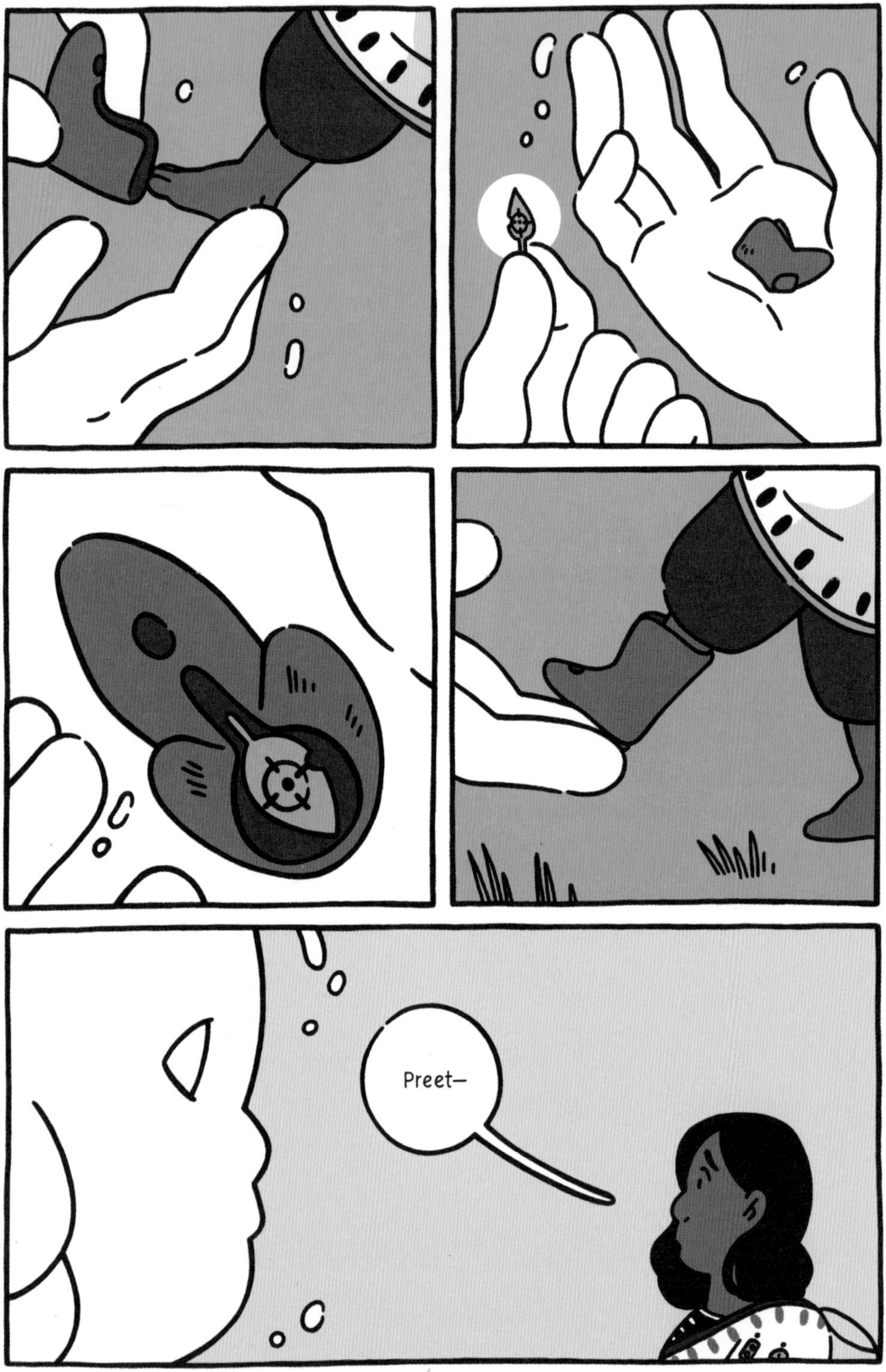
Preet—

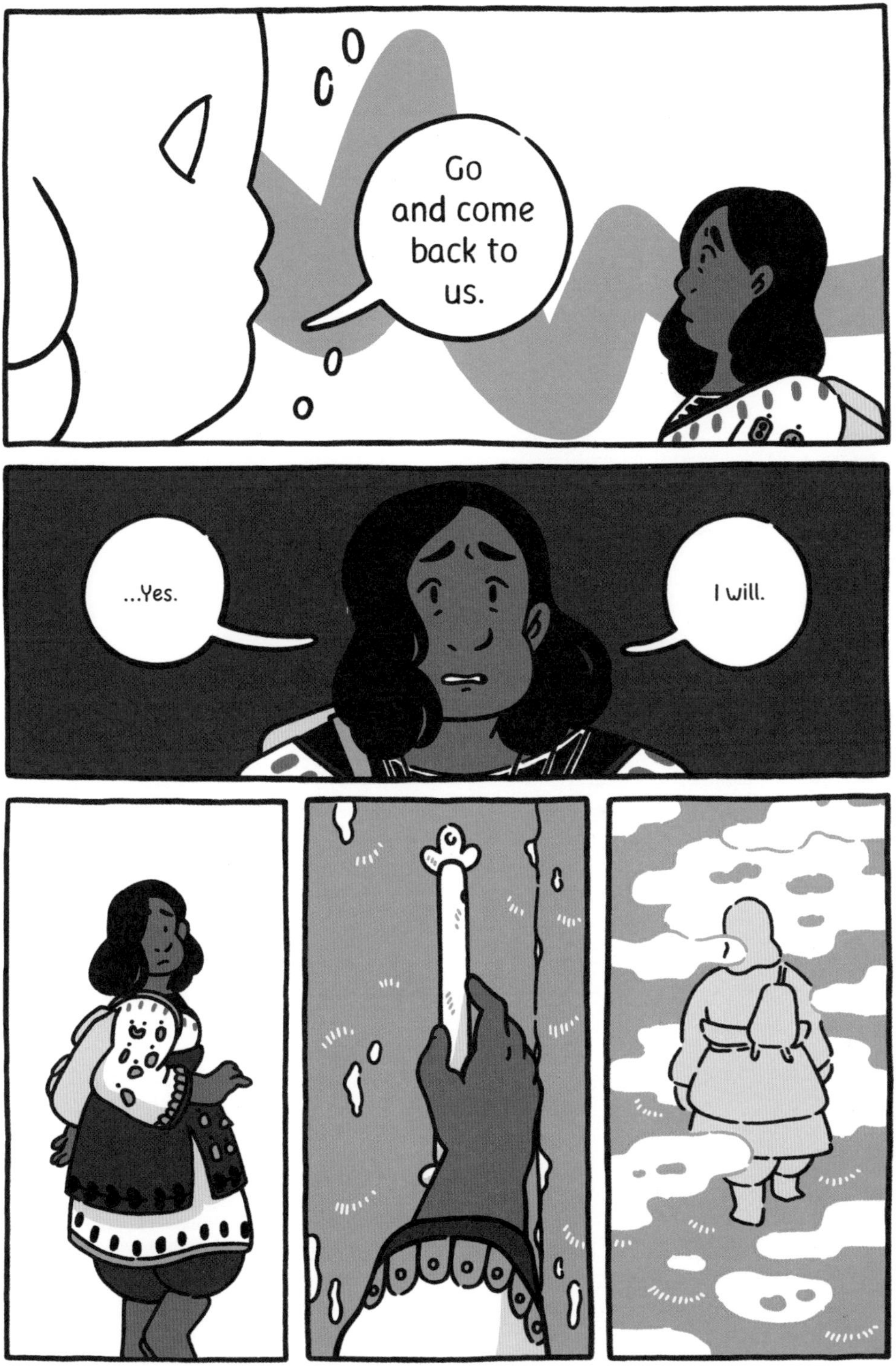
Go and come back to us.
...Yes.
I will.

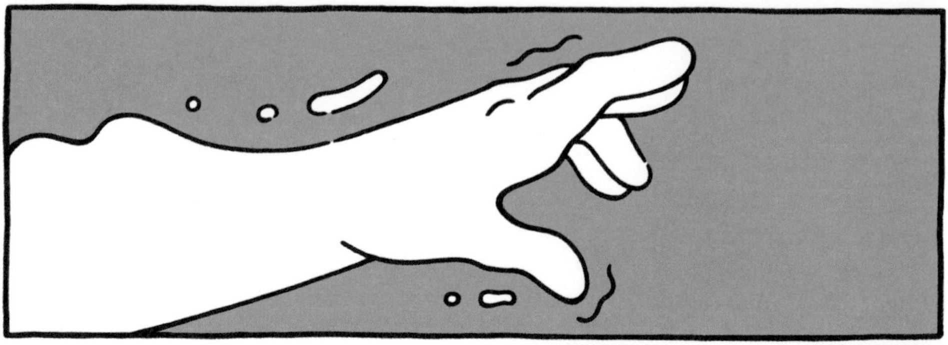

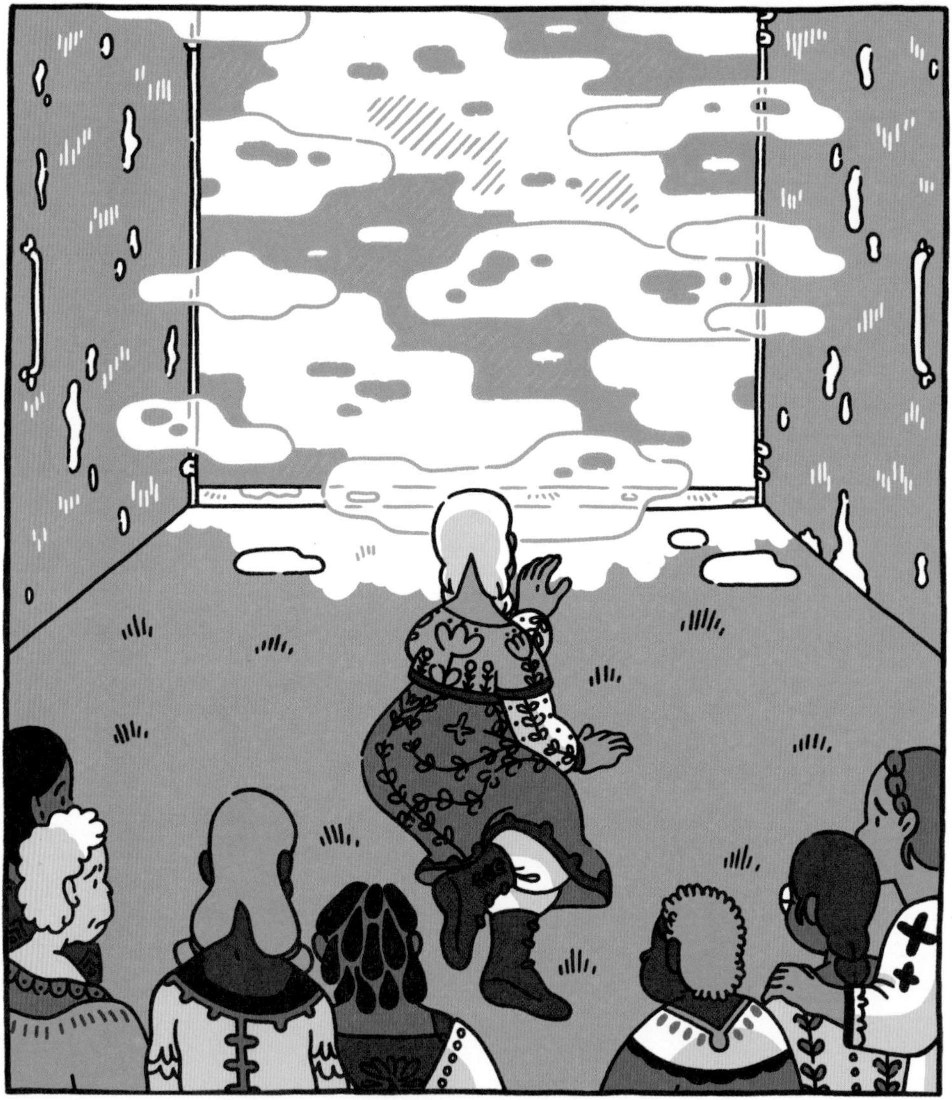

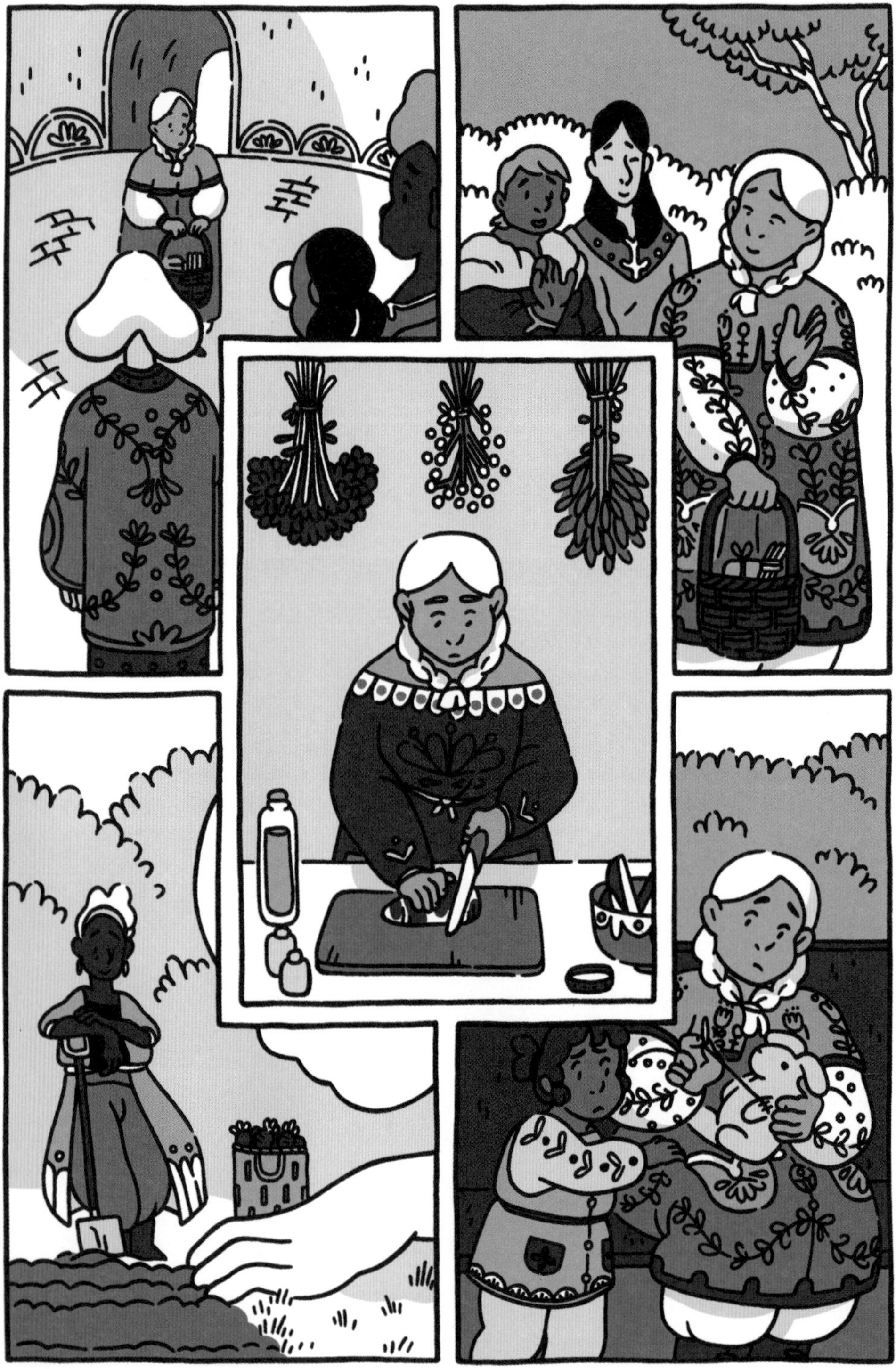

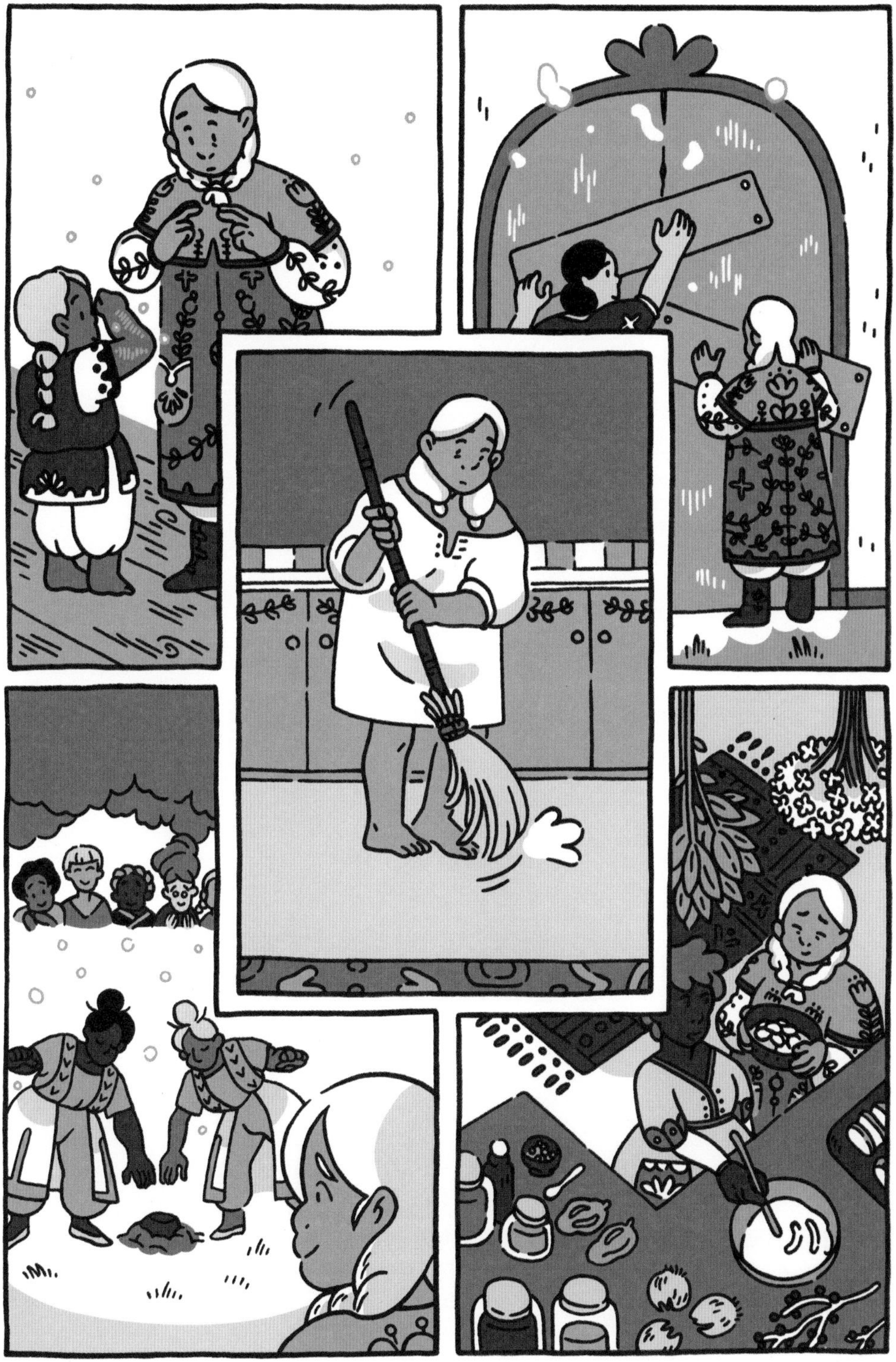

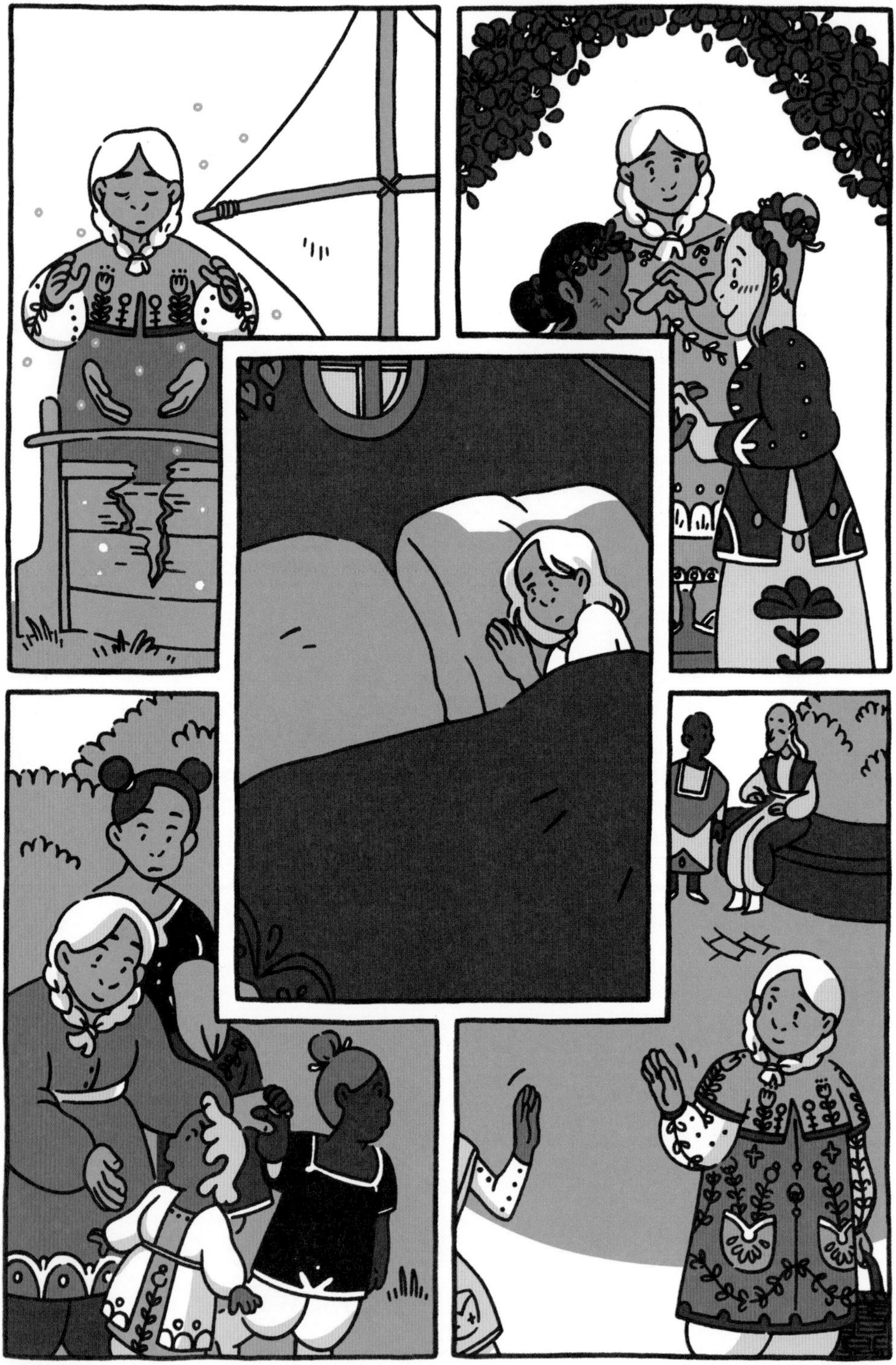

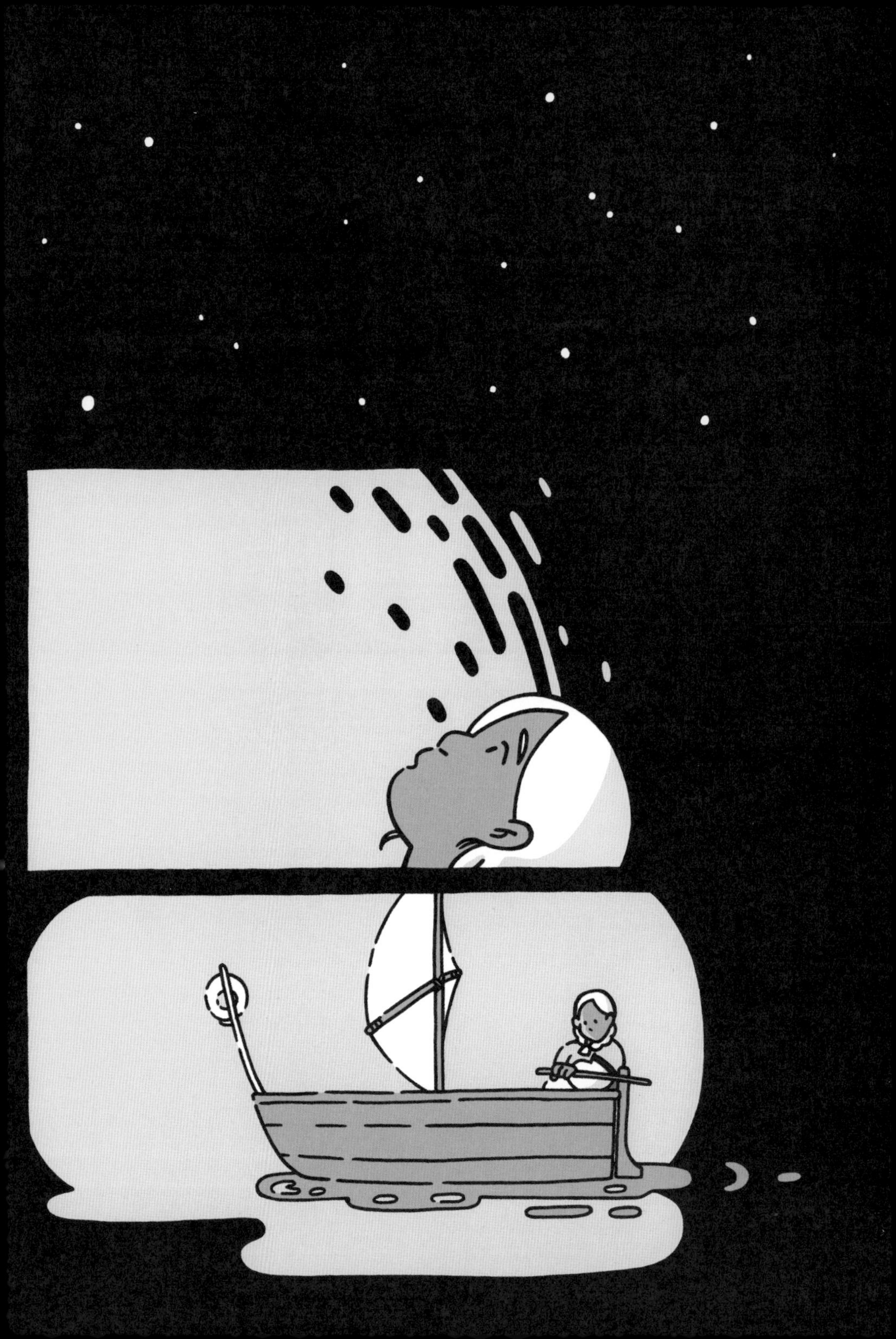

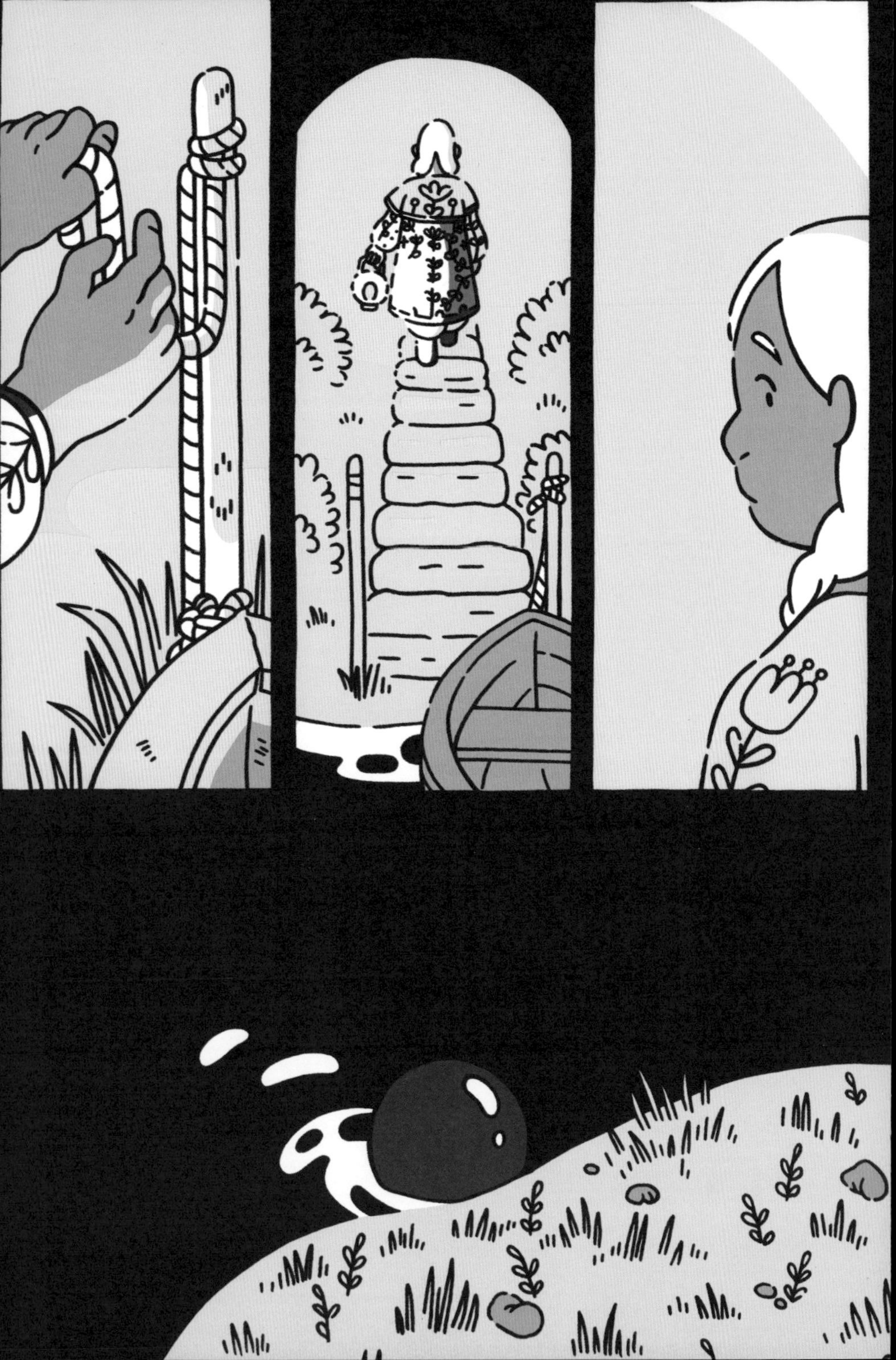

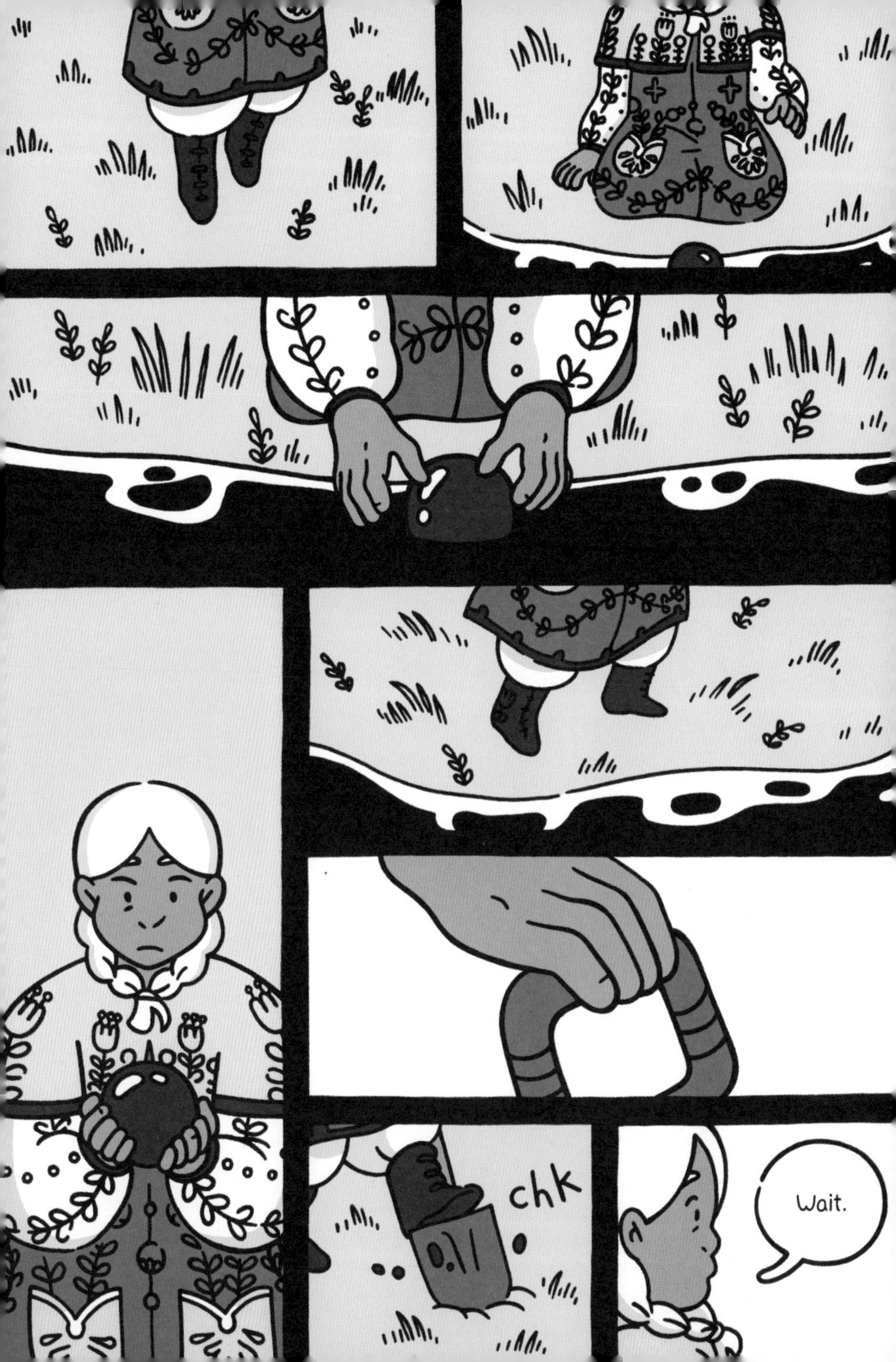
chk
Wait.

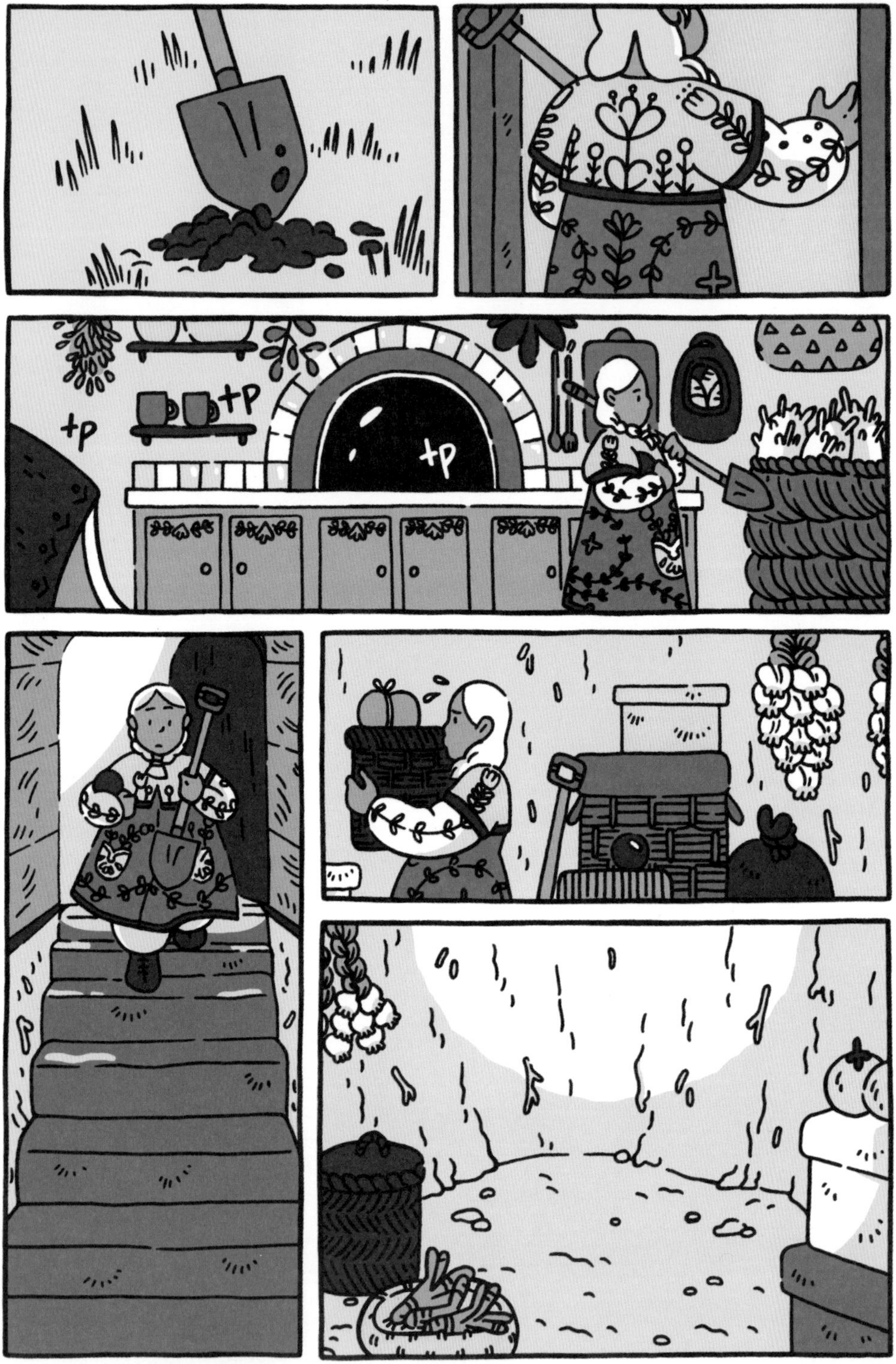
tp
tp
tp

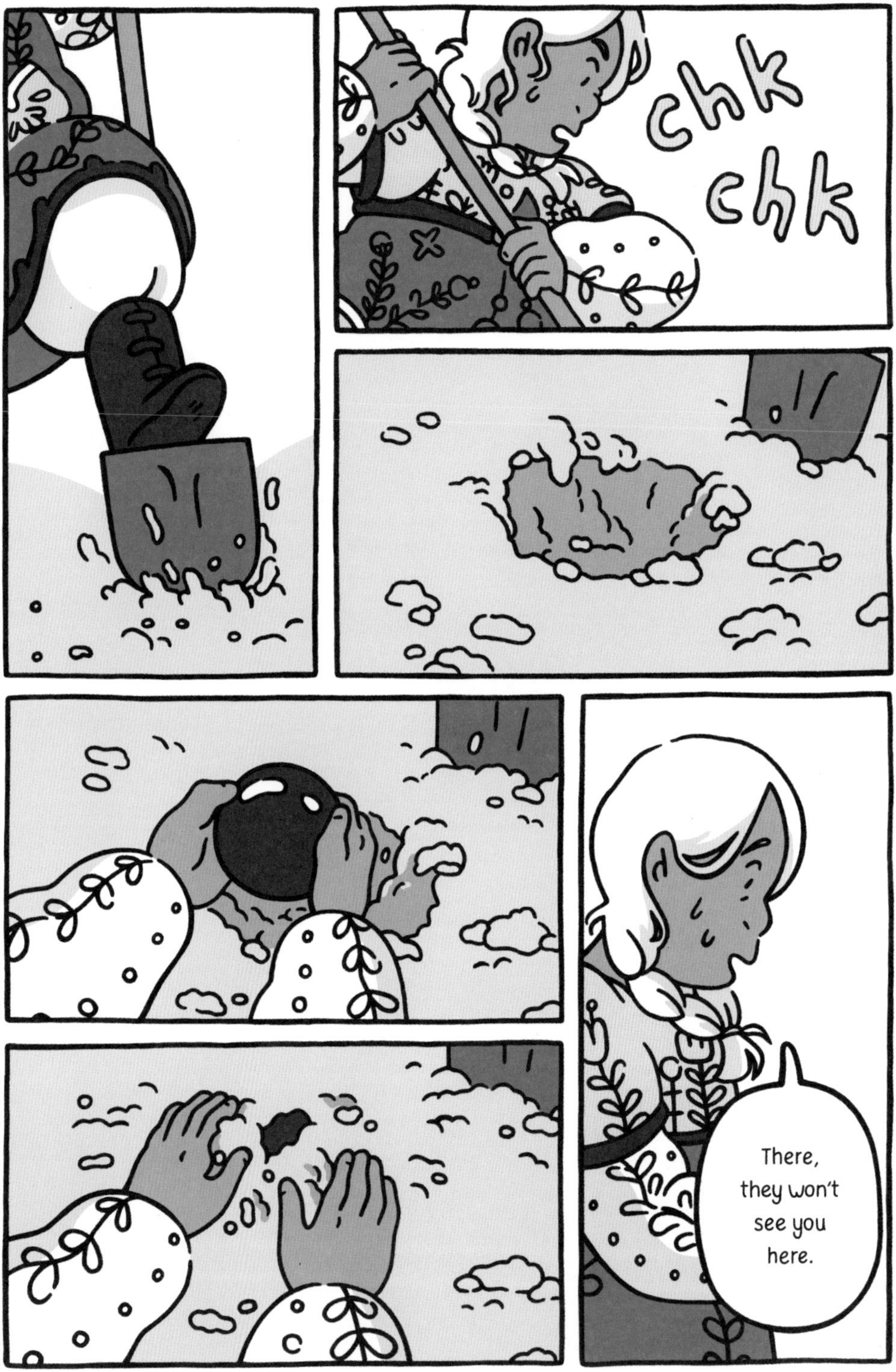
chk
chk
There, they won't see you here.

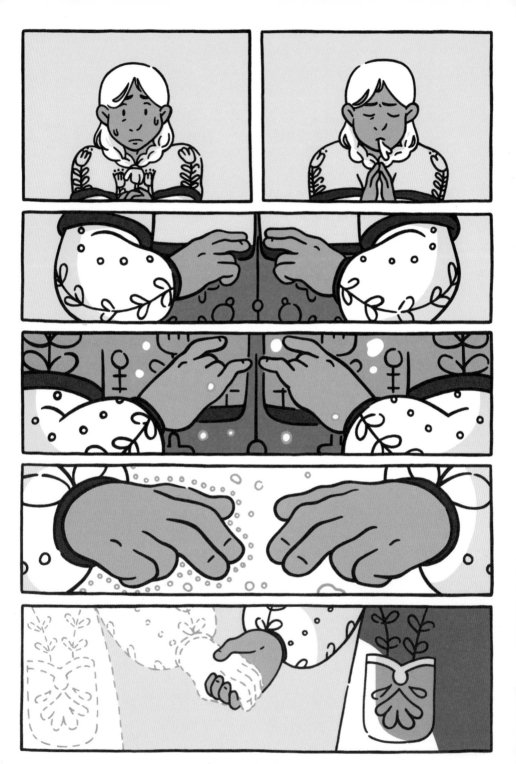

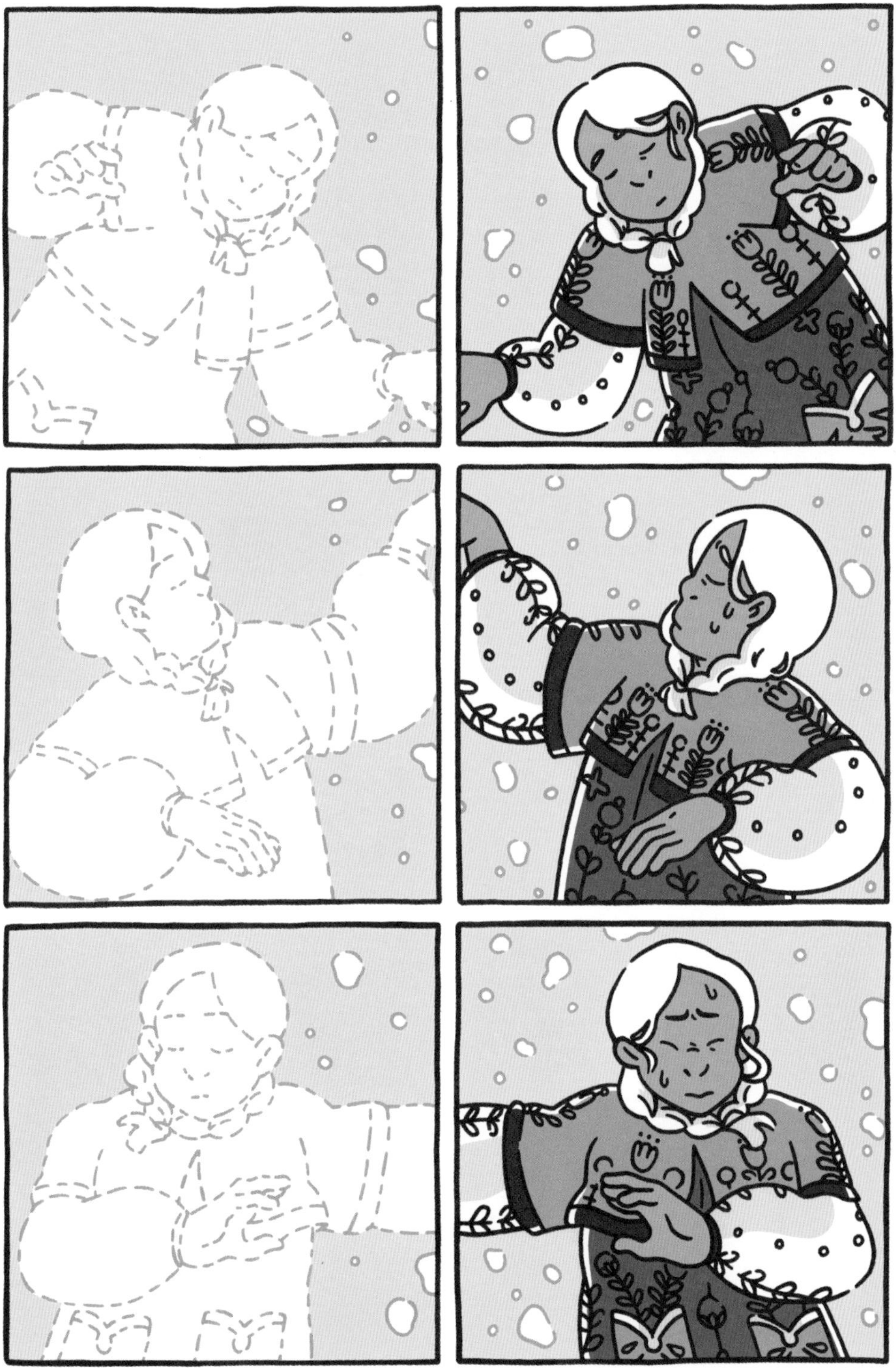

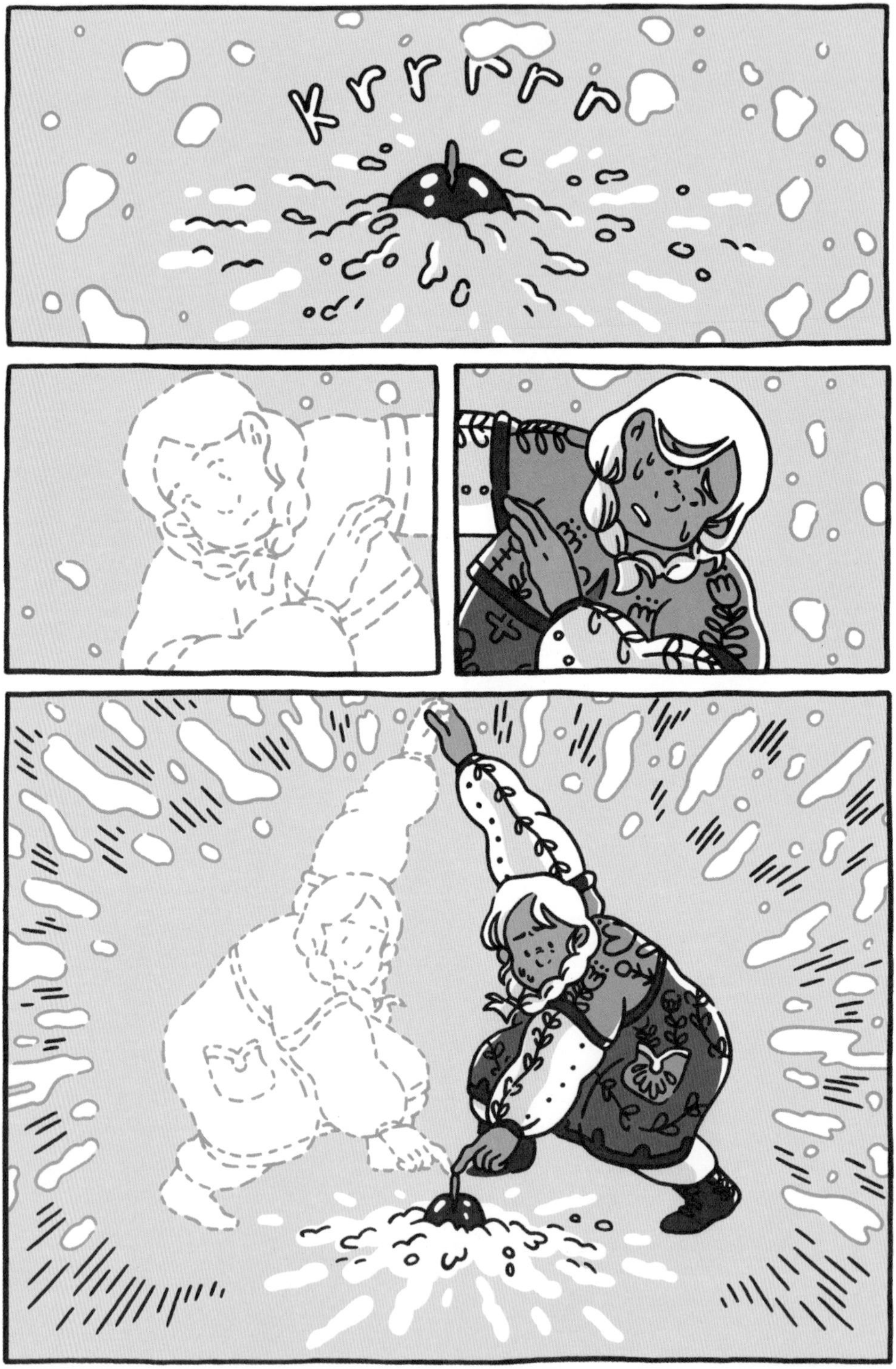
Krrrrrr

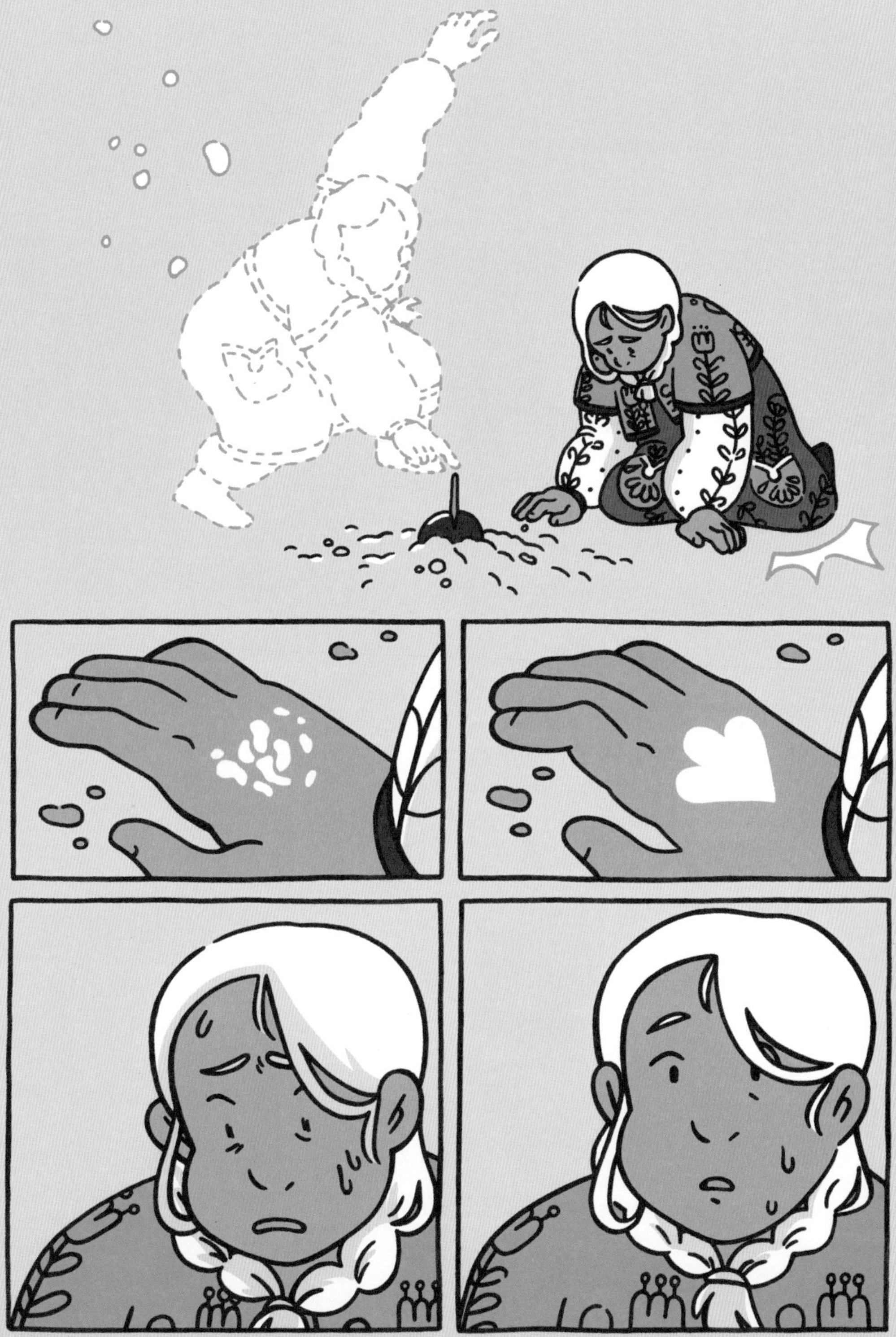

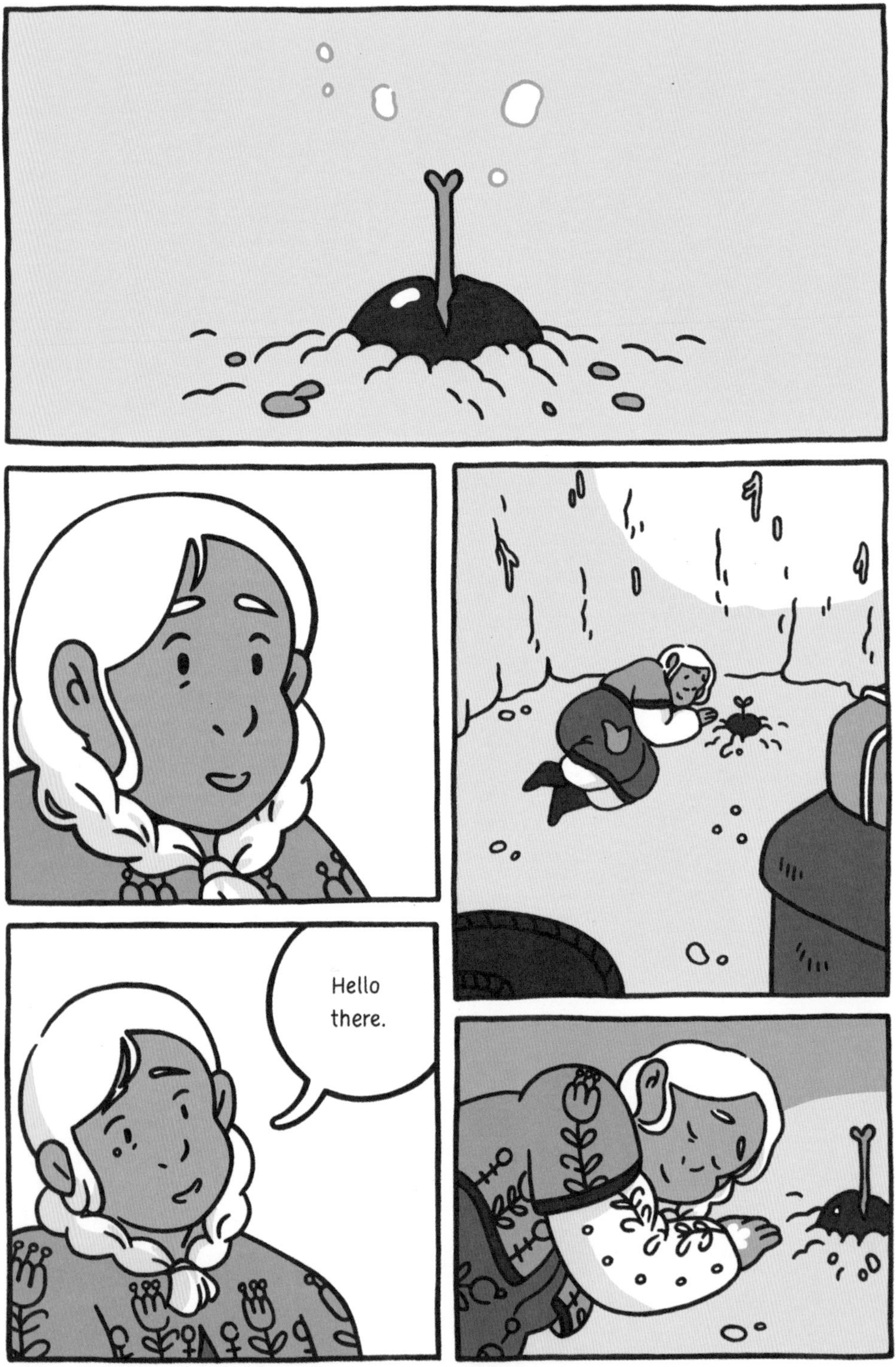
Hello
there.

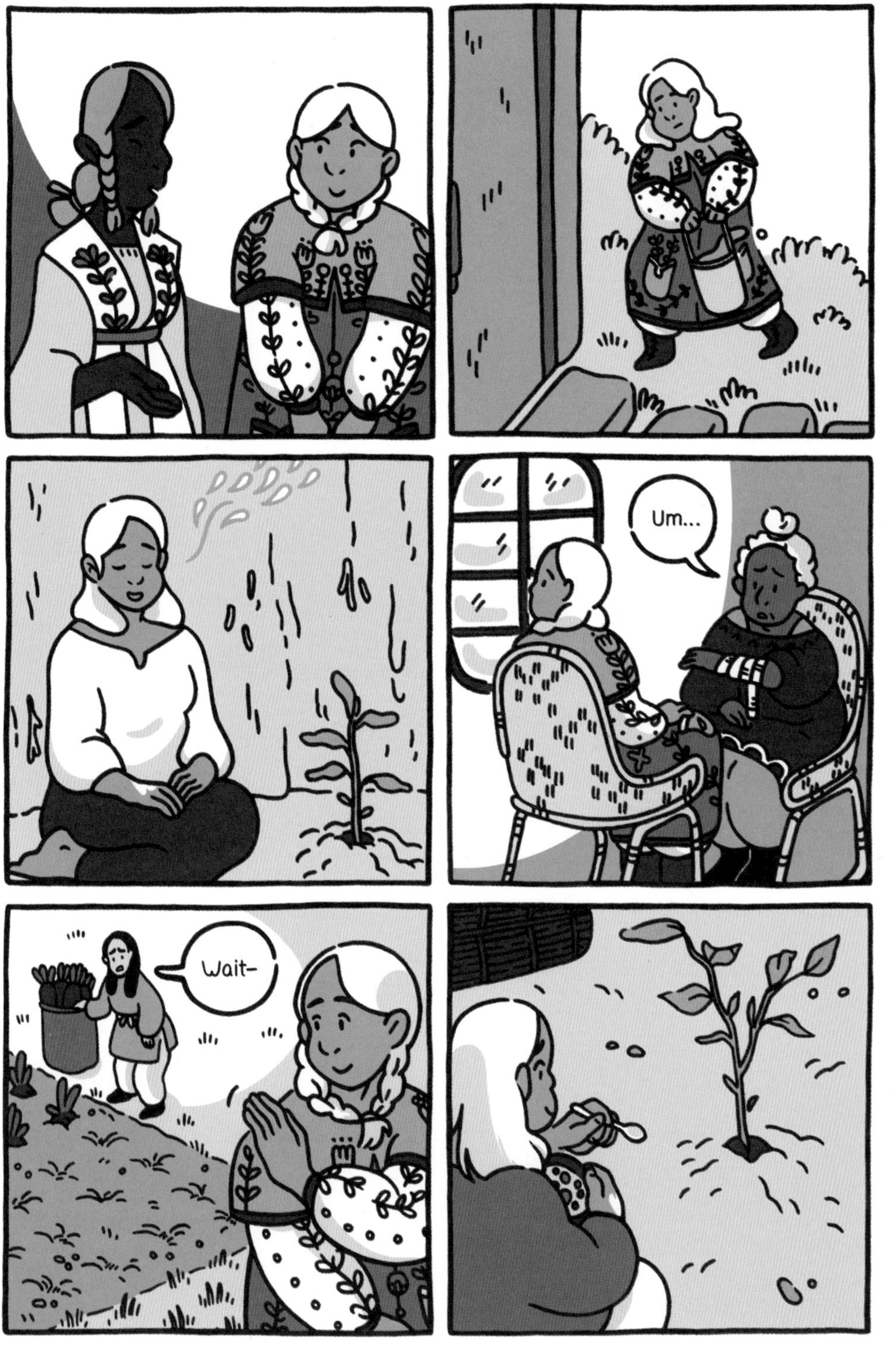
Um...
Wait-

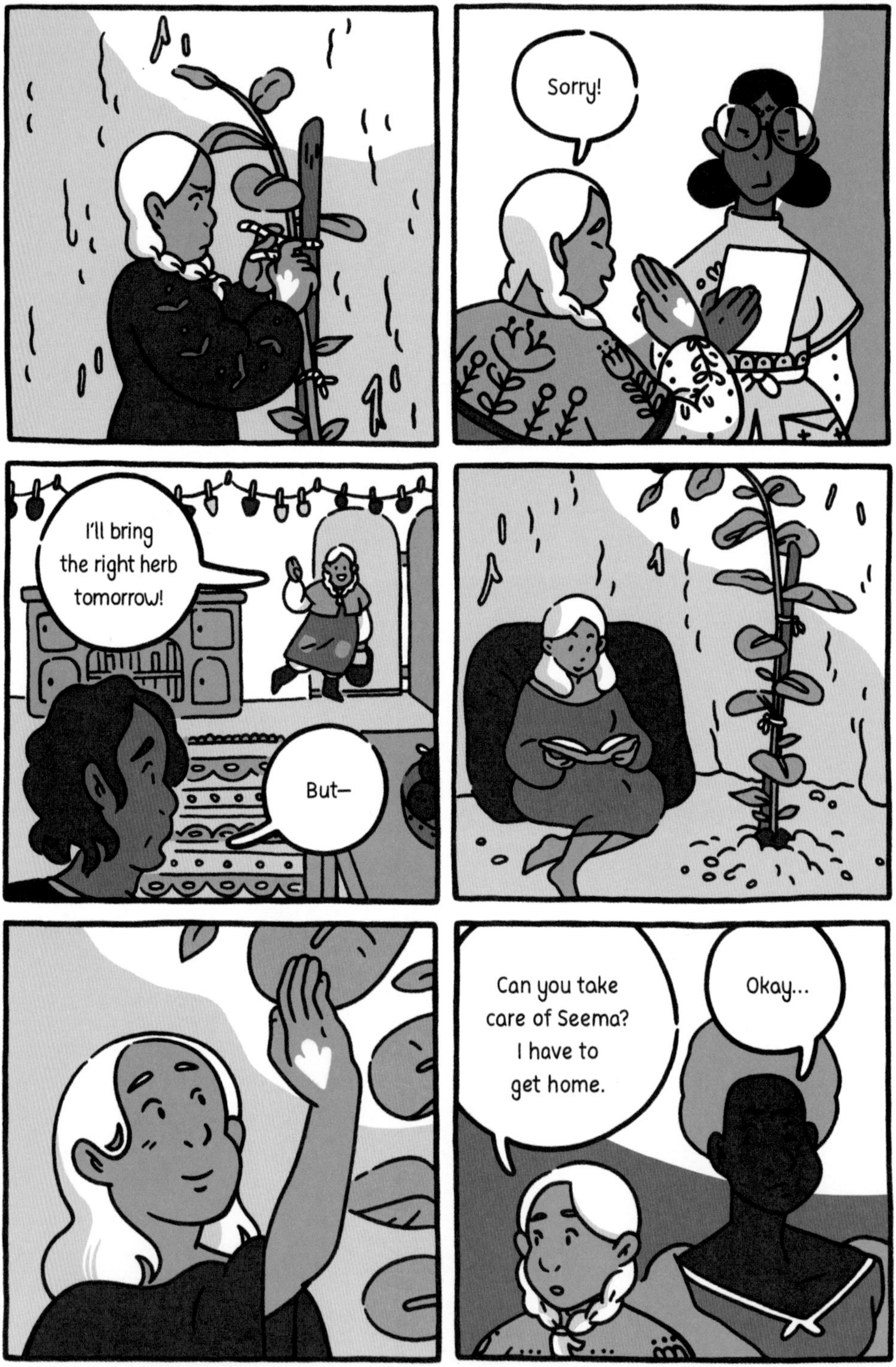
Sorry!
I'll bring the right herb tomorrow!
But—
Can you take care of Seema? I have to get home.
Okay...

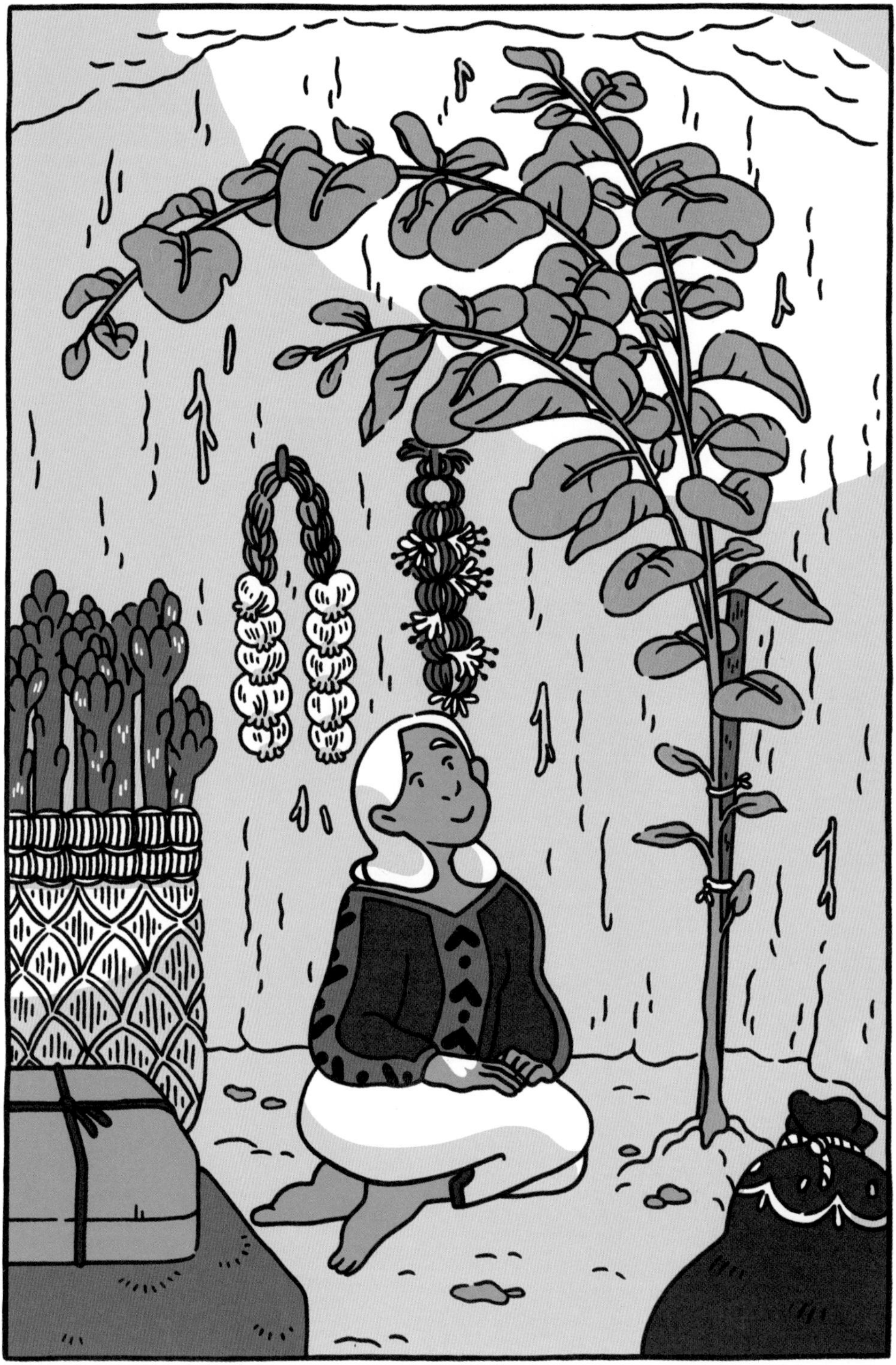

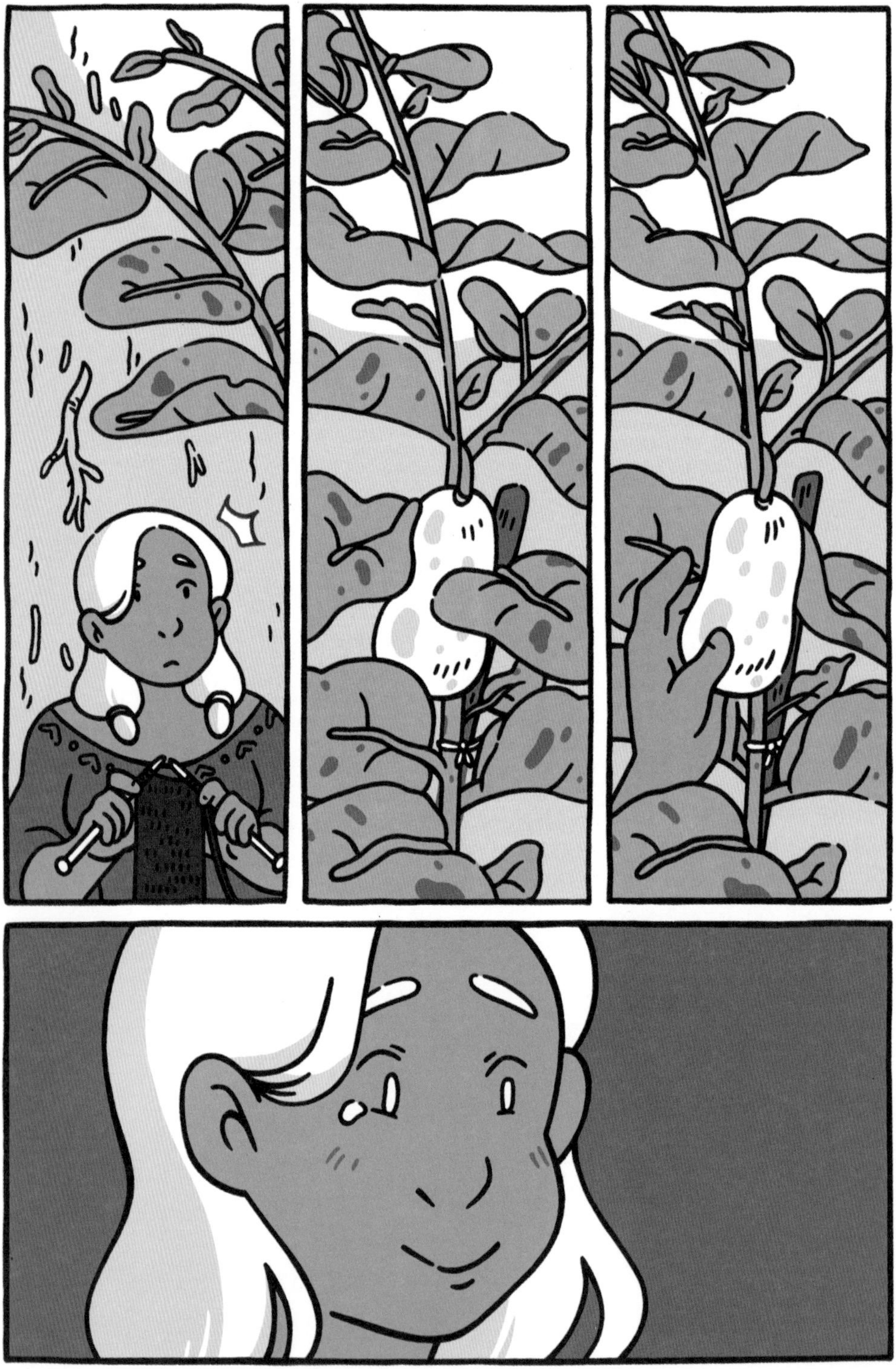

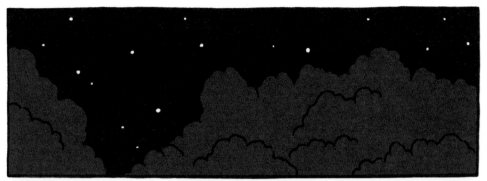

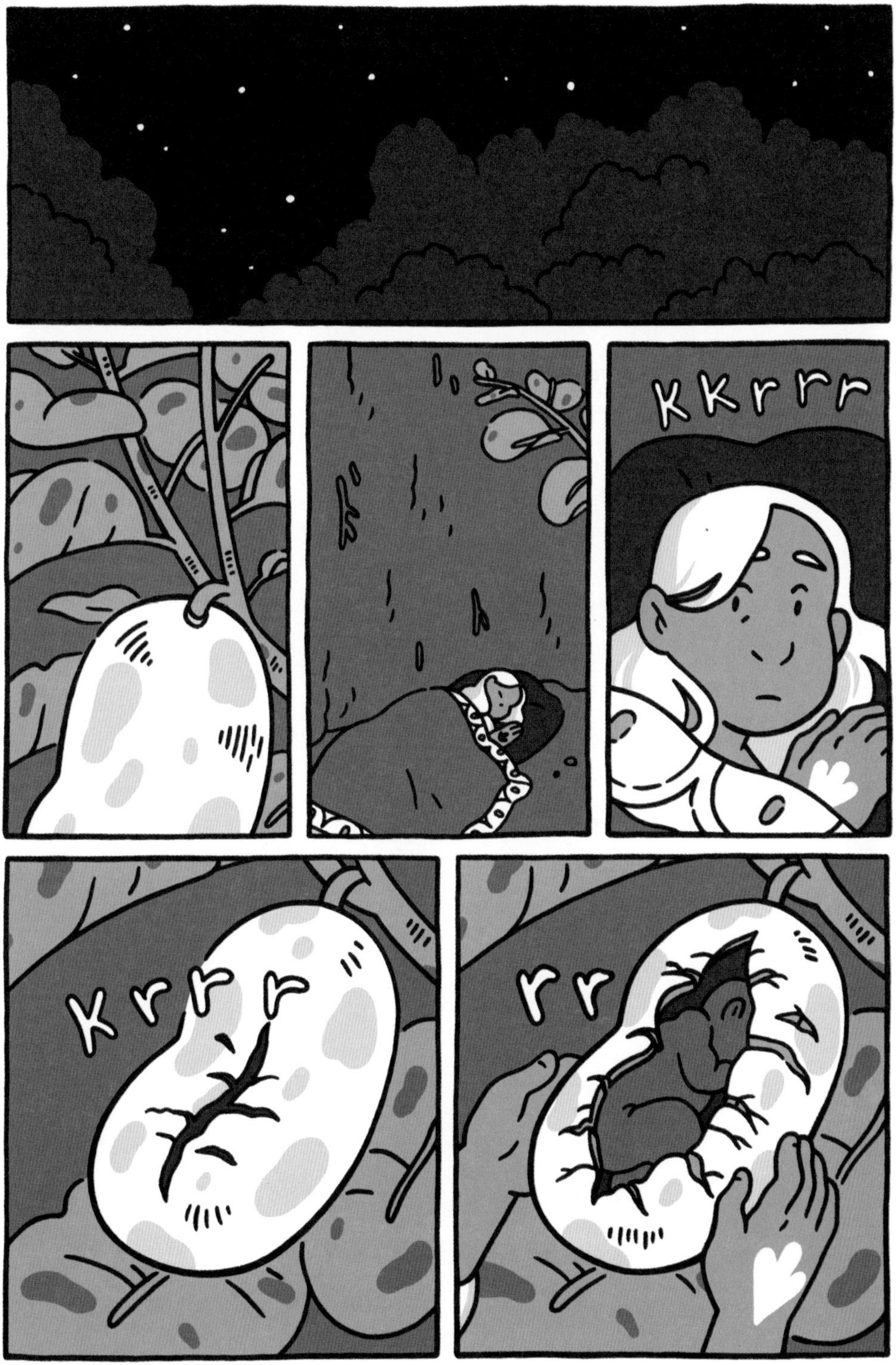
KKrrr
krrr
rr

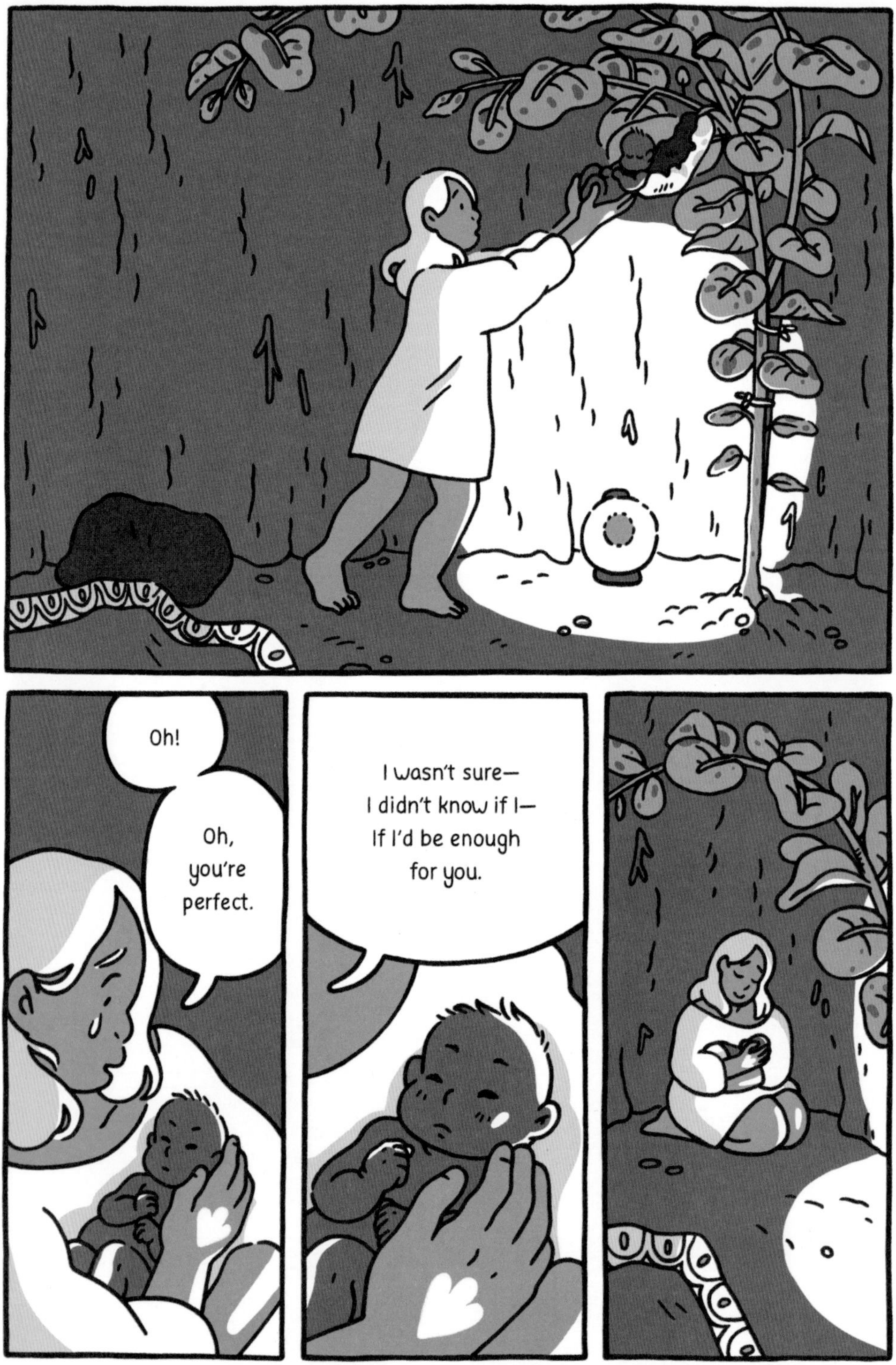
Oh!
Oh, you're perfect.
I wasn't sure— I didn't know if I— If I'd be enough for you.

Fellow Pillars,
I have taken very ill. I hope to rejoin you soon, but for now I must rest.

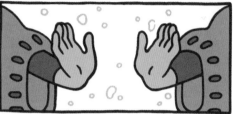

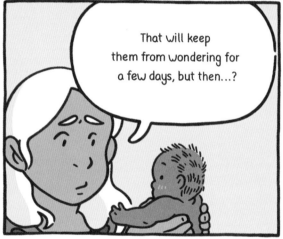

That will keep them from wondering for a few days, but then...?

What will we do, Lue?

They mustn't see you.

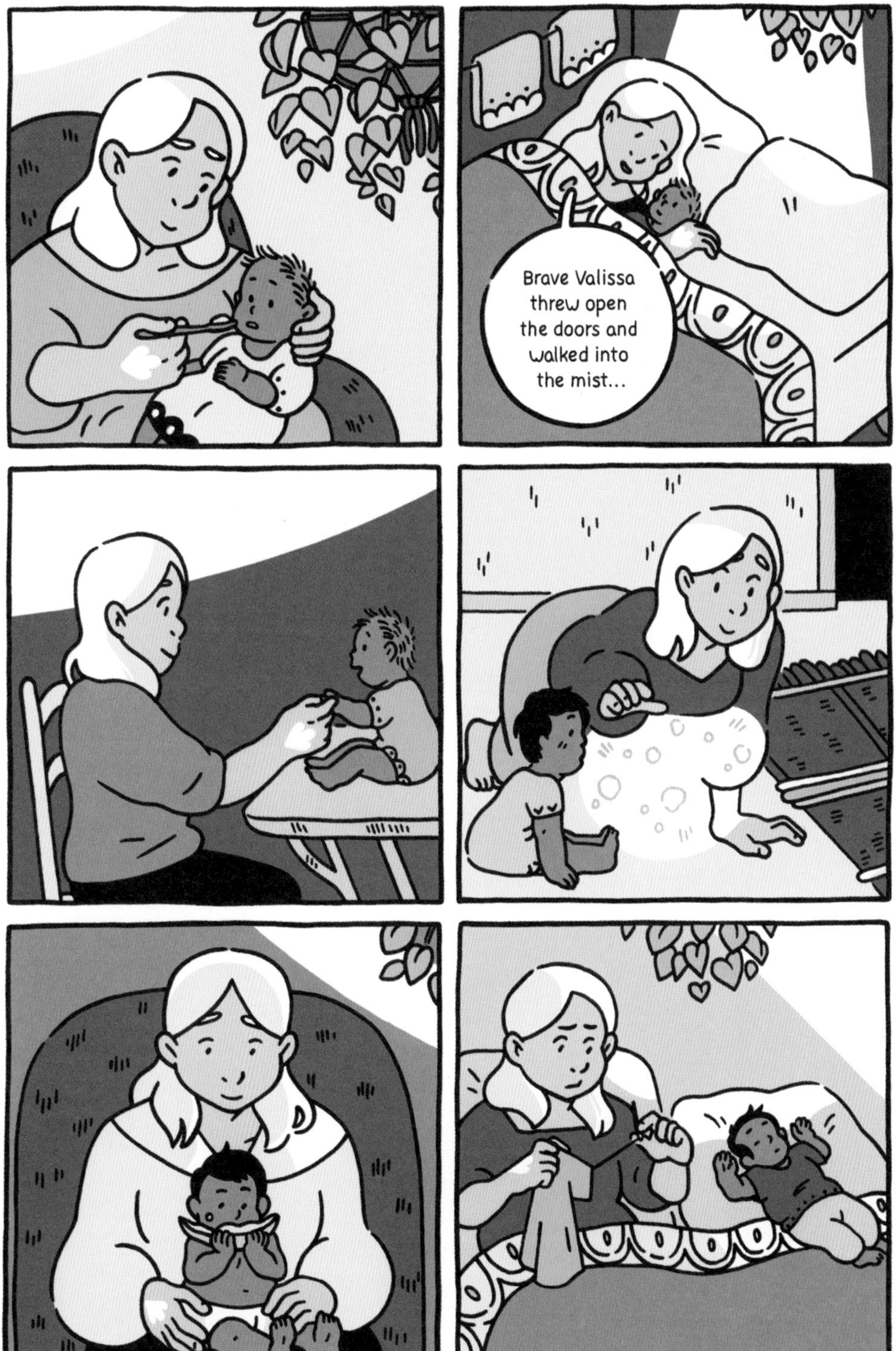
Brave Valissa threw open the doors and walked into the mist...

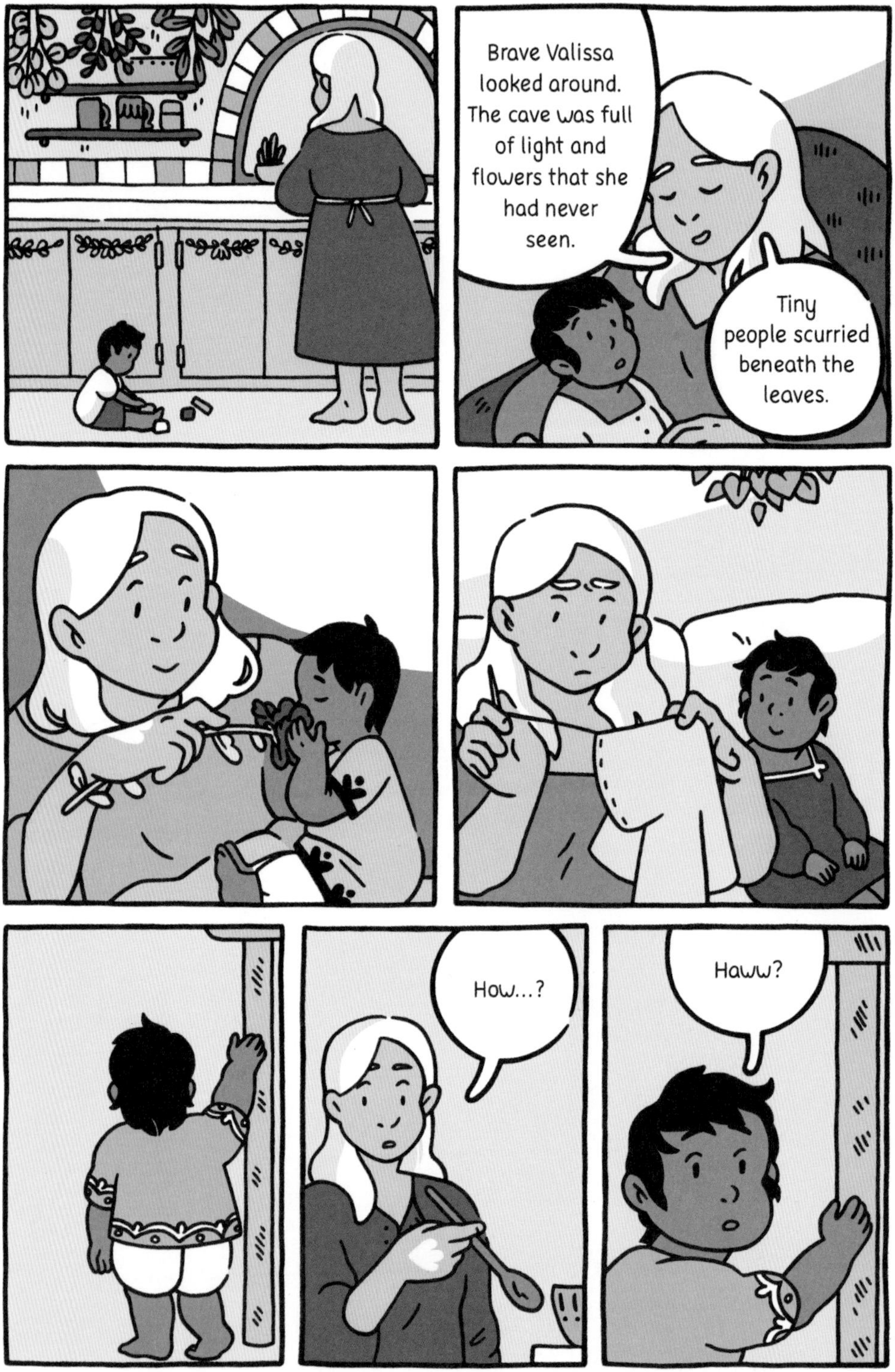
Brave Valissa looked around. The cave was full of light and flowers that she had never seen.
Tiny people scurried beneath the leaves.
How...?
Haww?

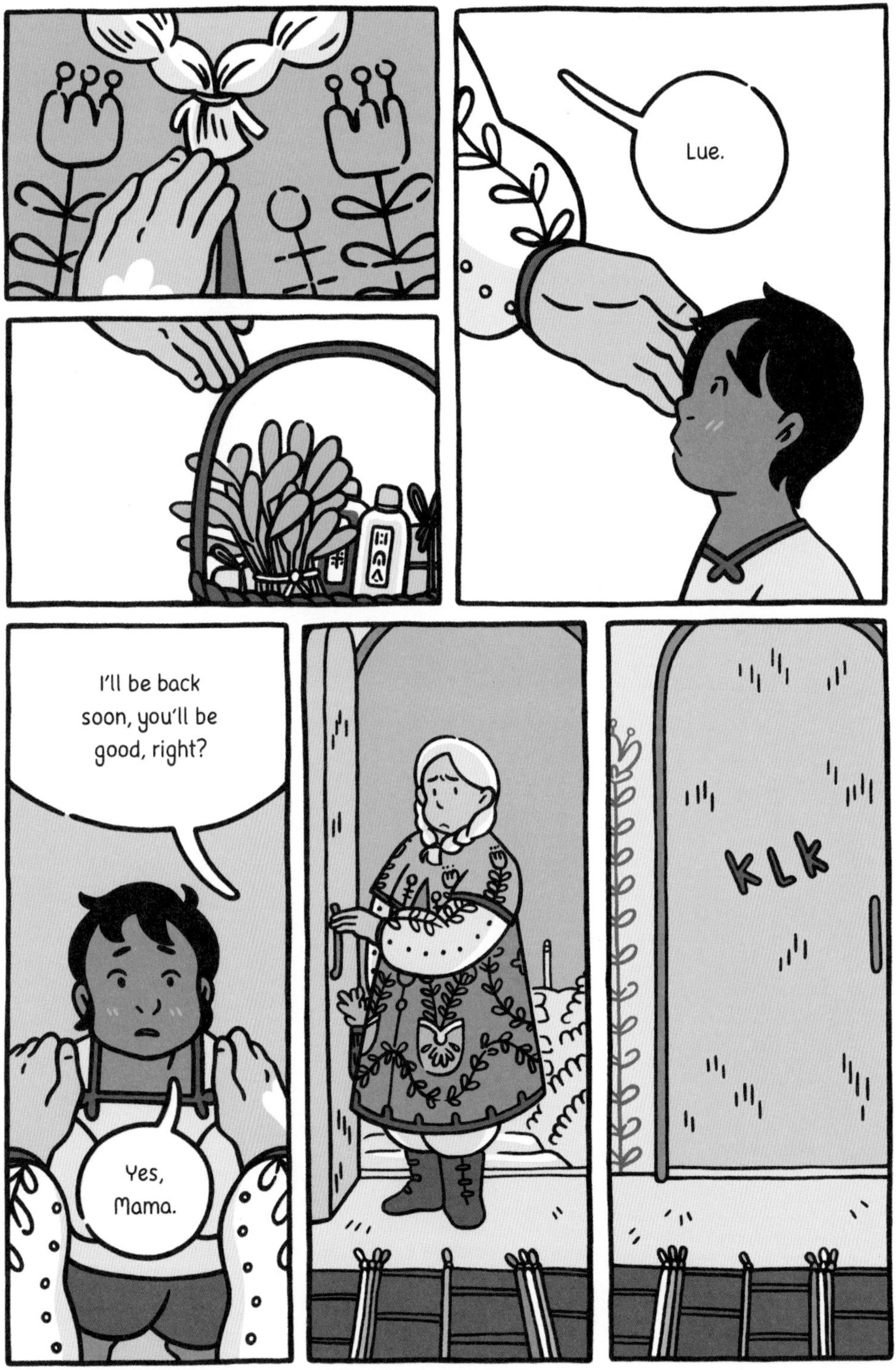
Lue.
I'll be back soon, you'll be good, right?
Yes, Mama.
KLK

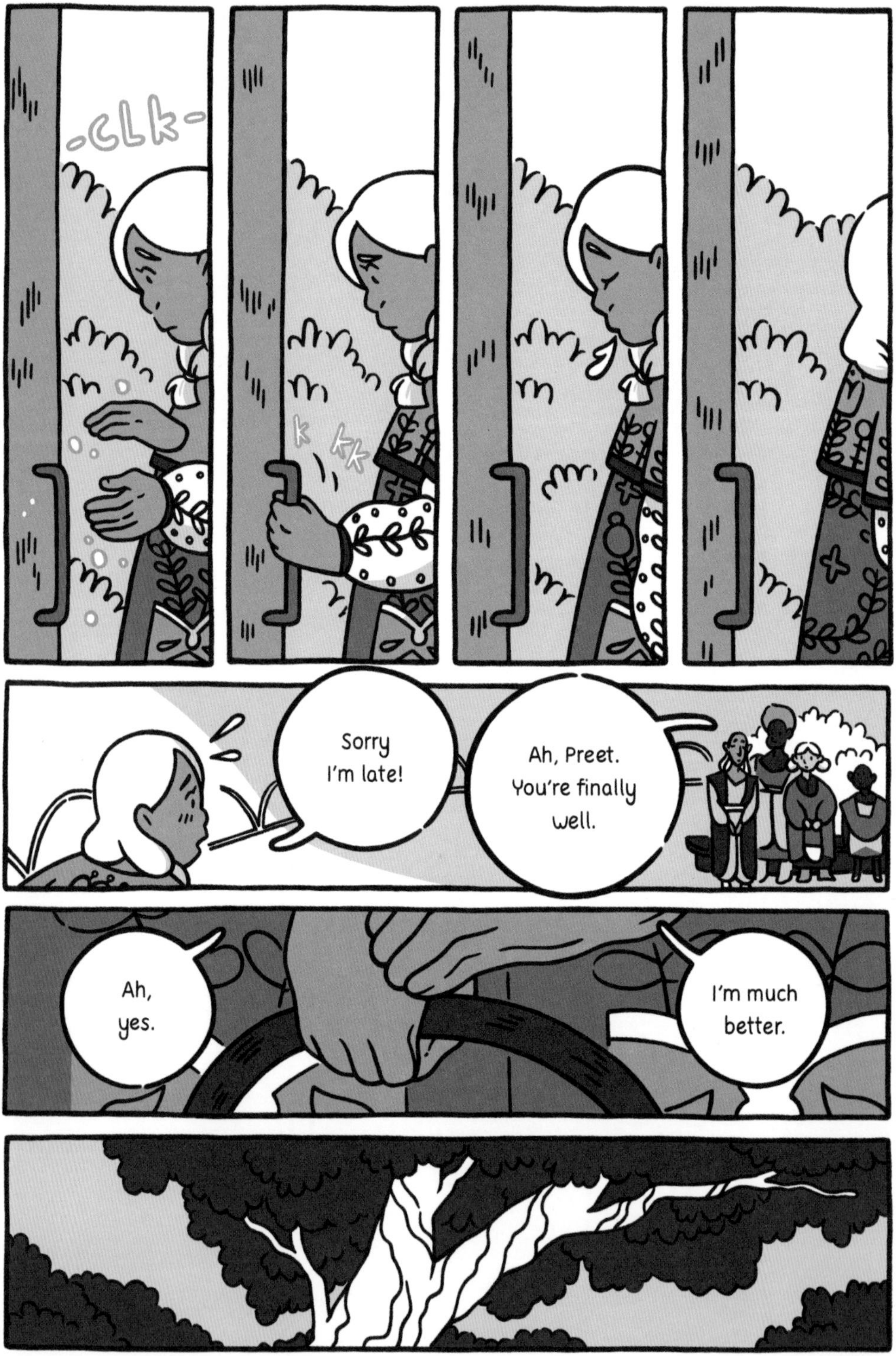
-CLK-
K
KK
Sorry I'm late!
Ah, Preet. You're finally well.
Ah, yes.
I'm much better.

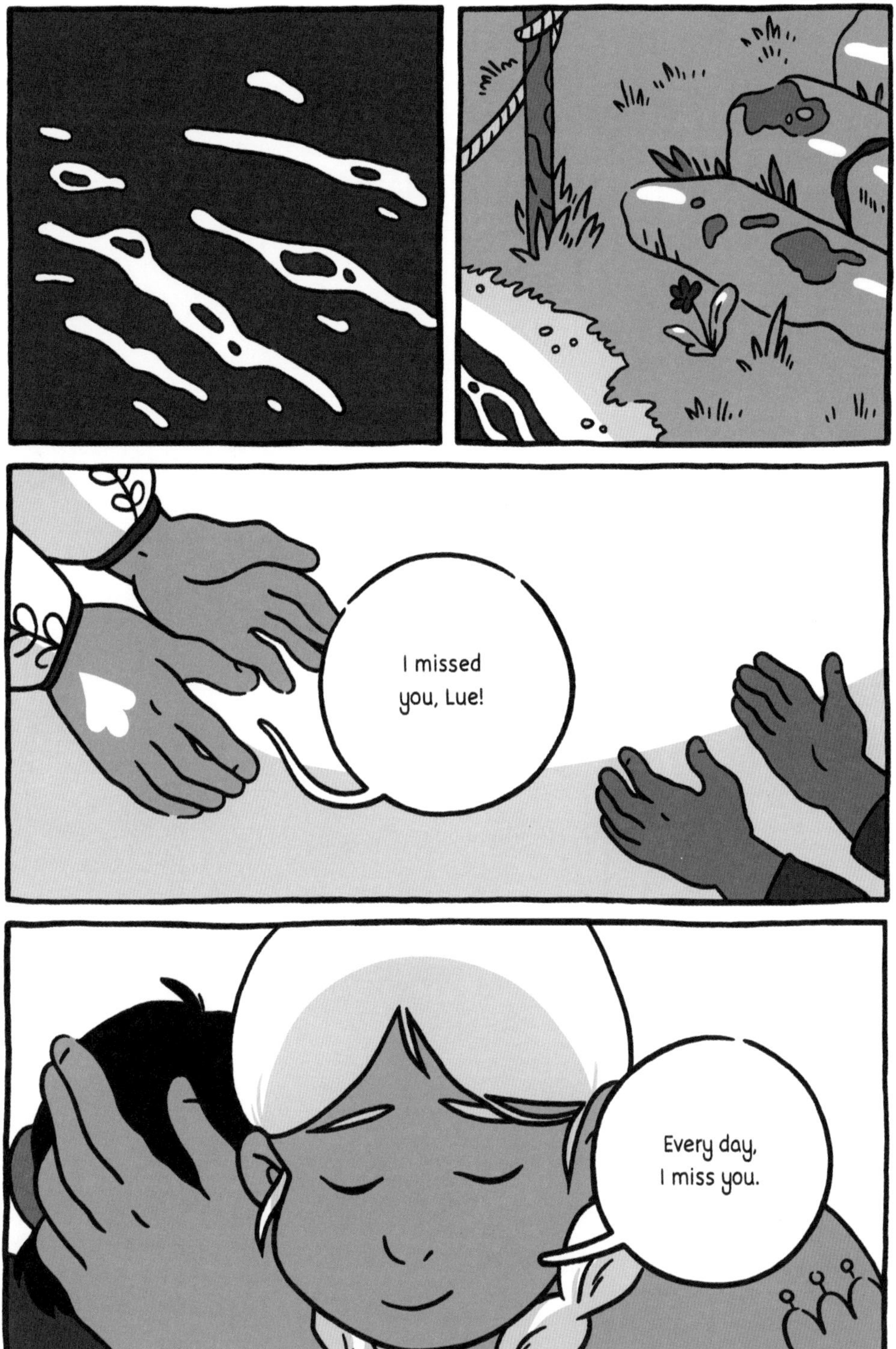
I missed you, Lue!
Every day, I miss you.

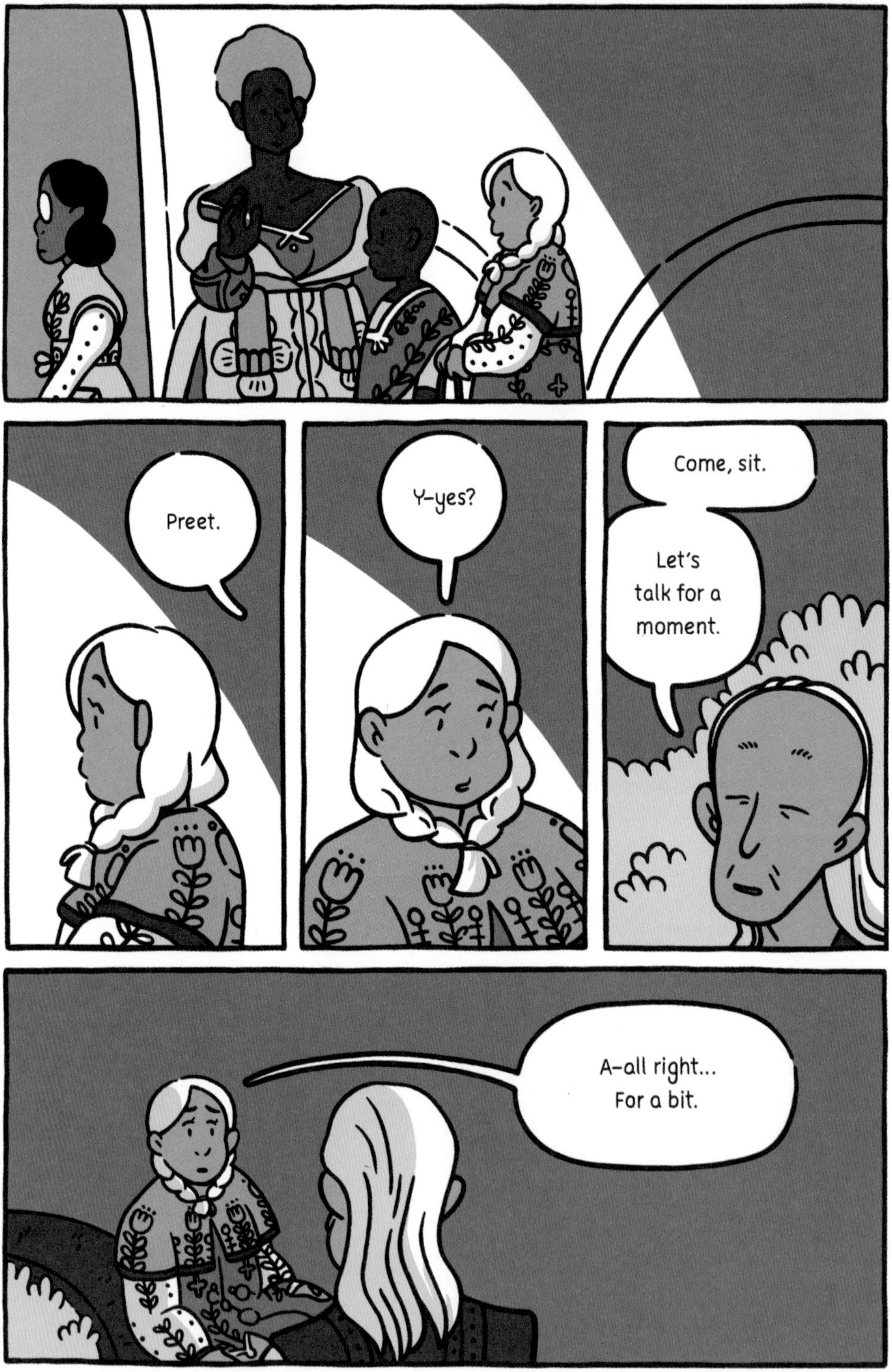
Preet.
Y-yes?
Come, sit.
Let's talk for a moment.
A-all right... For a bit.

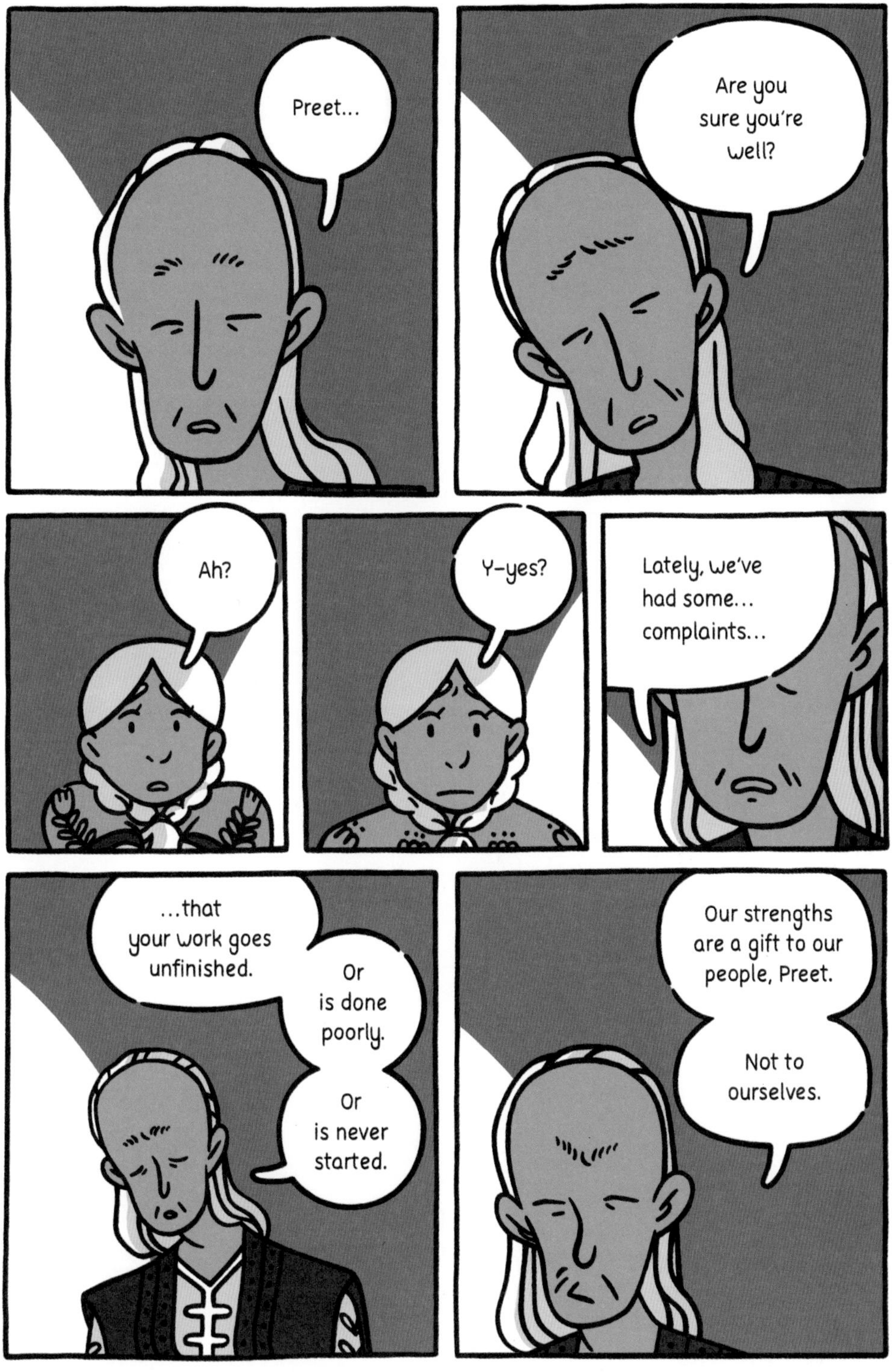
Preet...
Are you sure you're well?
Ah?
Y-yes?
Lately, we've had some... complaints...
...that your work goes unfinished.
Or is done poorly.
Or is never started.
Our strengths are a gift to our people, Preet.
Not to ourselves.

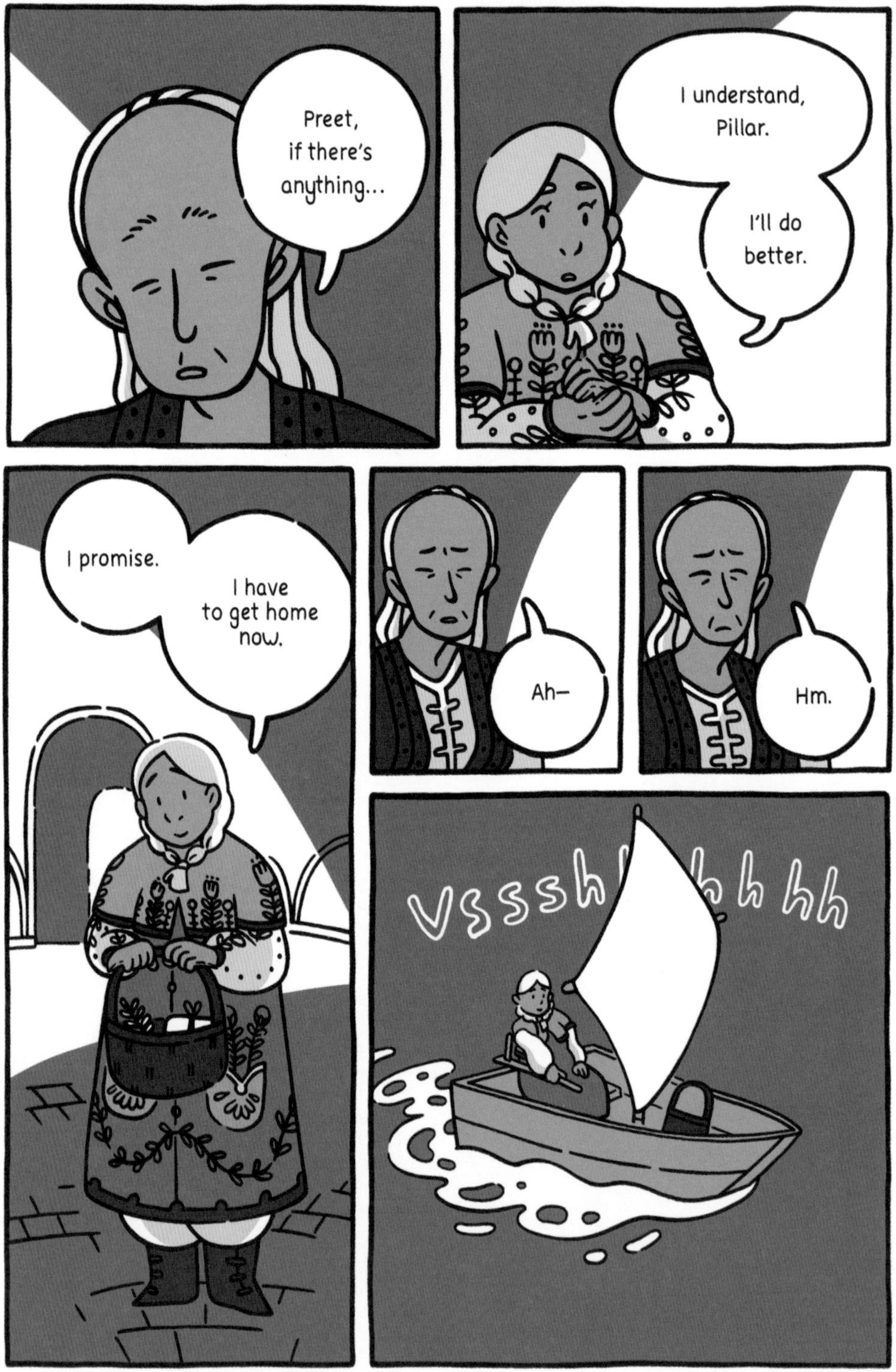
Preet, if there's anything...
I understand, Pillar.
I'll do better.
I promise.
I have to get home now.
Ah–
Hm.
Vssshhhhhh

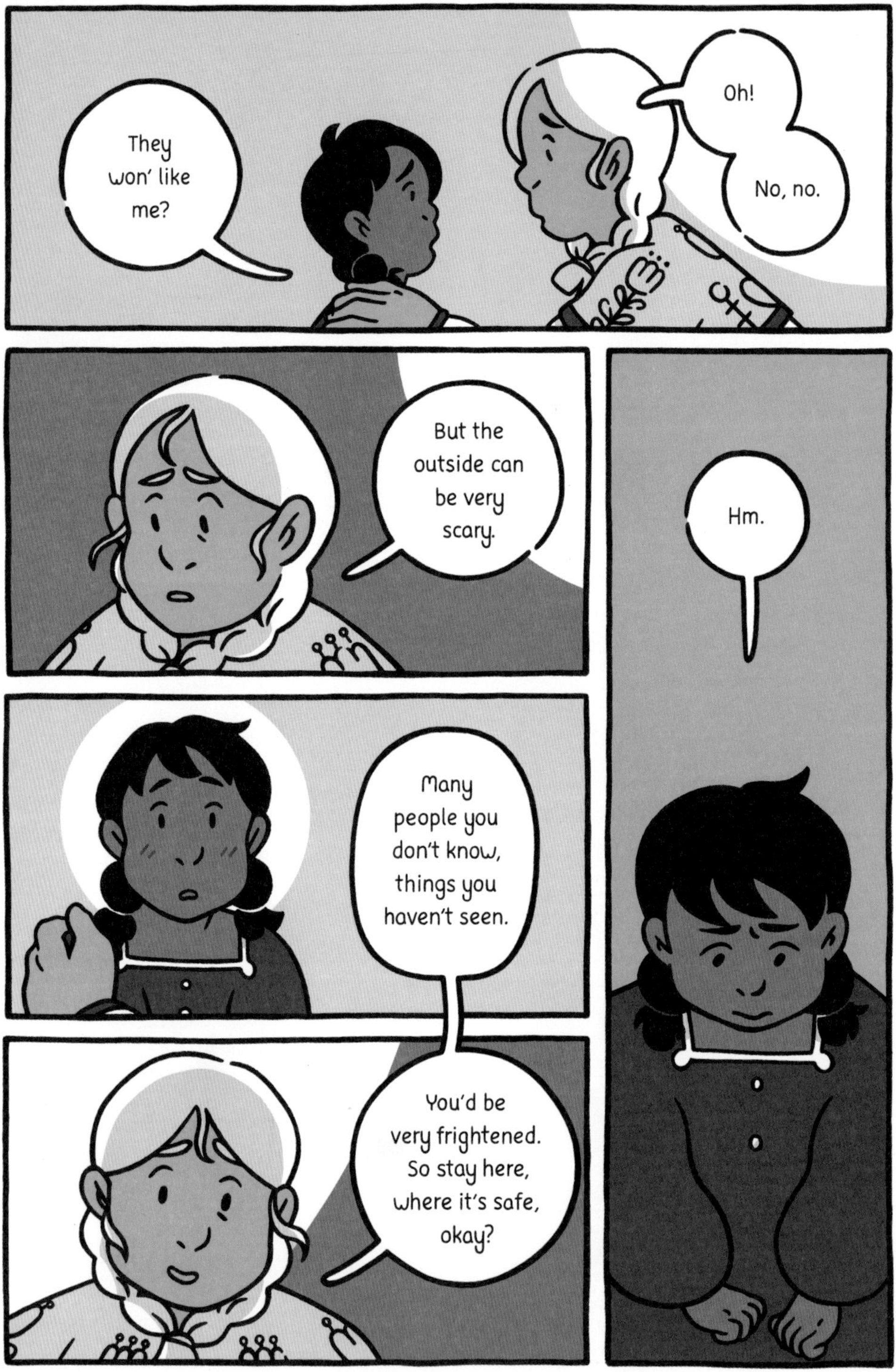
They won' like me?
Oh!
No, no.
But the outside can be very scary.
Hm.
Many people you don't know, things you haven't seen.
You'd be very frightened. So stay here, where it's safe, okay?

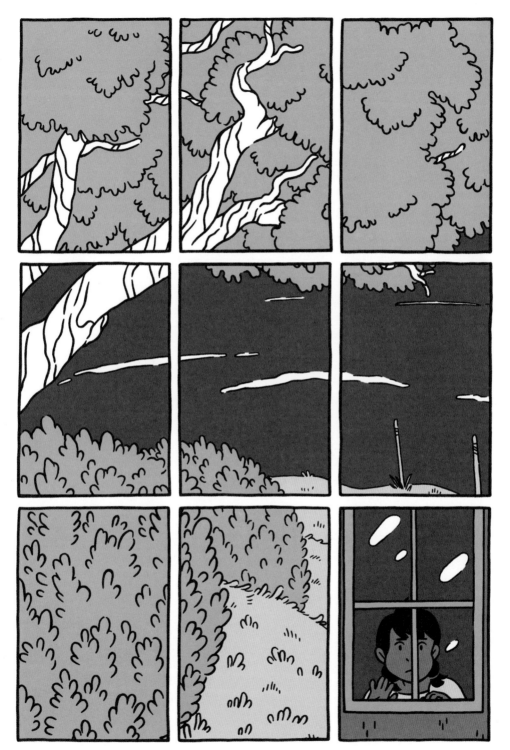

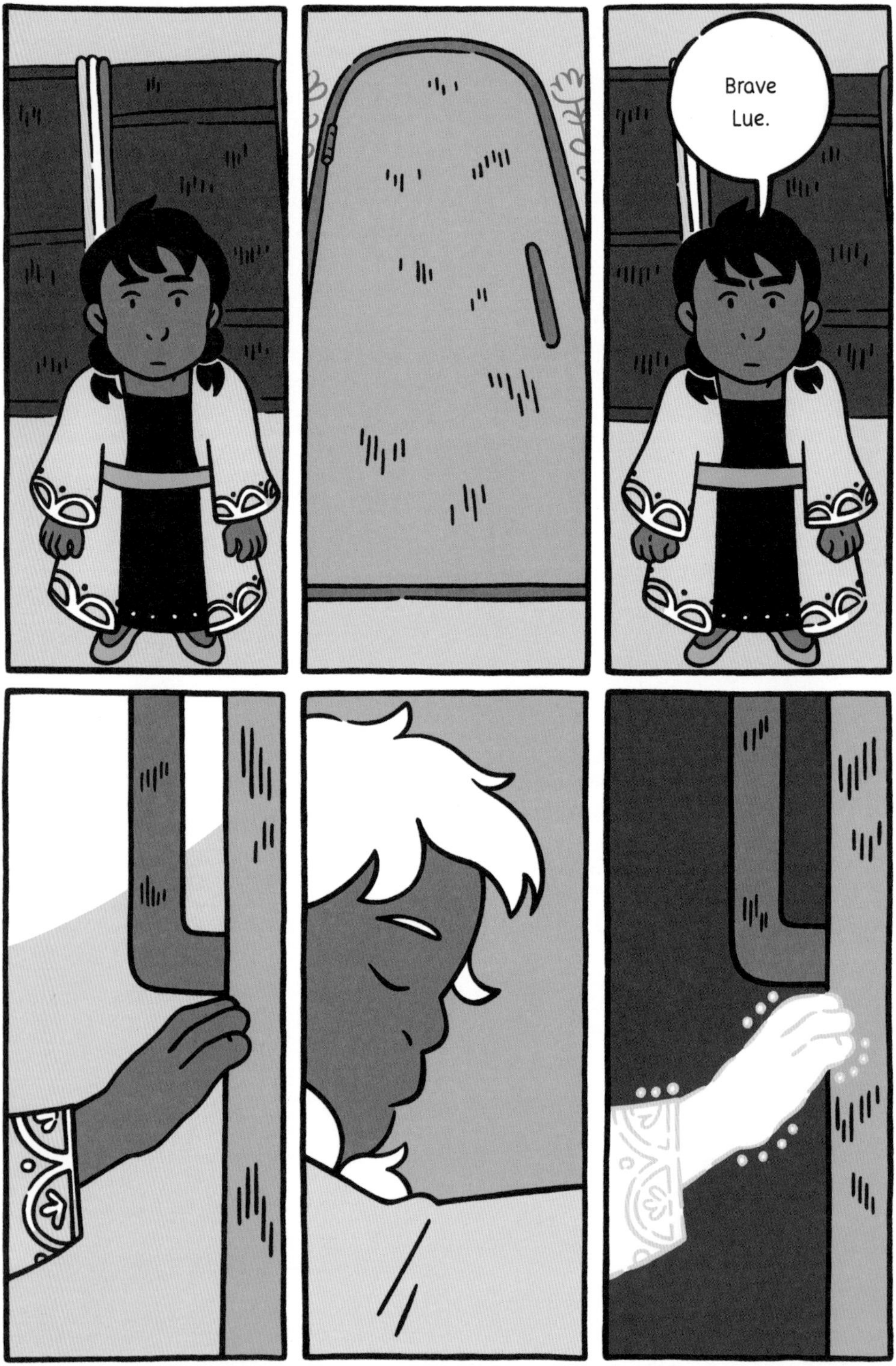
Brave
Lue.

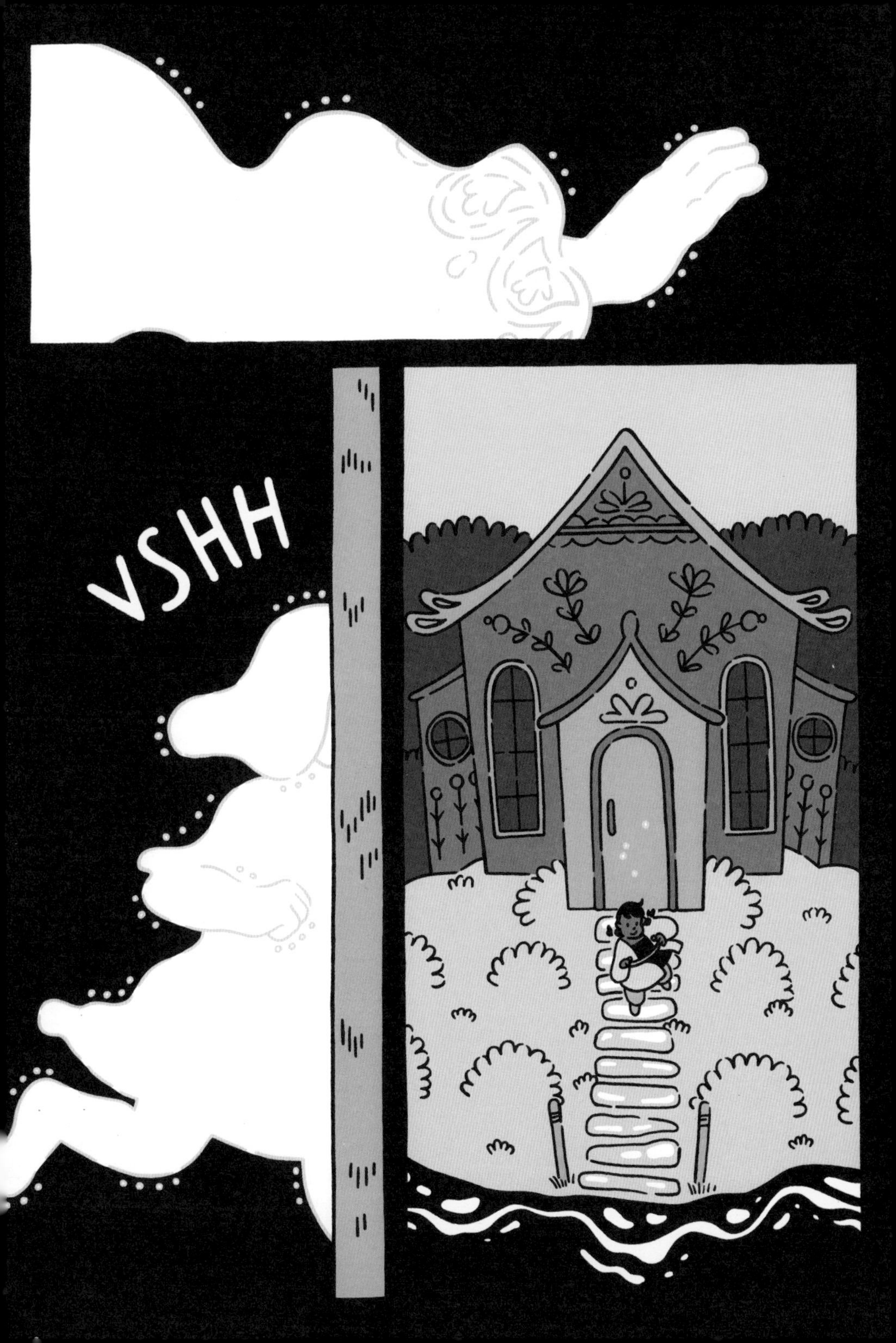
VSHH

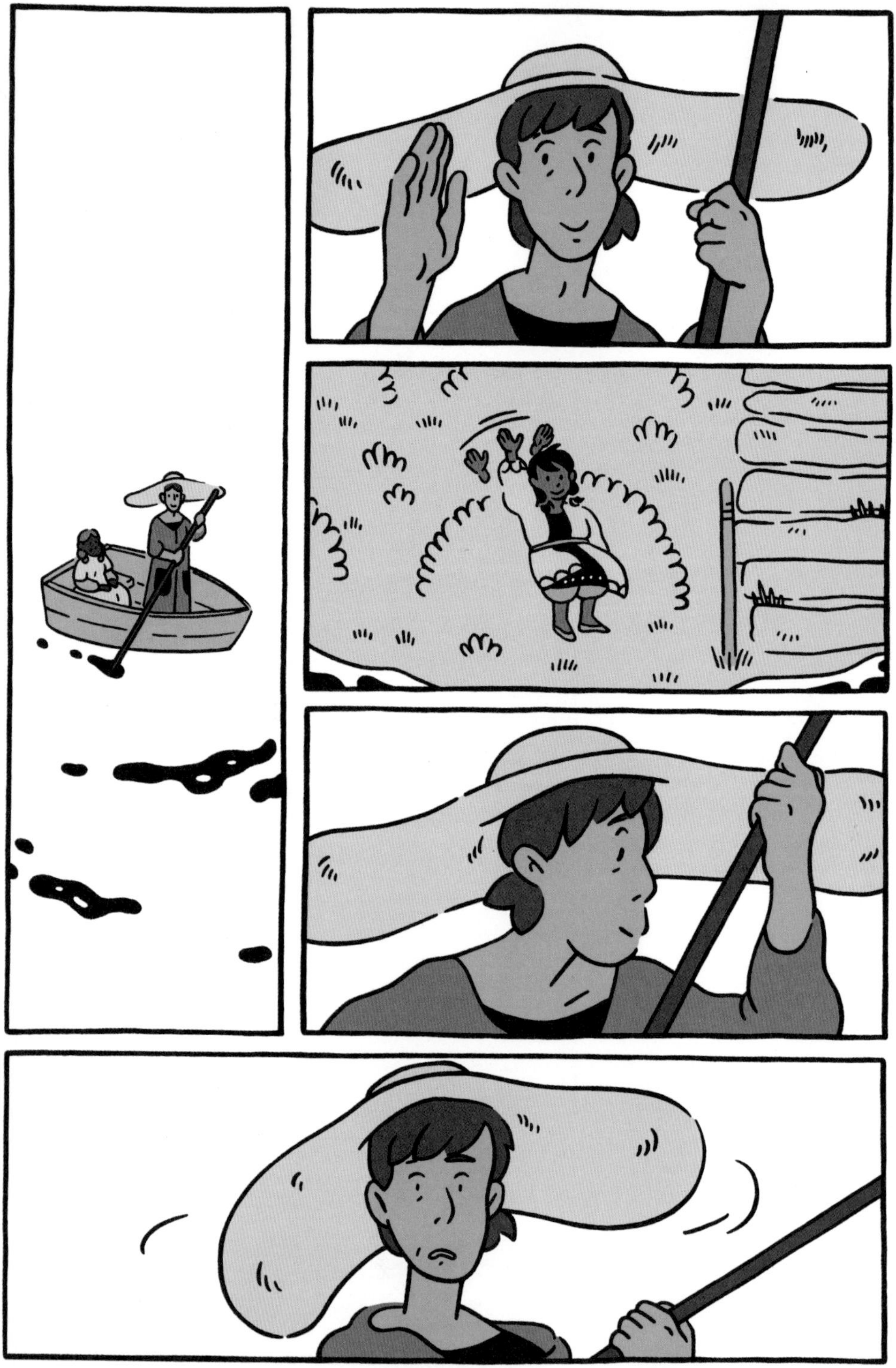

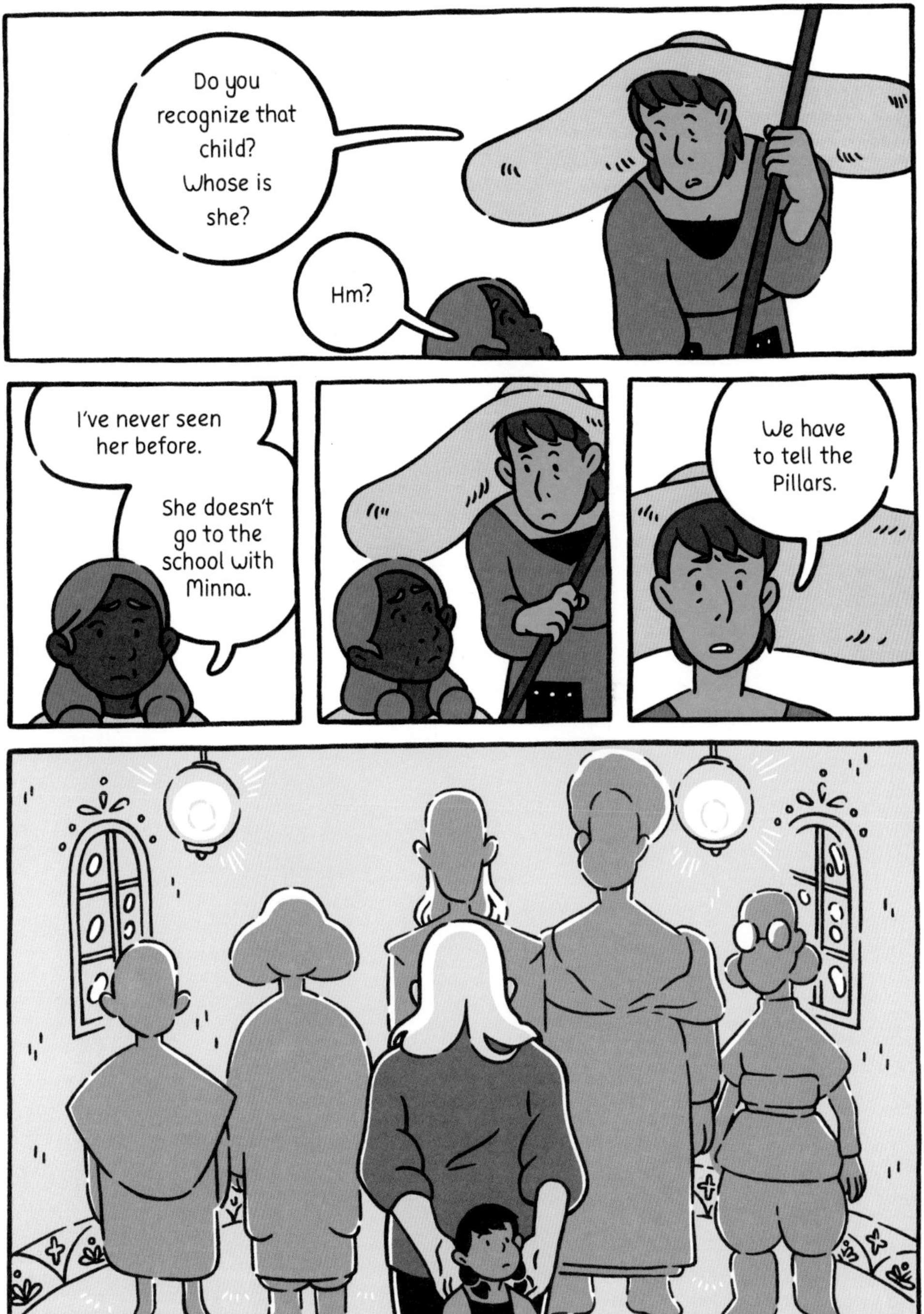
Do you recognize that child? Whose is she?
Hm?
I've never seen her before.
She doesn't go to the school with Minna.
We have to tell the Pillars.

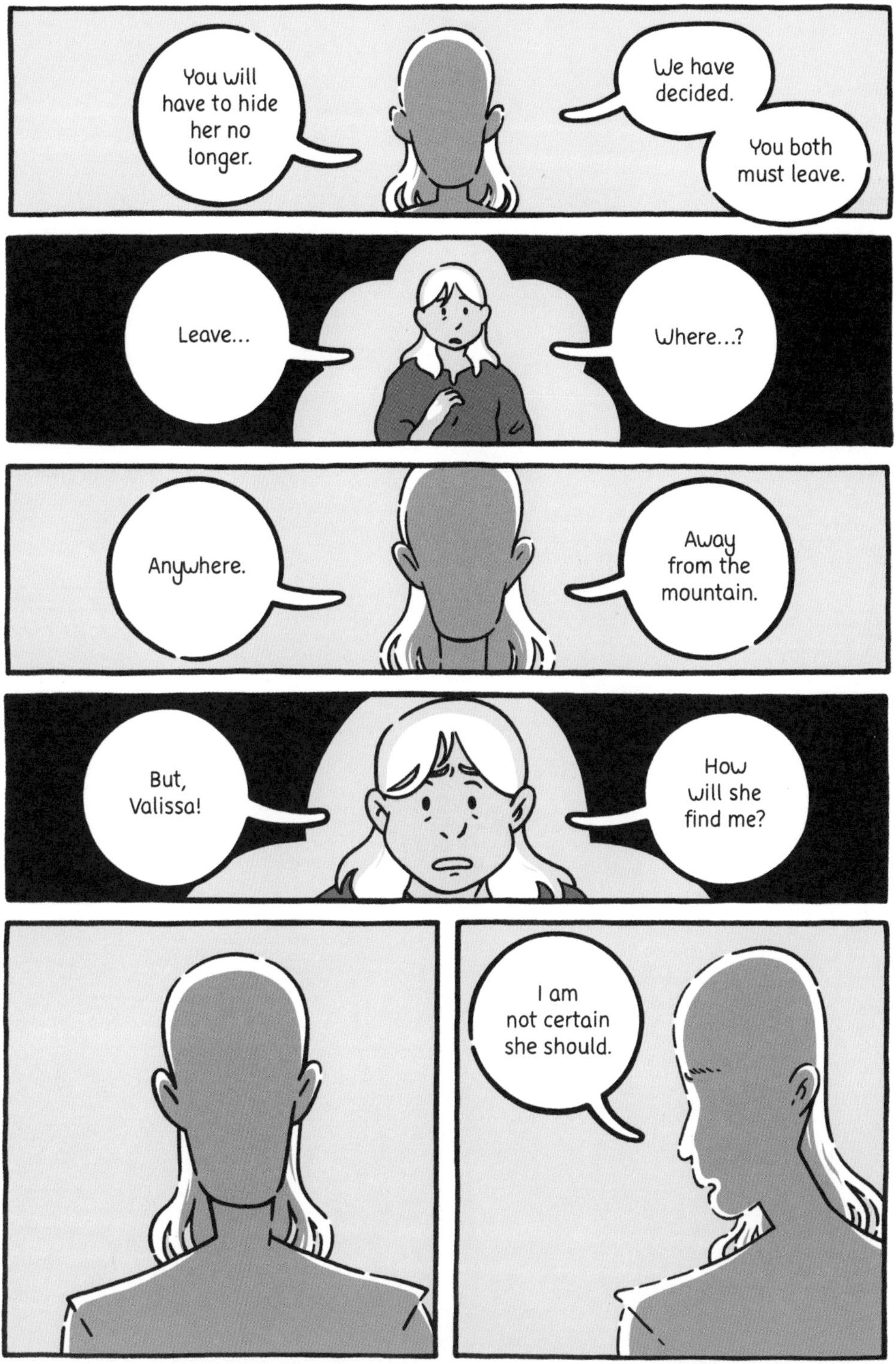
You will have to hide her no longer.
We have decided.
You both must leave.
Leave...
Where...?
Anywhere.
Away from the mountain.
But, Valissa!
How will she find me?
I am not certain she should.

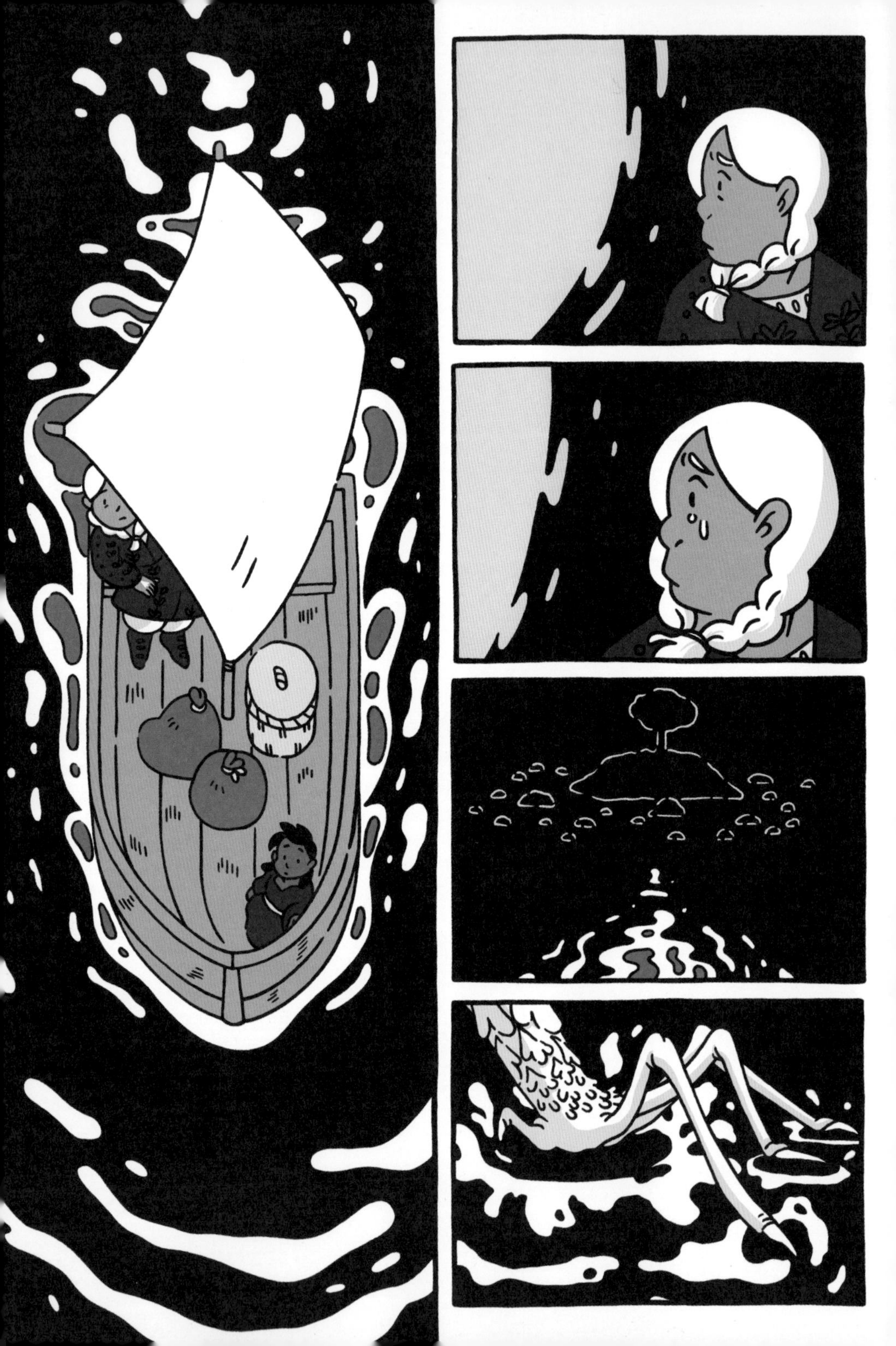

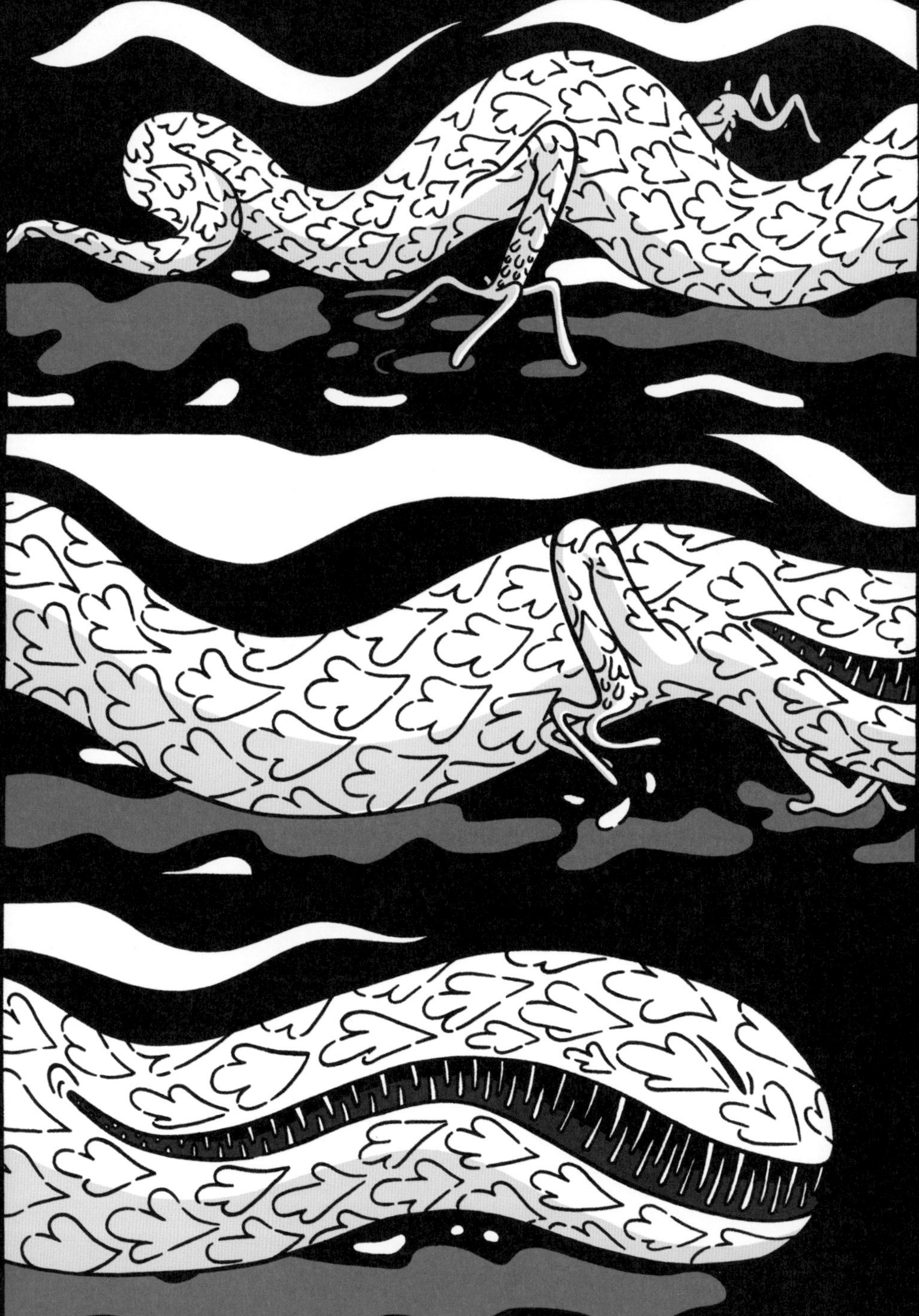

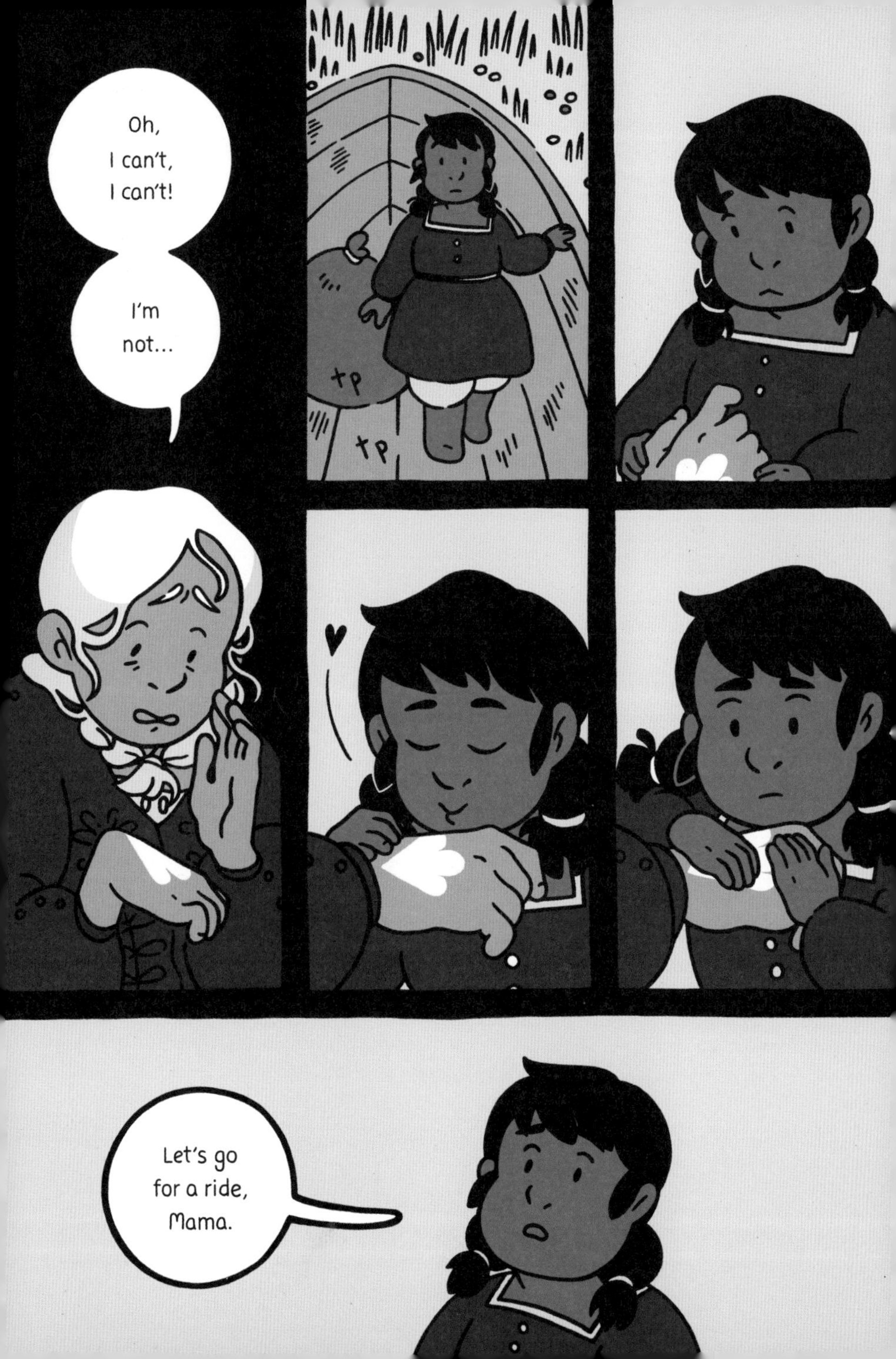
Oh, I can't, I can't!
I'm not...
tp
tp
Let's go for a ride, Mama.

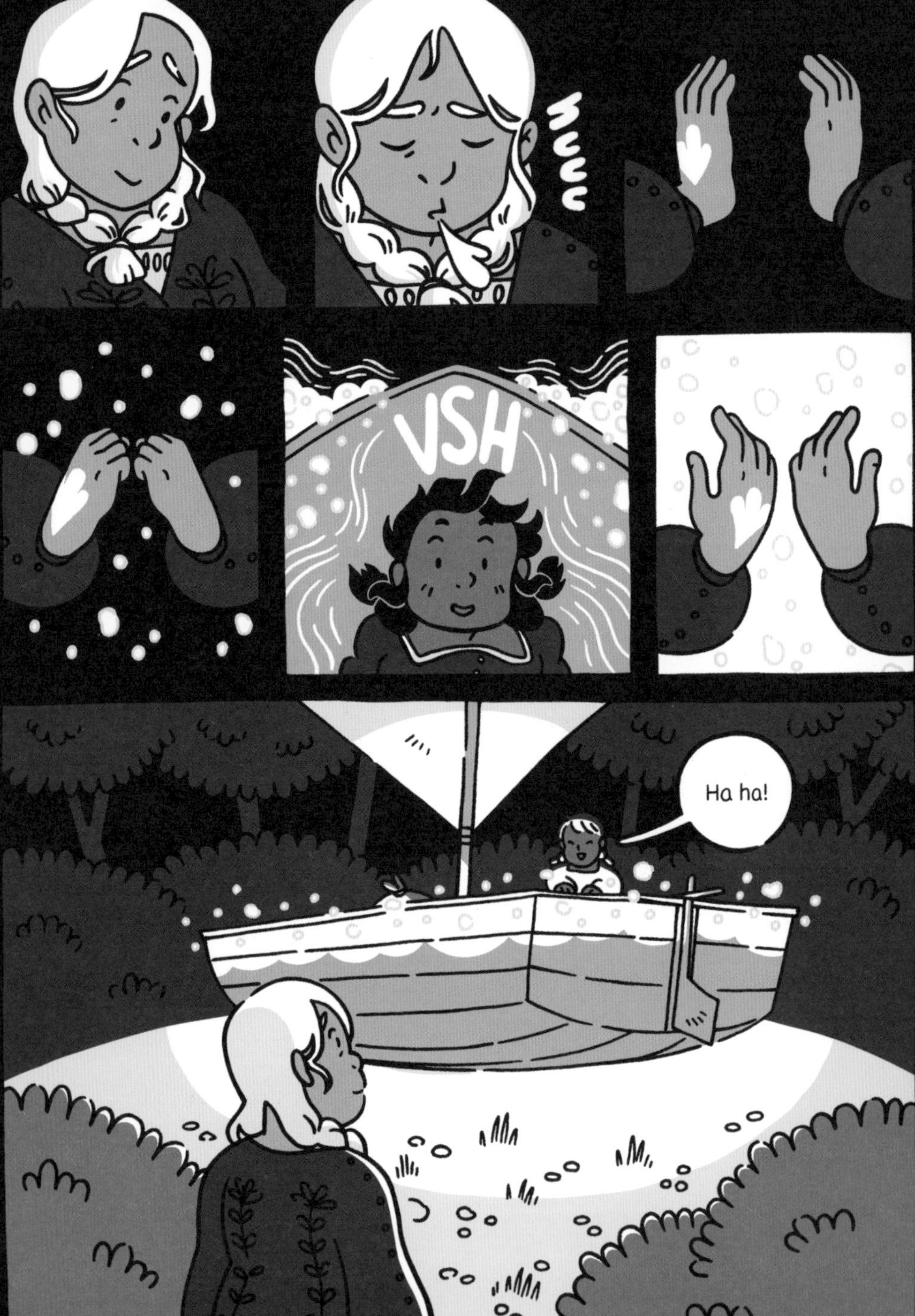
huuu
VSH
Ha ha!

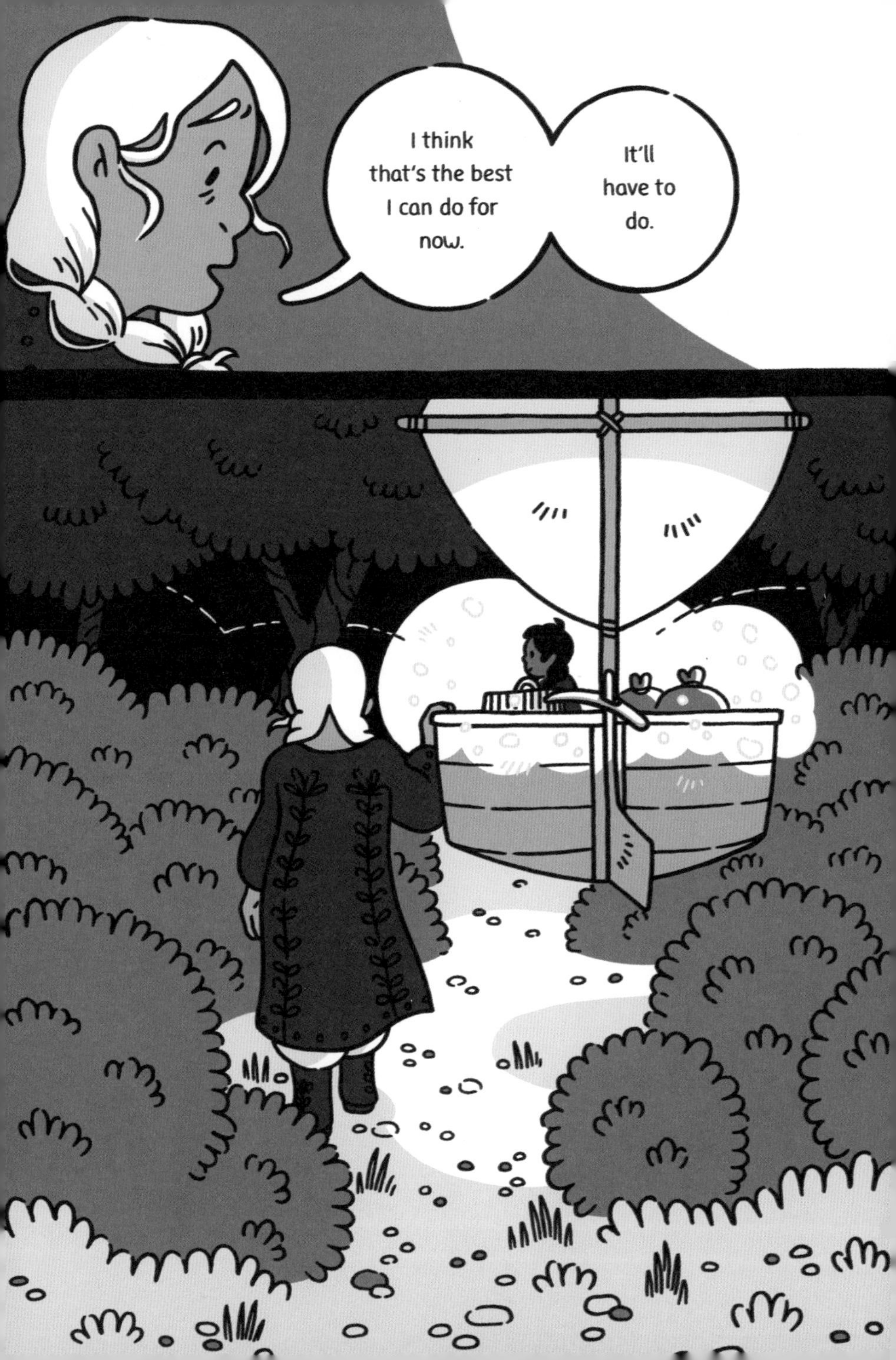
I think that's the best I can do for now.
It'll have to do.

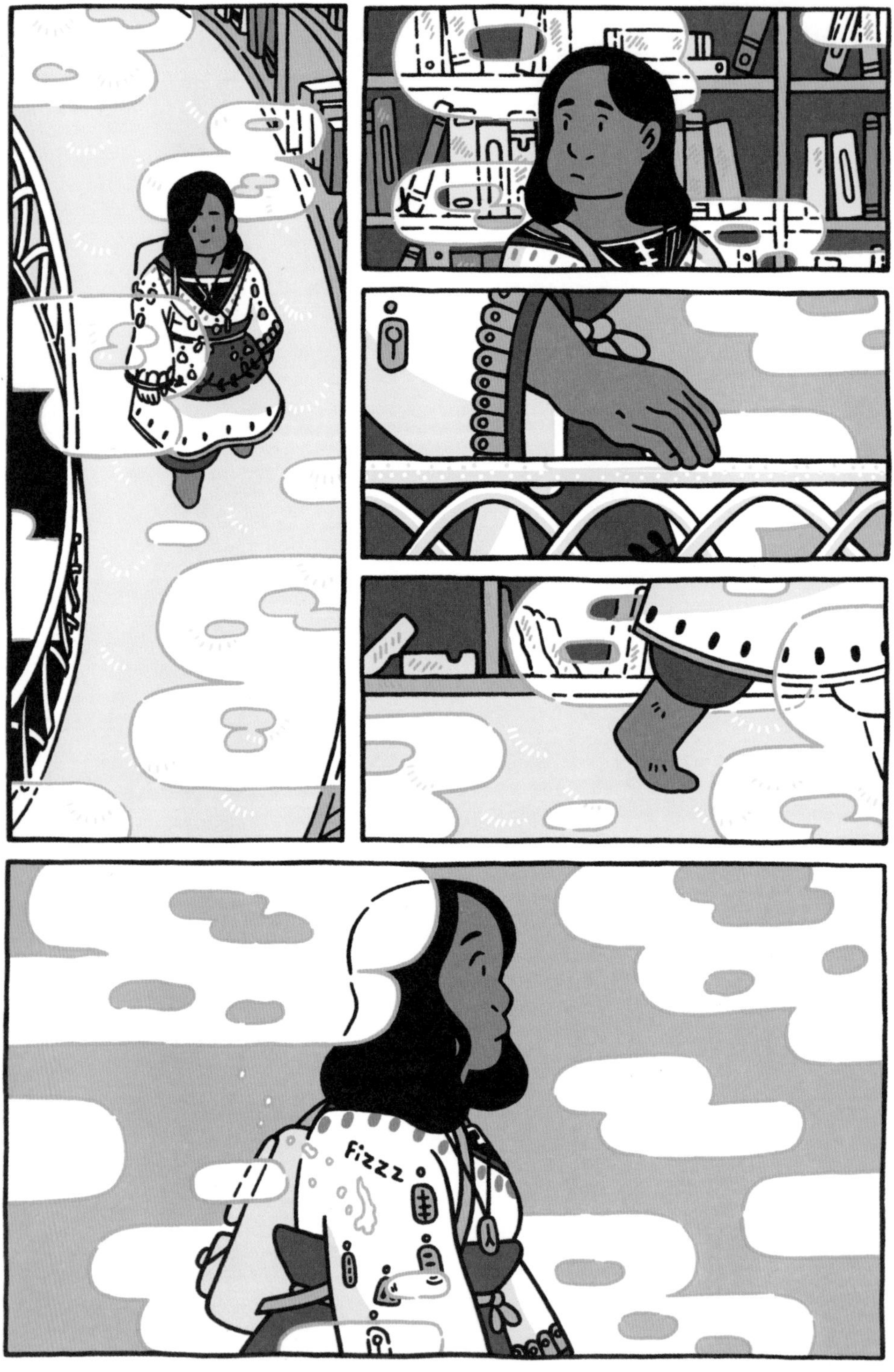
Fizzz

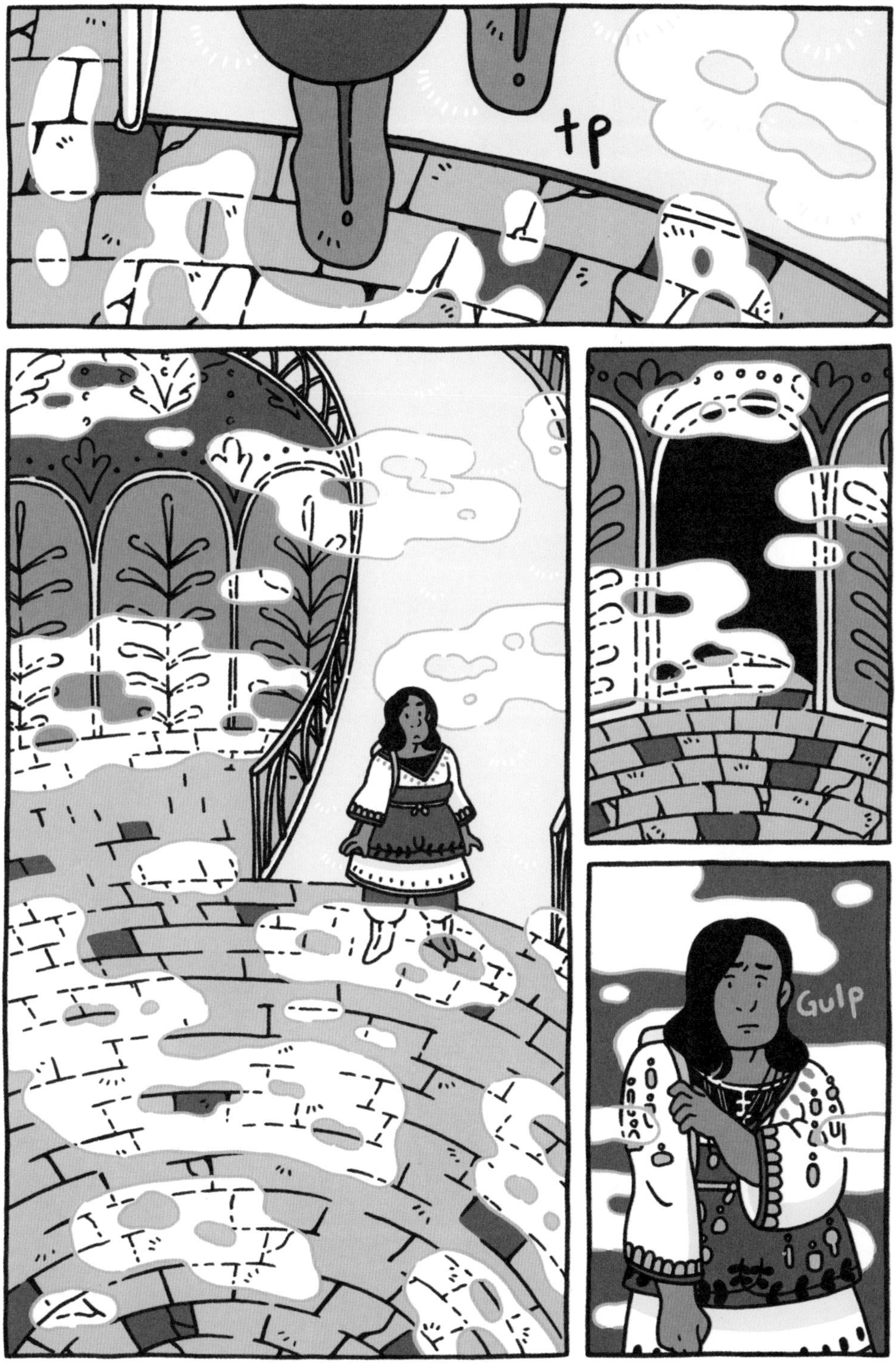
tp
Gulp

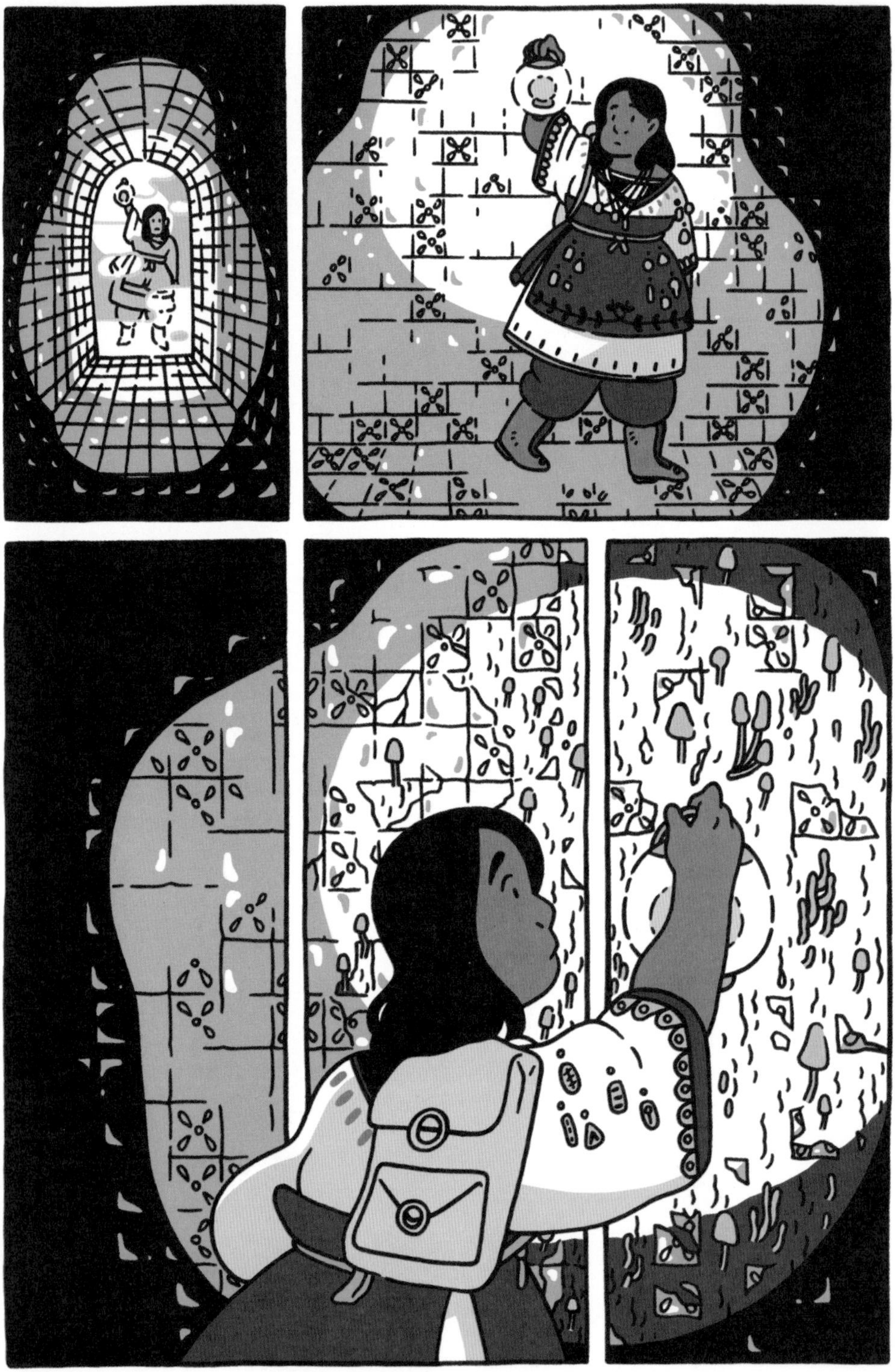

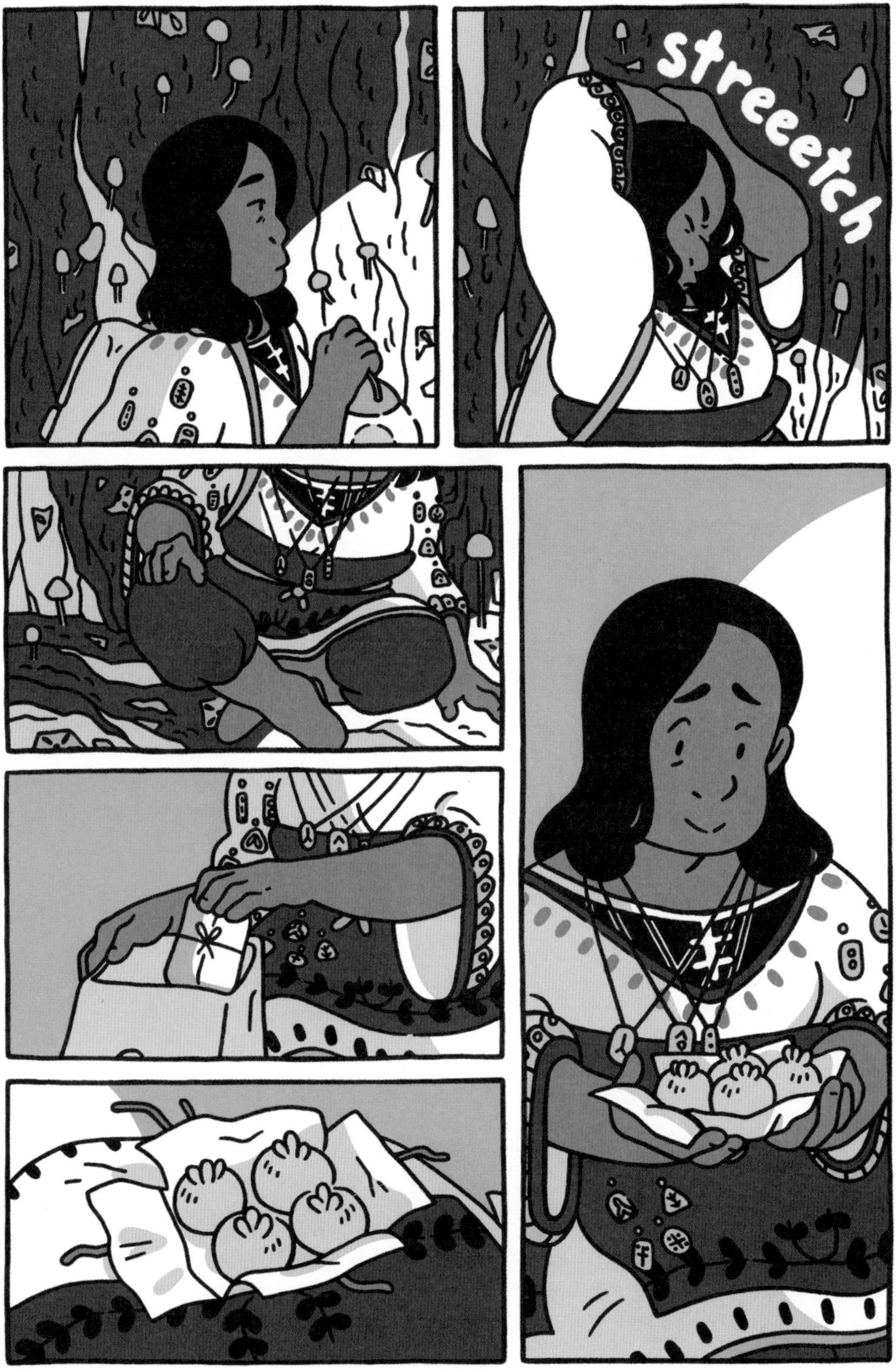
streeetch

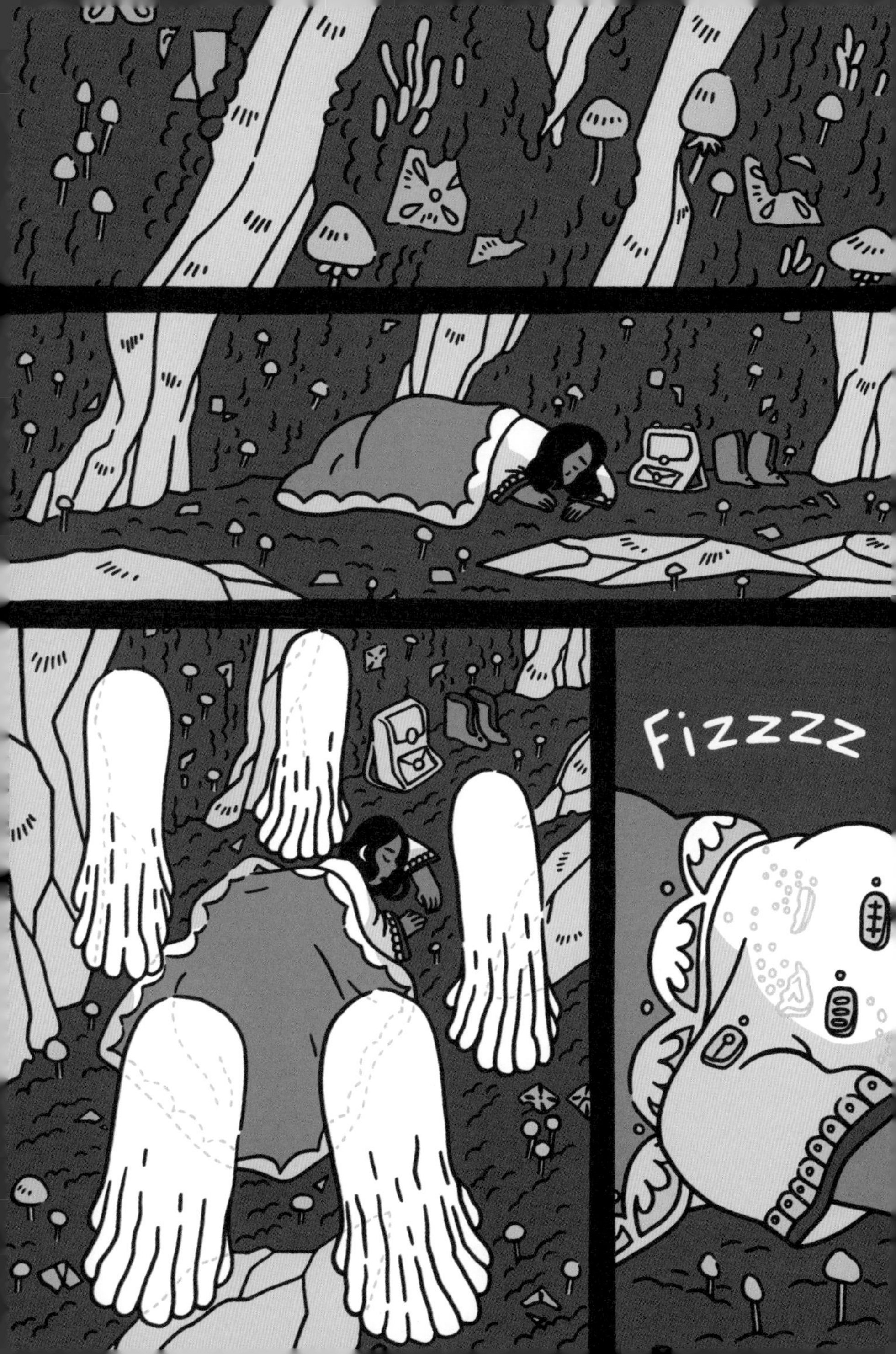
Fizzzz

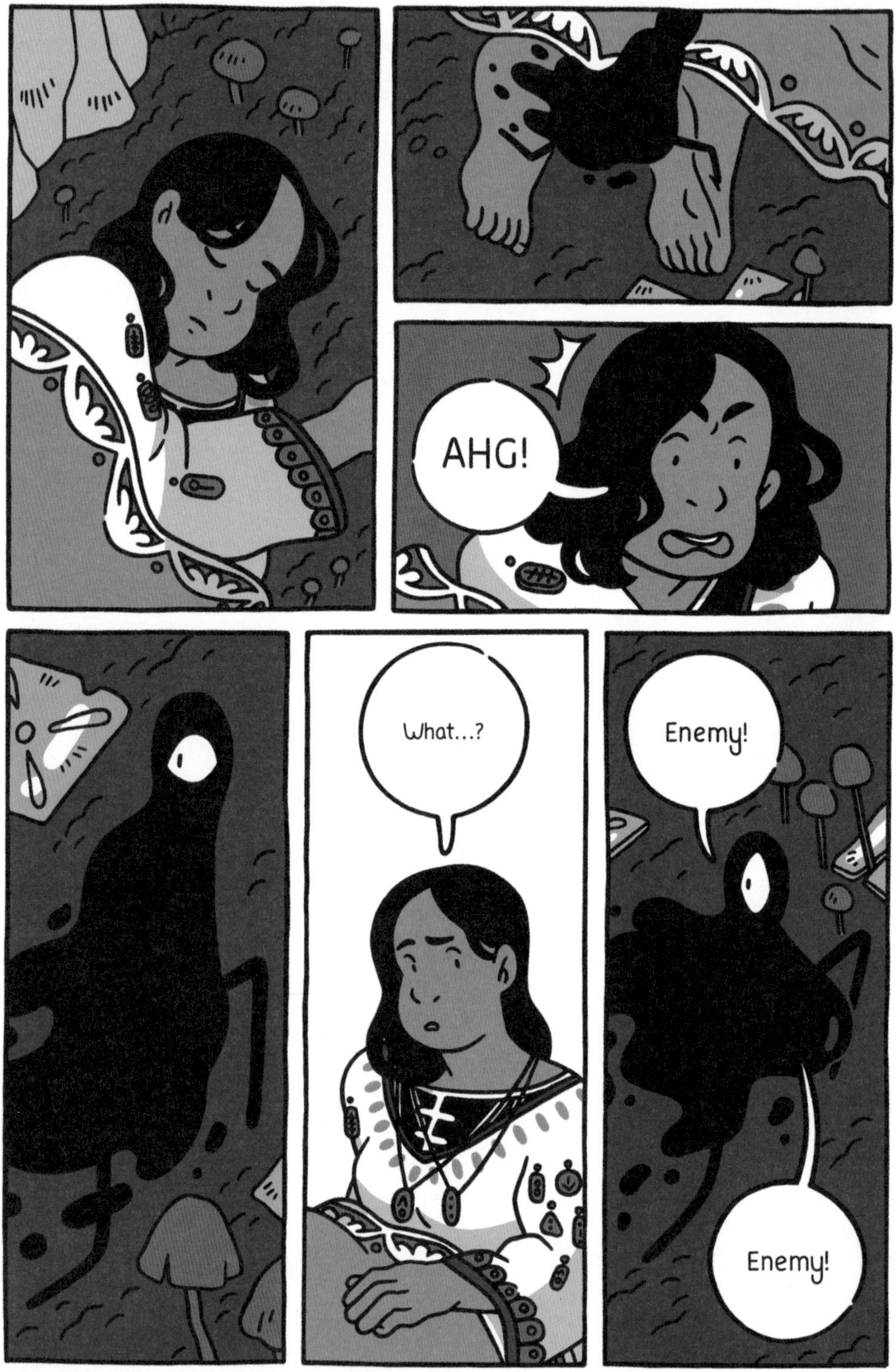
AHG!
What...?
Enemy!
Enemy!

Curses, already?

Enemy!

Your. Your!

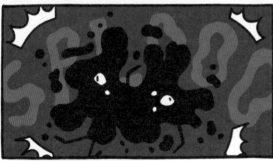

Eh?

Your enemy!

Your enemy!

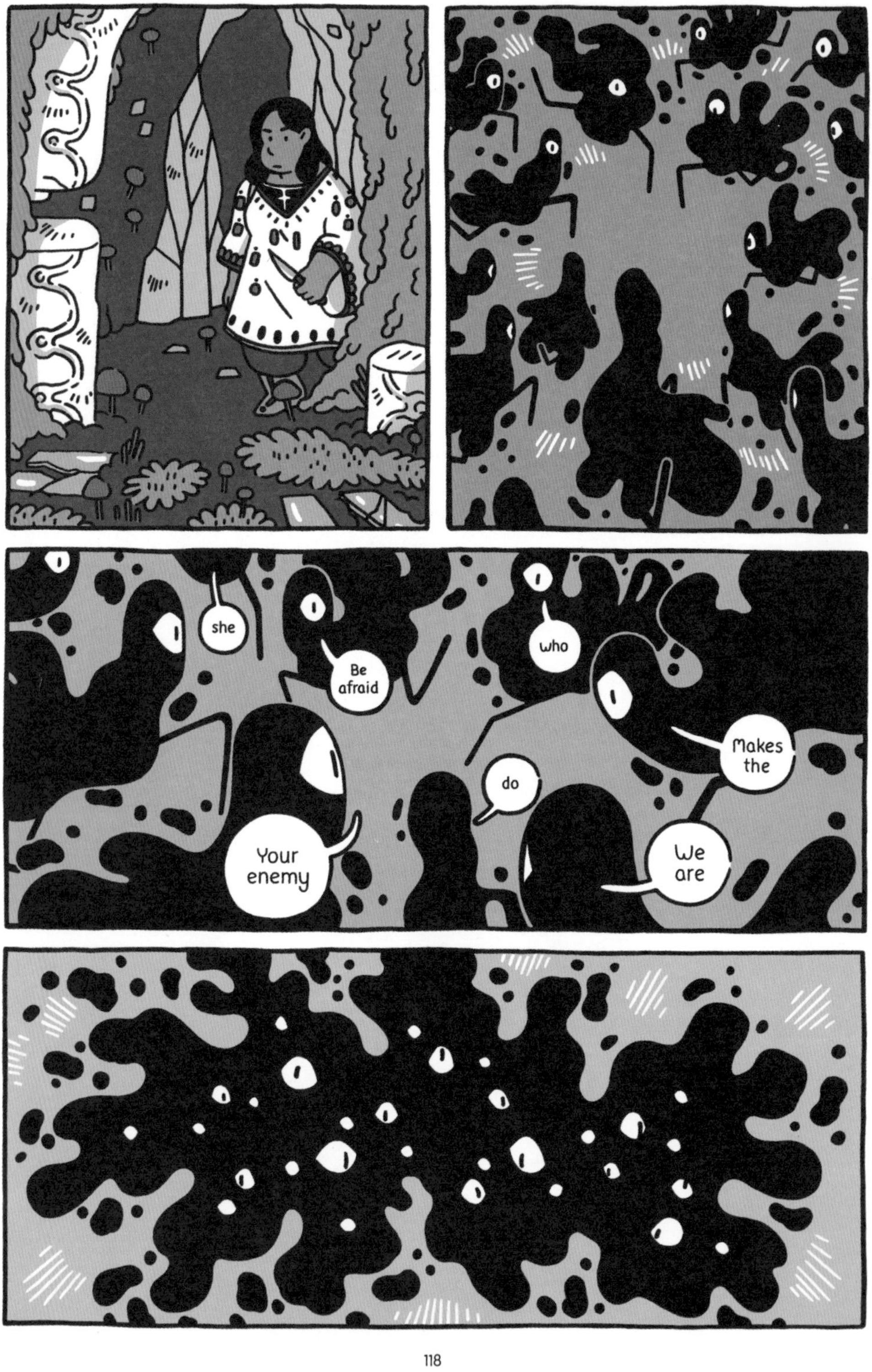
she
Be afraid
who
Makes the
do
Your enemy
We are

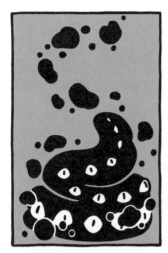

Do not be afraid. We are not your enemy.

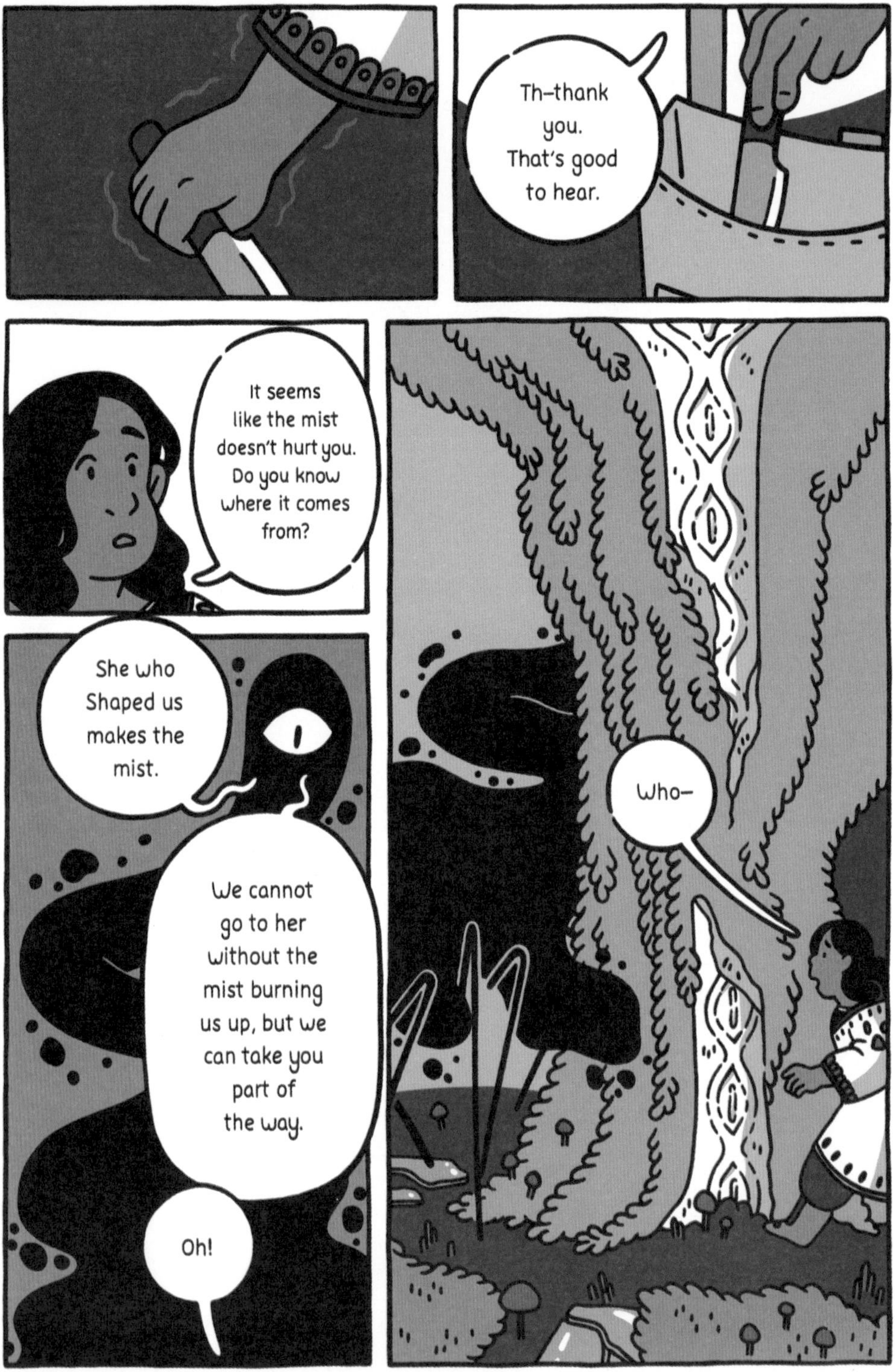
Th–thank you. That's good to hear.
It seems like the mist doesn't hurt you. Do you know where it comes from?
She who Shaped us makes the mist.
We cannot go to her without the mist burning us up, but we can take you part of the way.
Oh!
Who–

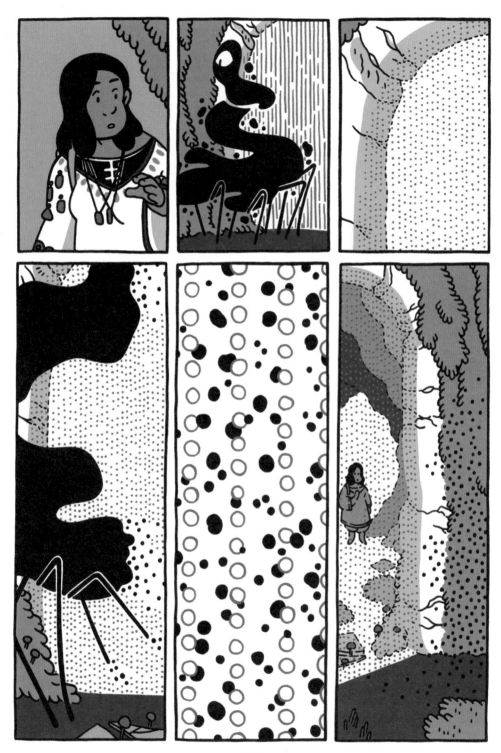

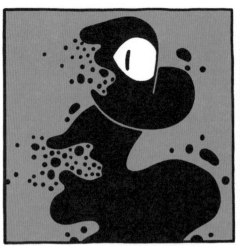

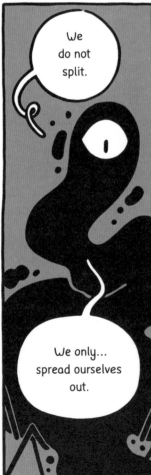

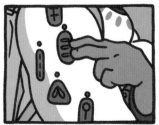

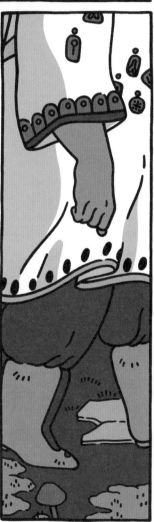

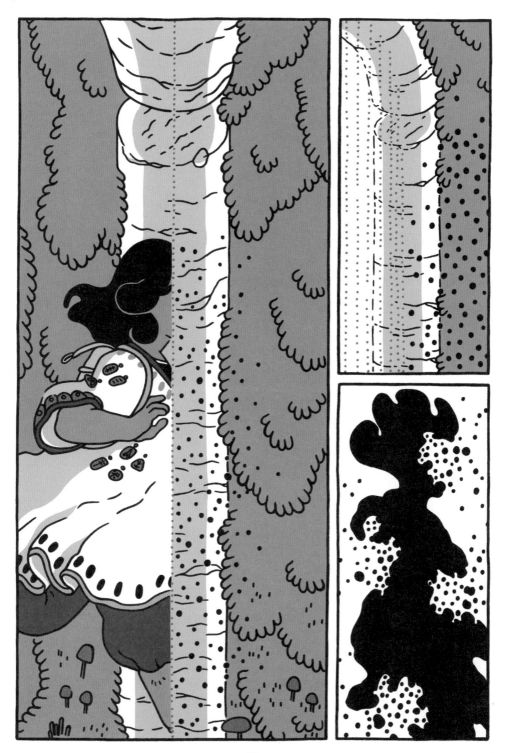

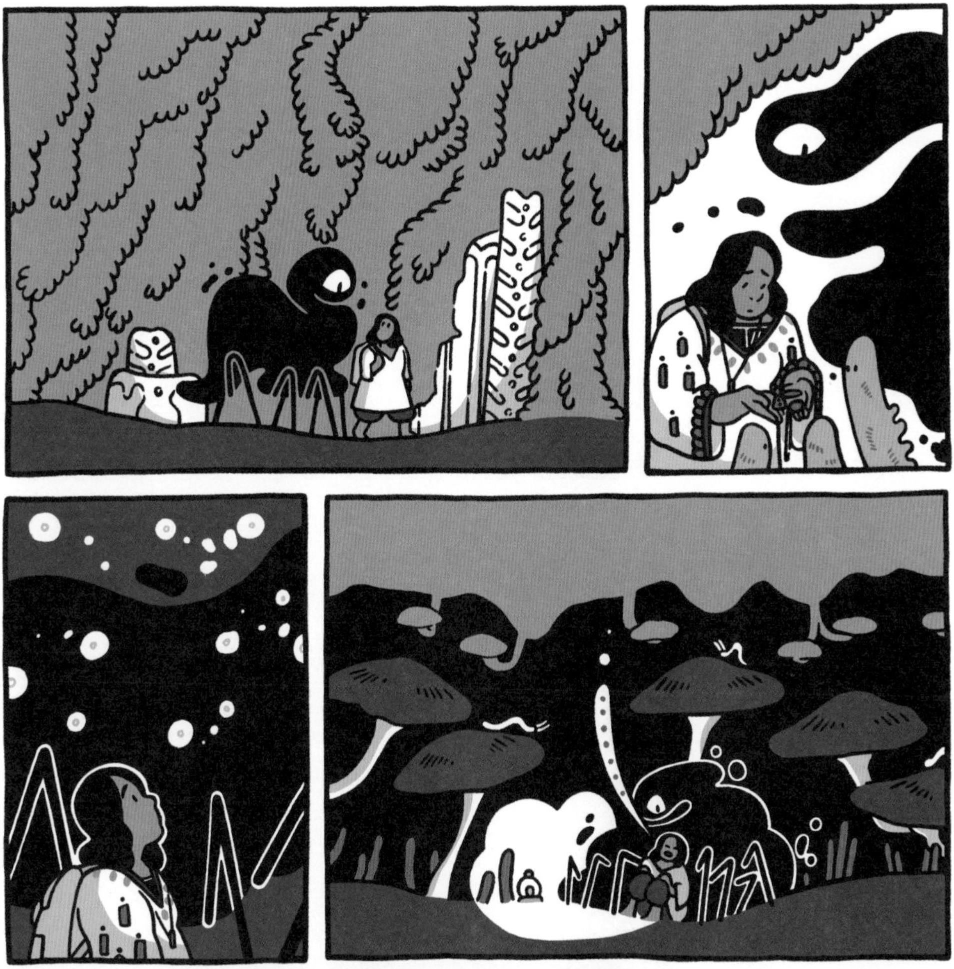

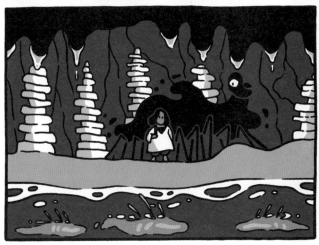

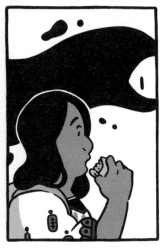

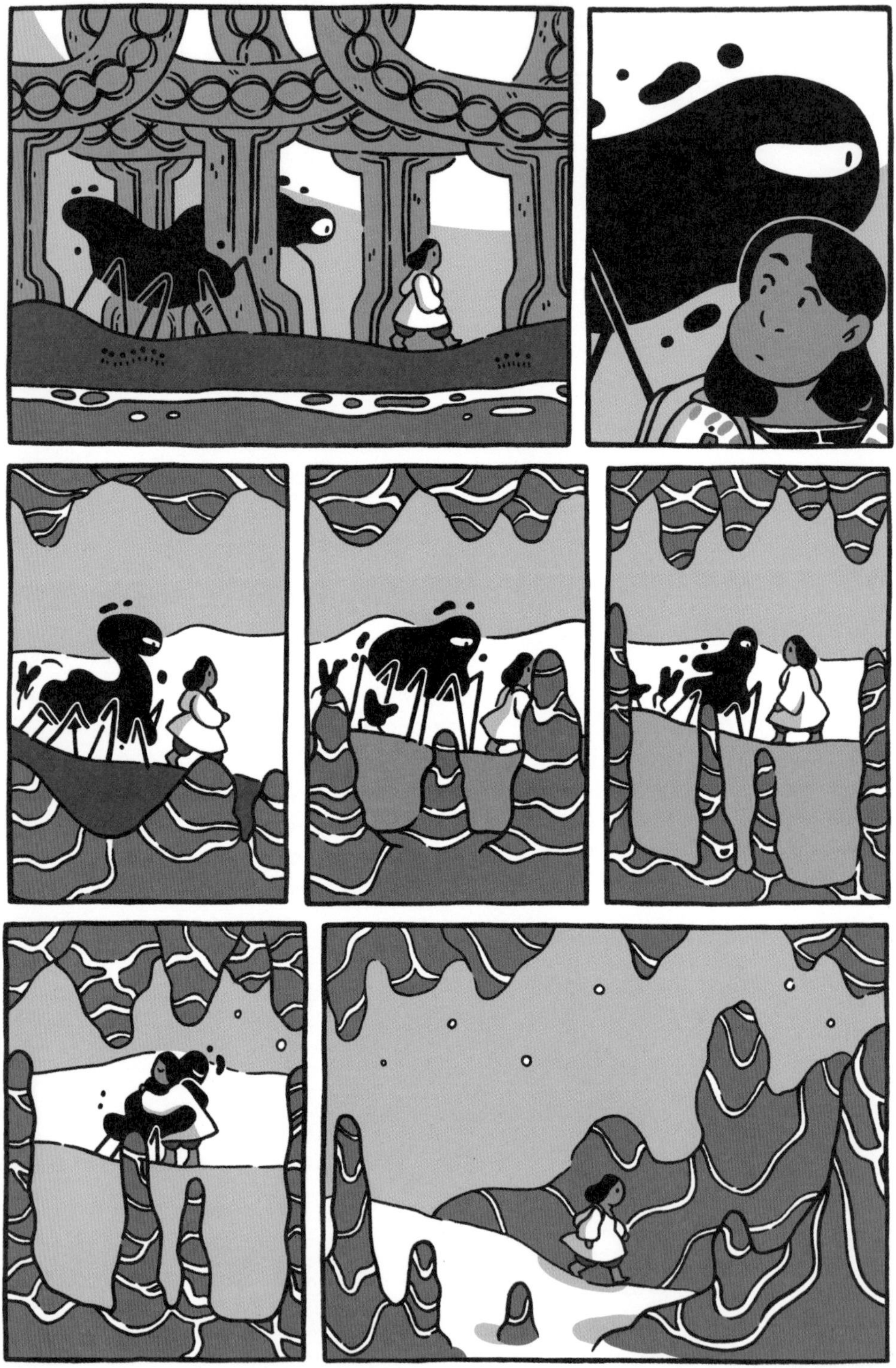

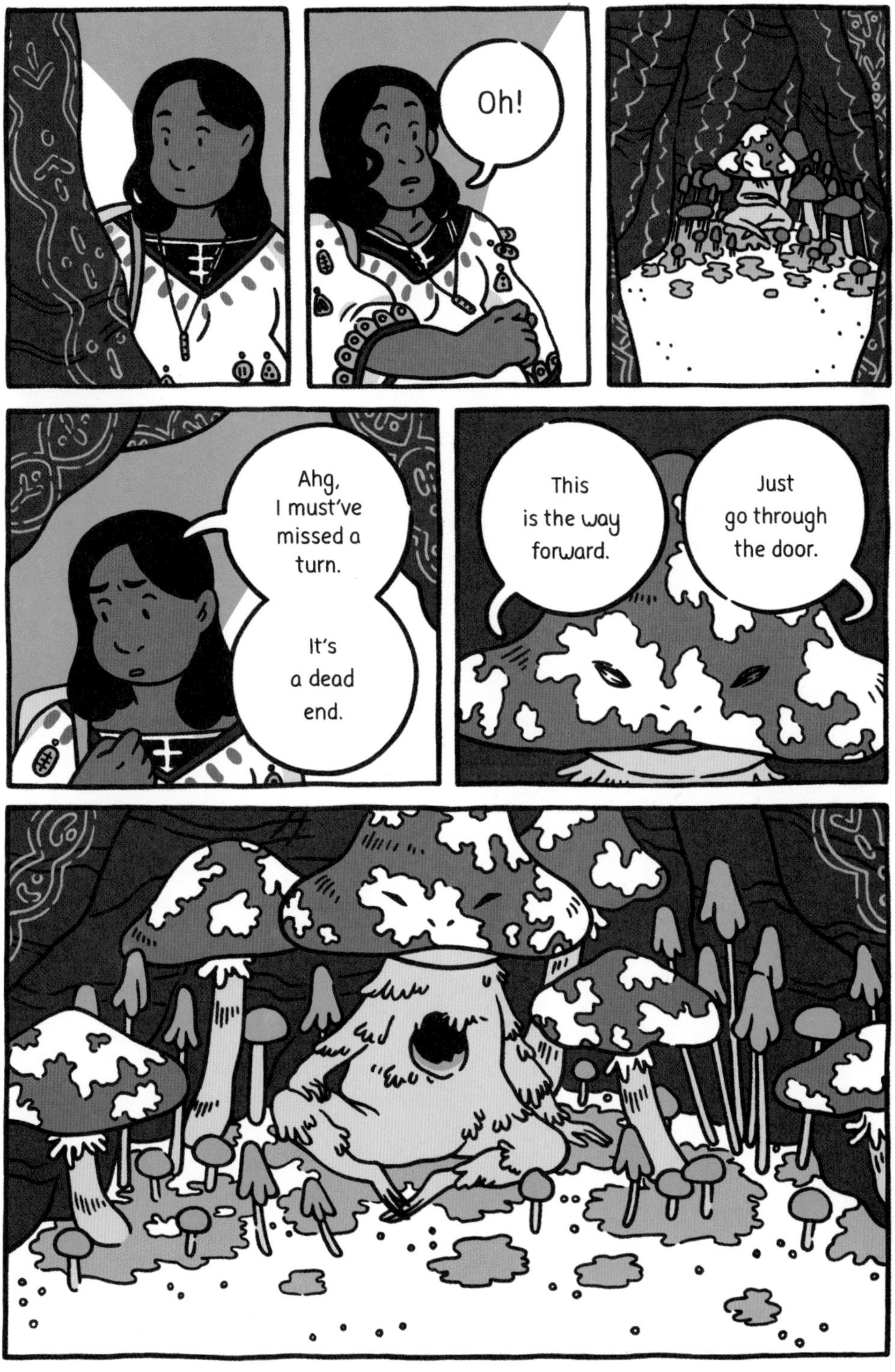
Oh!
Ahg, I must've missed a turn.
It's a dead end.
This is the way forward.
Just go through the door.

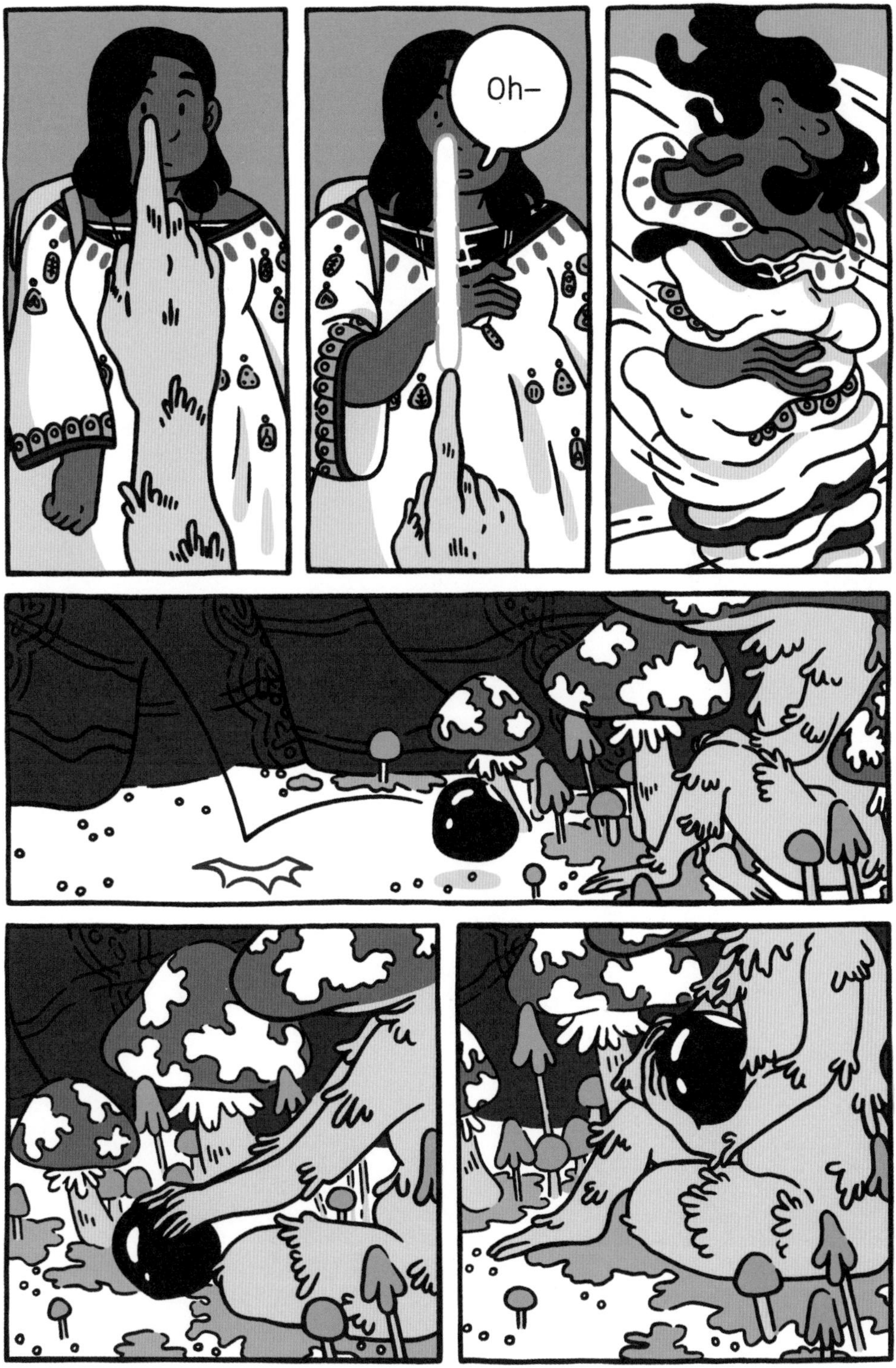
Oh–

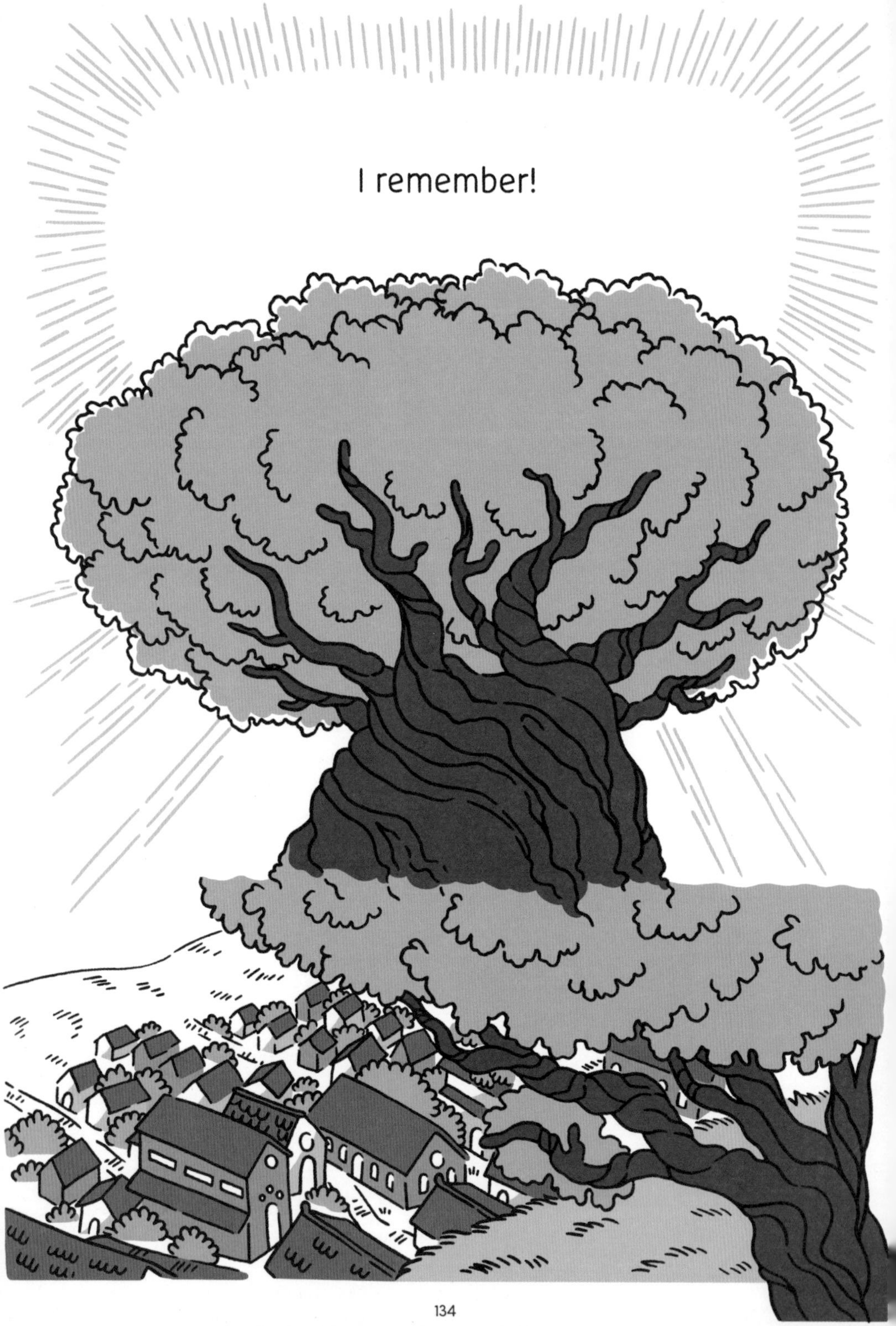
I remember!

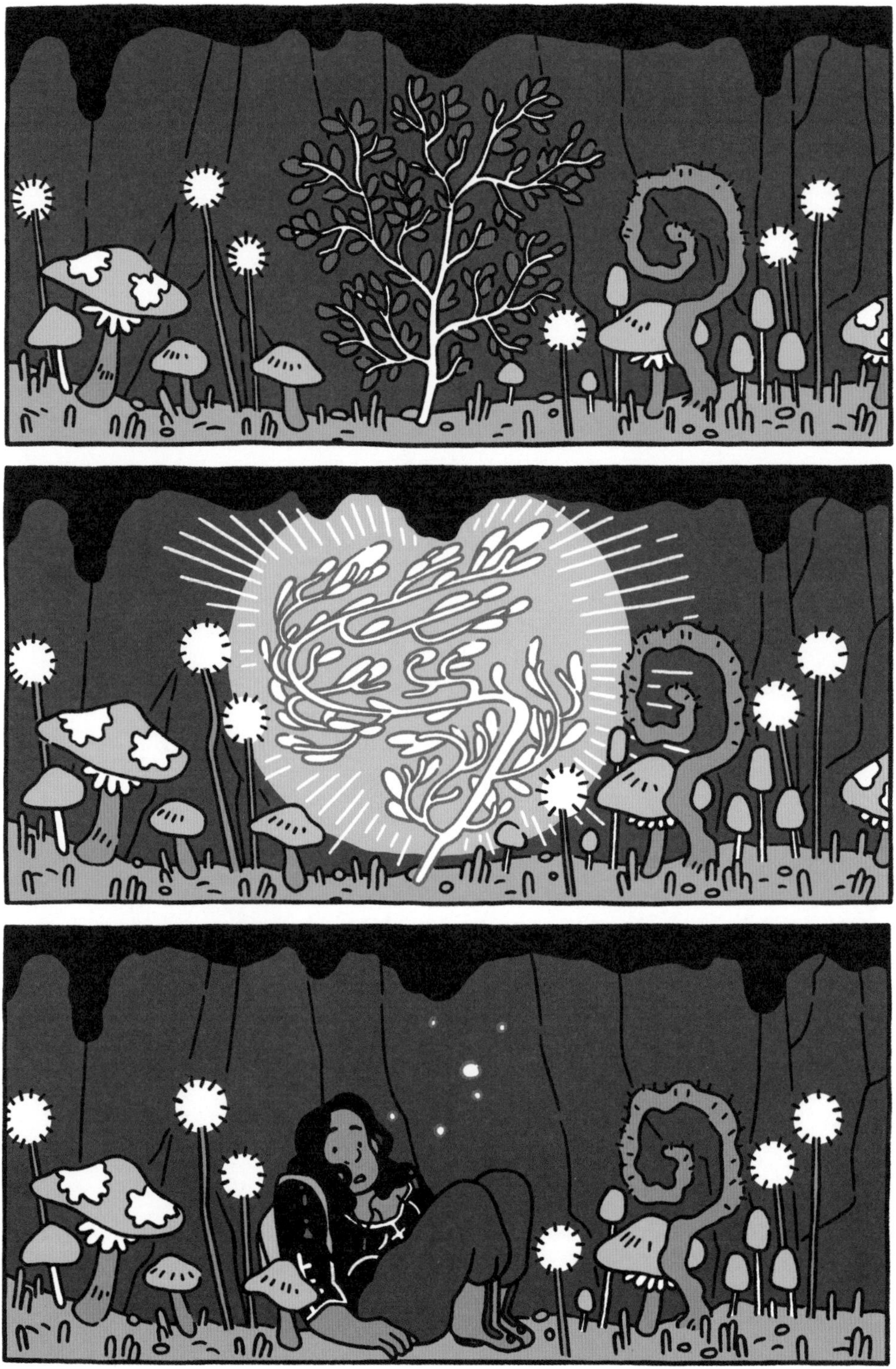

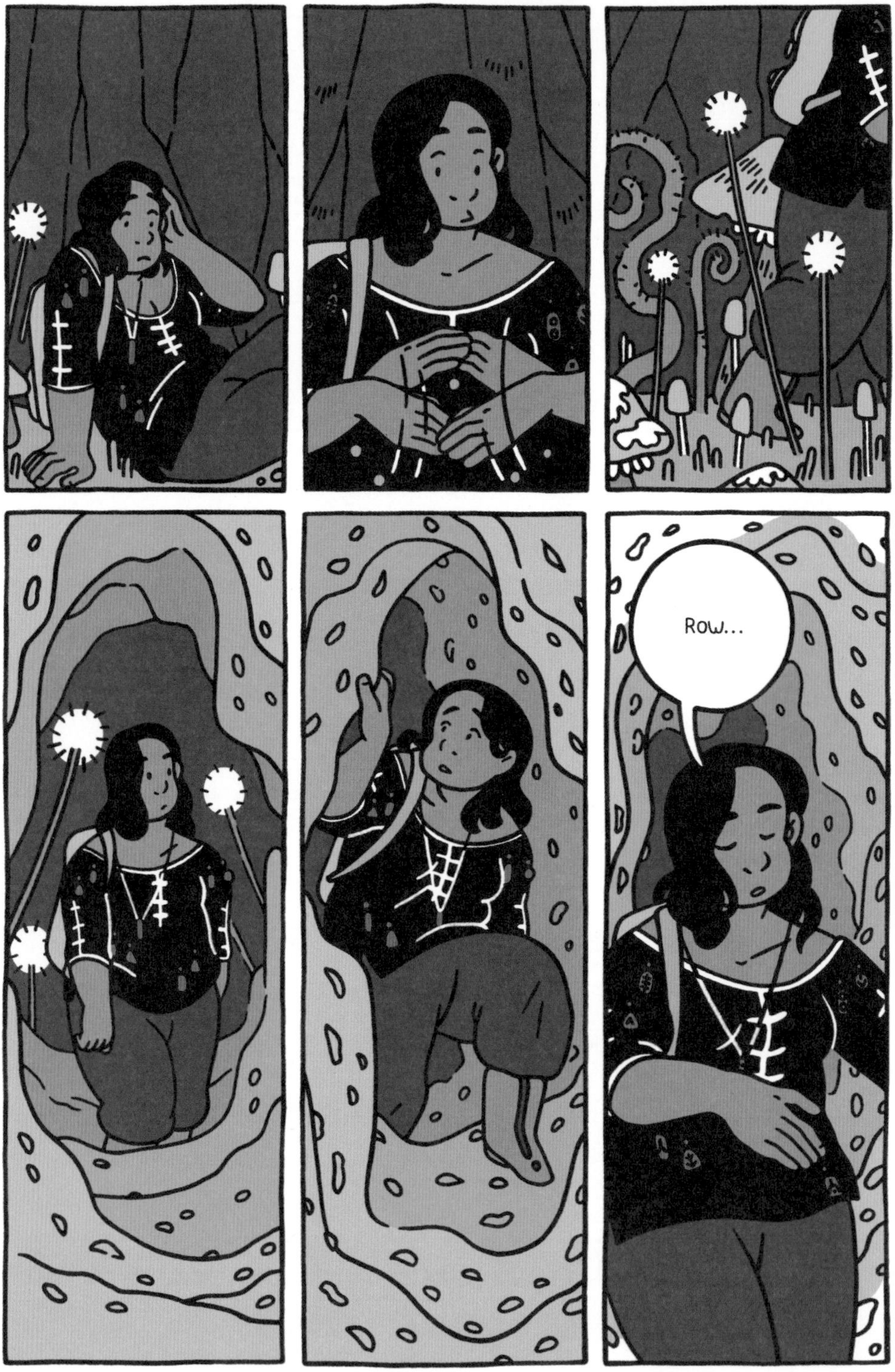
Row...

Row and row, come on—

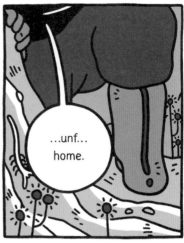

...unf... home.

Through the fog, through the snow.

Little... boat, little leaf,

Through the night... home to...

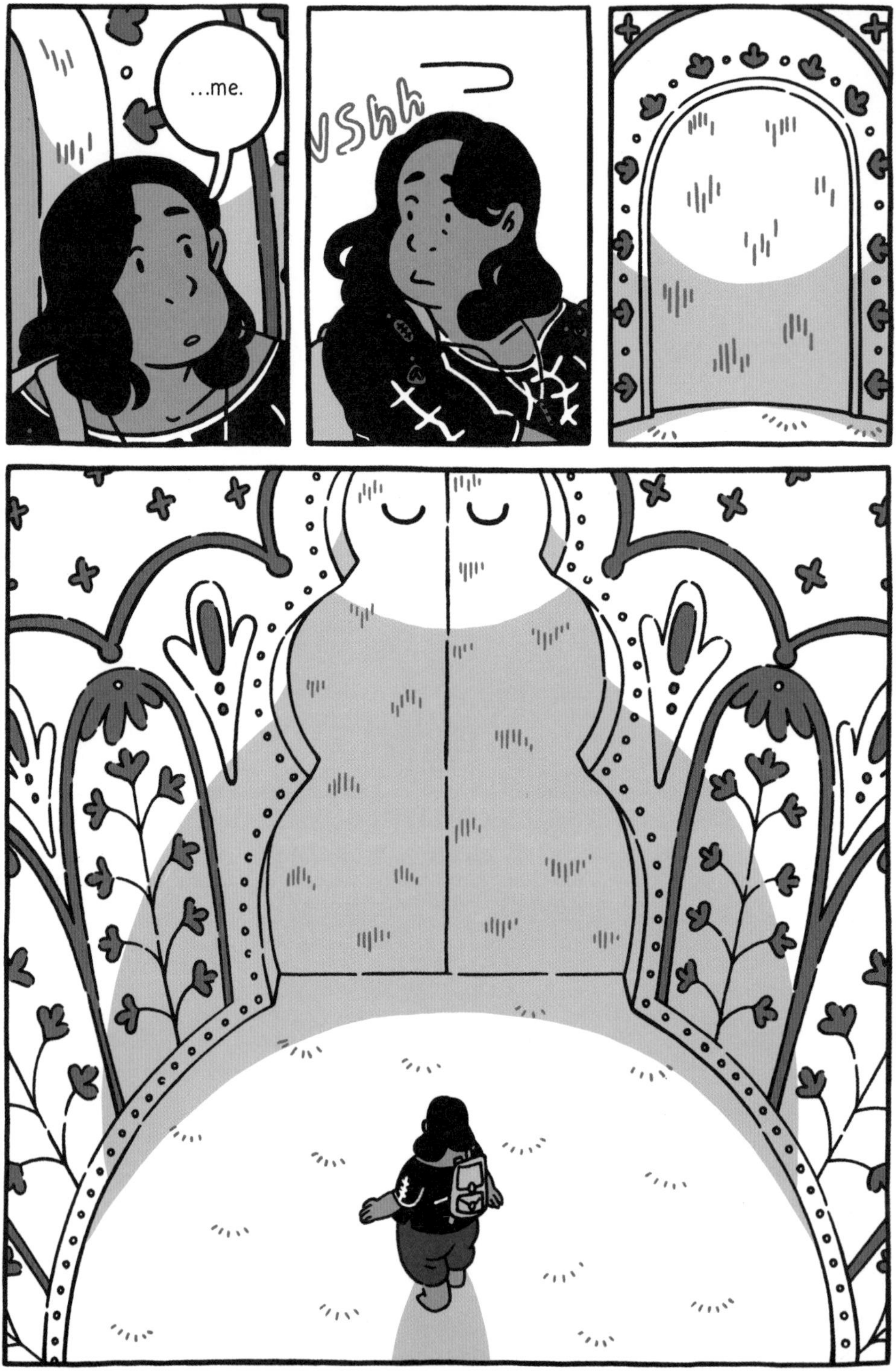
...me.
VSHH

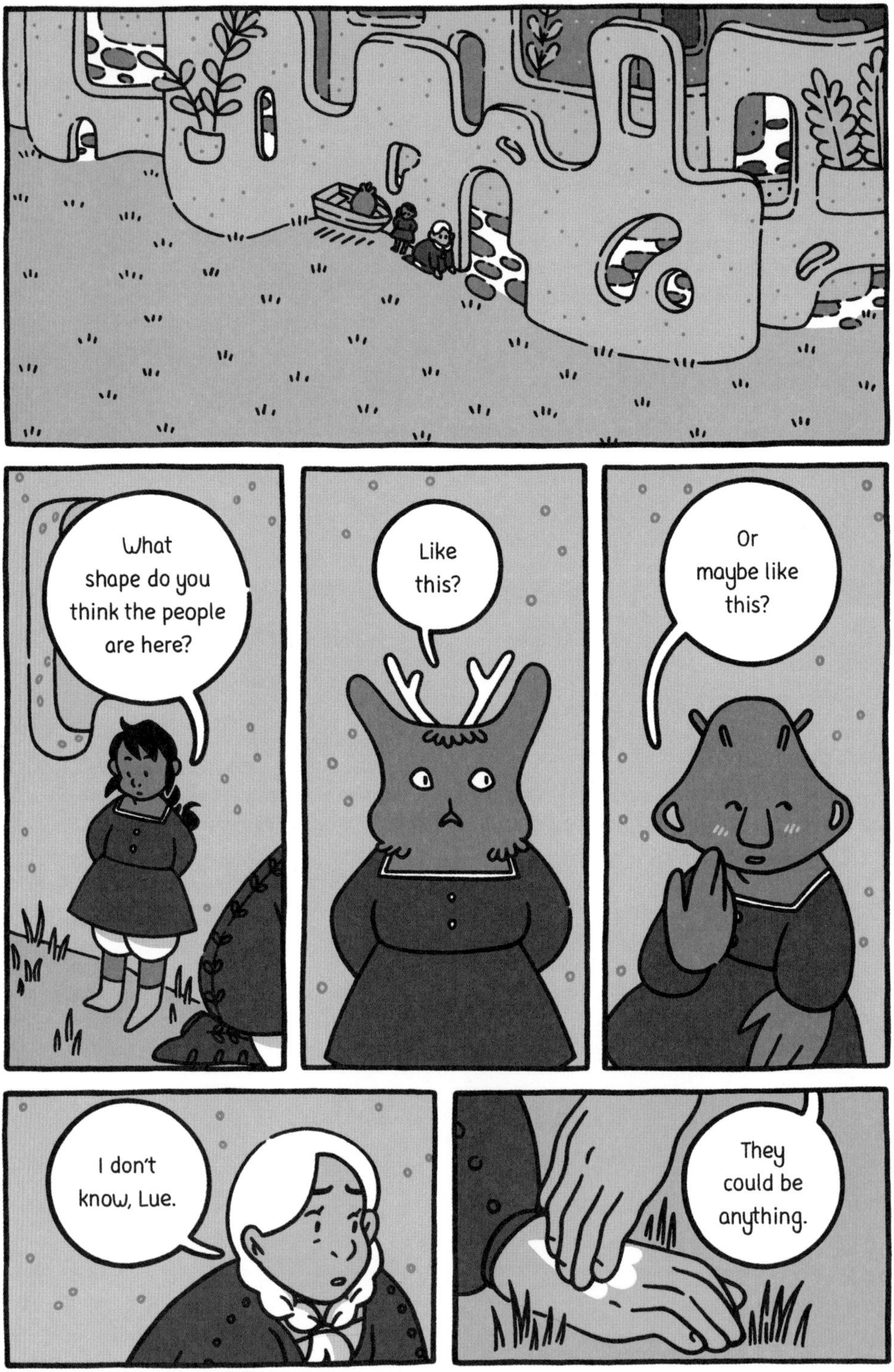
What shape do you think the people are here?
Like this?
Or maybe like this?
I don't know, Lue.
They could be anything.

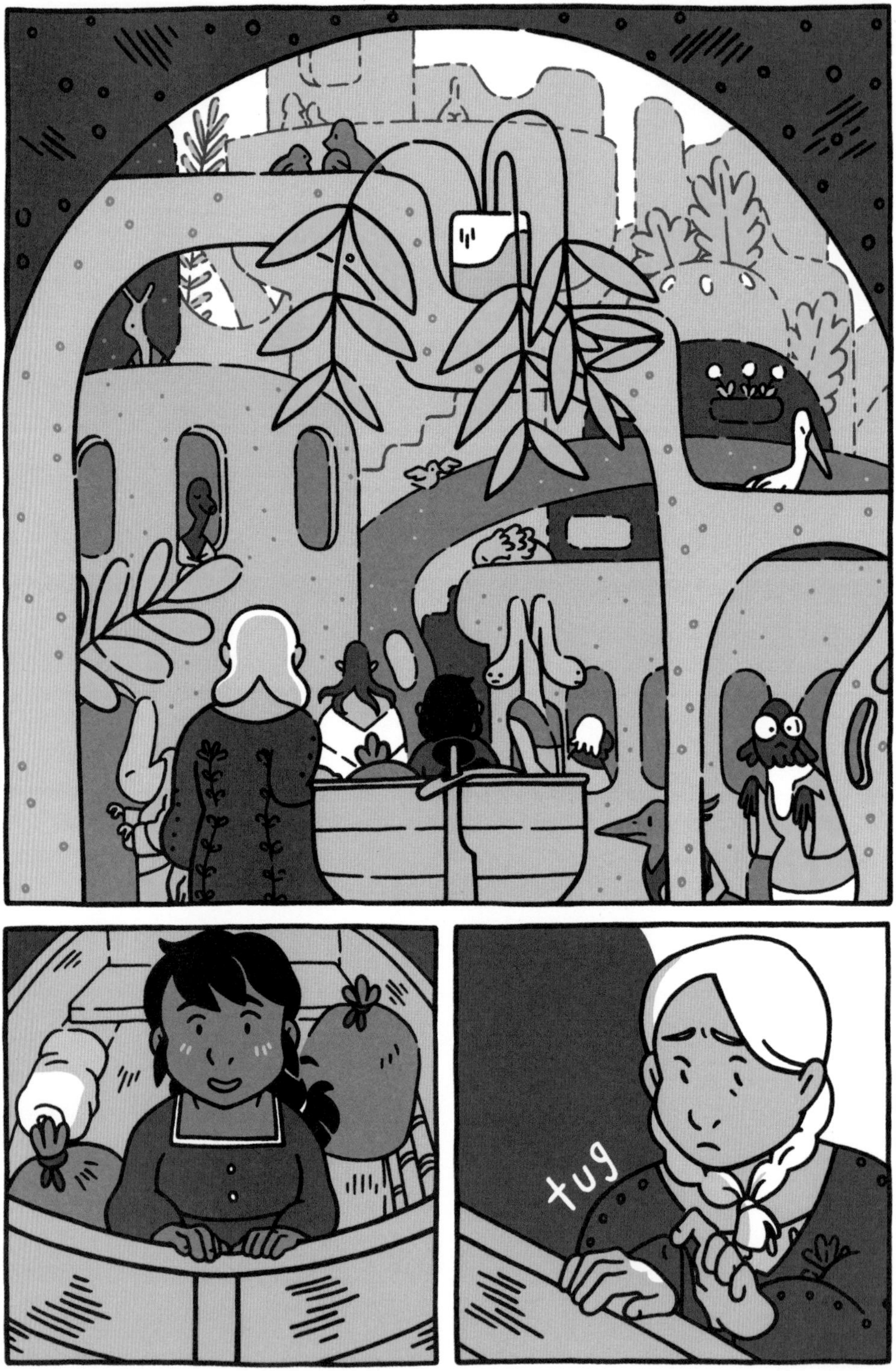
tug

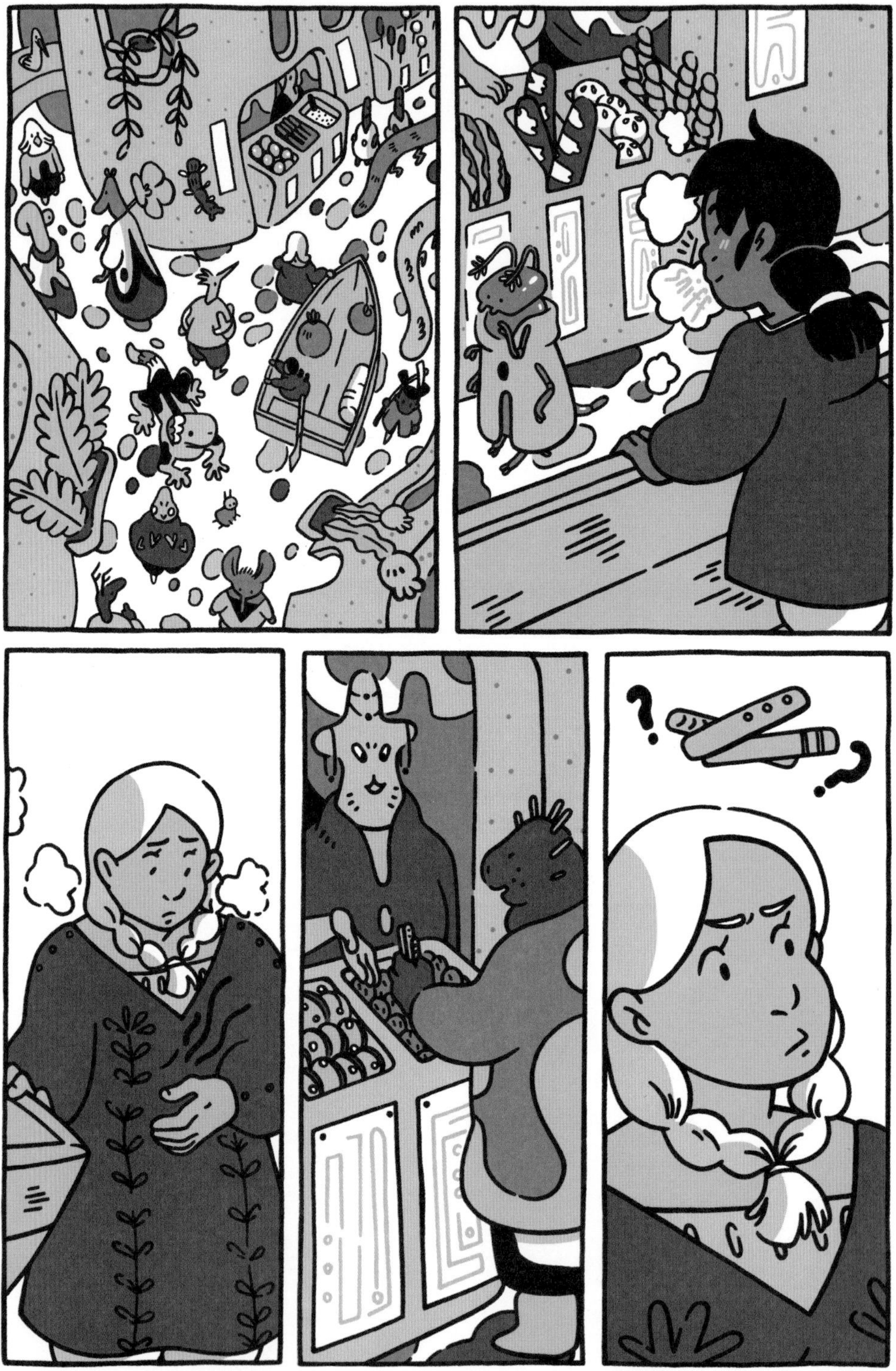
sniff

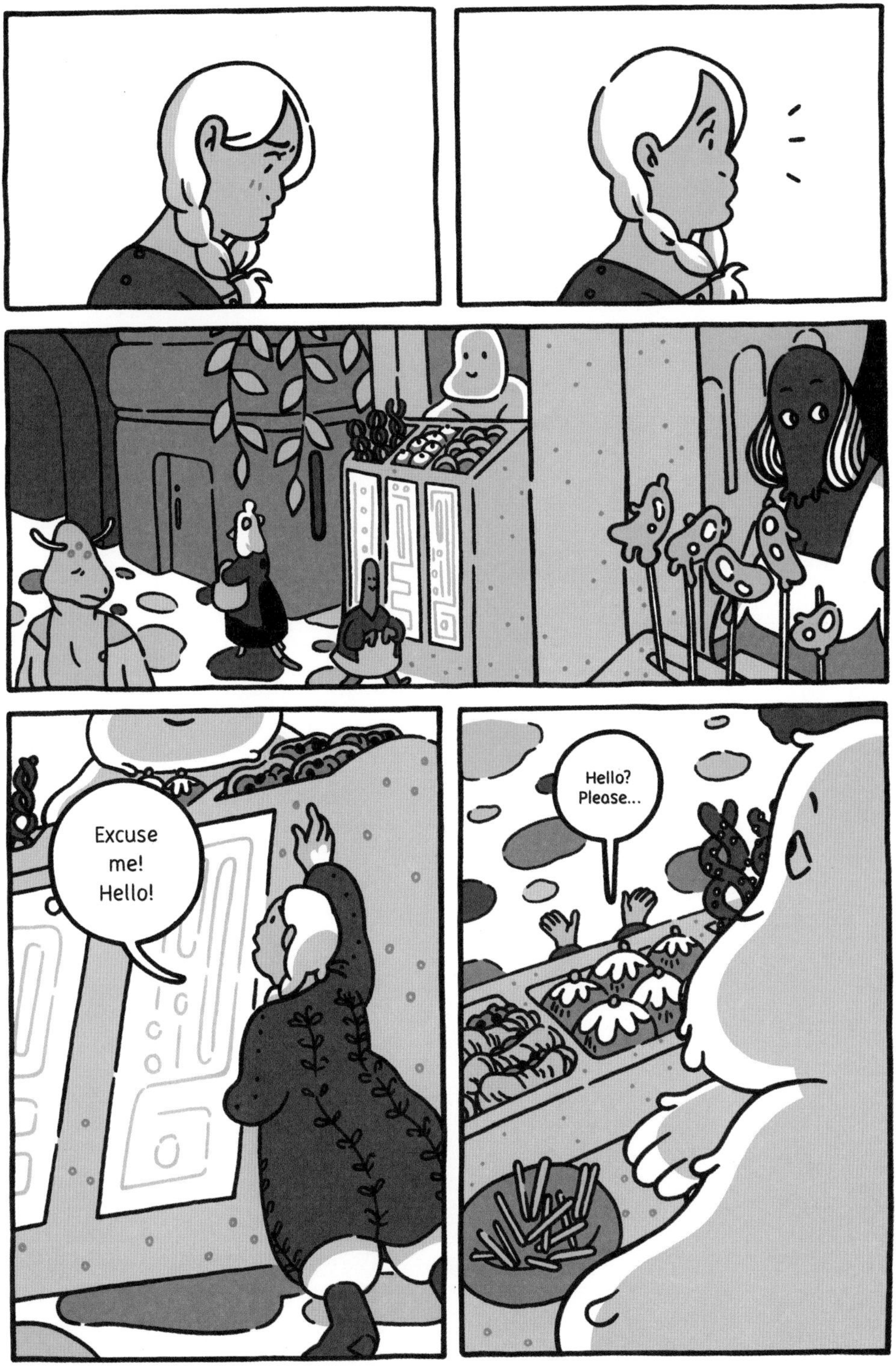
Excuse me! Hello!
Hello? Please...

H–hello!

Ah! Hello!

Grena, look!

A familiar face!

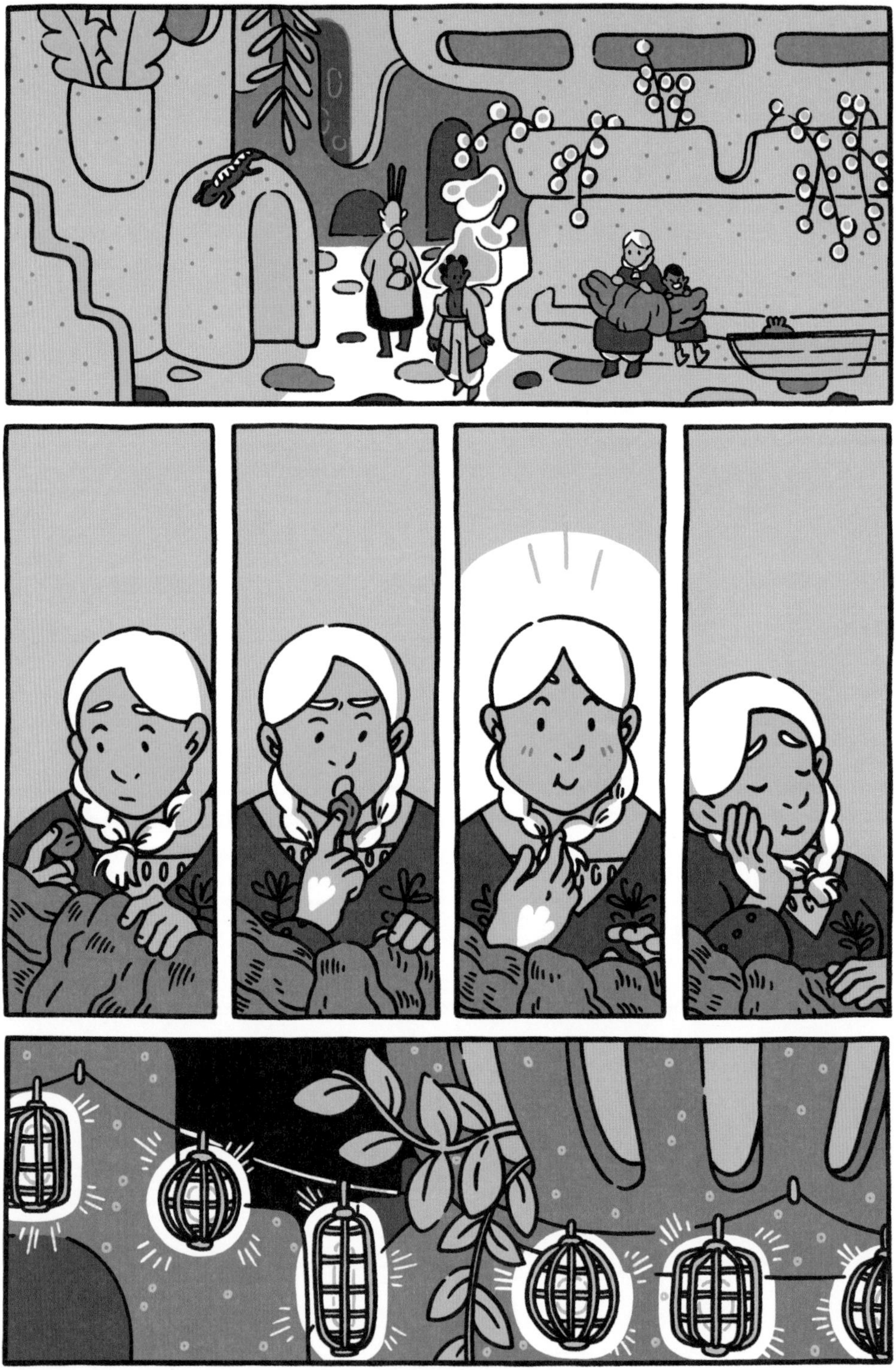

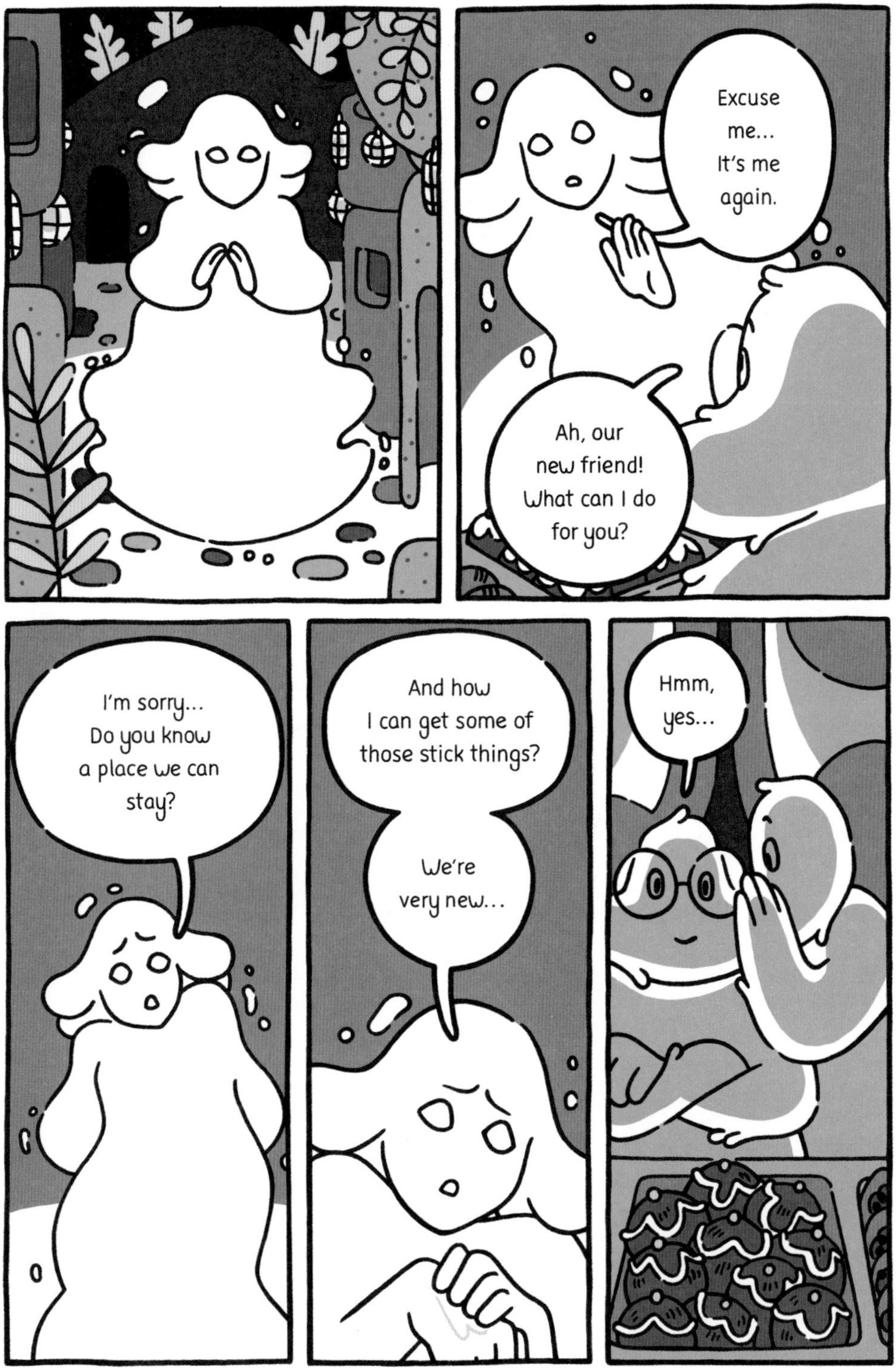
Excuse me... It's me again.
Ah, our new friend! What can I do for you?
I'm sorry... Do you know a place we can stay?
And how I can get some of those stick things?
We're very new...
Hmm, yes...

We have a room up top you could stay in as well, at least for a while.

Actually, we can give you a job if you'd like.

We need help in the back, and so few people here are strong enough to carry the barrels.

Truly? Thank you, thank you so much!

Ha ha!

Well, get your small friend and come on up, I'll show you the room.

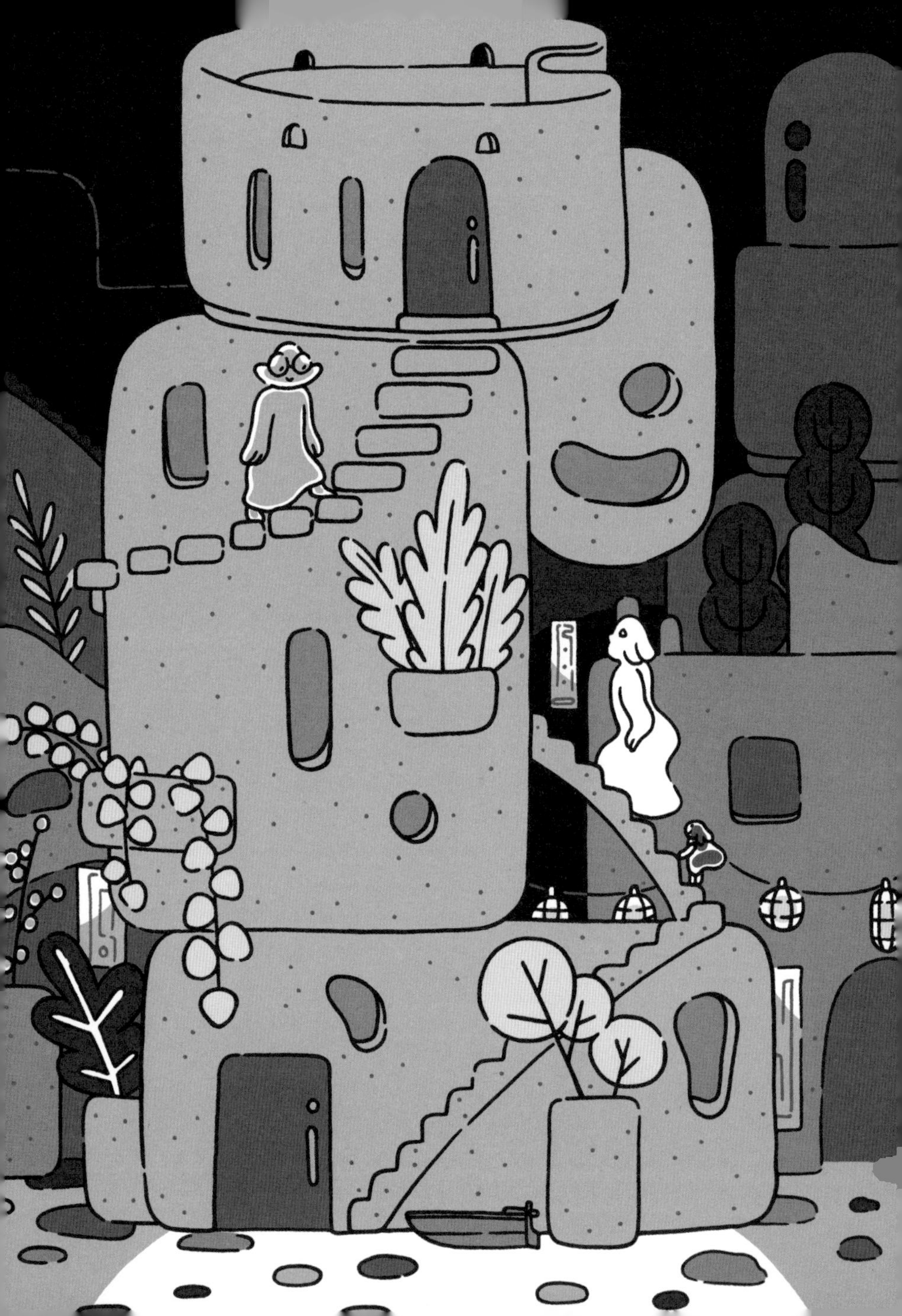

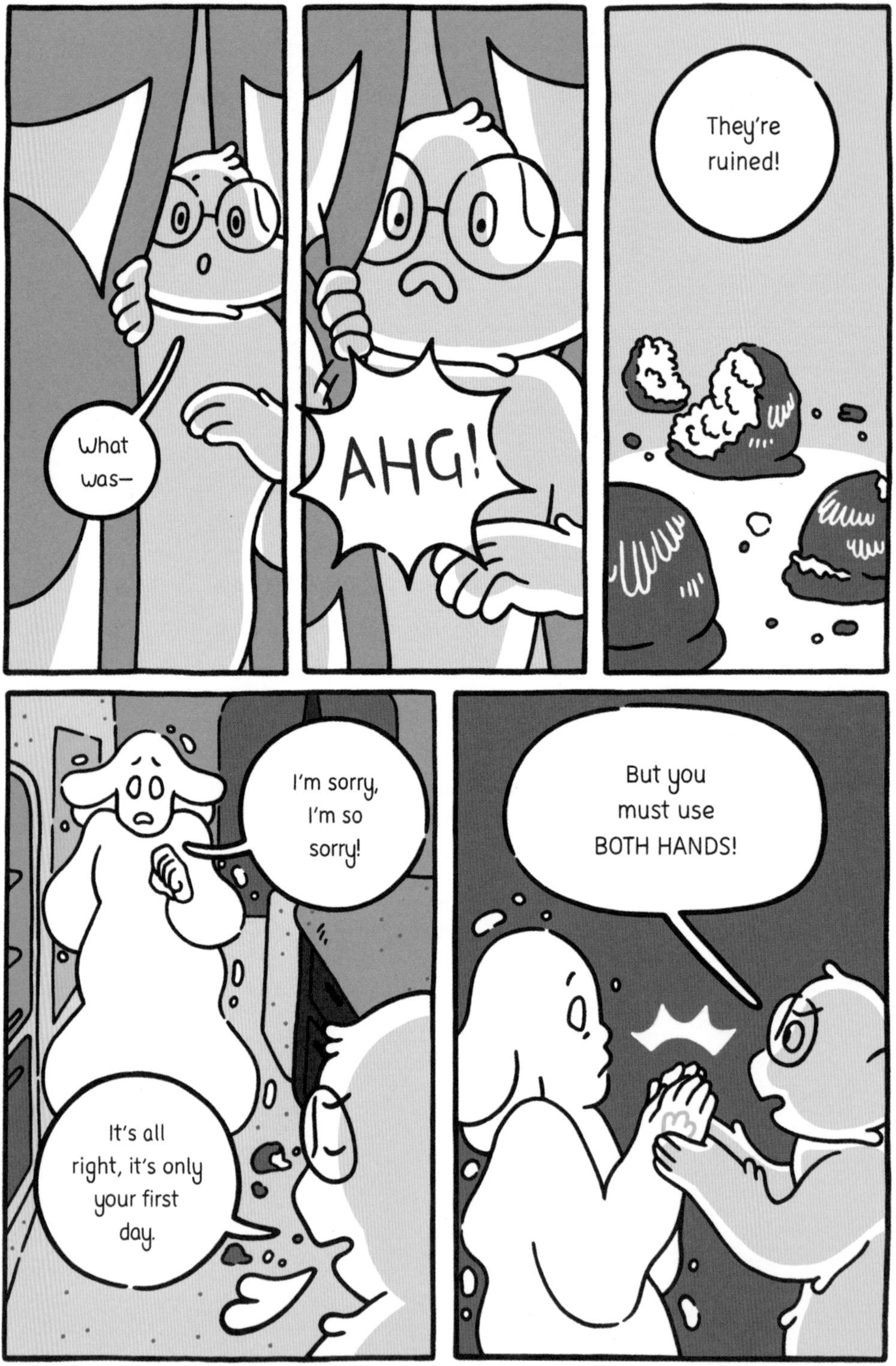
What was—
AHG!
They're ruined!
I'm sorry, I'm so sorry!
It's all right, it's only your first day.
But you must use BOTH HANDS!

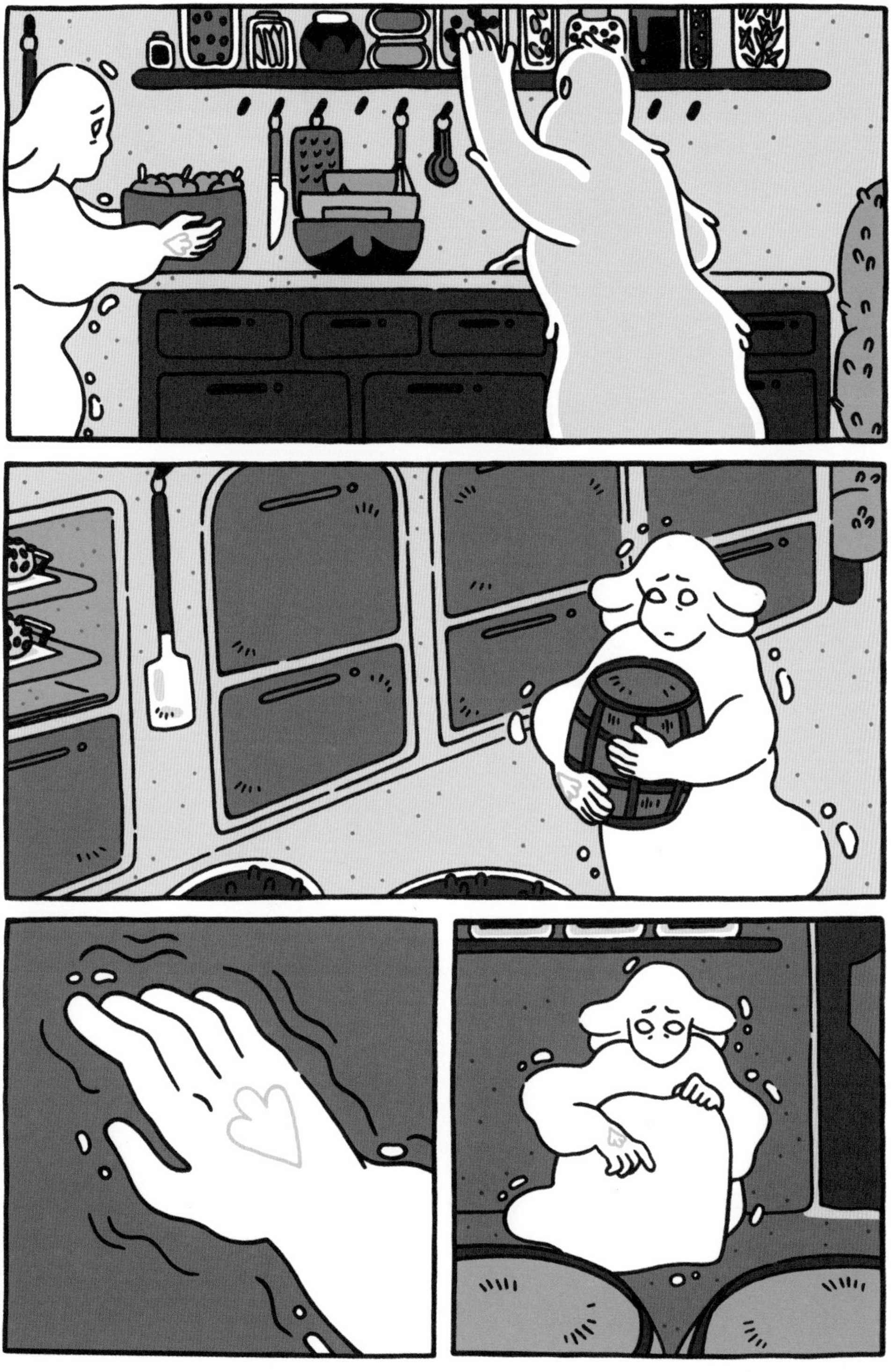

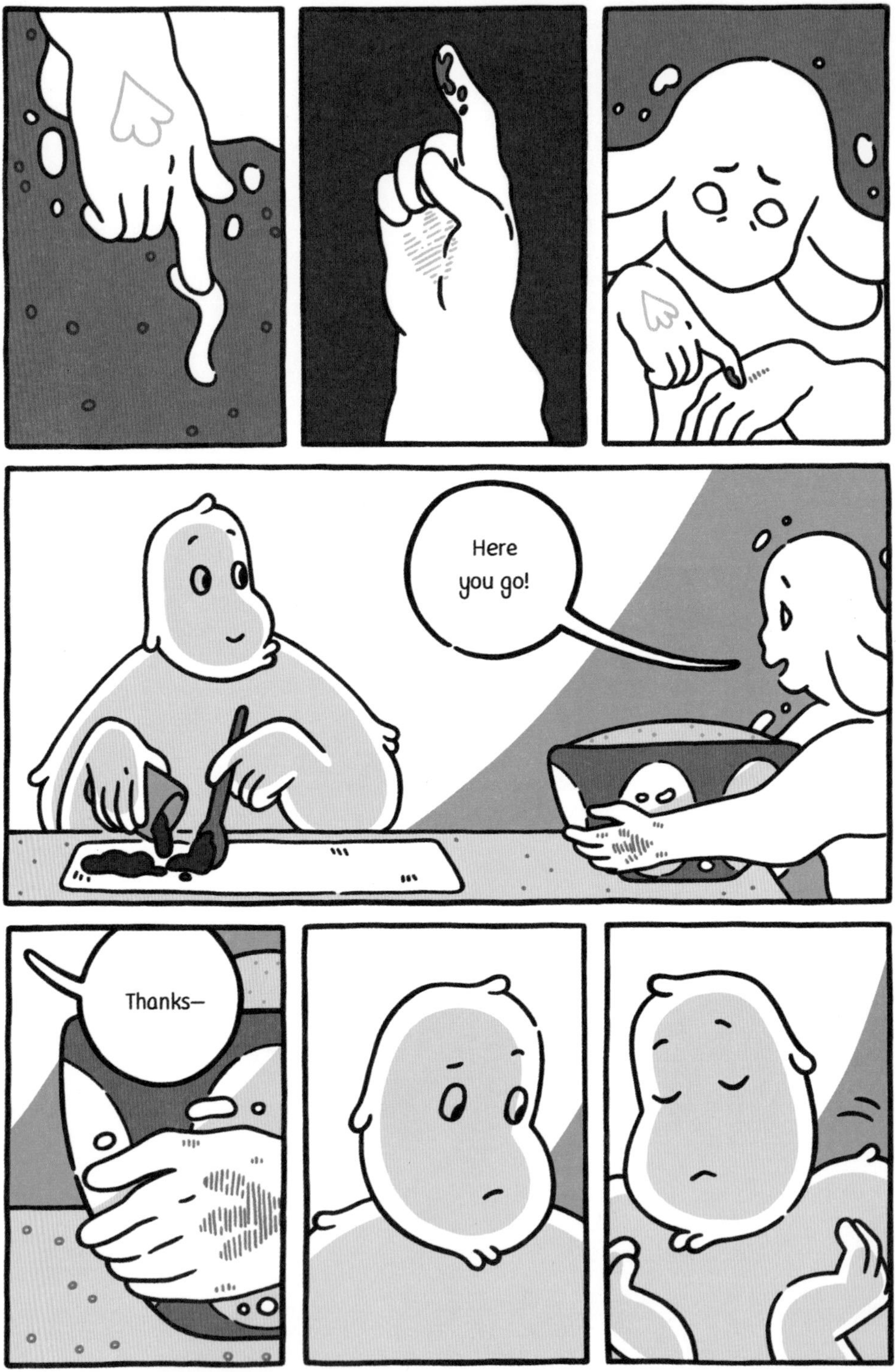
Here you go!
Thanks—

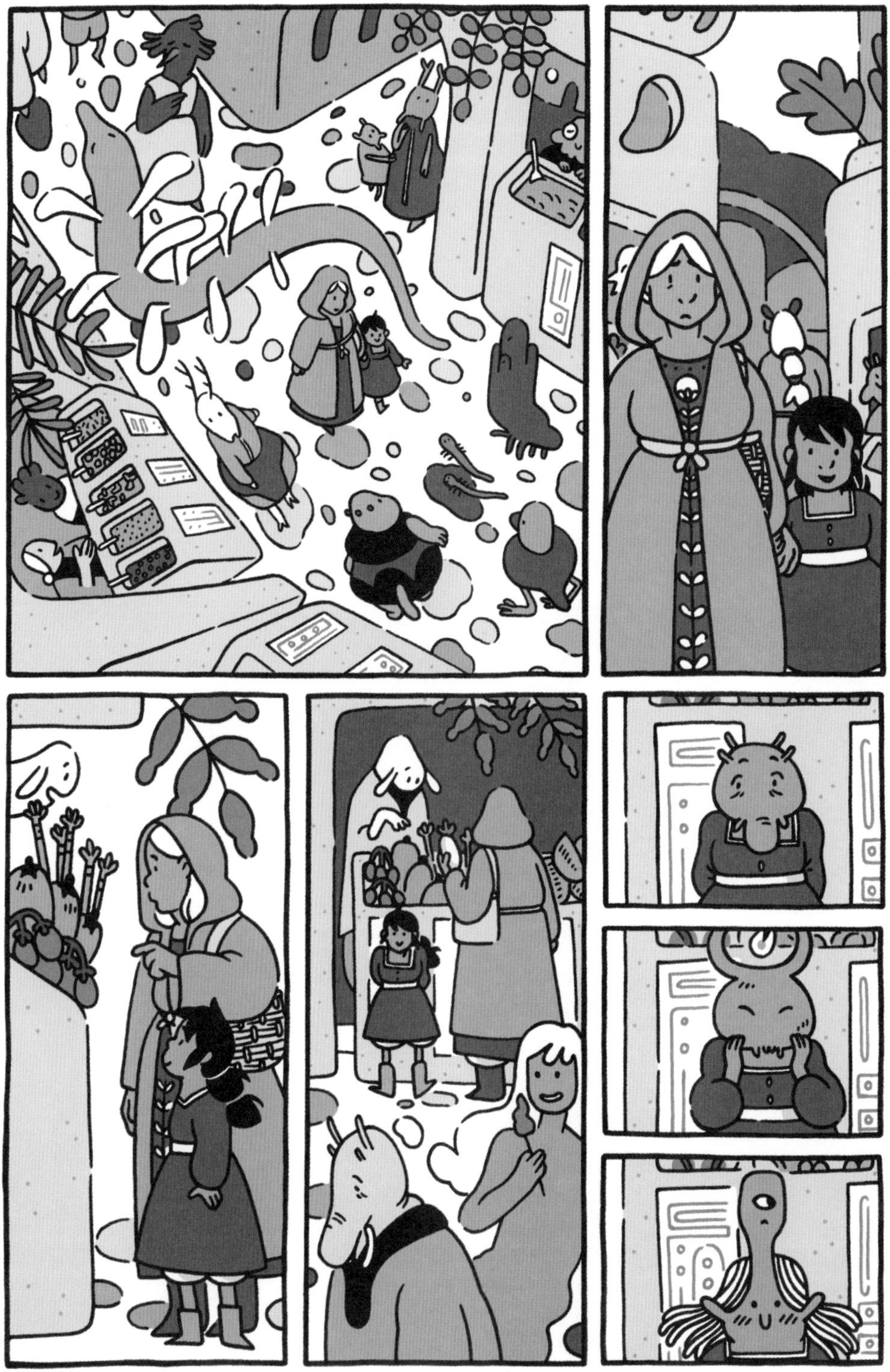

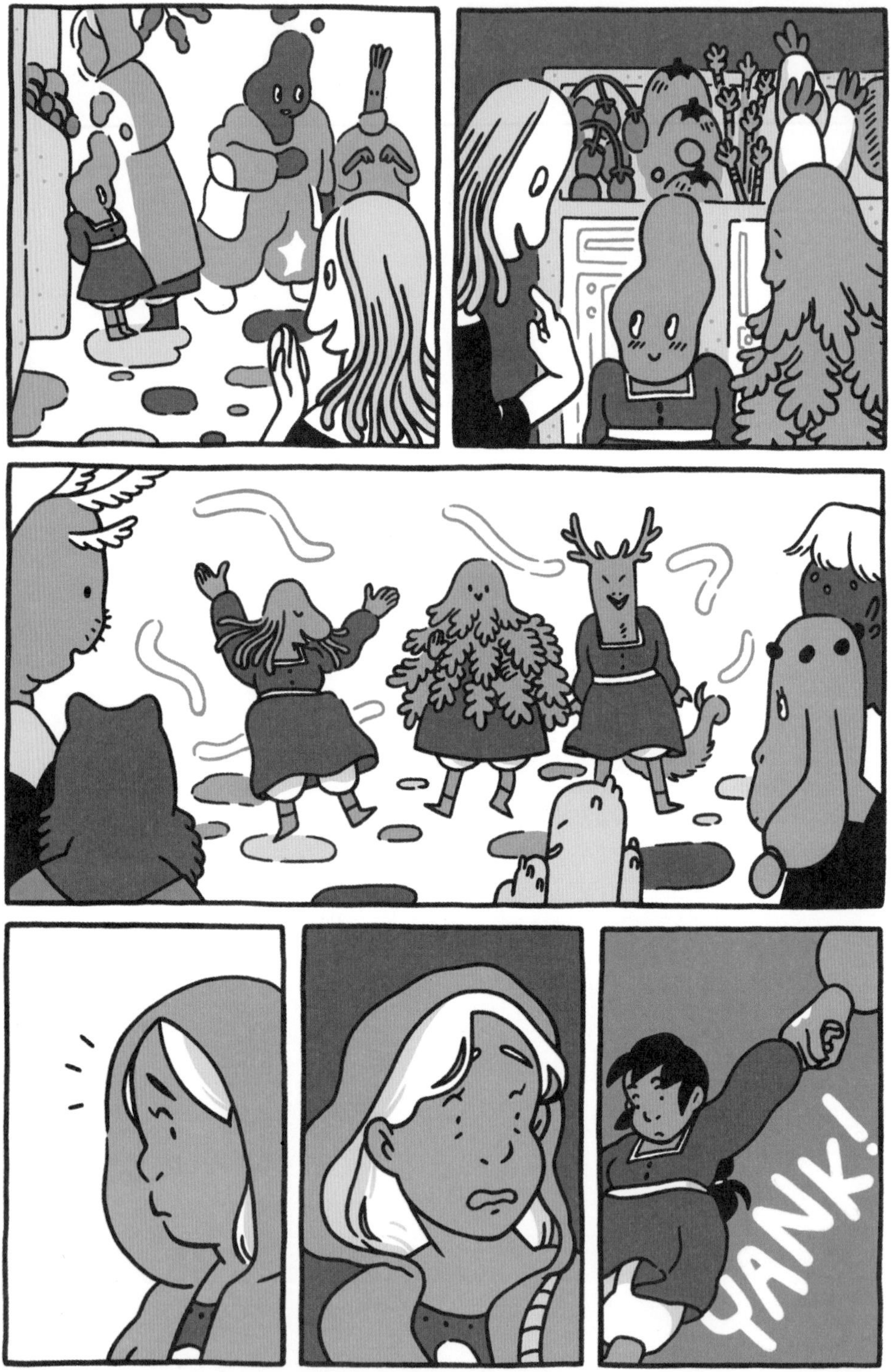
YANK!

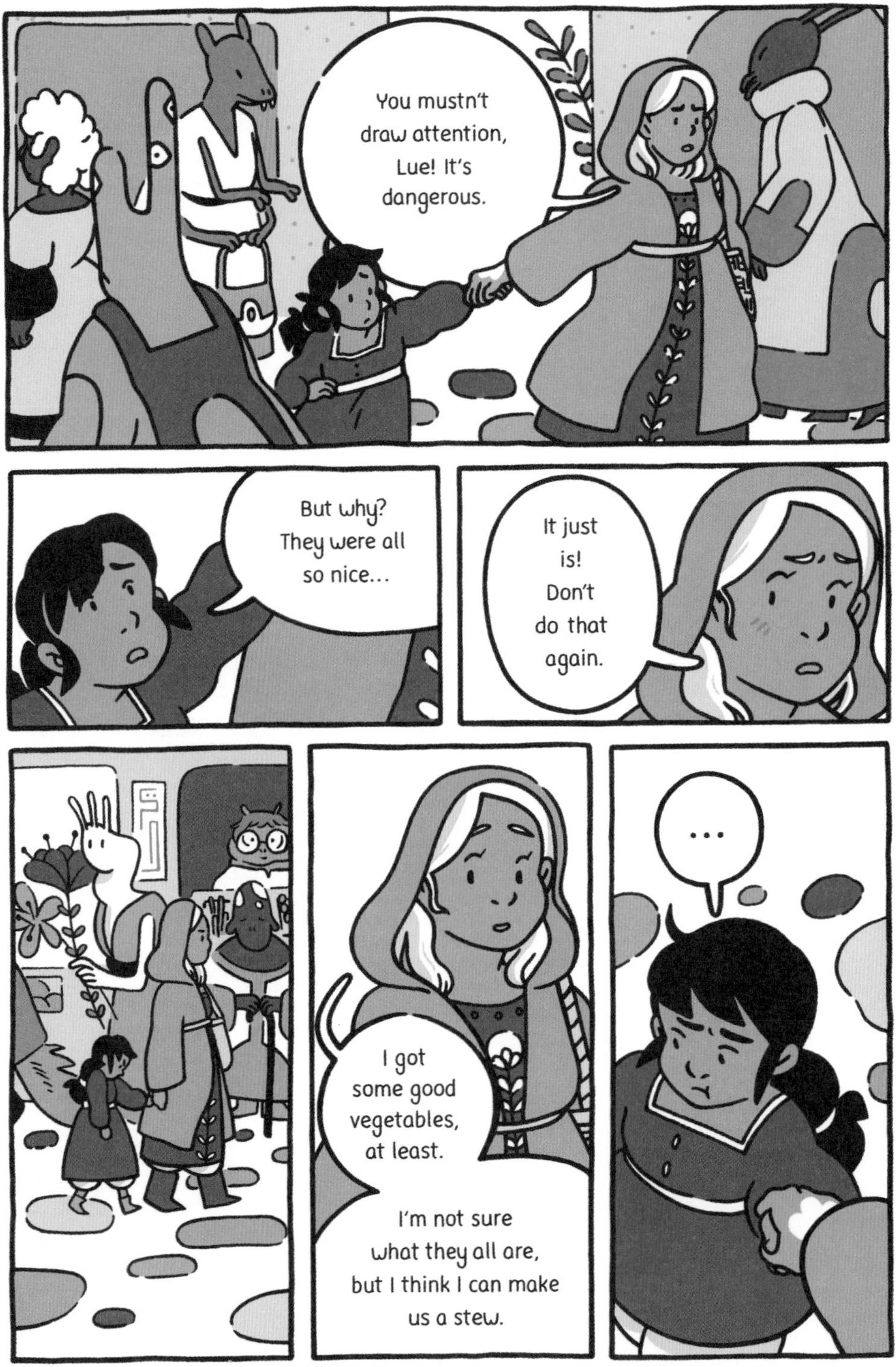
You mustn't draw attention, Lue! It's dangerous.
But why? They were all so nice...
It just is! Don't do that again.
I got some good vegetables, at least.
I'm not sure what they all are, but I think I can make us a stew.
...

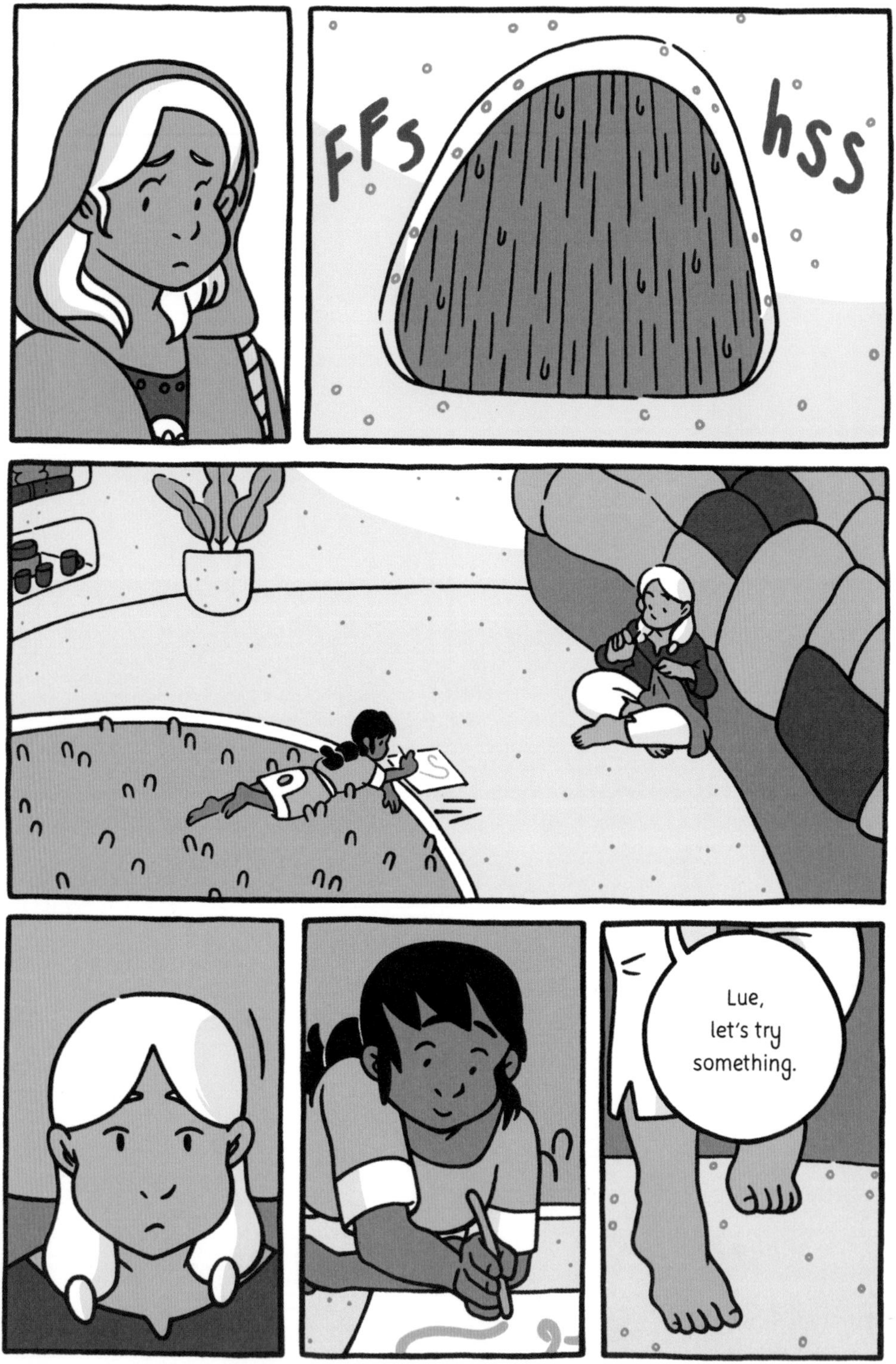
FFS
hss
Lue, let's try something.

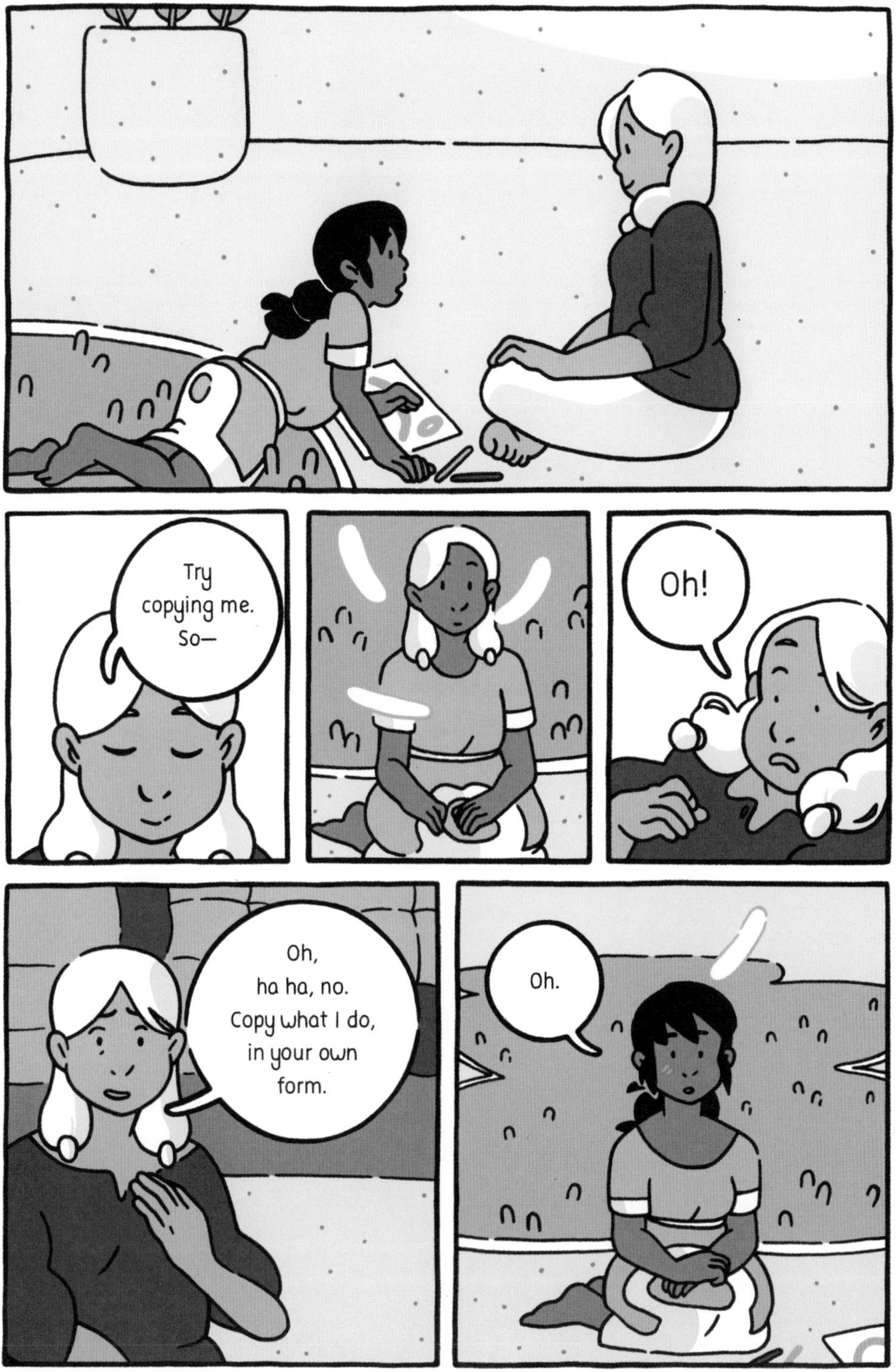
Try copying me. So—
Oh!
Oh, ha ha, no. Copy what I do, in your own form.
Oh.

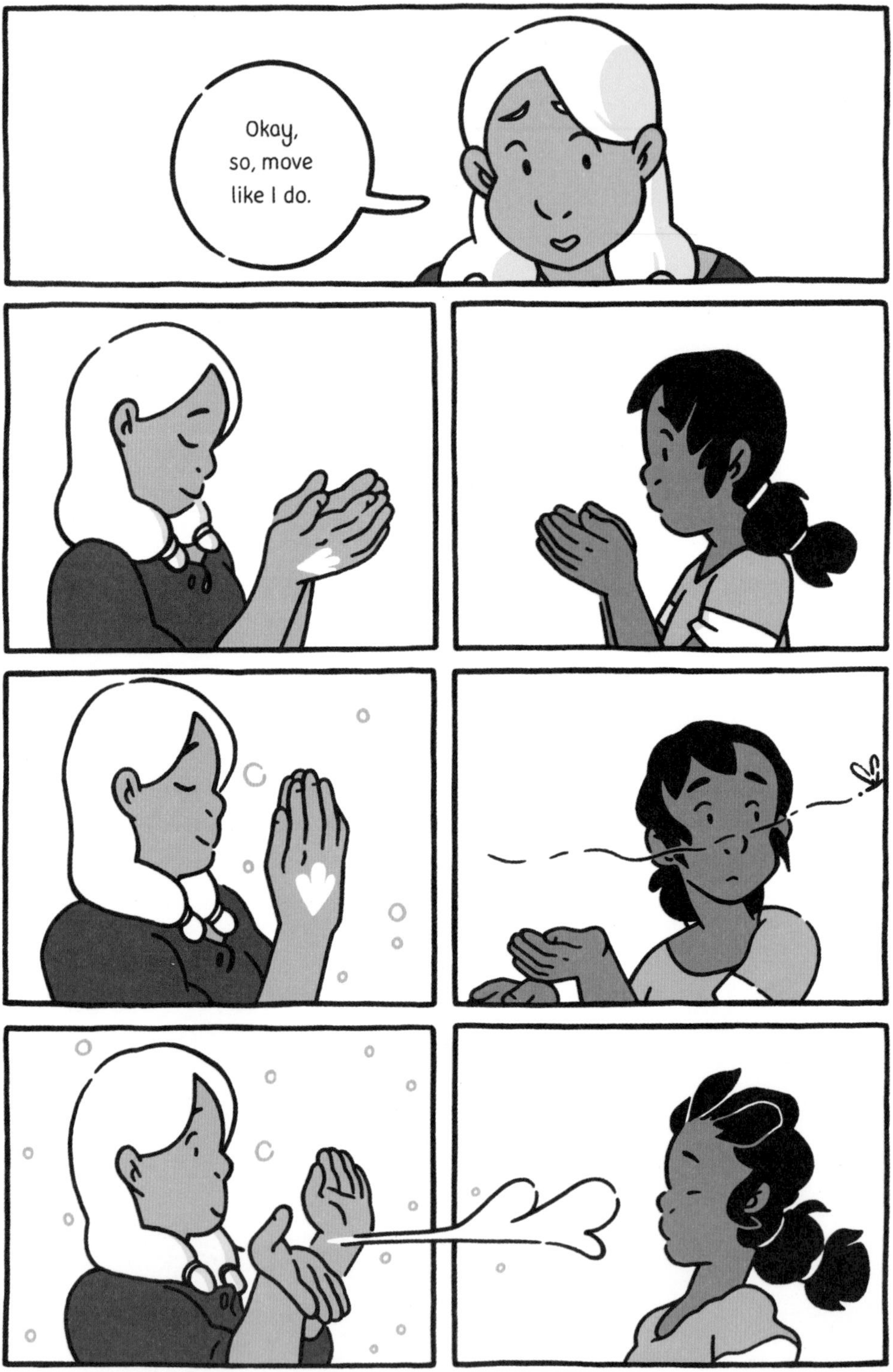
Okay, so, move like I do.

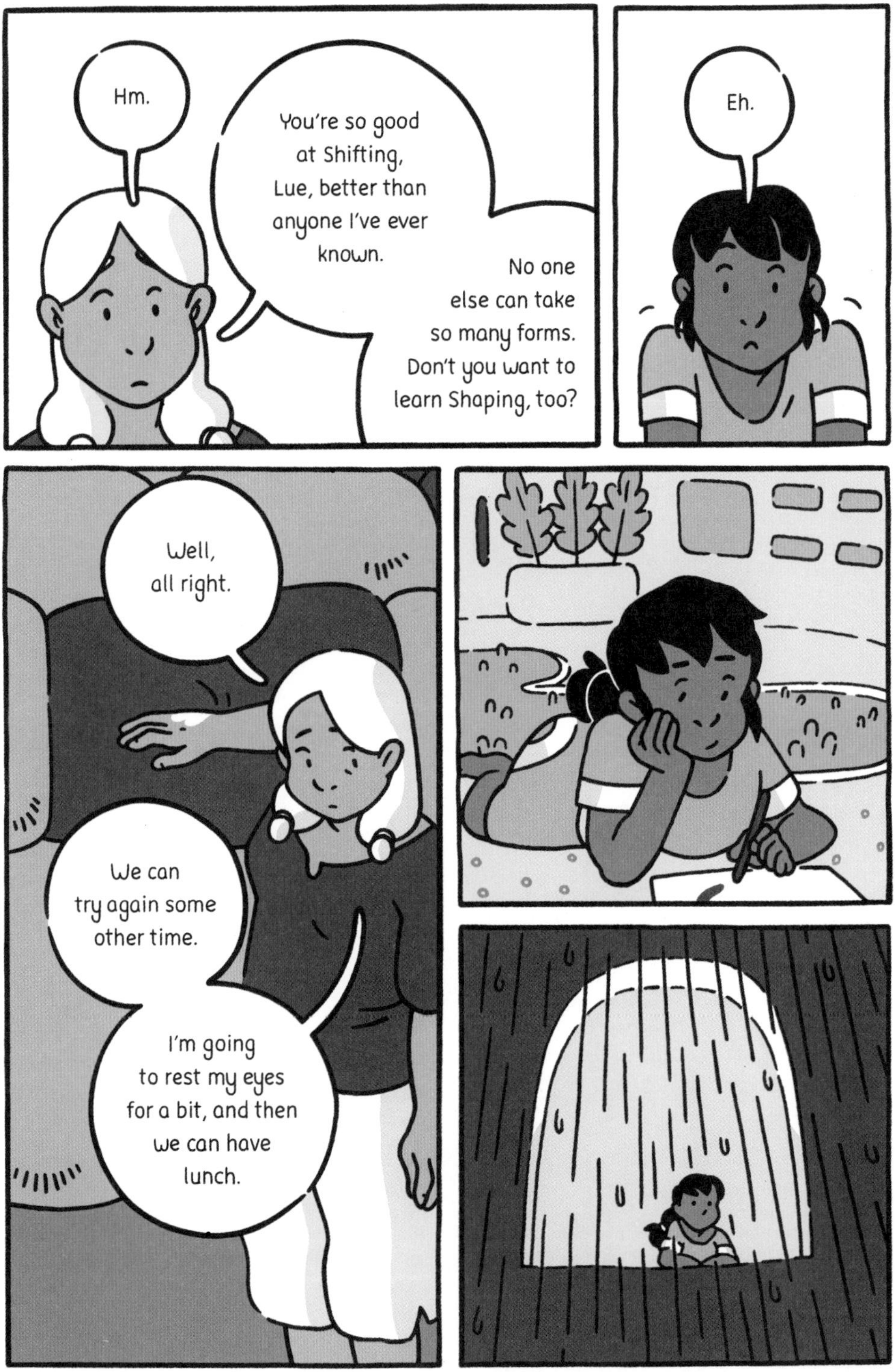
Hm.
You're so good at Shifting, Lue, better than anyone I've ever known.
No one else can take so many forms. Don't you want to learn Shaping, too?
Eh.
Well, all right.
We can try again some other time.
I'm going to rest my eyes for a bit, and then we can have lunch.

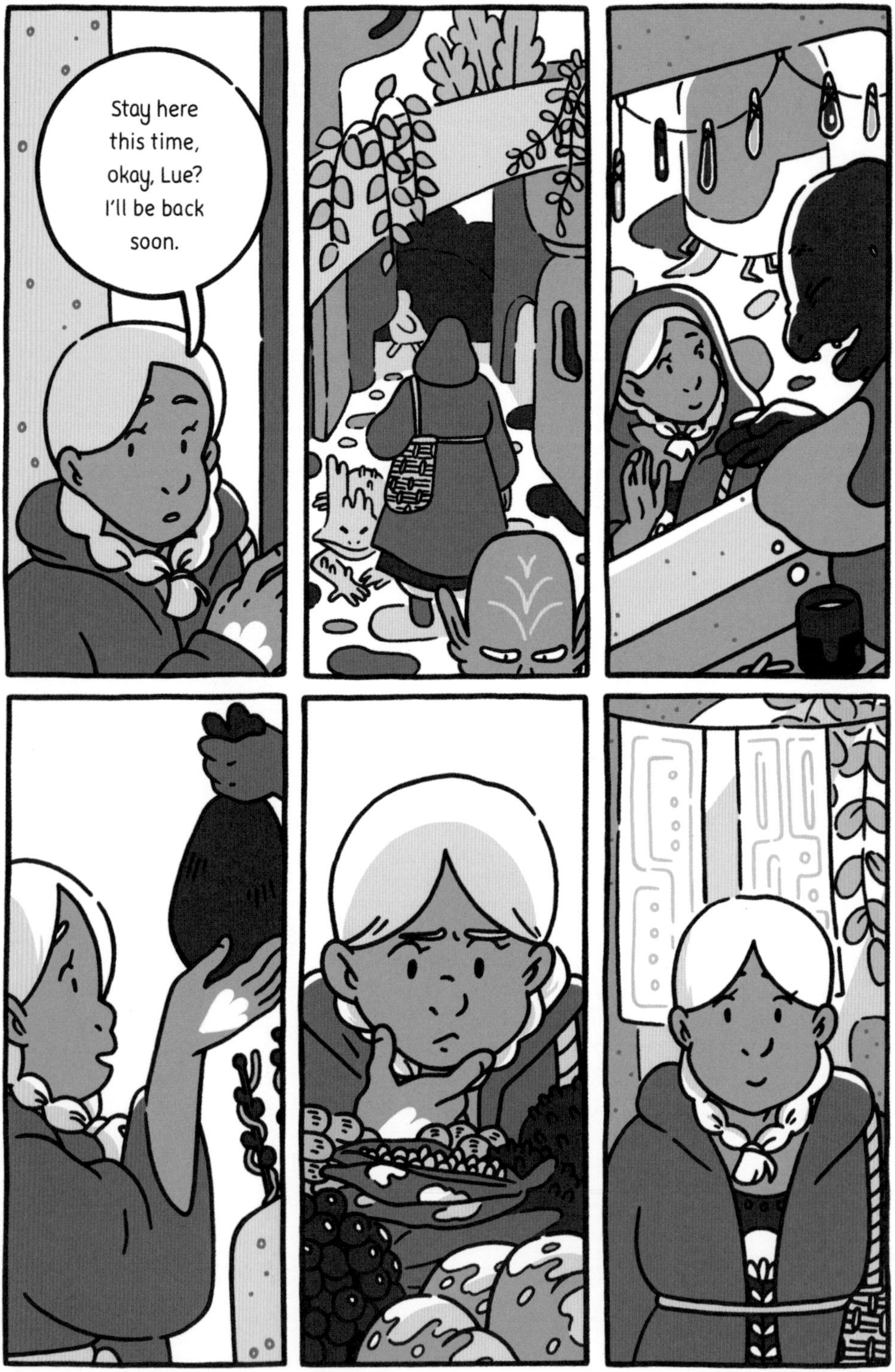
Stay here this time, okay, Lue? I'll be back soon.

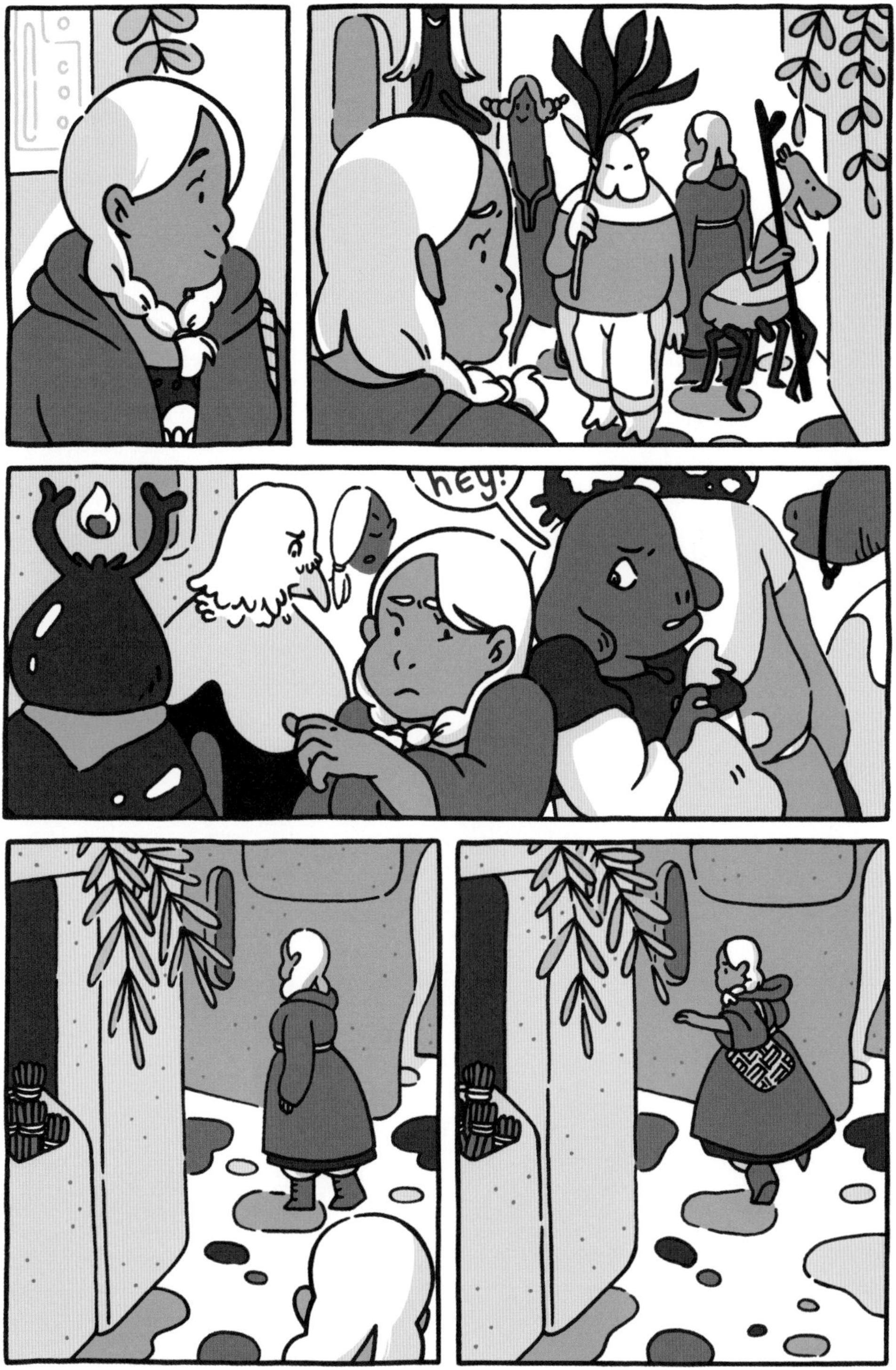
hey!

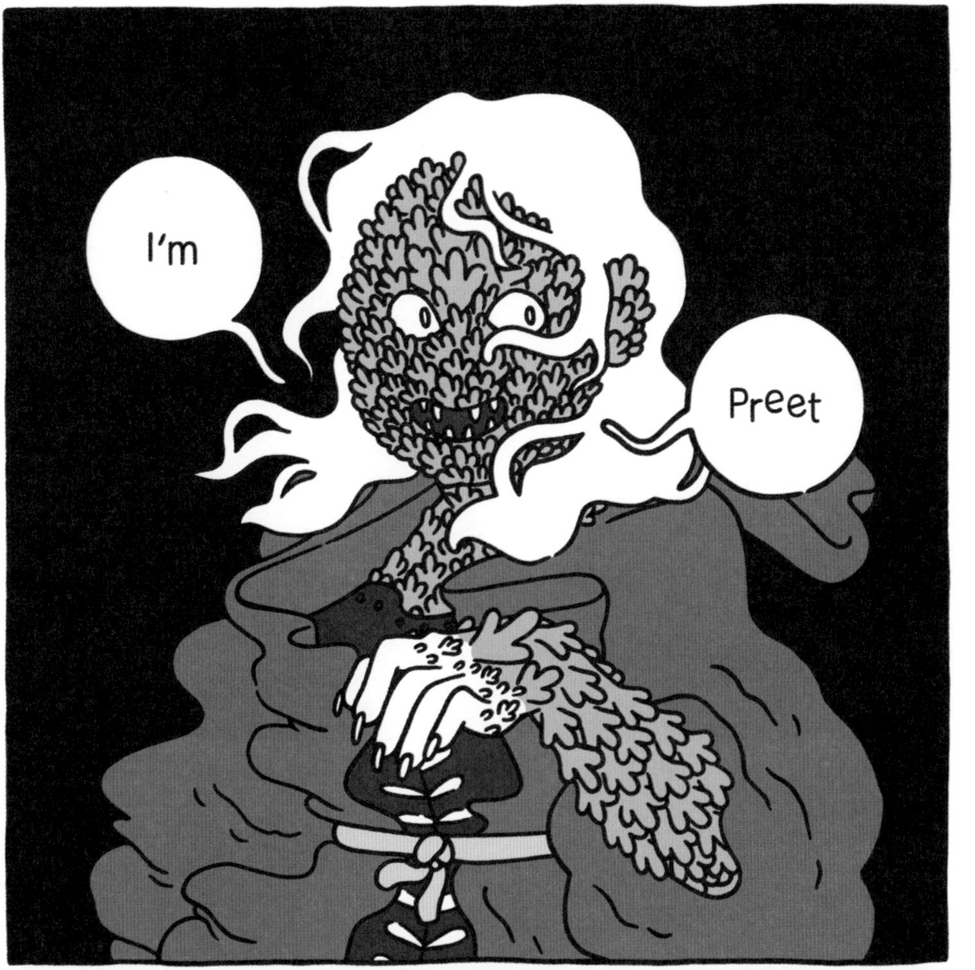
I'm
Preet
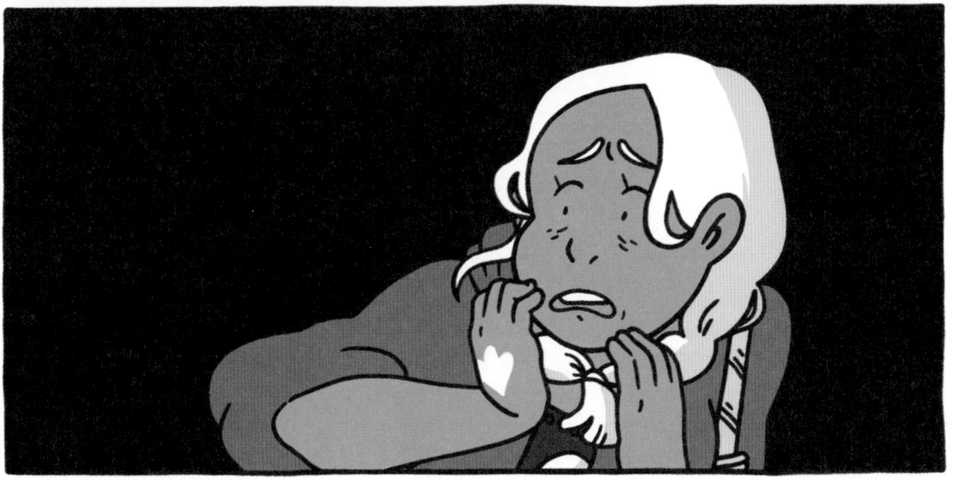

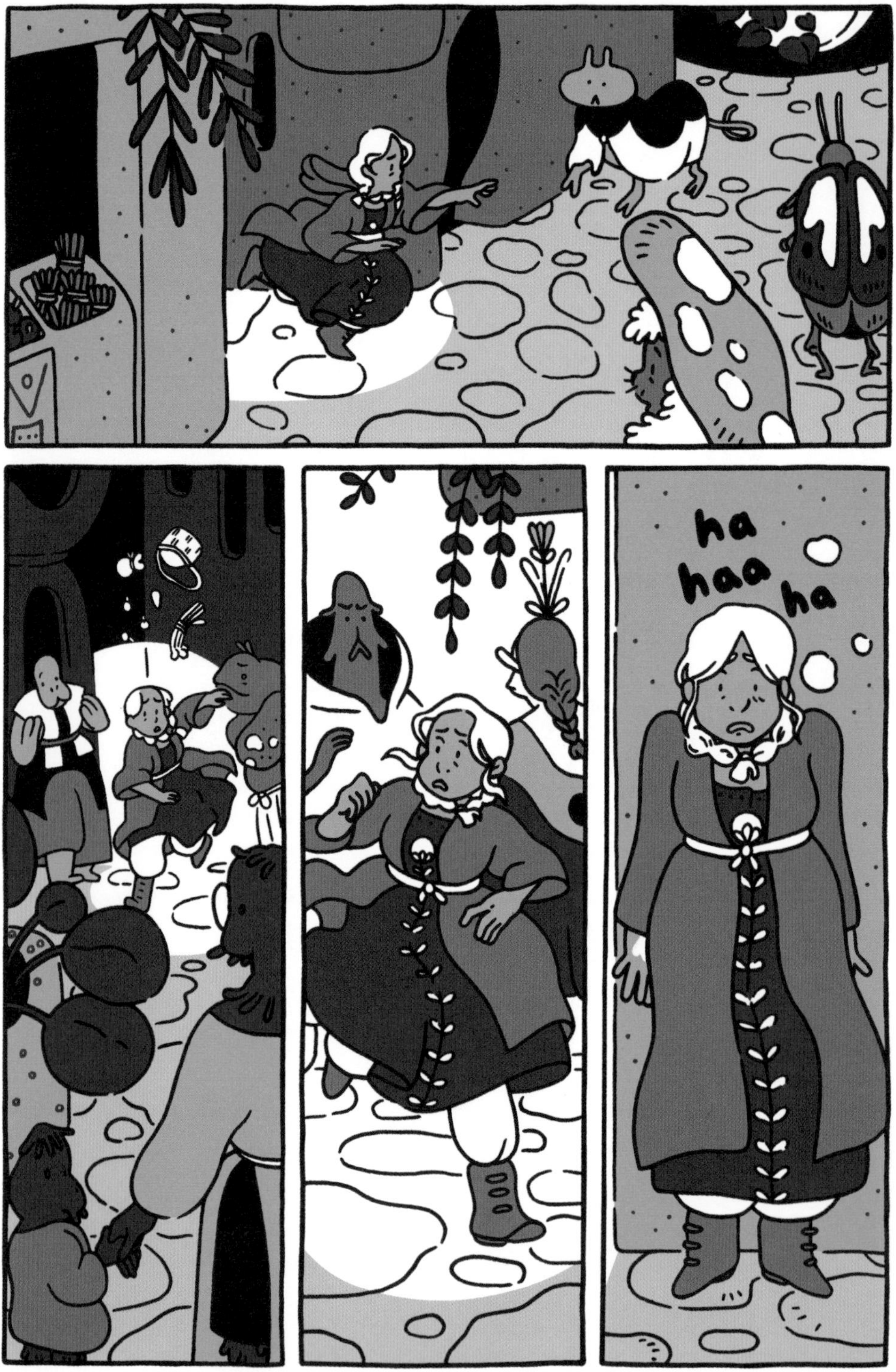
ha
haa
ha

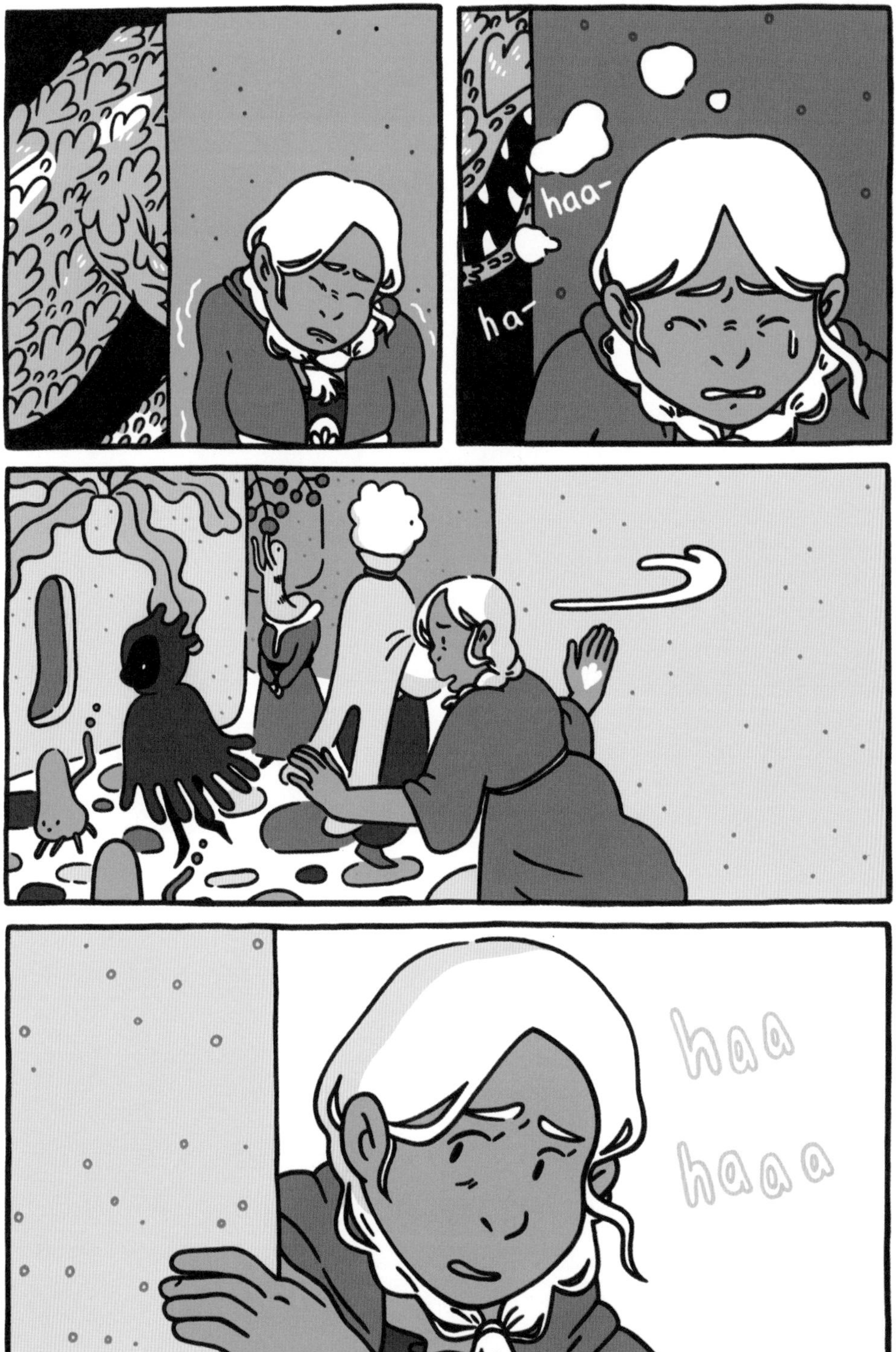
haa-
ha-
haa
haaa

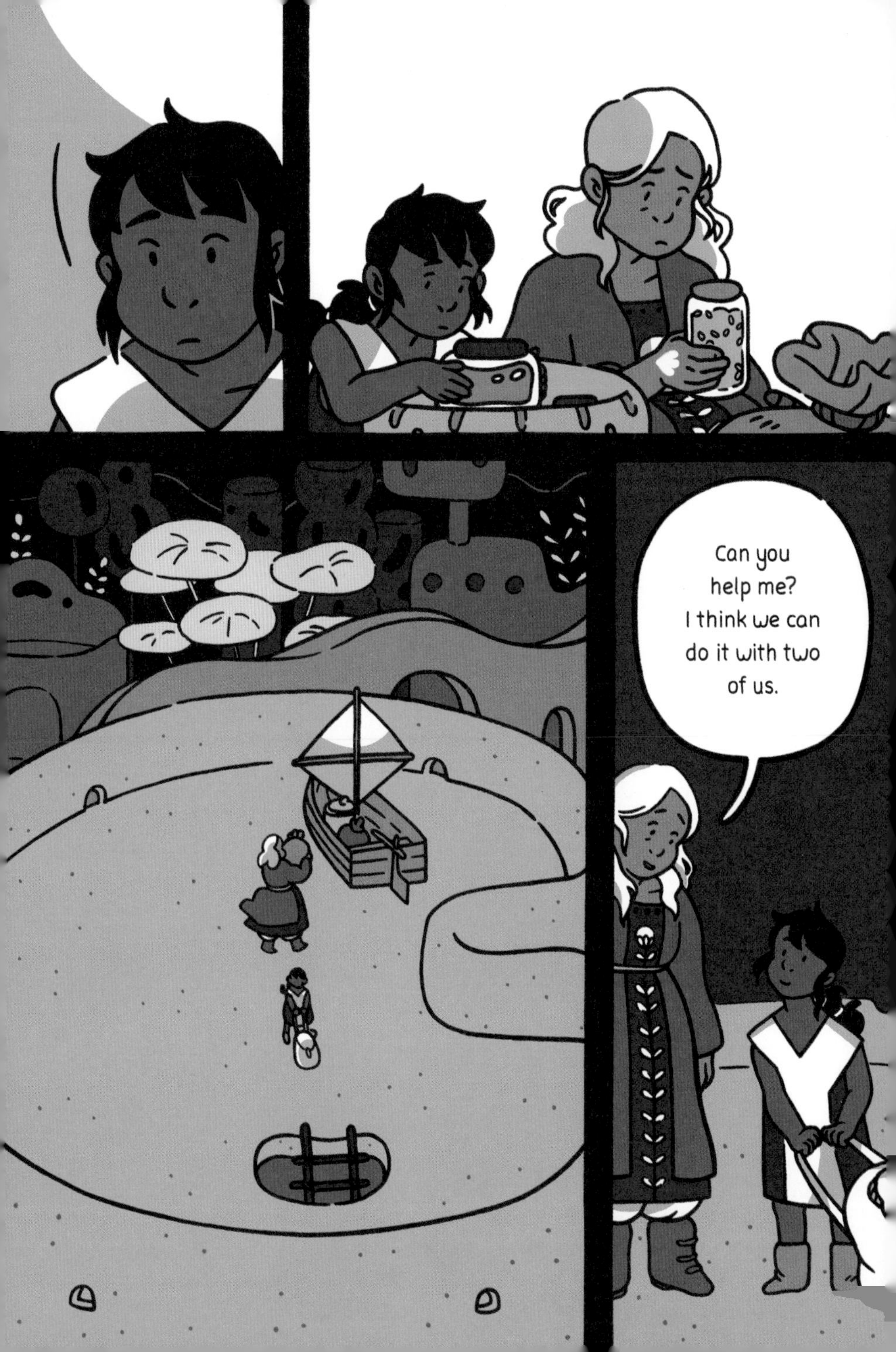
Can you help me? I think we can do it with two of us.

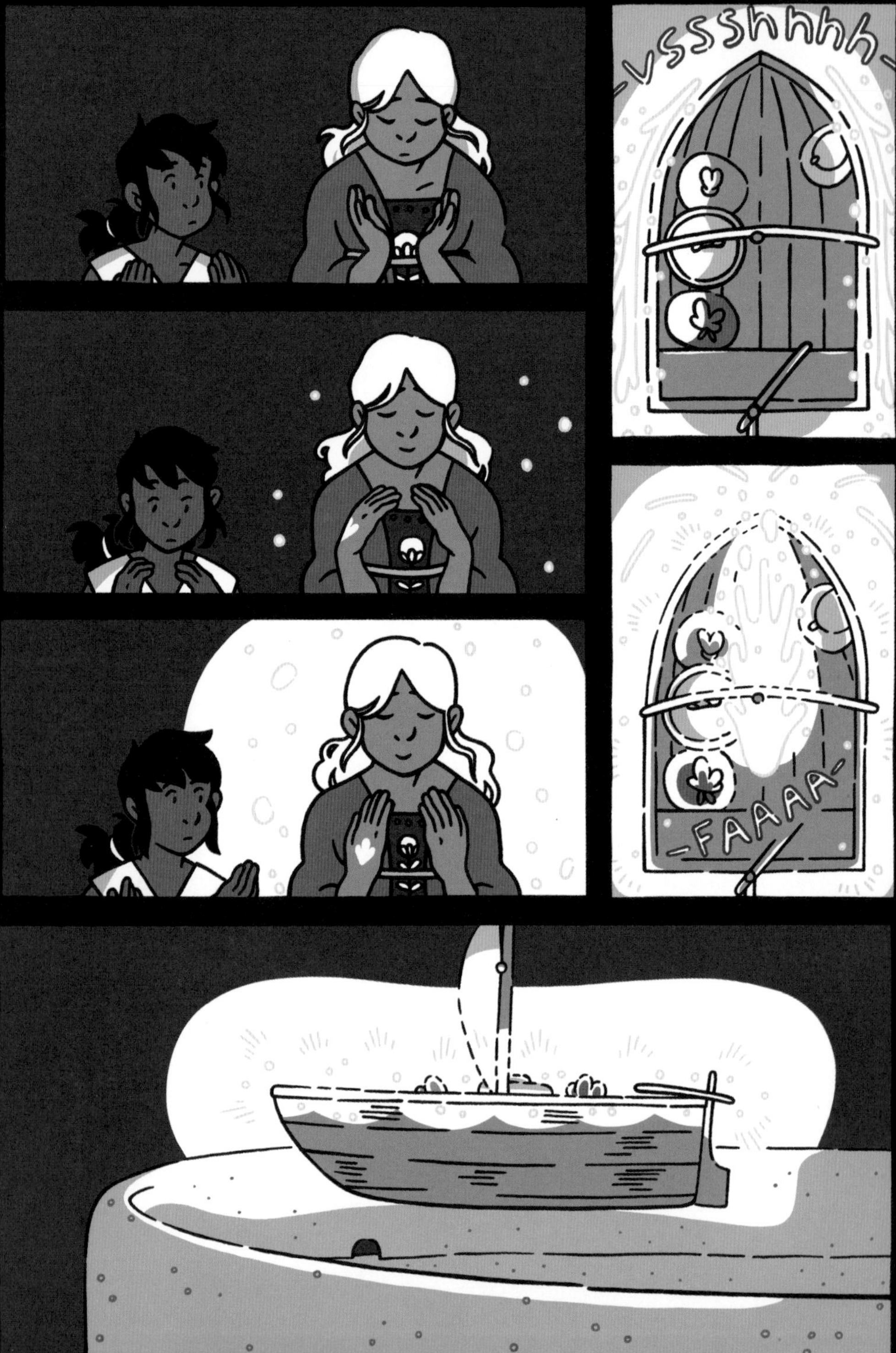
-VSSShhhh-
-FAAAA-

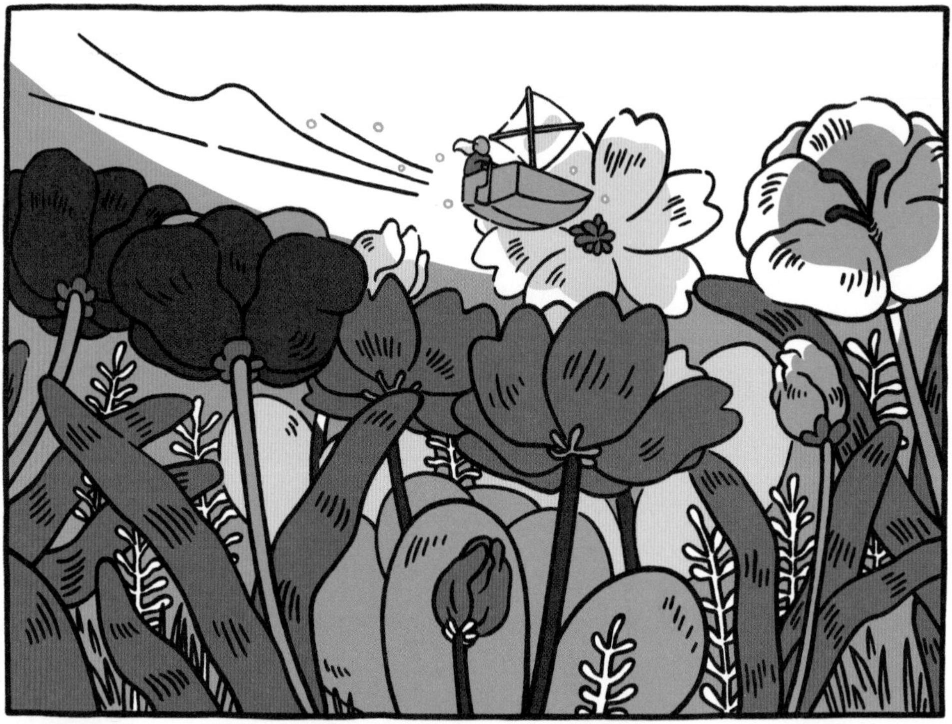

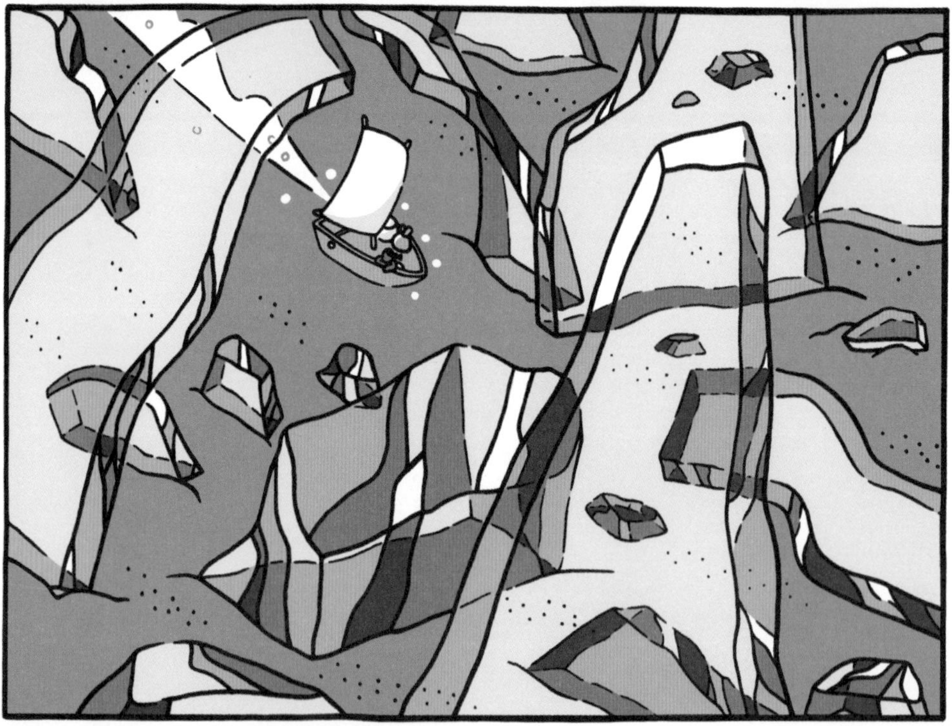

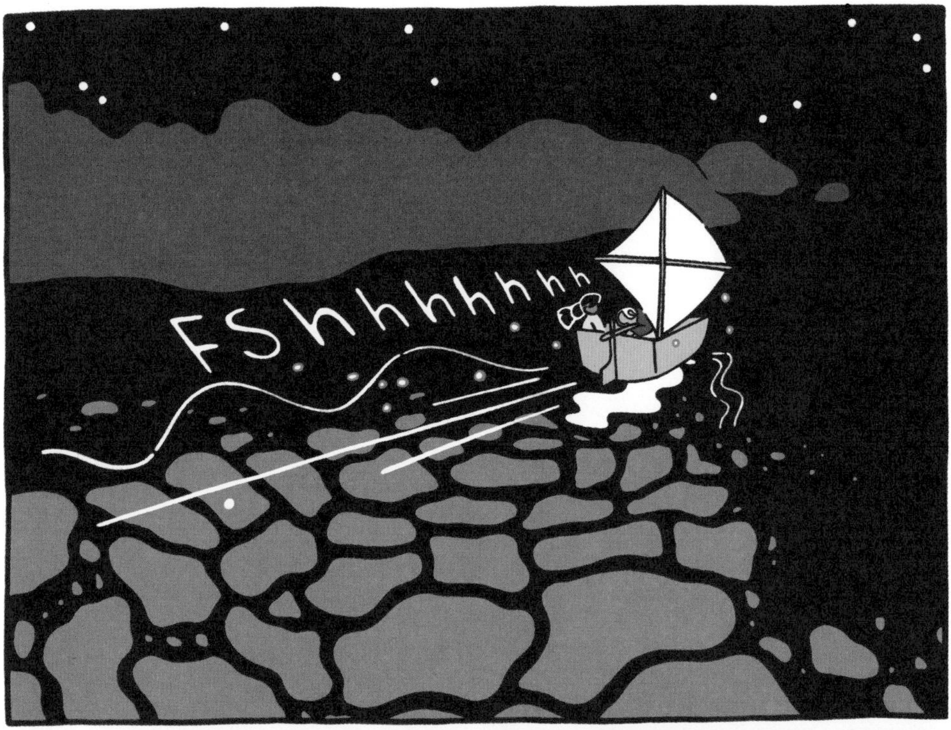
FShhhhhhhh

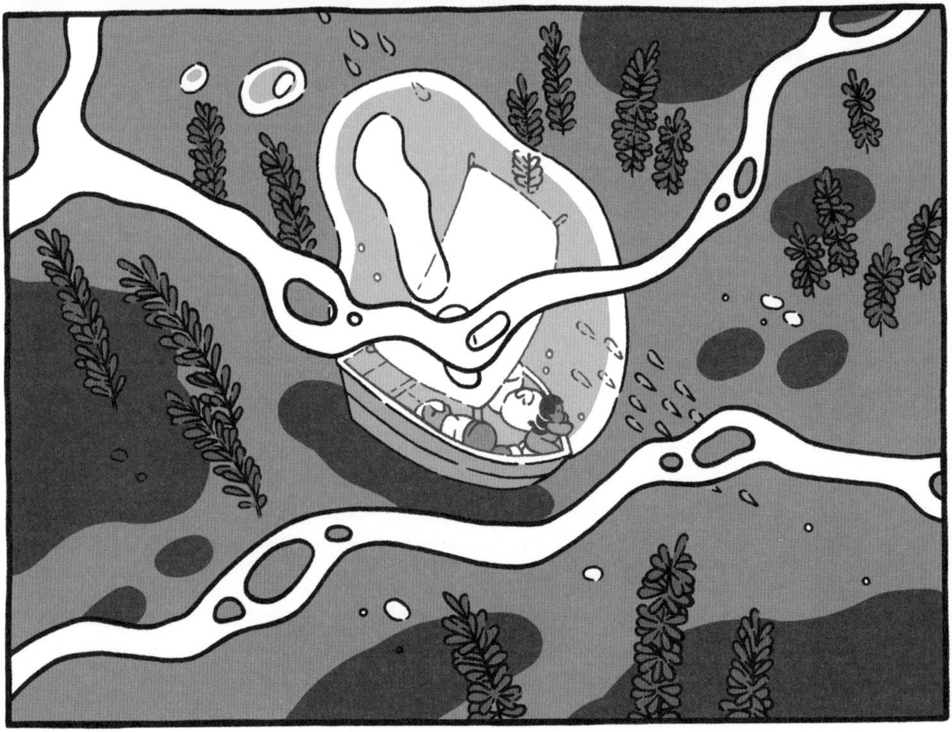

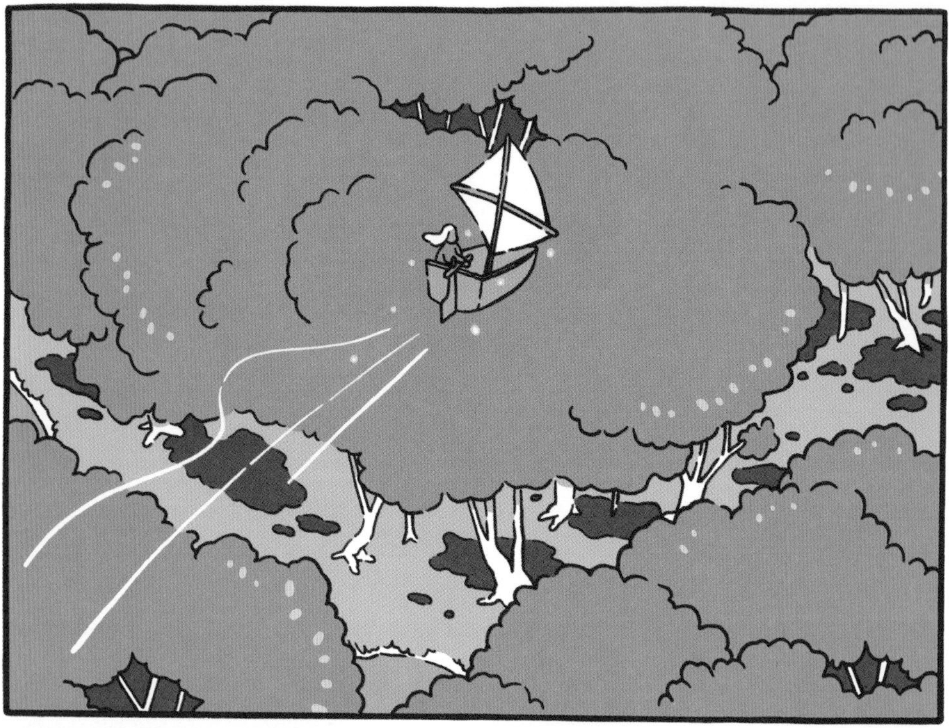

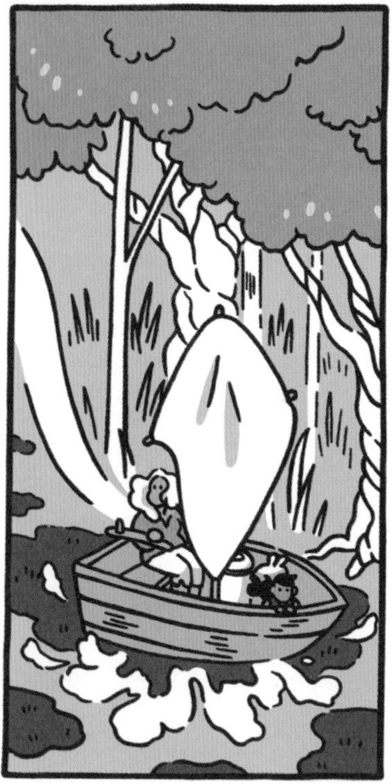

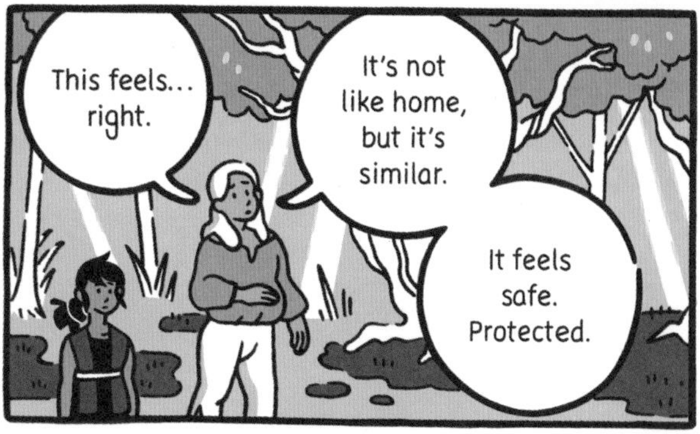
This feels... right.
It's not like home, but it's similar.
It feels safe. Protected.

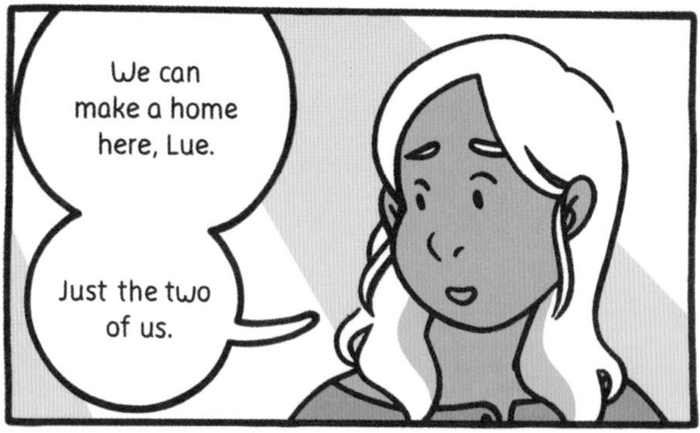
We can make a home here, Lue.
Just the two of us.

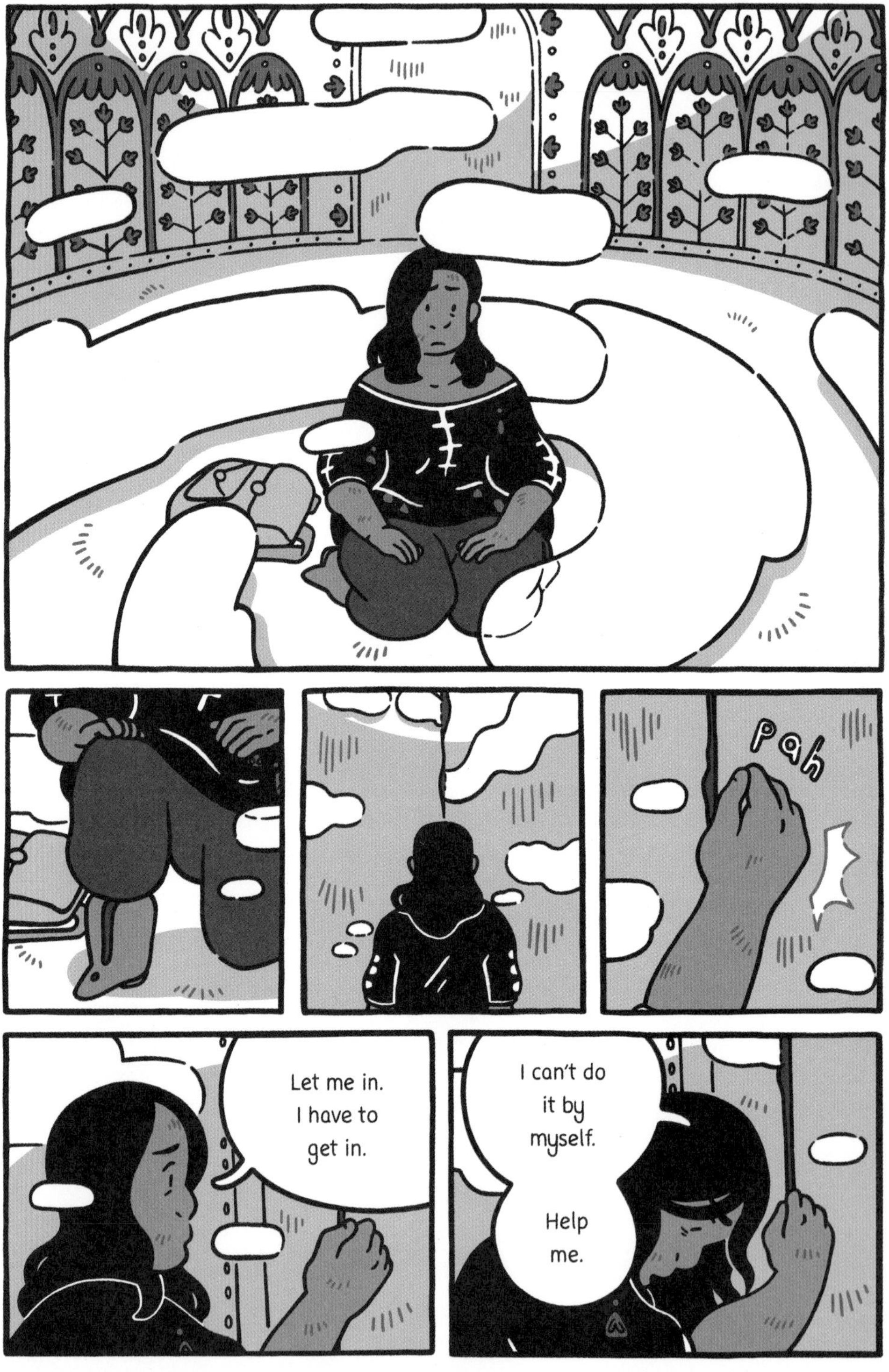
pah
Let me in. I have to get in.
I can't do it by myself.
Help me.

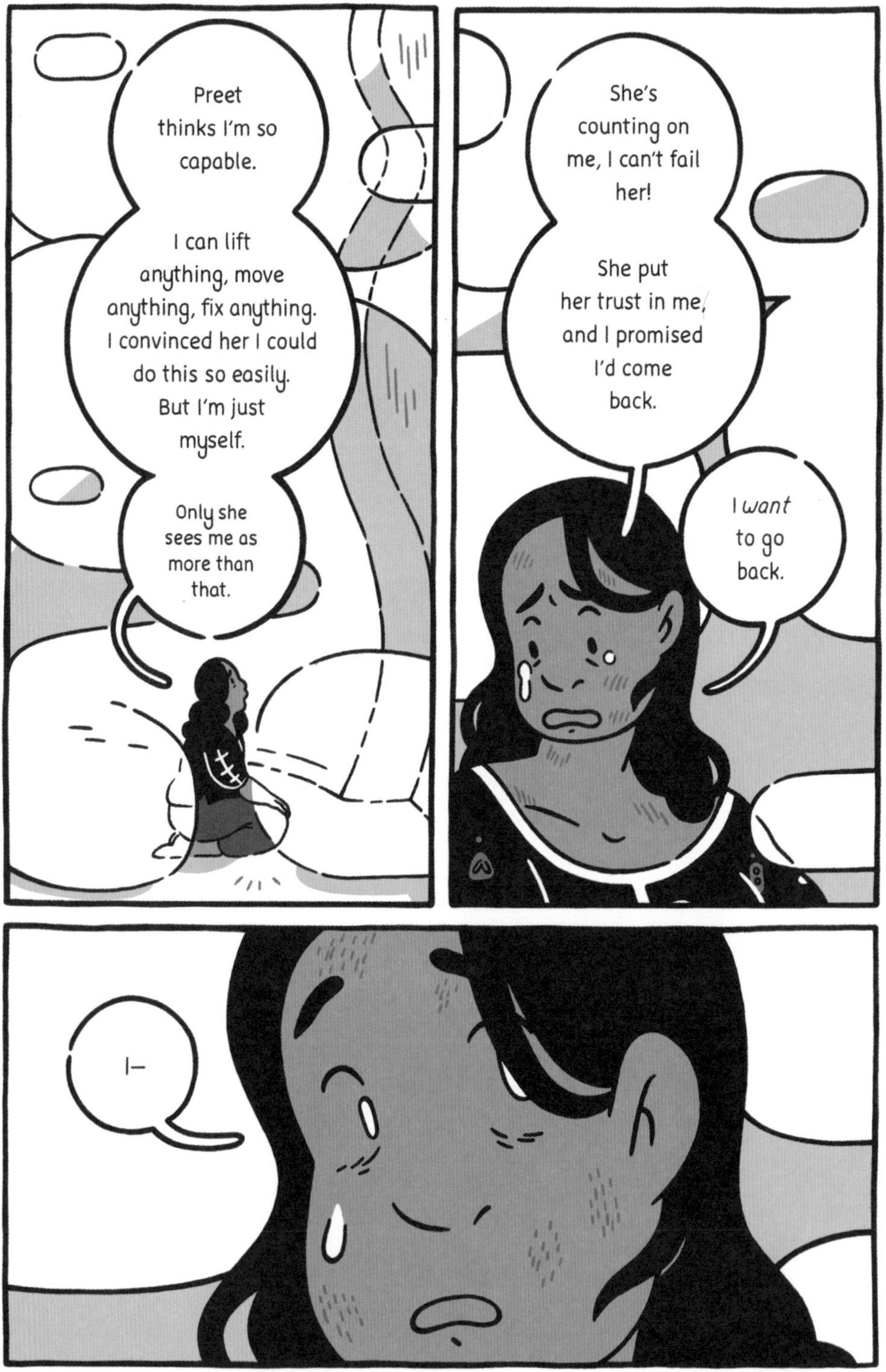
Preet thinks I'm so capable.
I can lift anything, move anything, fix anything. I convinced her I could do this so easily. But I'm just myself.
Only she sees me as more than that.
She's counting on me, I can't fail her!
She put her trust in me, and I promised I'd come back.
I *want* to go back.
I—

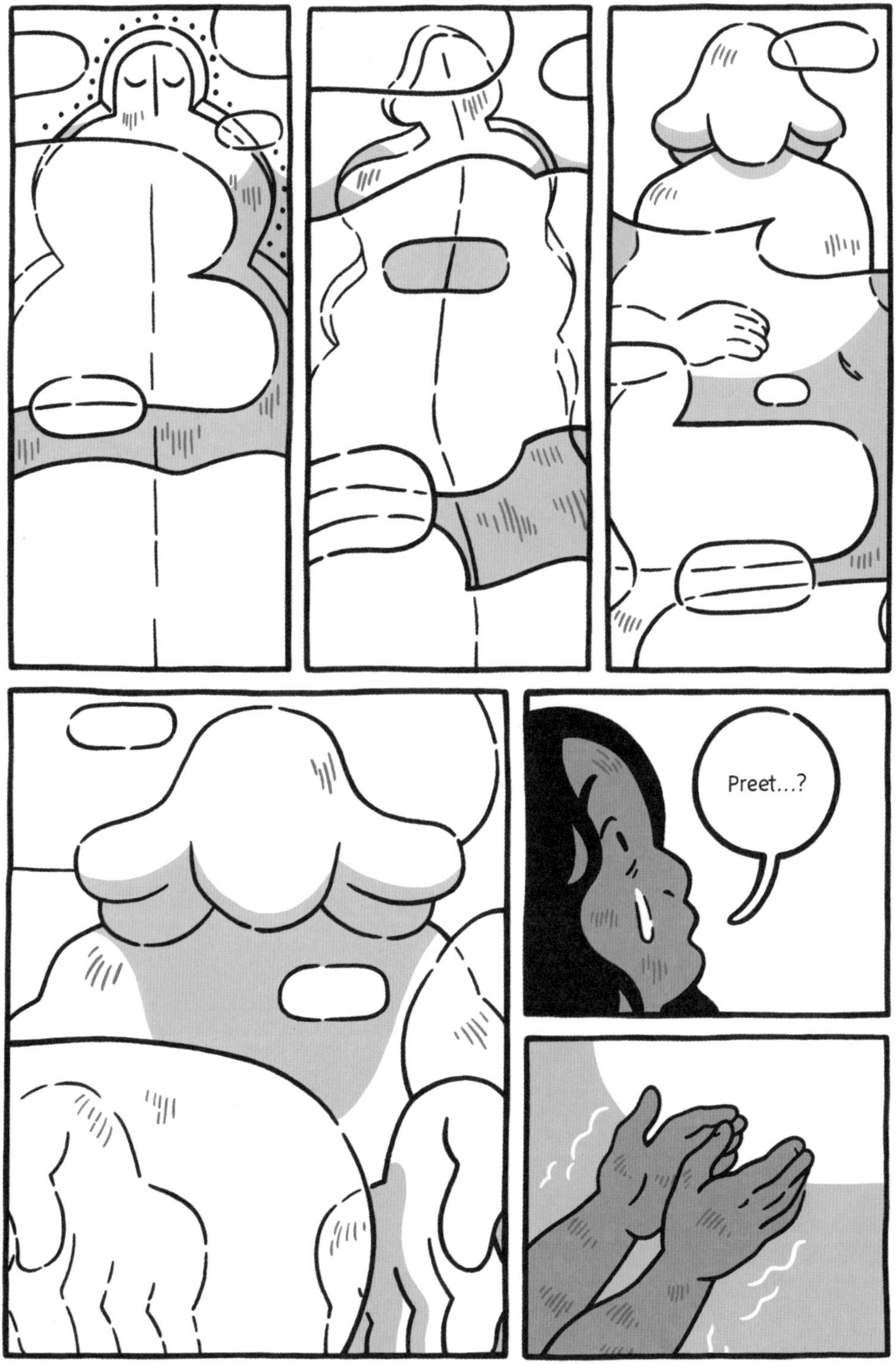
Preet...?

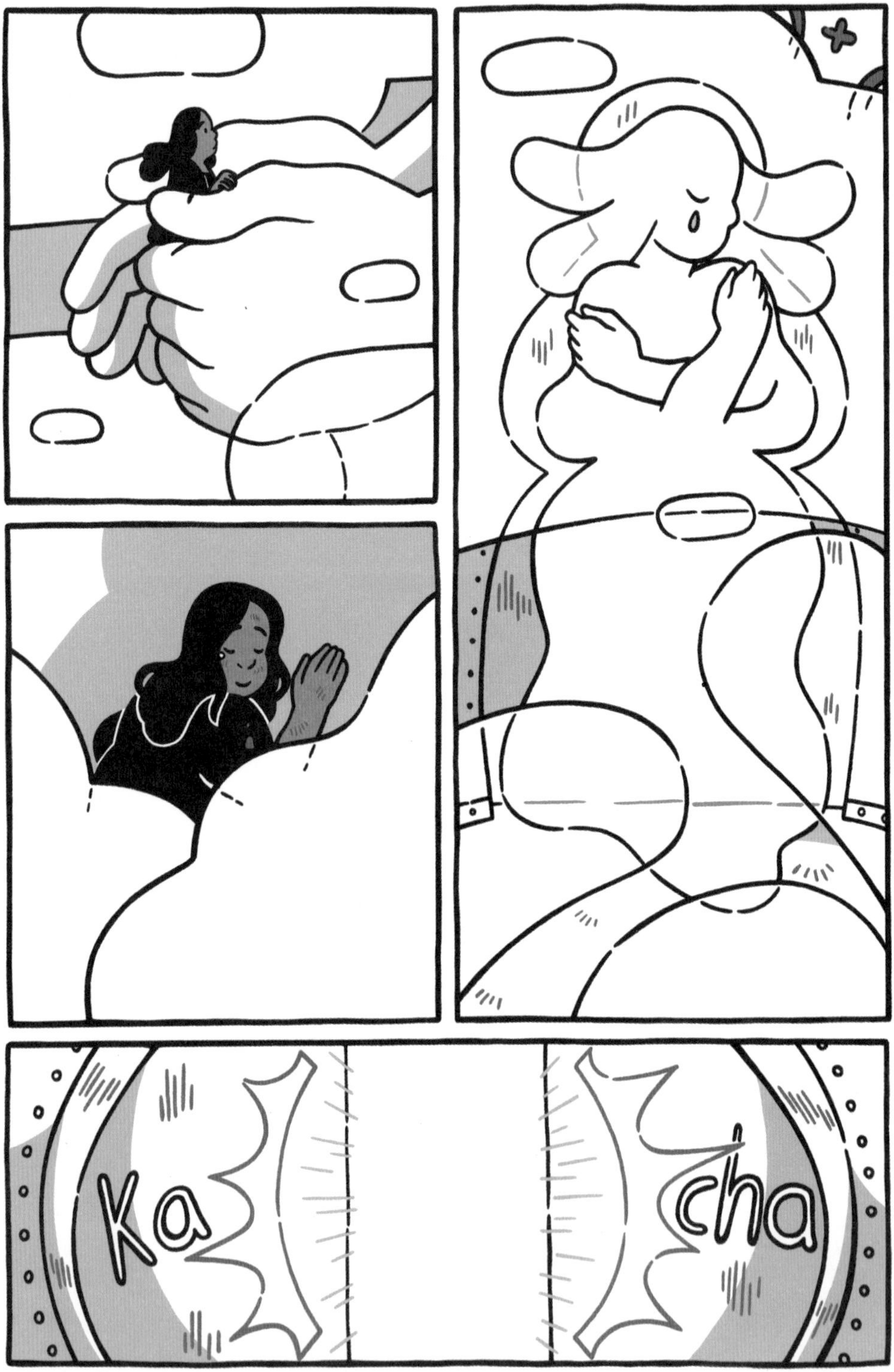
Ka
cha

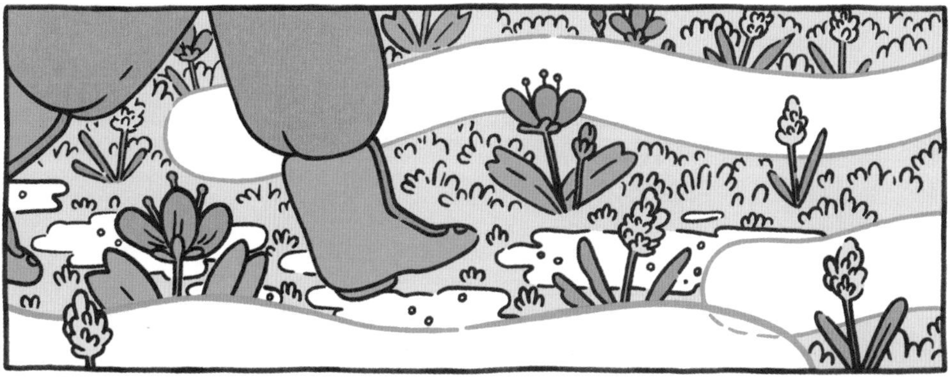

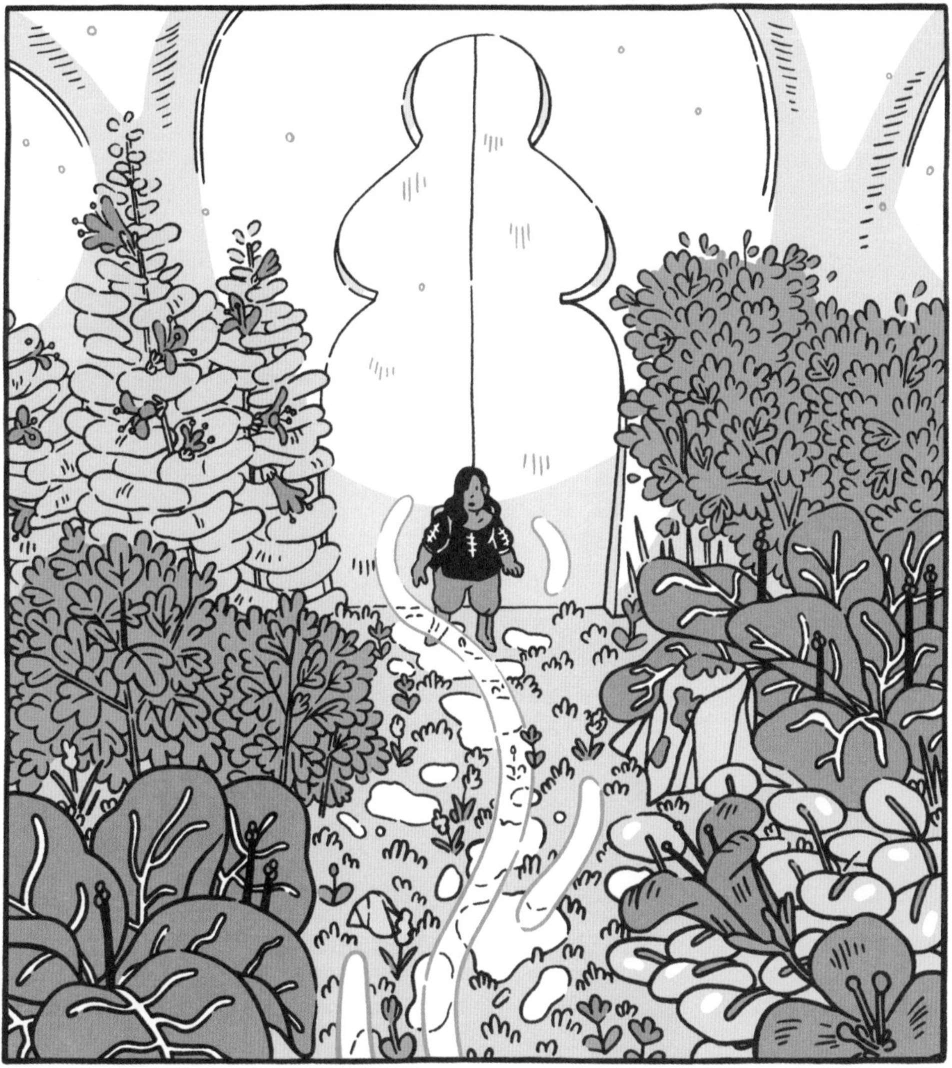

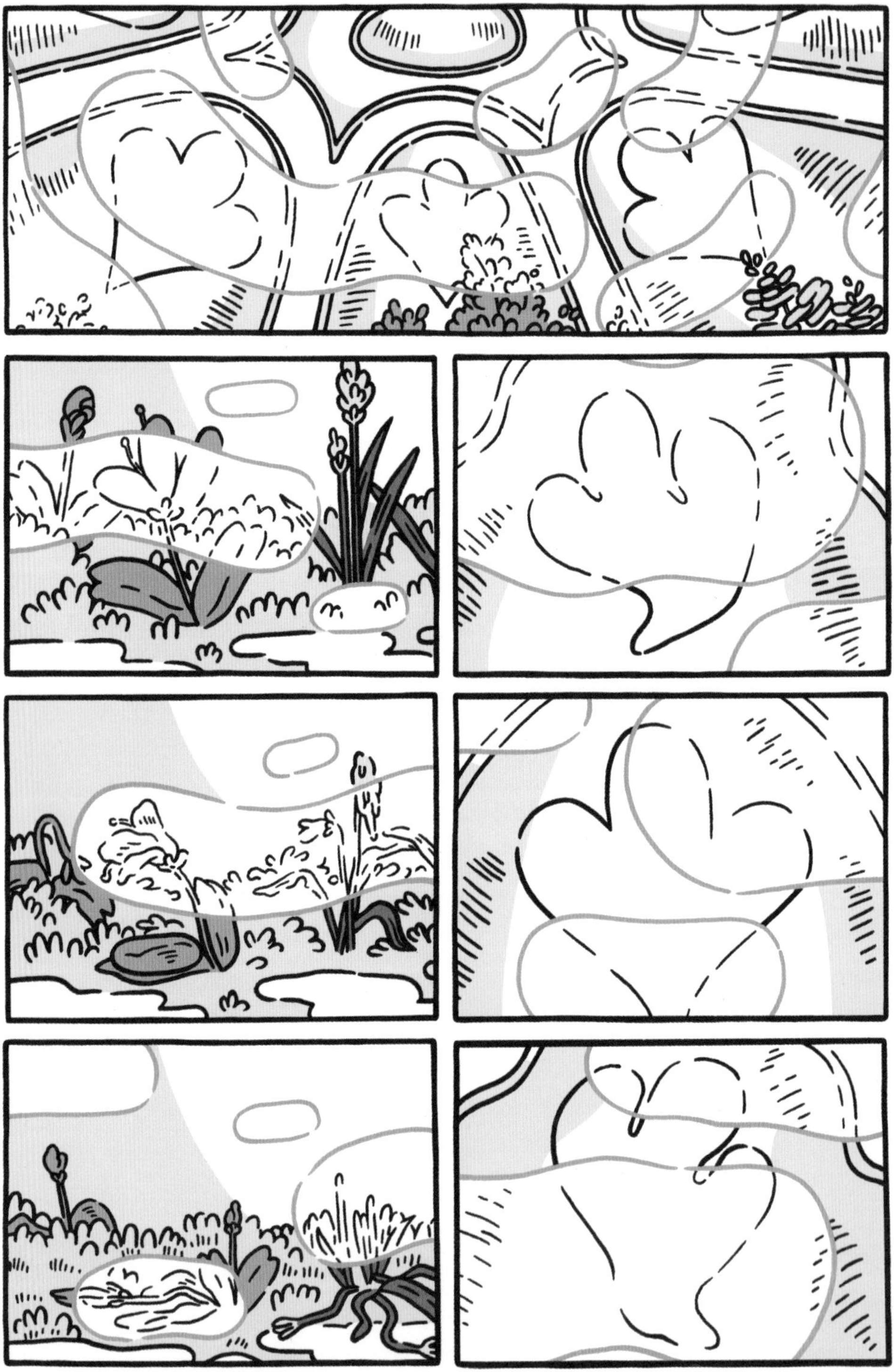

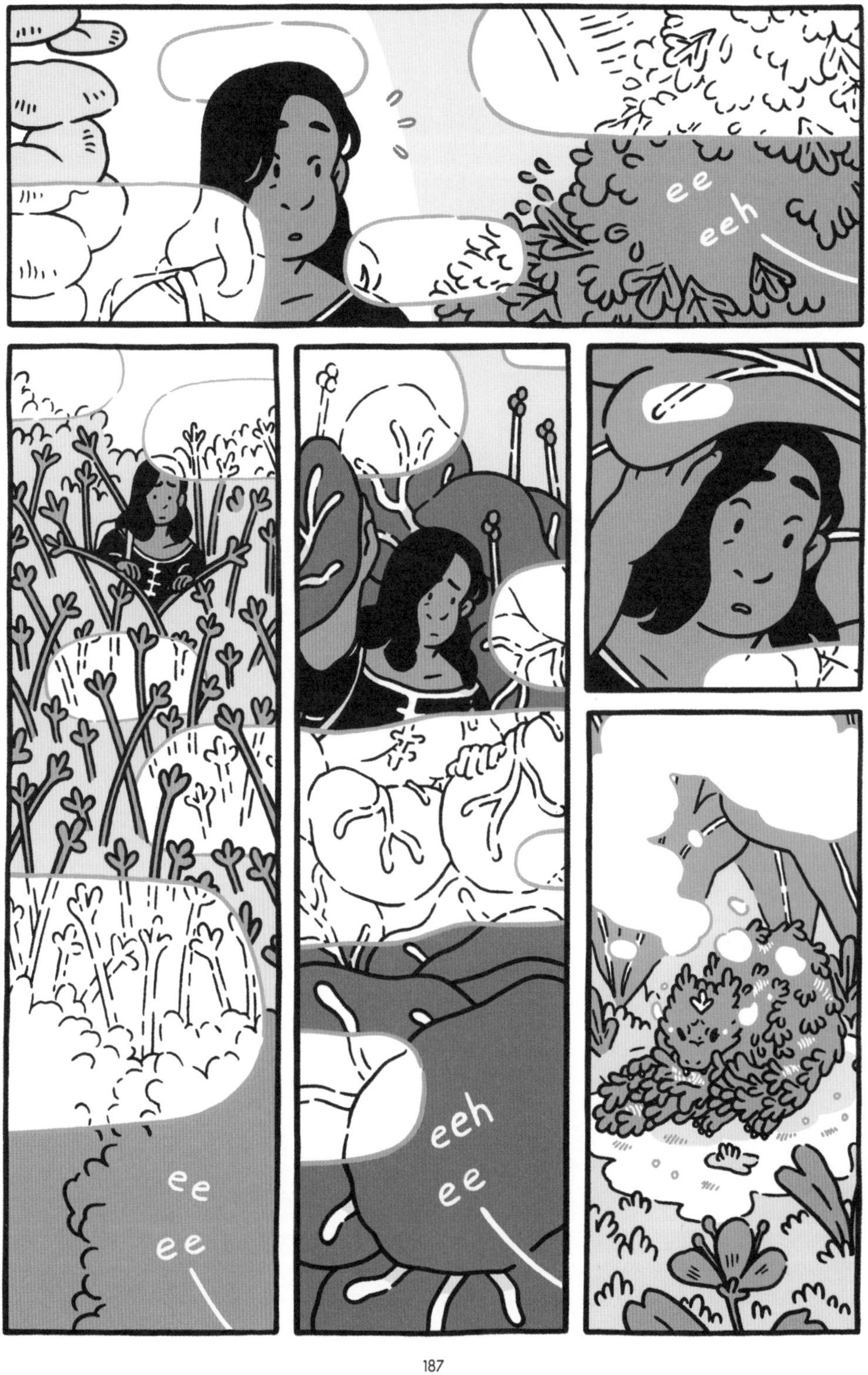
ee
eeh
ee
ee
eeh
ee

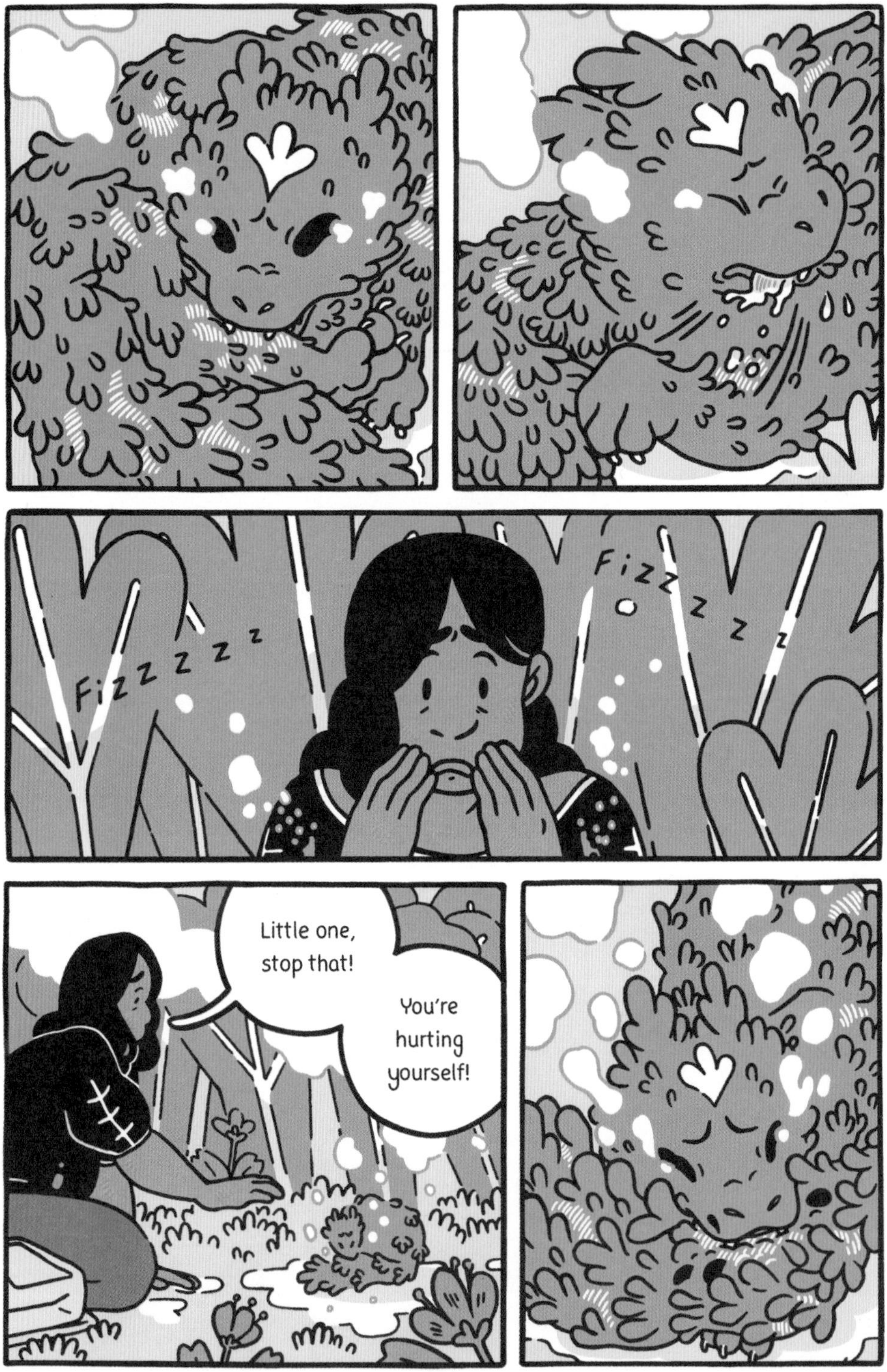
Fizzzzz
Fizzzzz
Little one, stop that!
You're hurting yourself!

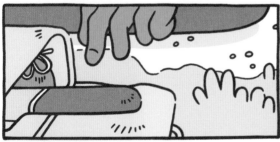

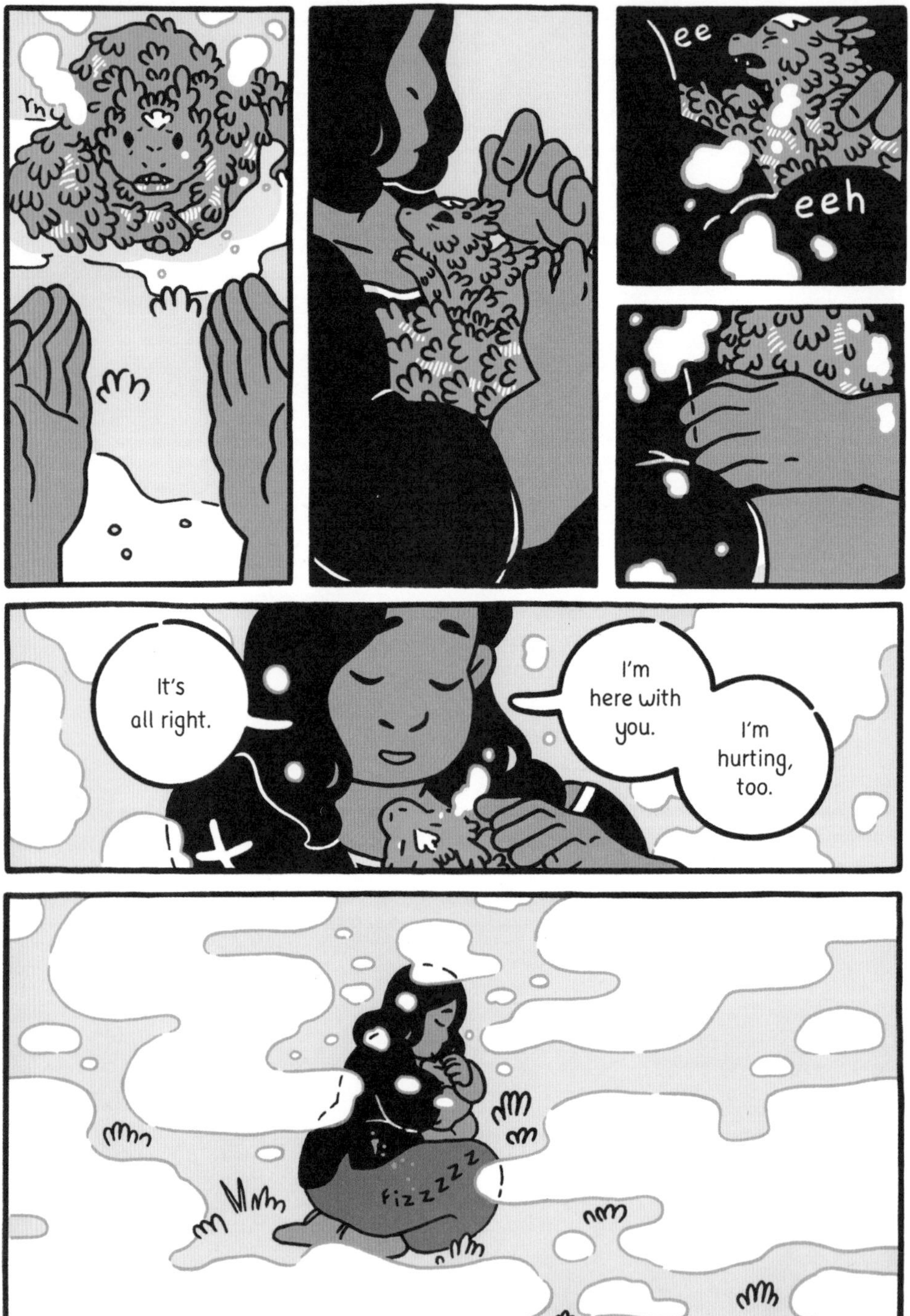
ee
eeh
It's all right.
I'm here with you.
I'm hurting, too.
Fizzzzz

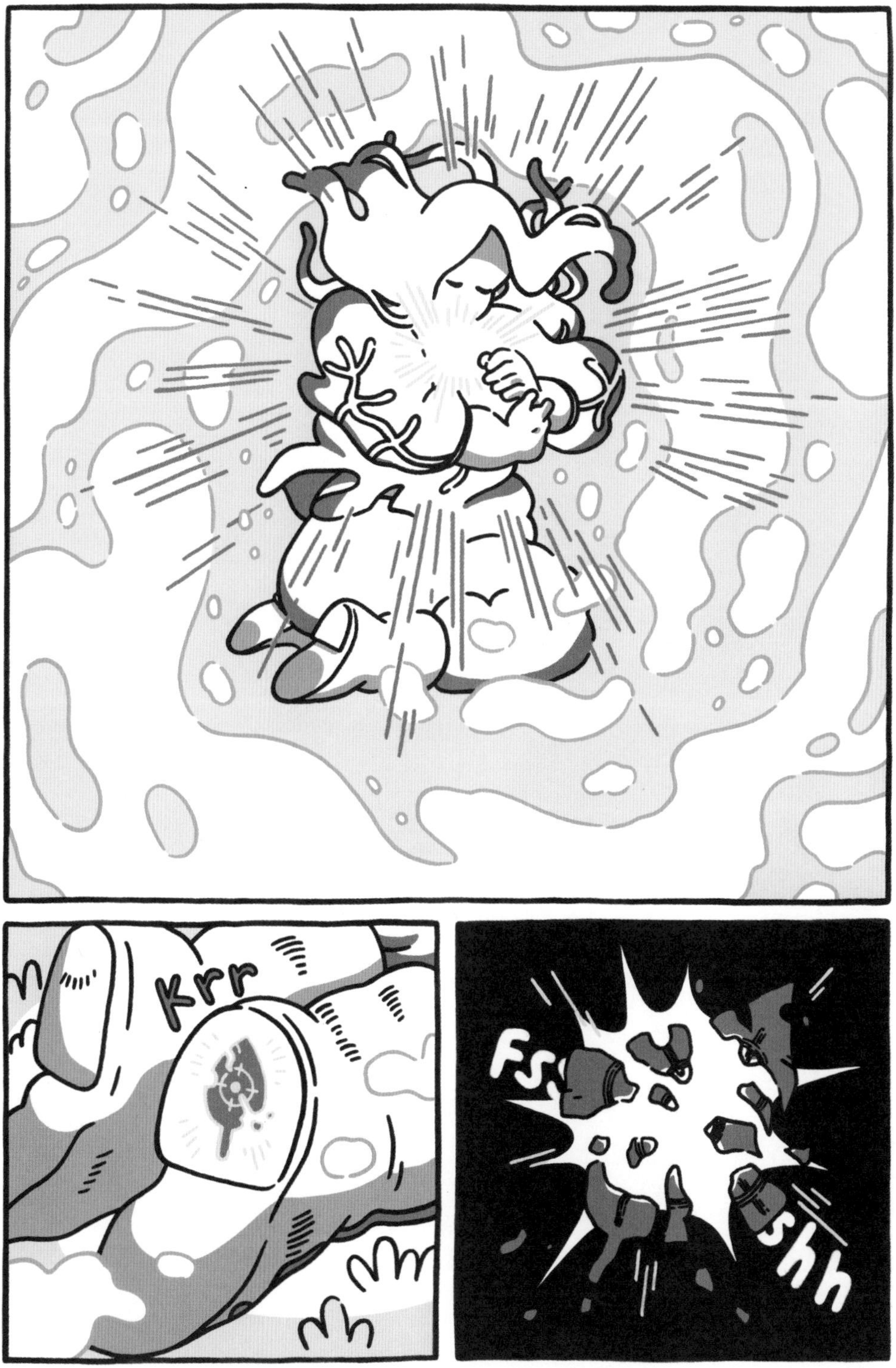
Krr
FS
shh

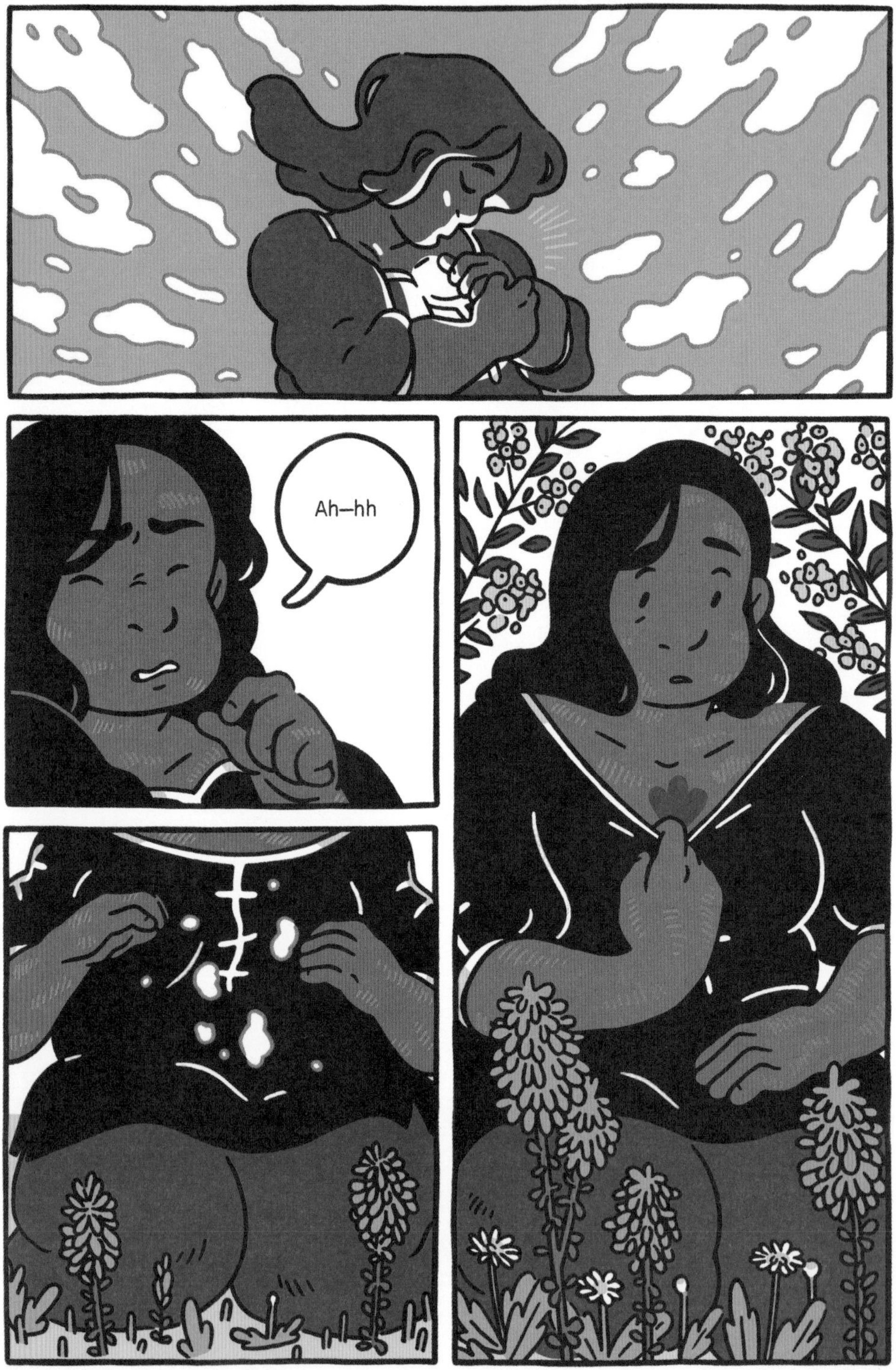
Ah—hh

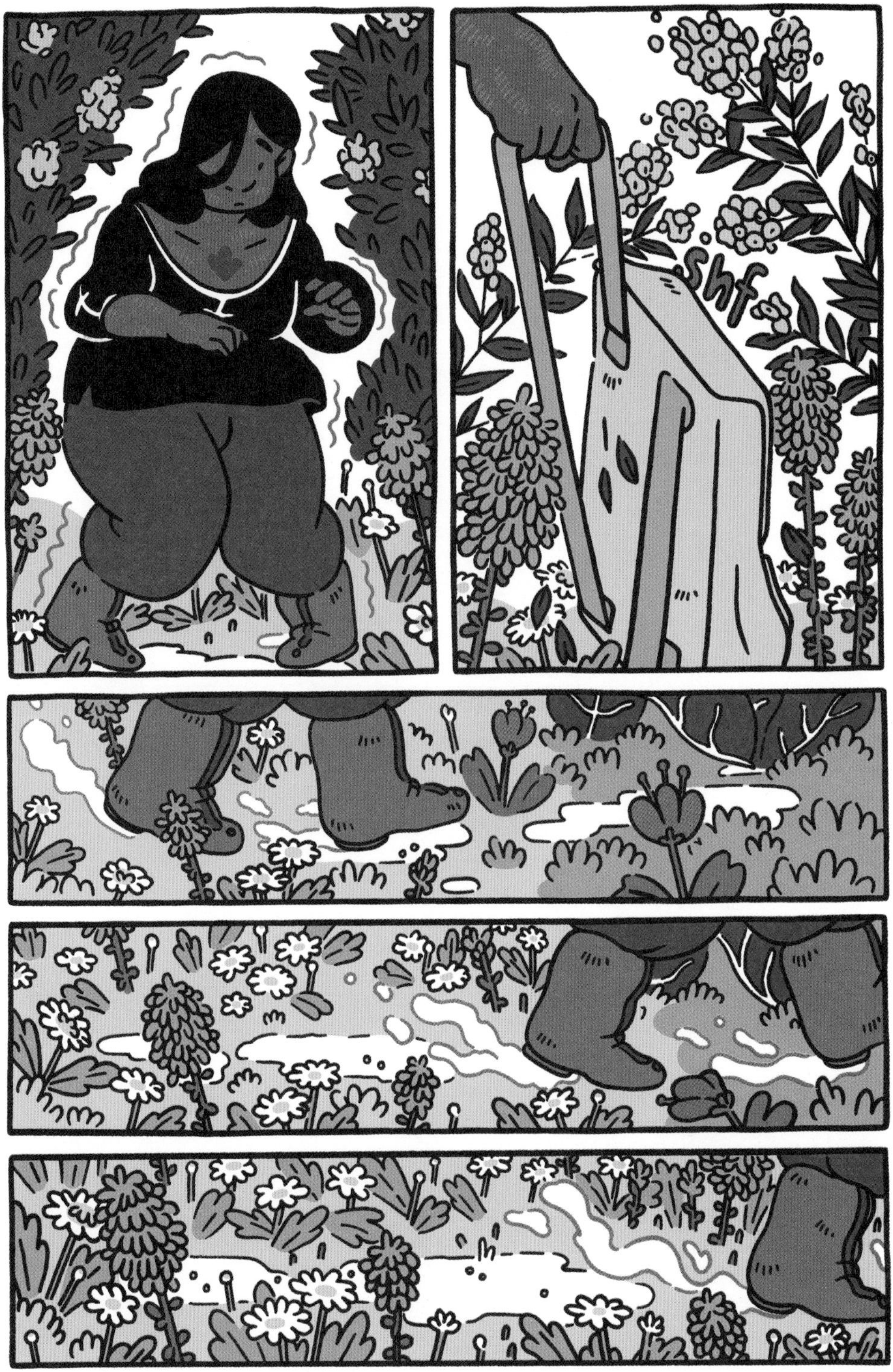
shf

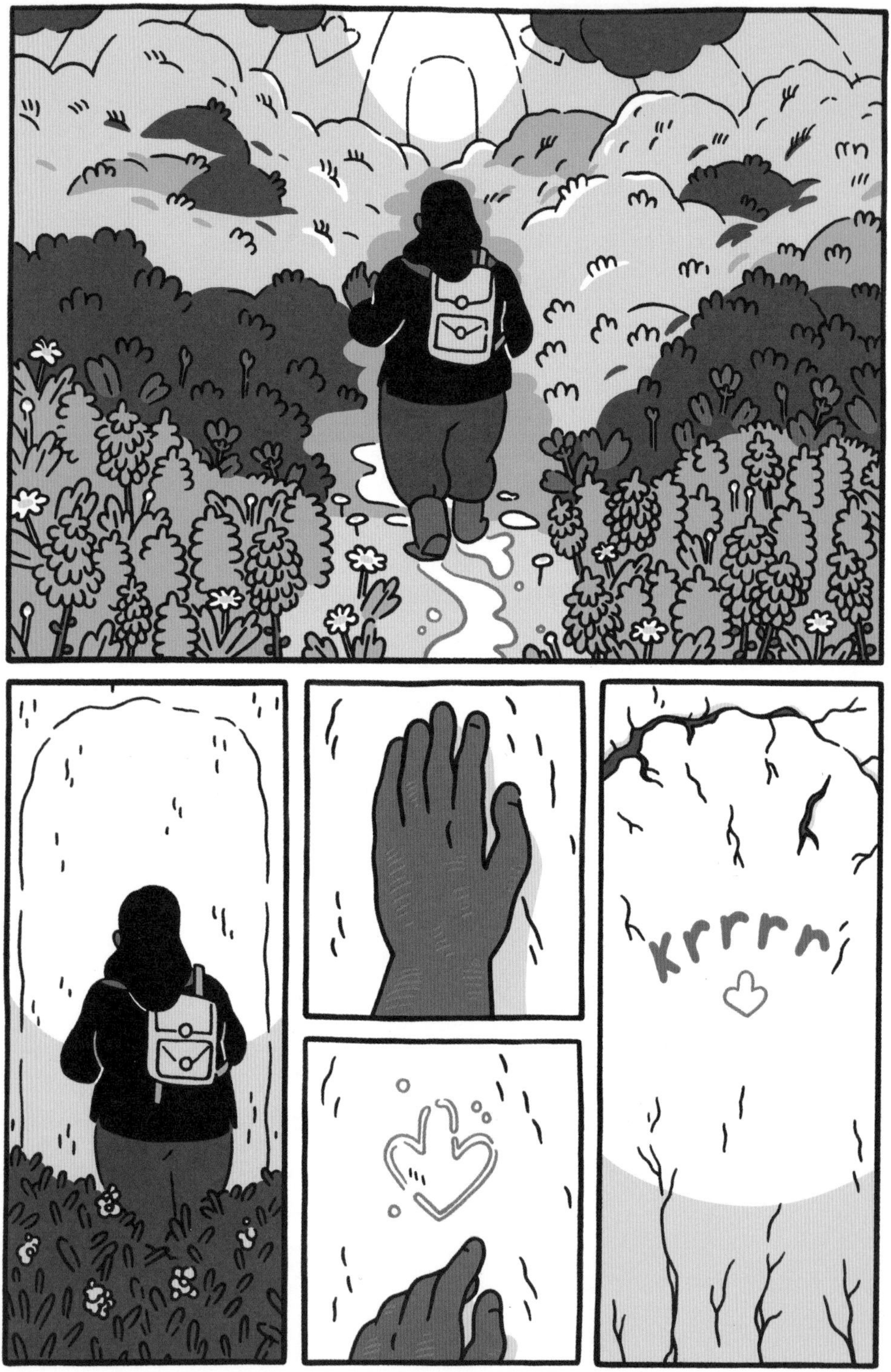
krrrn

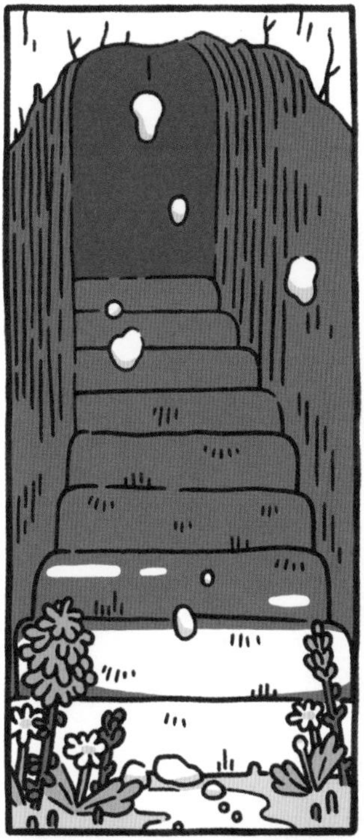
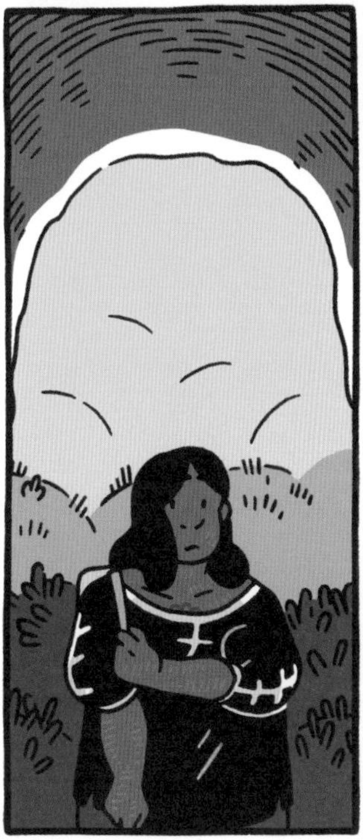
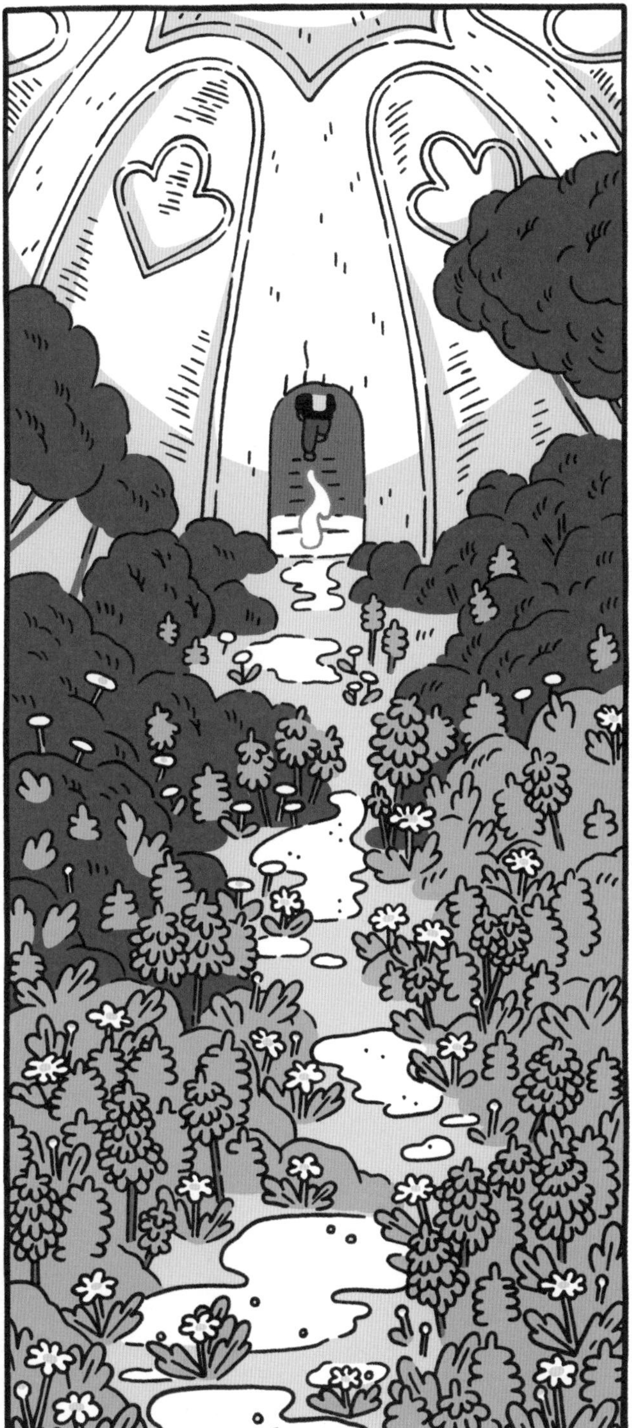

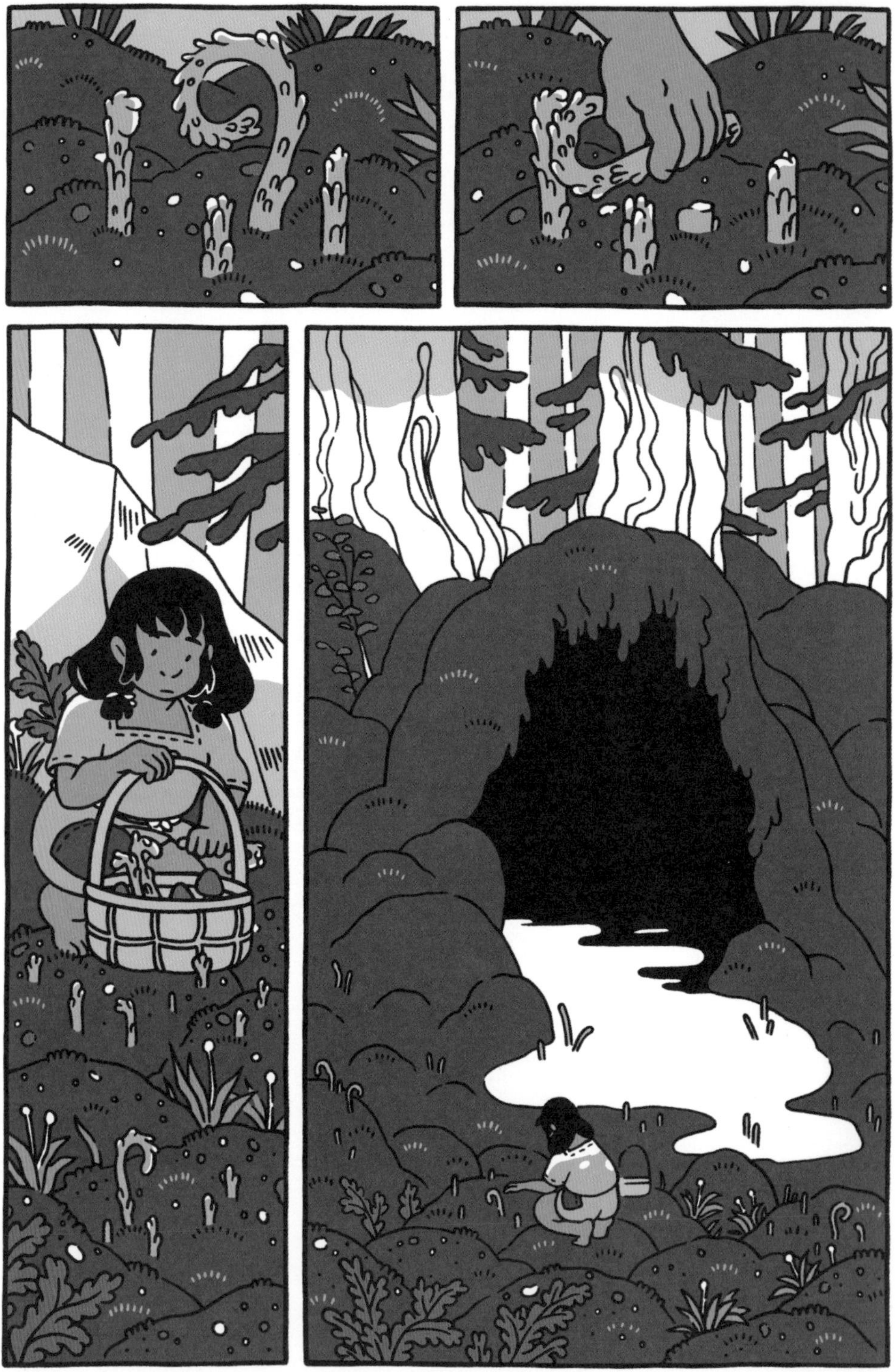

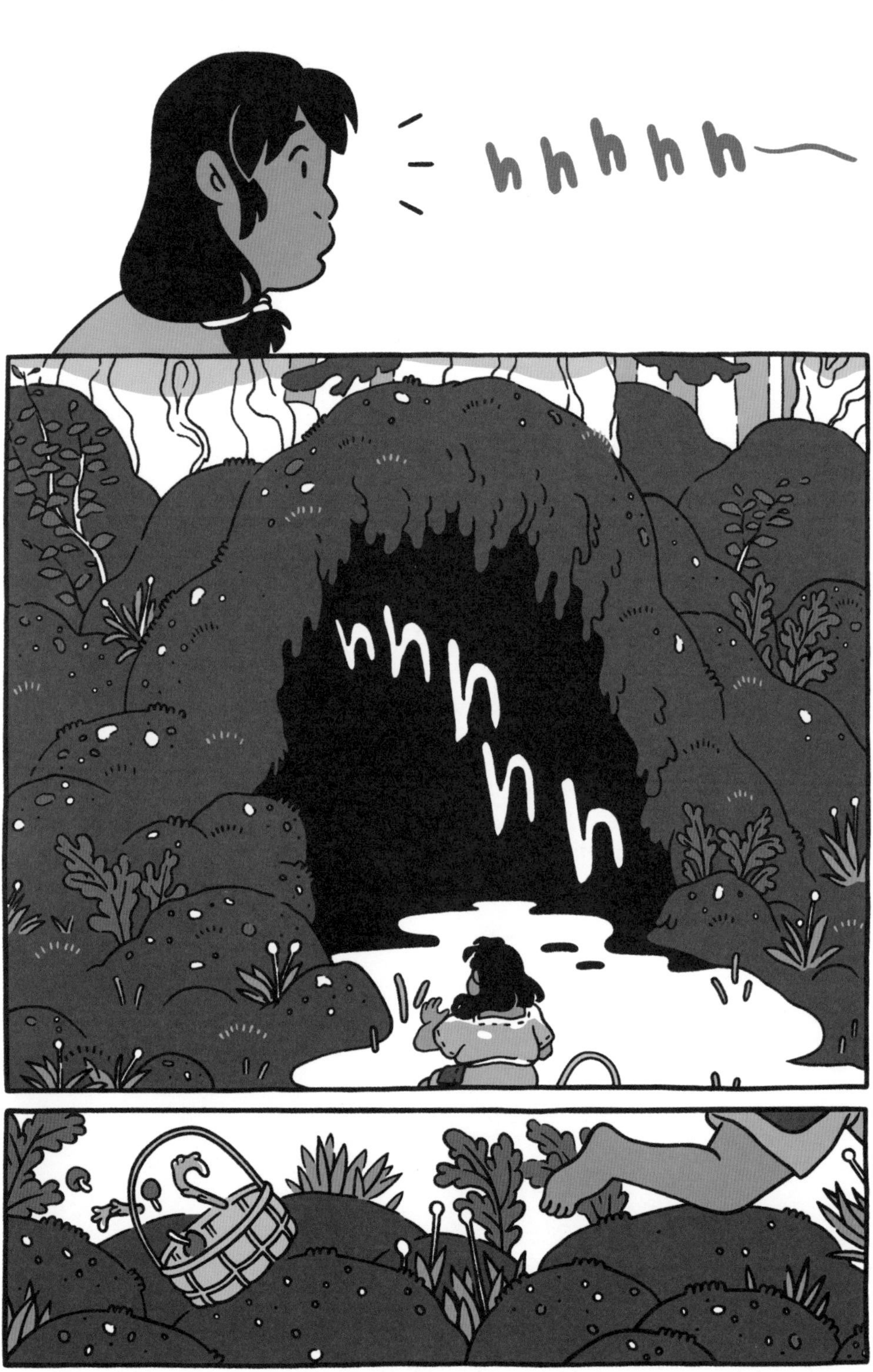
hhhhh—
hhhhhhh

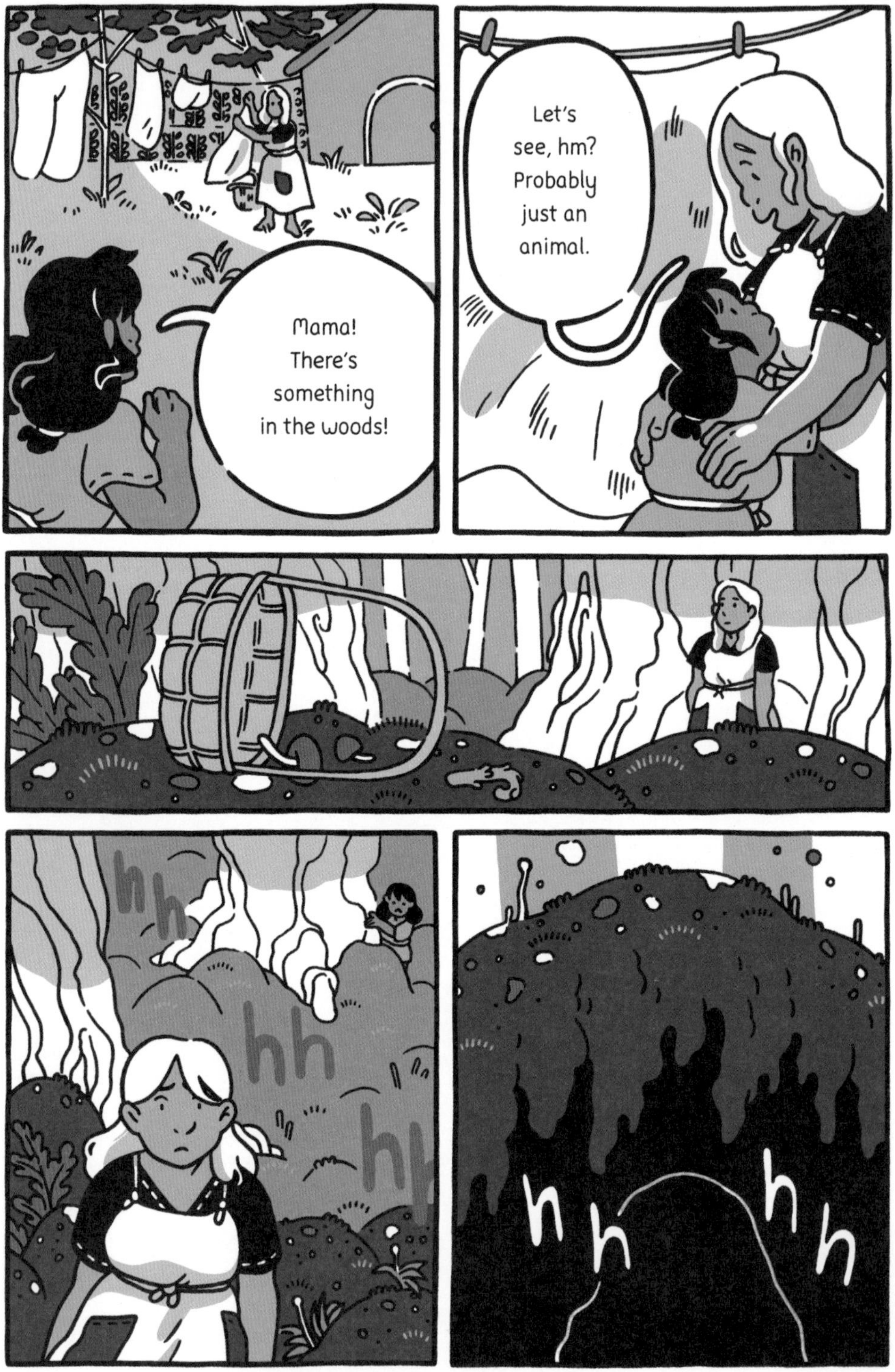
Mama! There's something in the woods!
Let's see, hm? Probably just an animal.
hh
hh
h
hh
hh

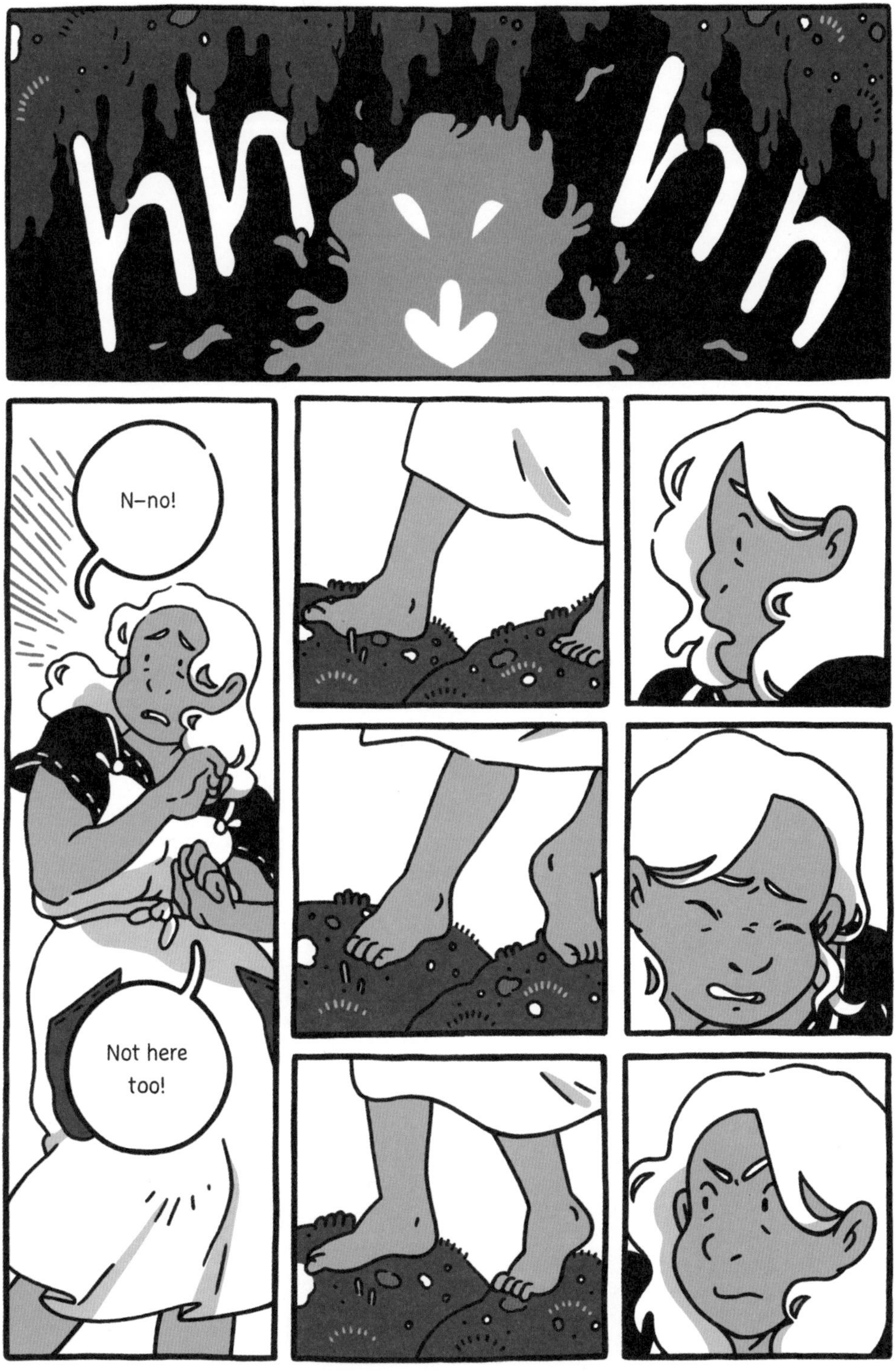
hhhhh
N–no!
Not here too!

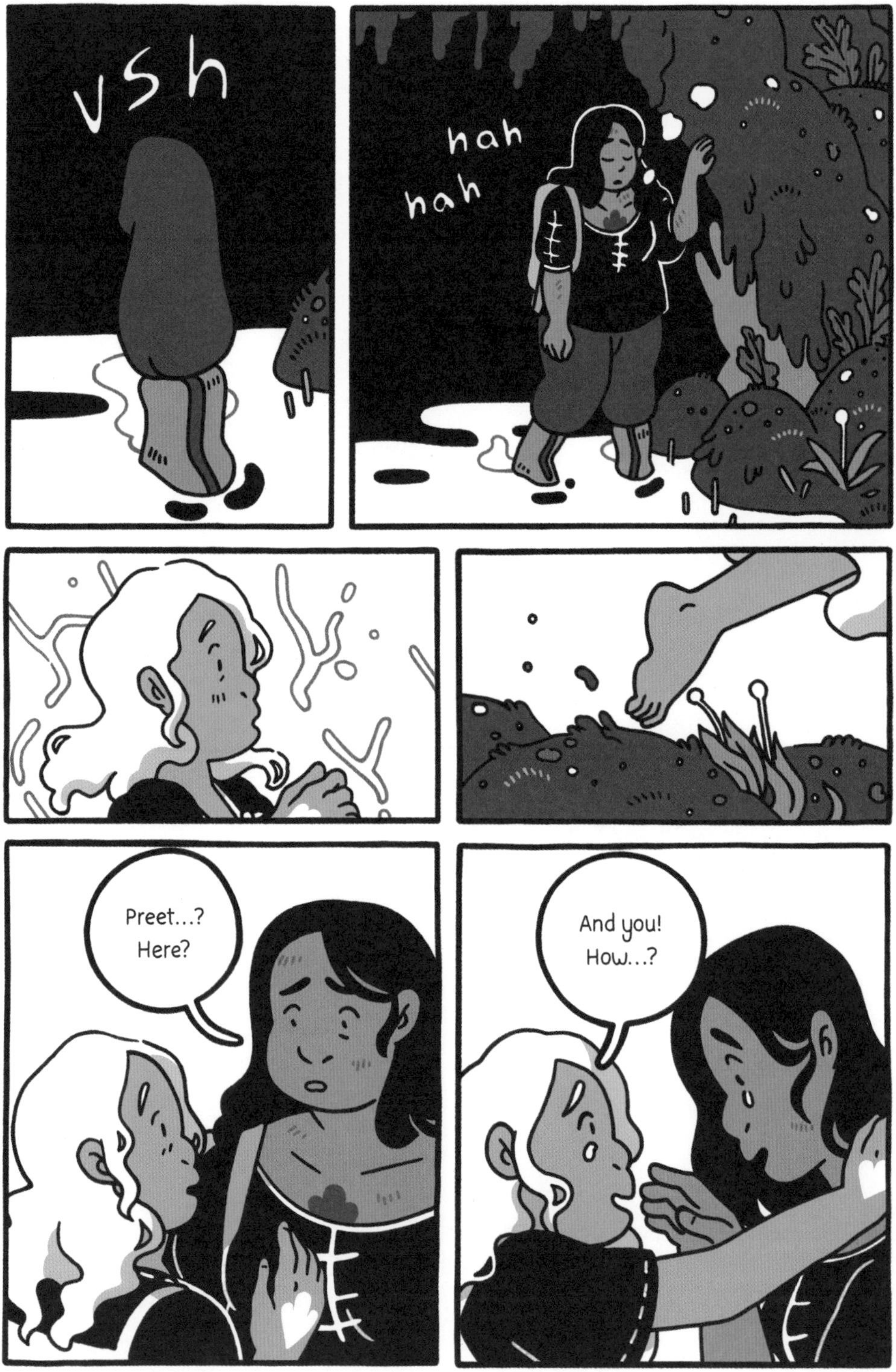
vsh
hah
hah
Preet...? Here?
And you! How...?

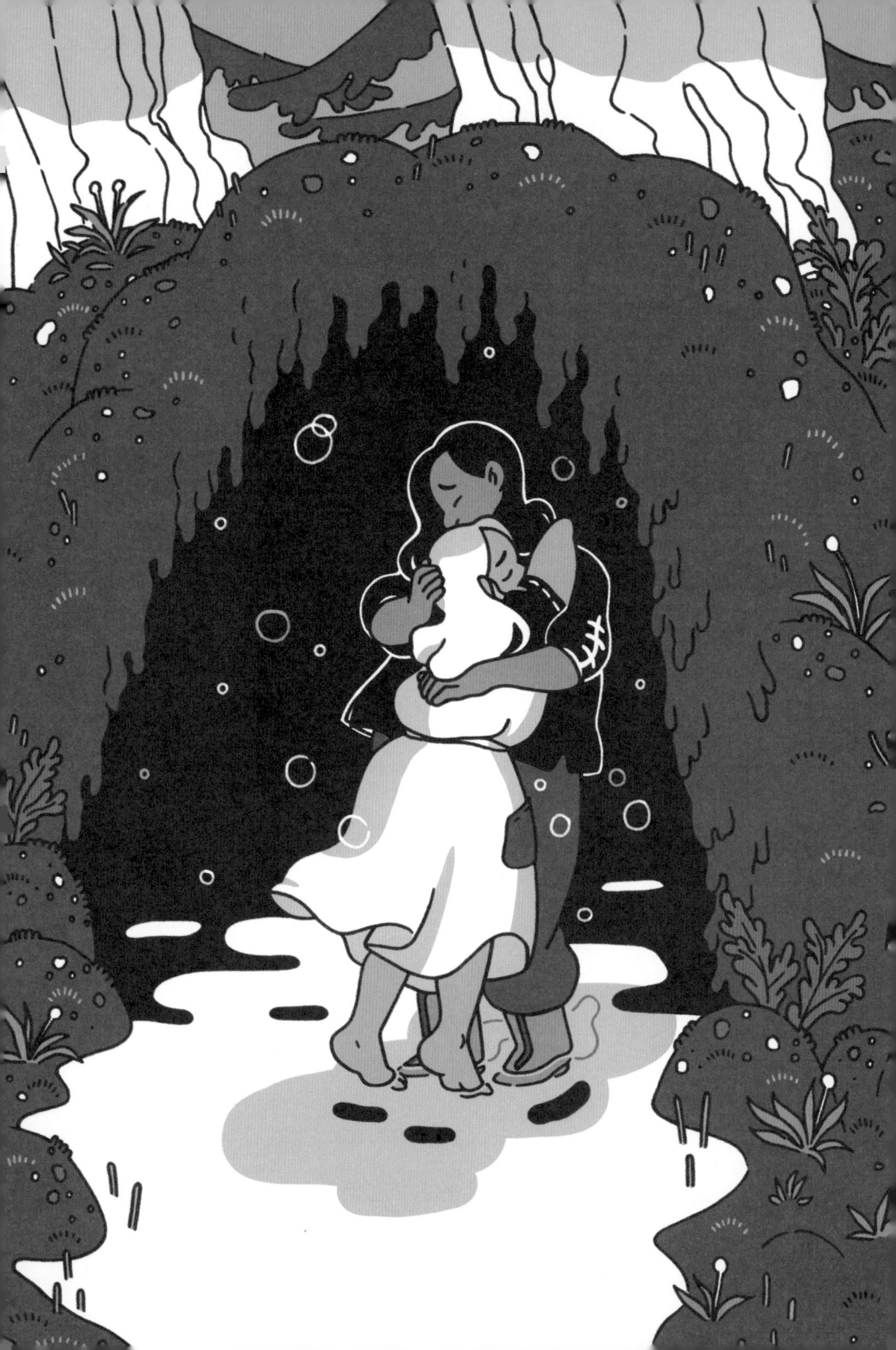

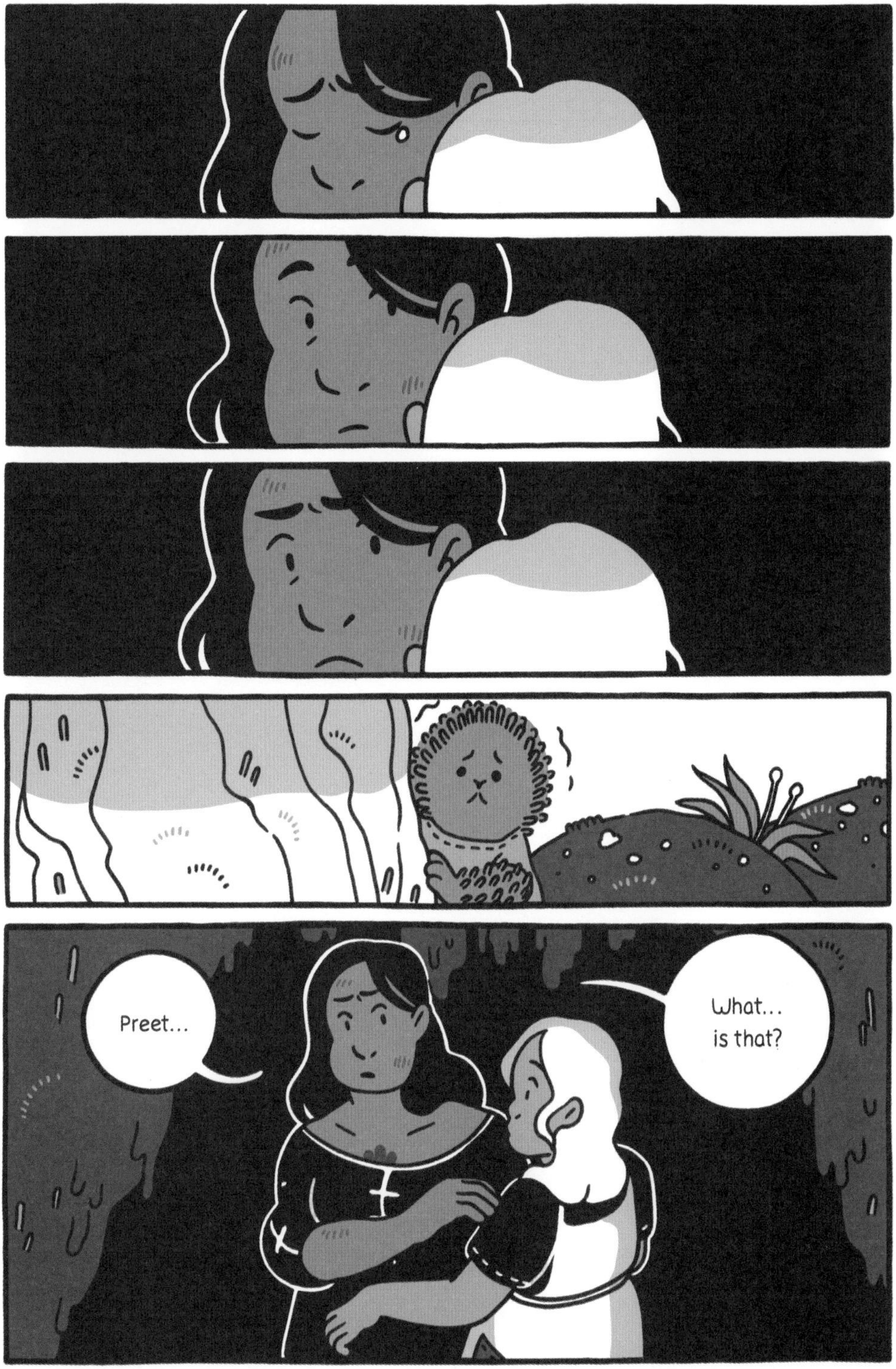
Preet...
What... is that?

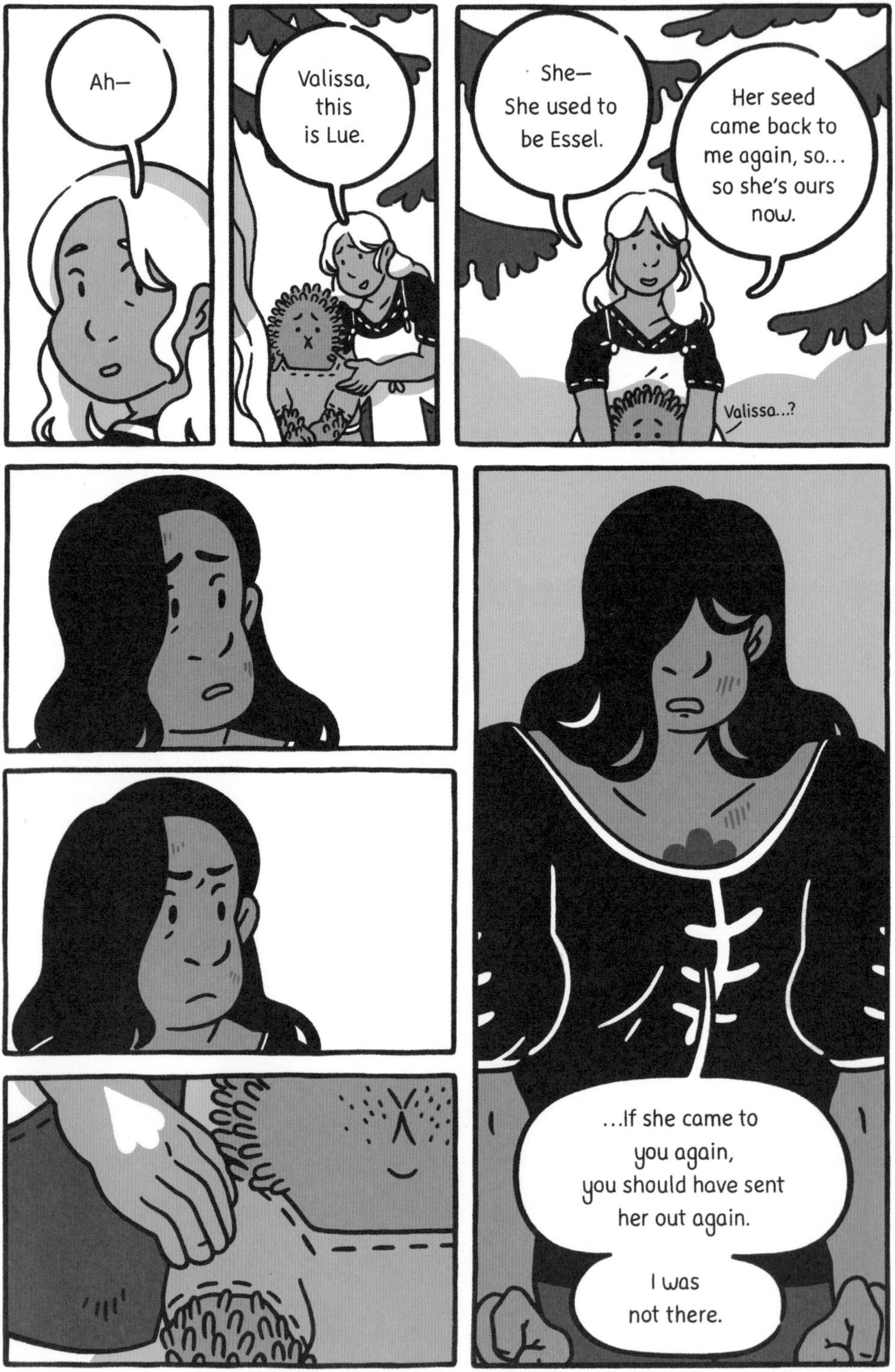
Ah—
Valissa, this is Lue.
She— She used to be Essel.
Her seed came back to me again, so... so she's ours now.
Valissa...?
...If she came to you again, you should have sent her out again.
I was not there.

But—

It's our way, Preet!

I can guess now why you're here, so far from home!

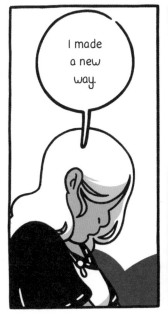

I made a new way.

I feel guilty and ashamed, and I have suffered for it, but I don't regret what I chose to do.

I will never regret Lue.

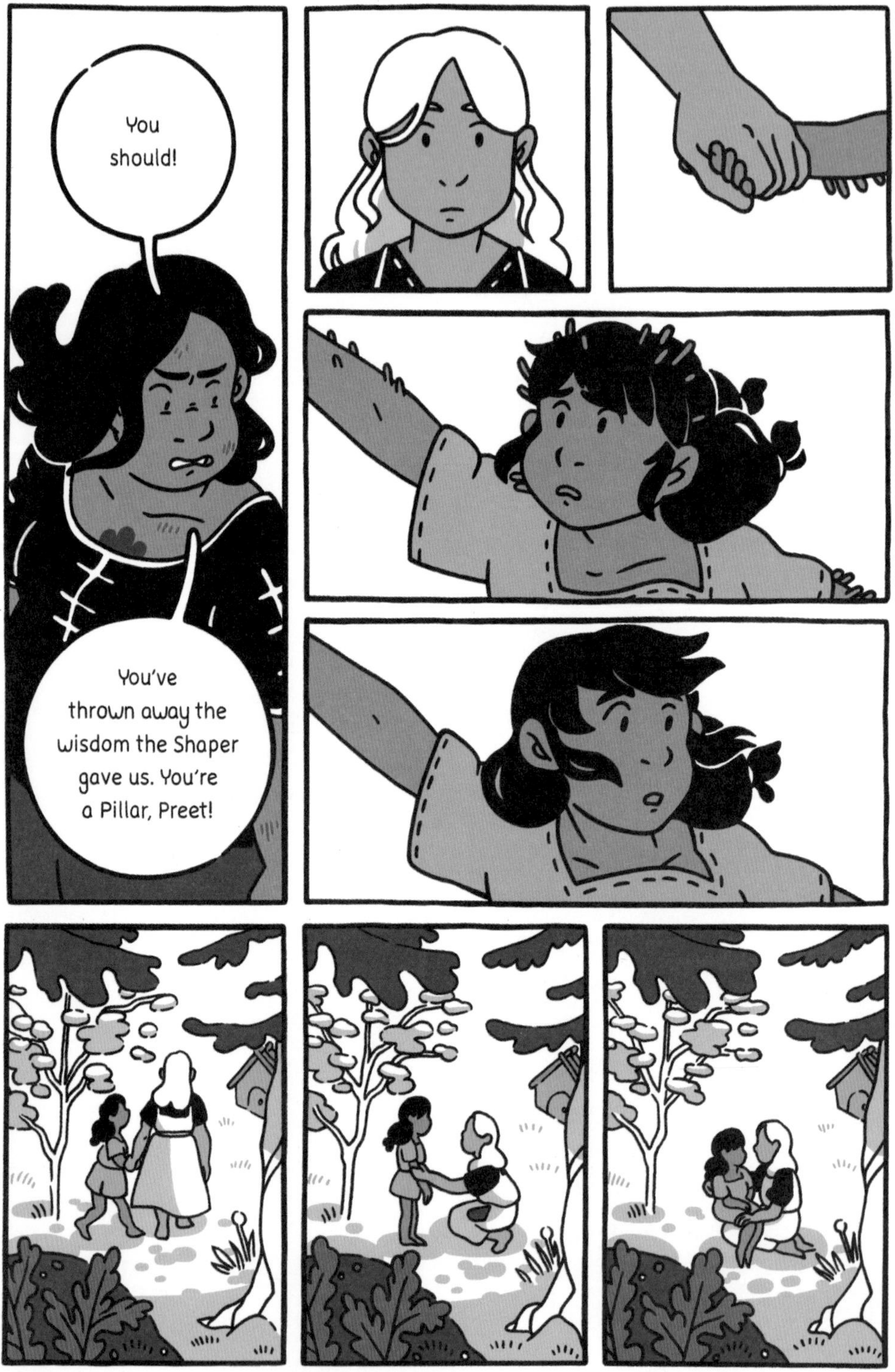
You should!
You've thrown away the wisdom the Shaper gave us. You're a Pillar, Preet!

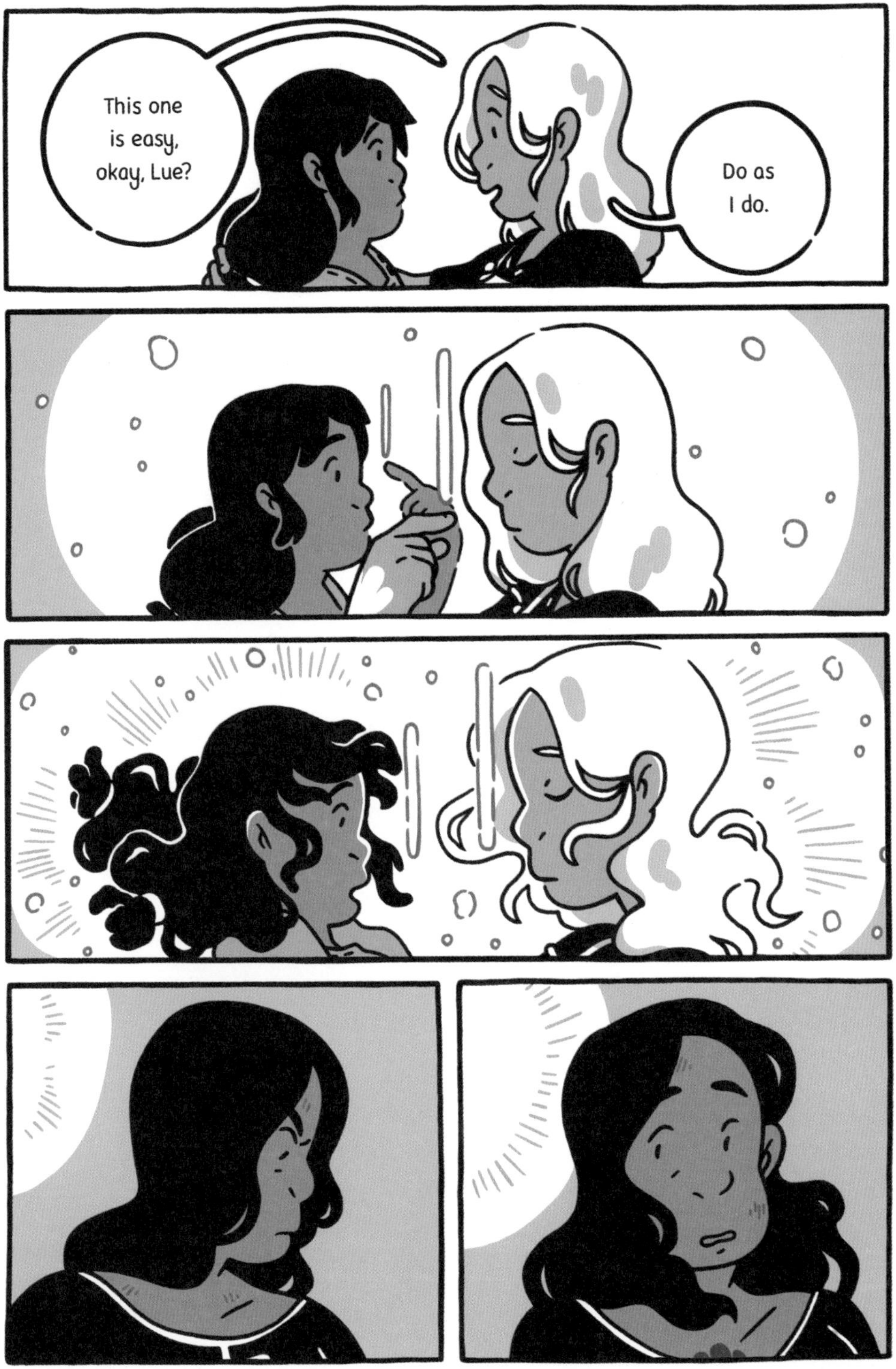
This one is easy, okay, Lue?
Do as I do.

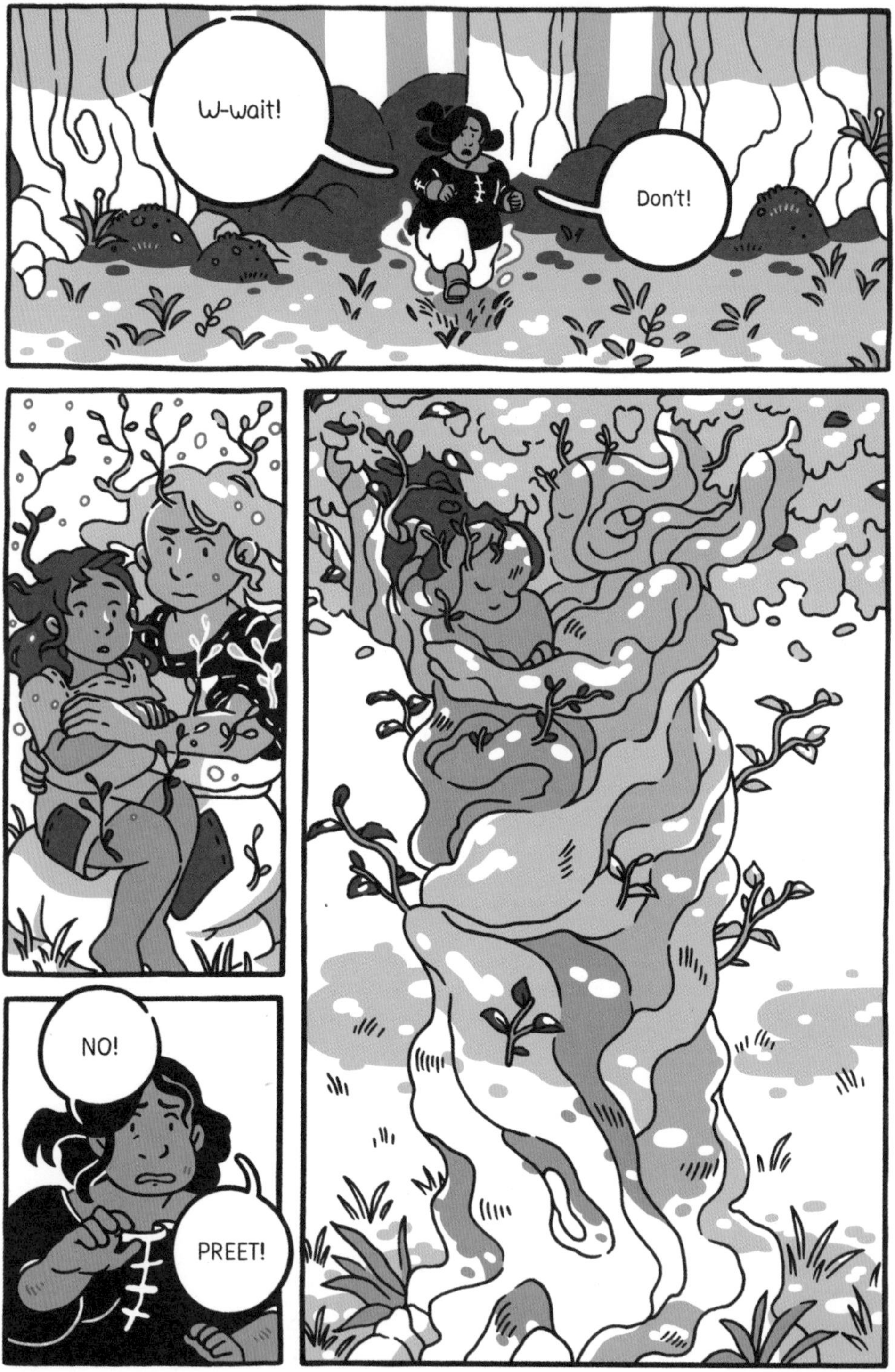
W-wait!
Don't!
NO!
PREET!

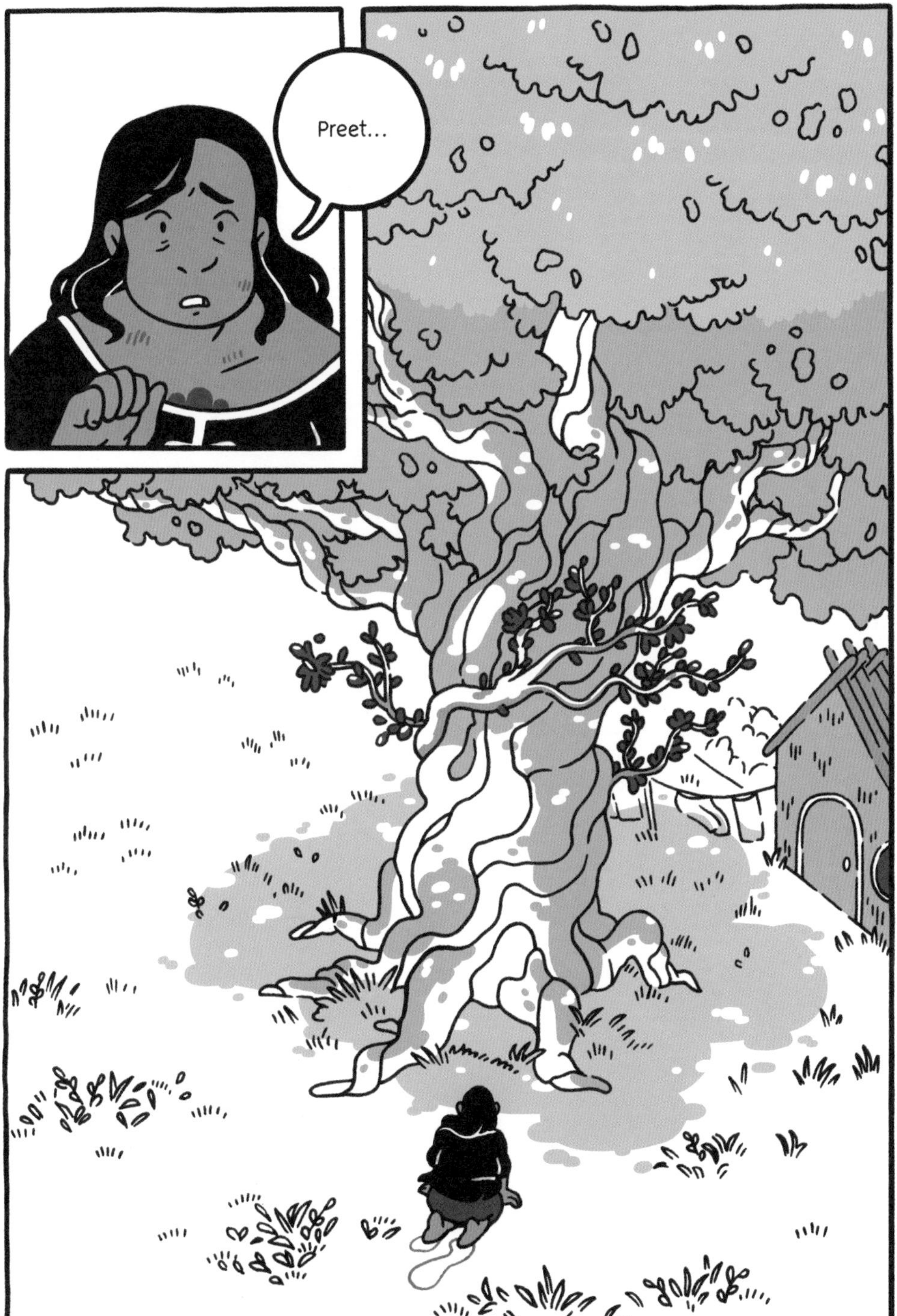
Preet...

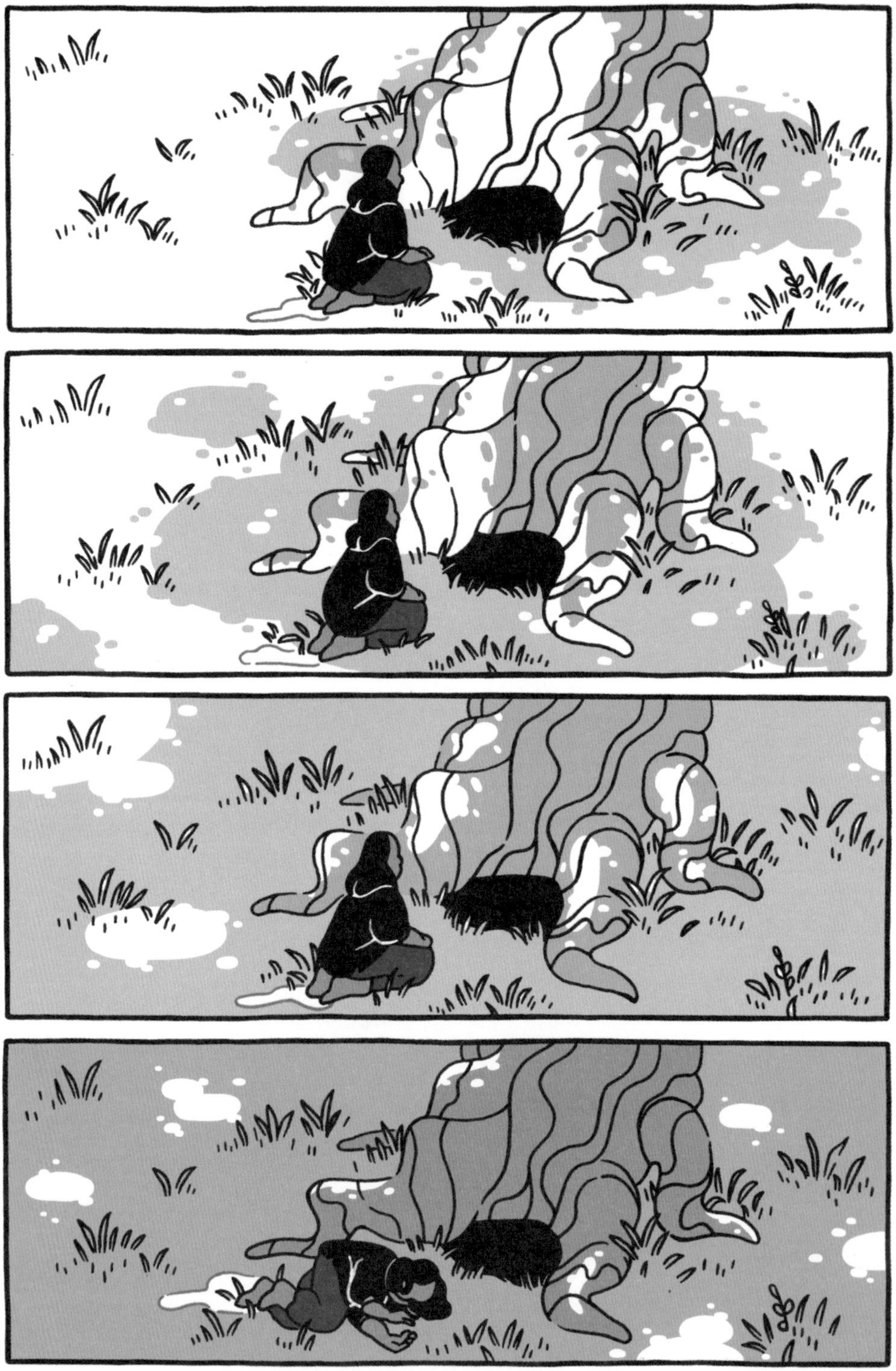

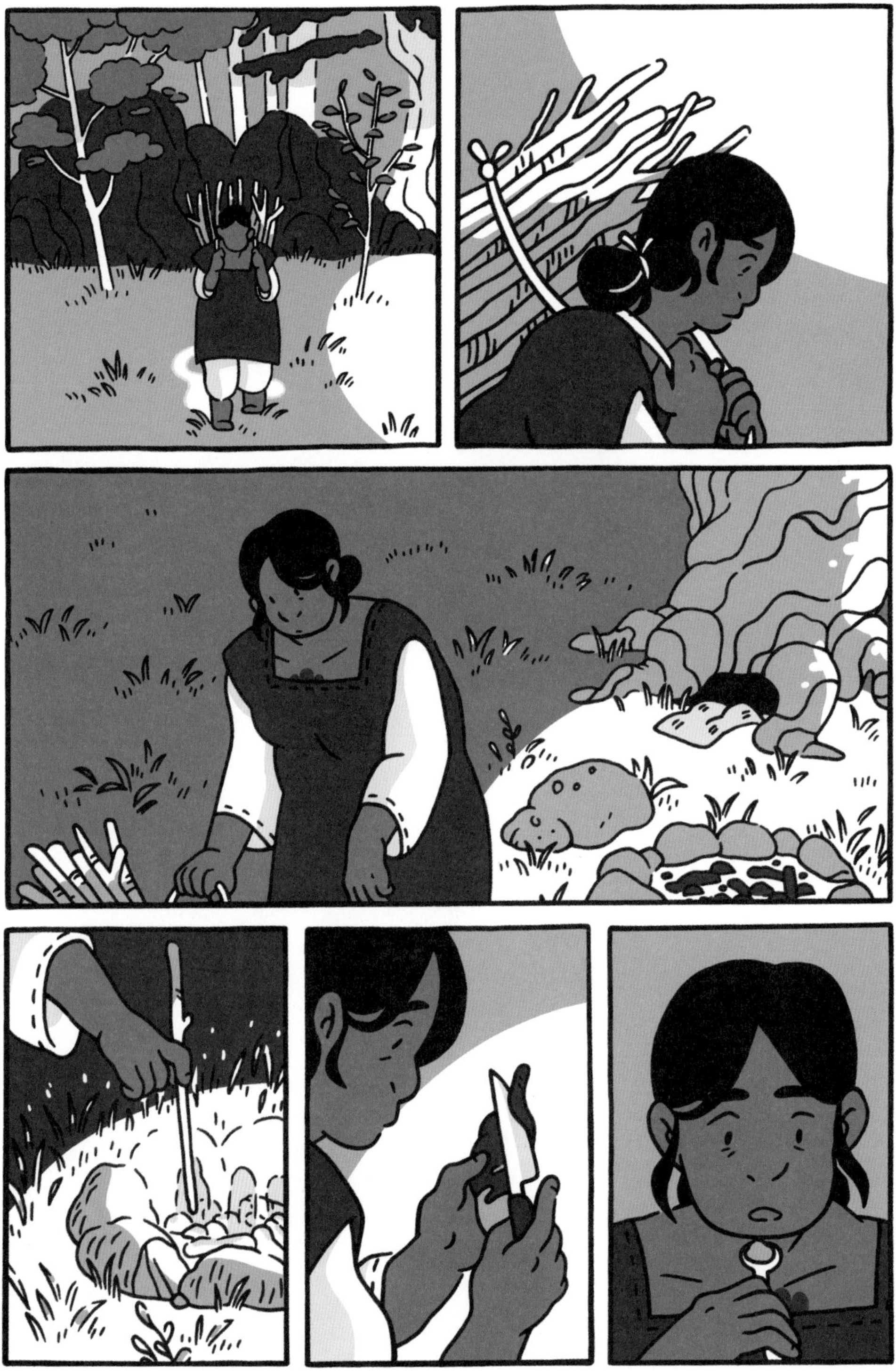

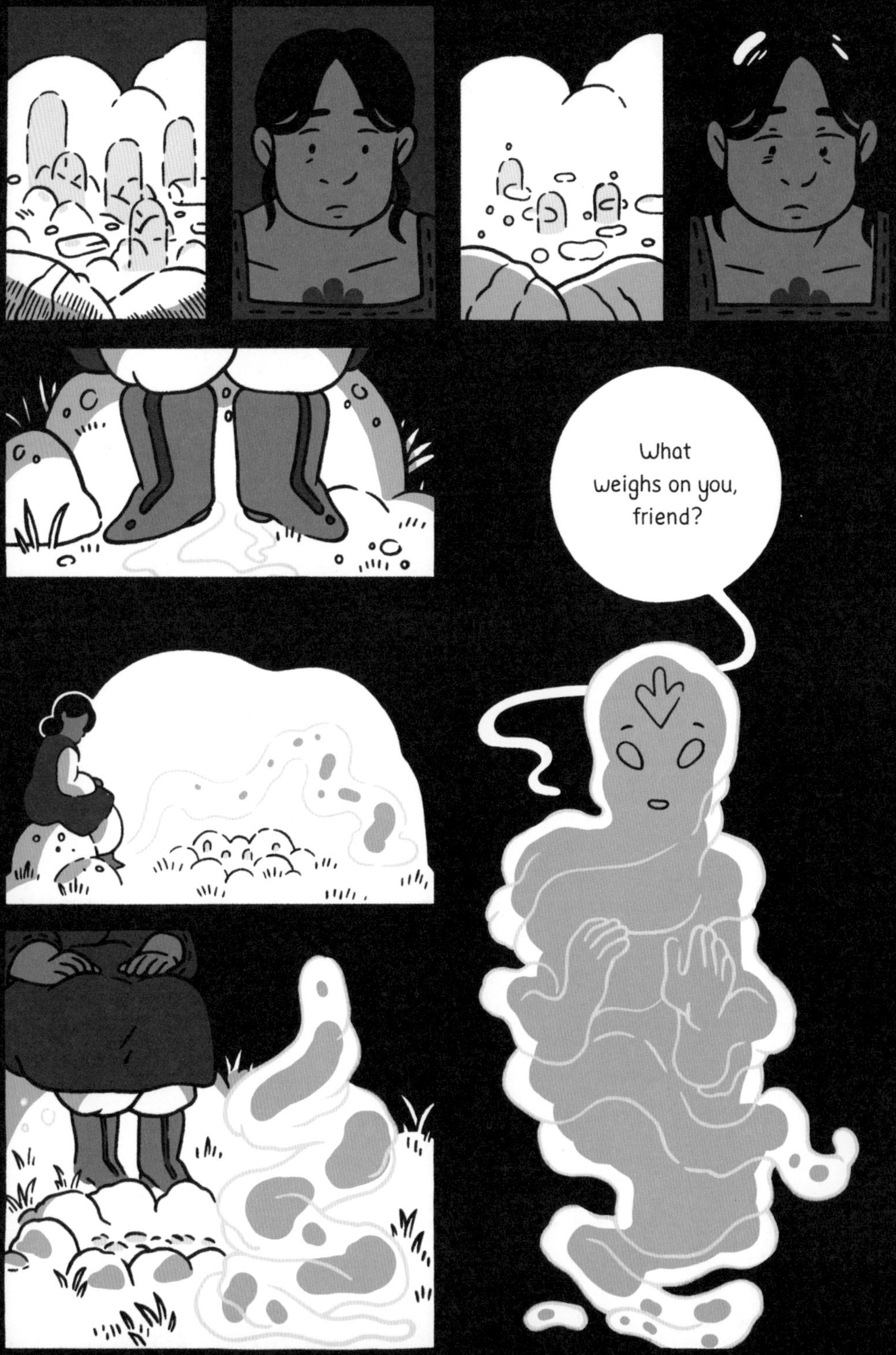
What weighs on you, friend?

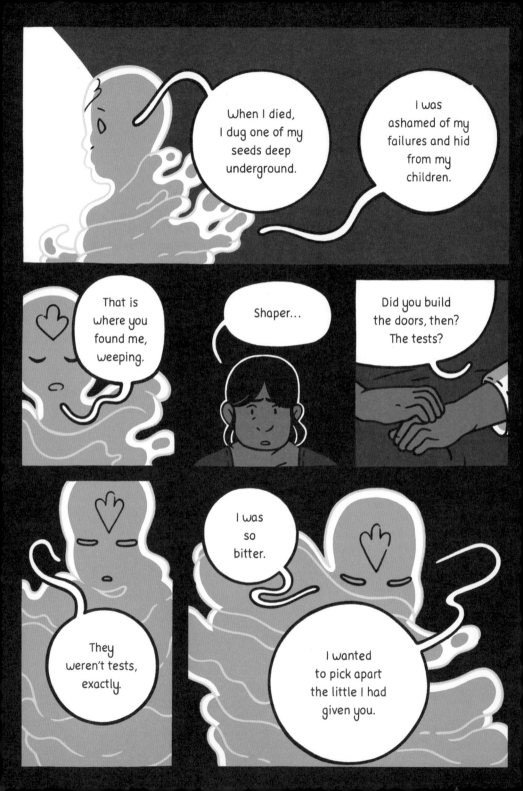

Ya

own

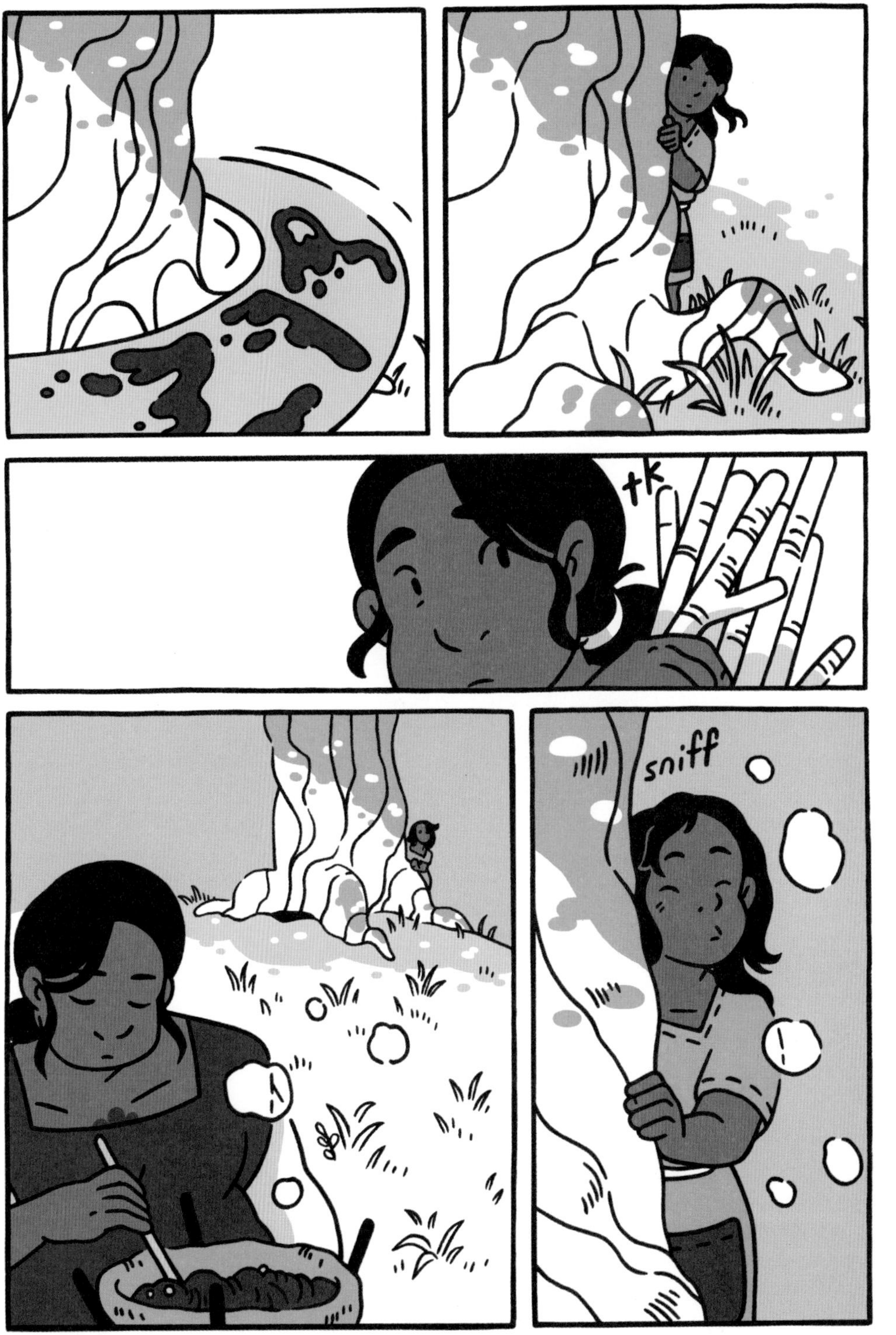
tk
sniff

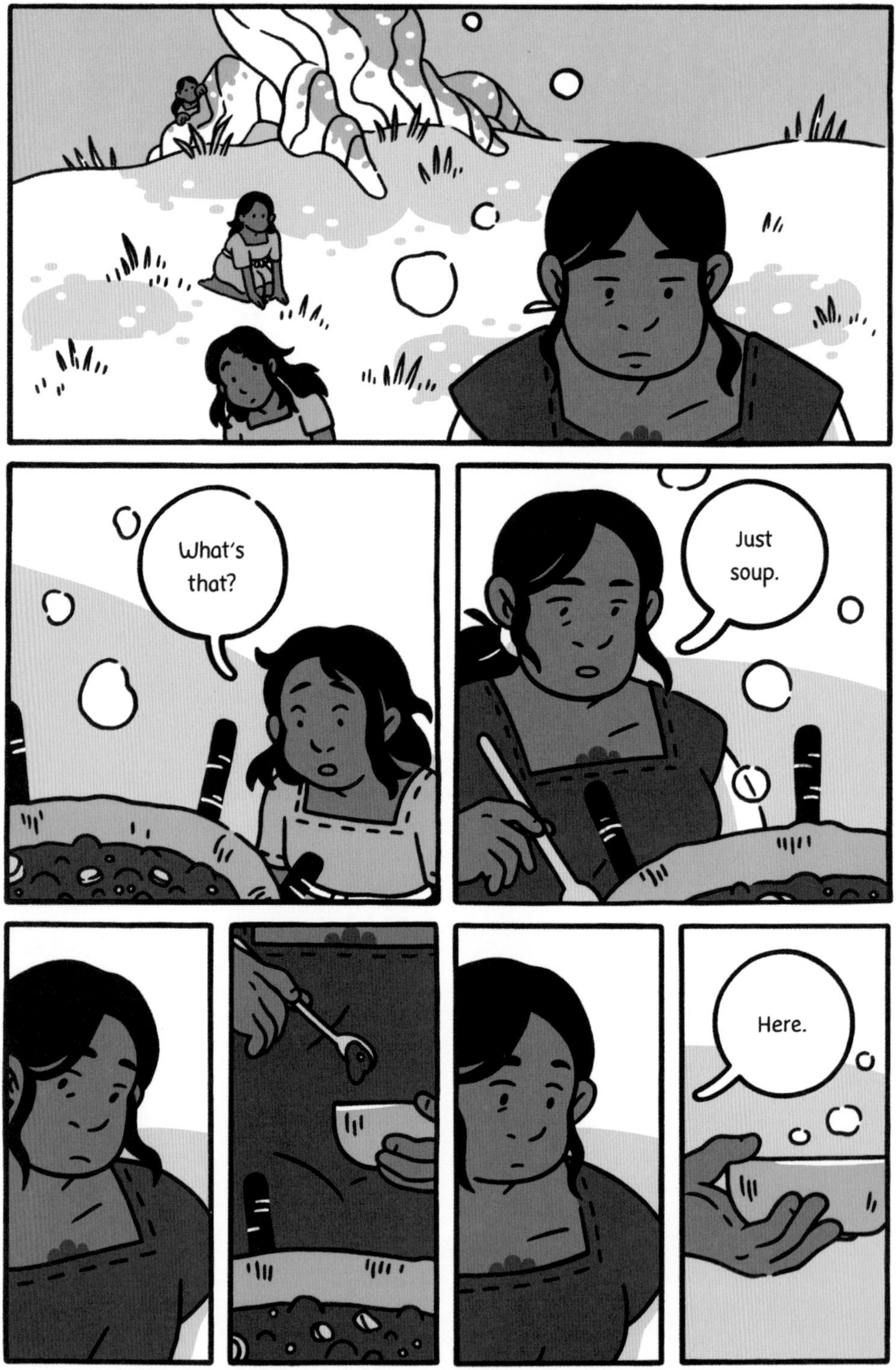
What's that?
Just soup.
Here.

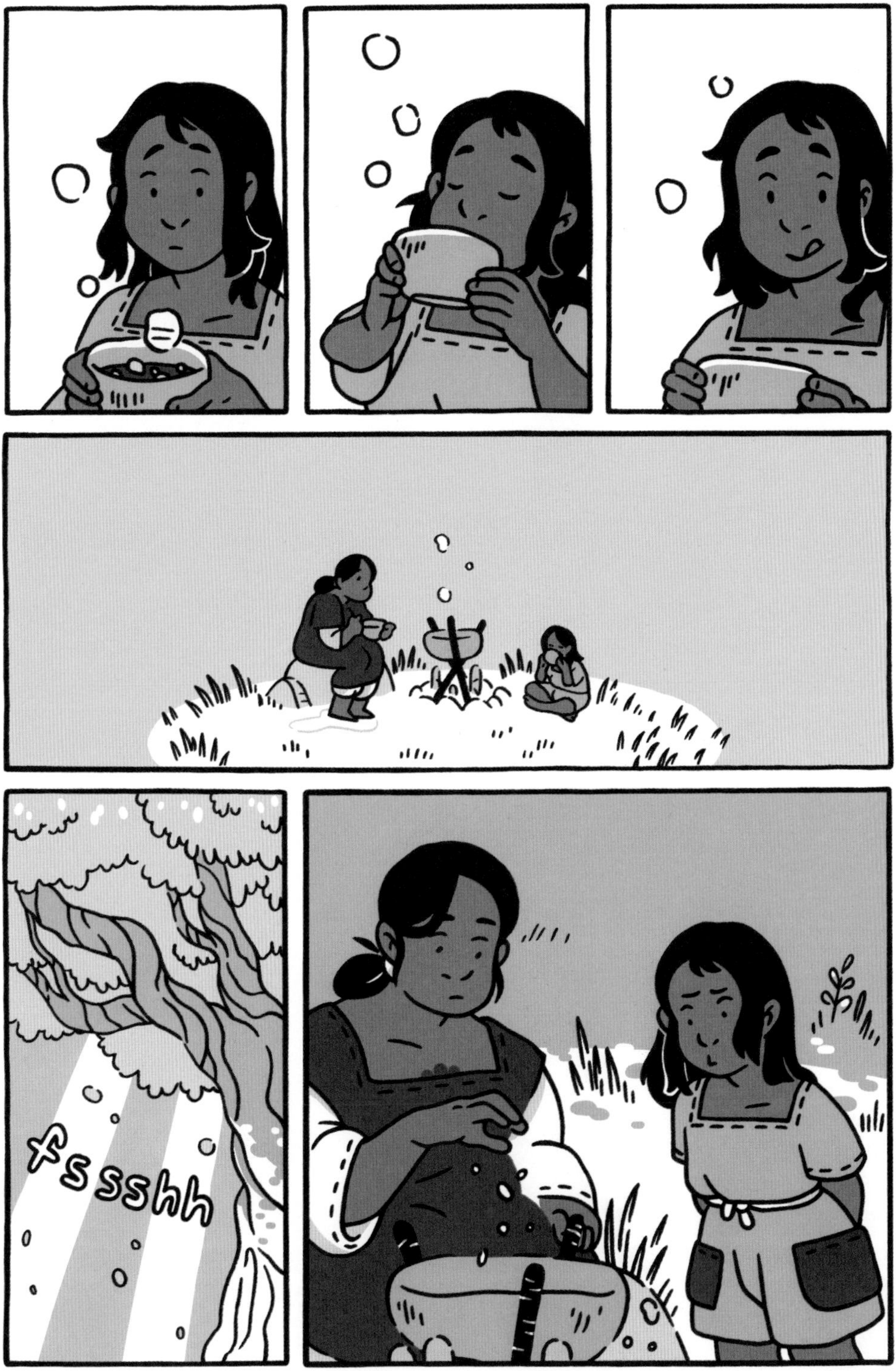
fssshh

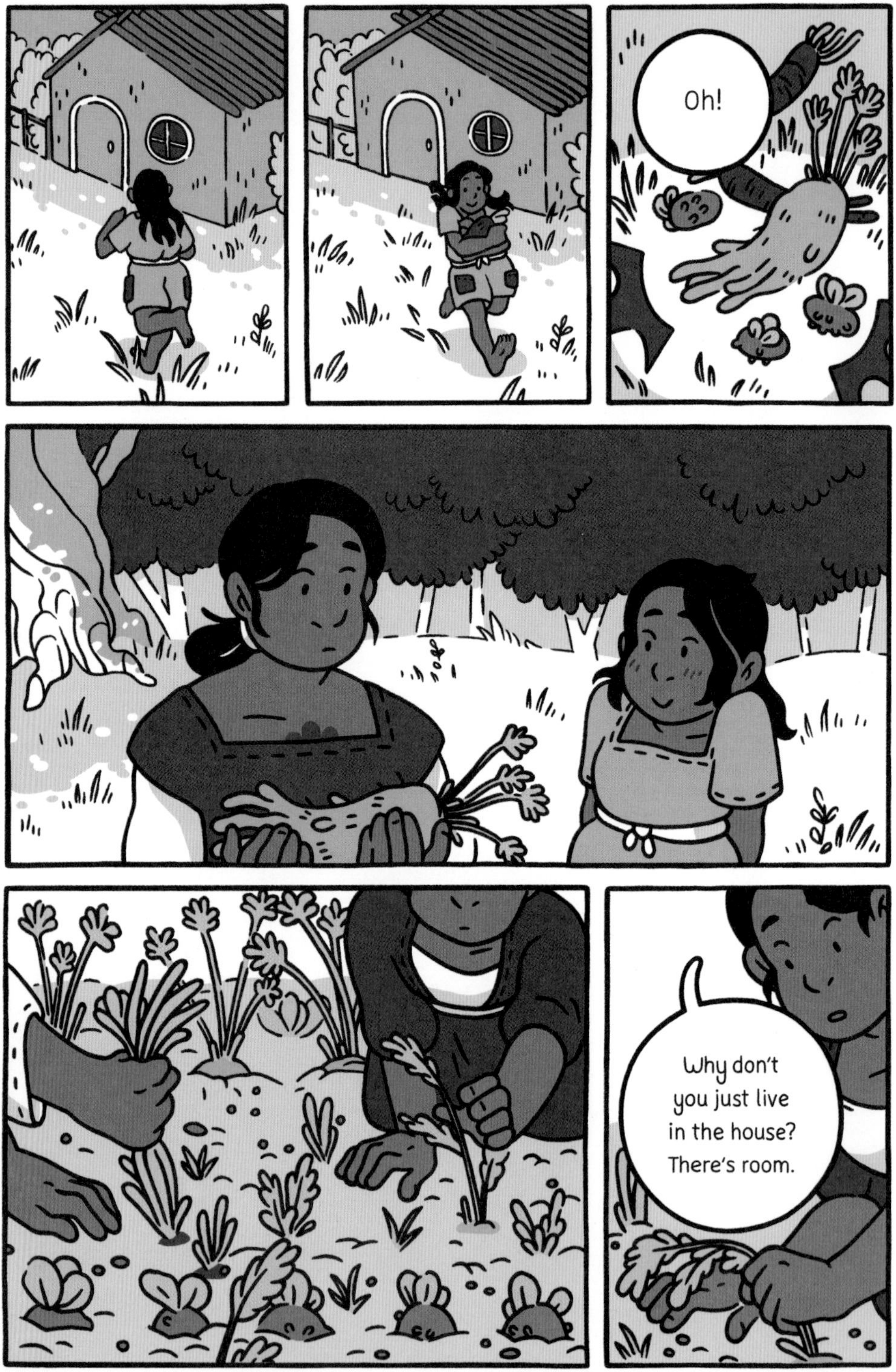
Oh!
Why don't you just live in the house? There's room.

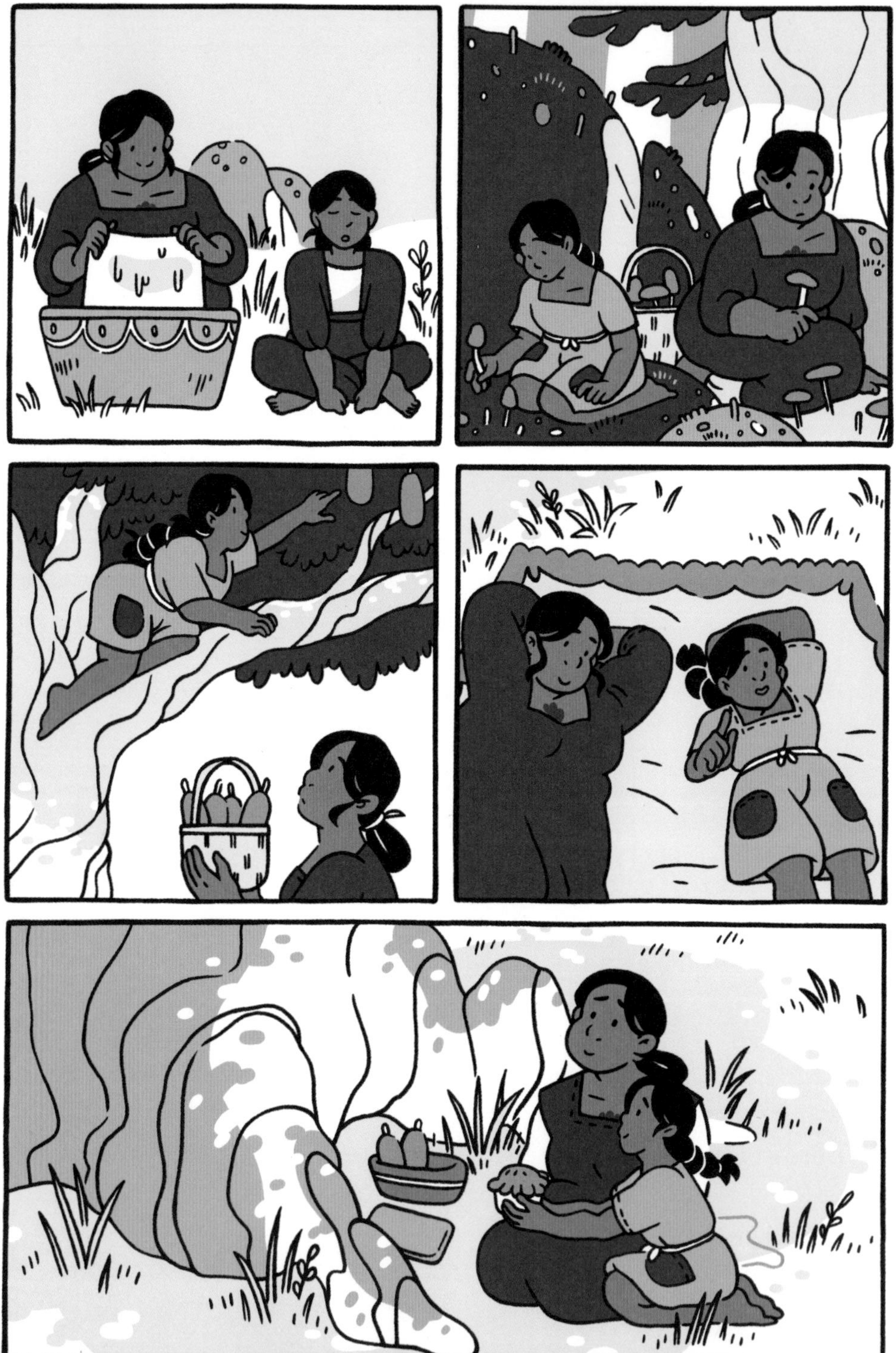

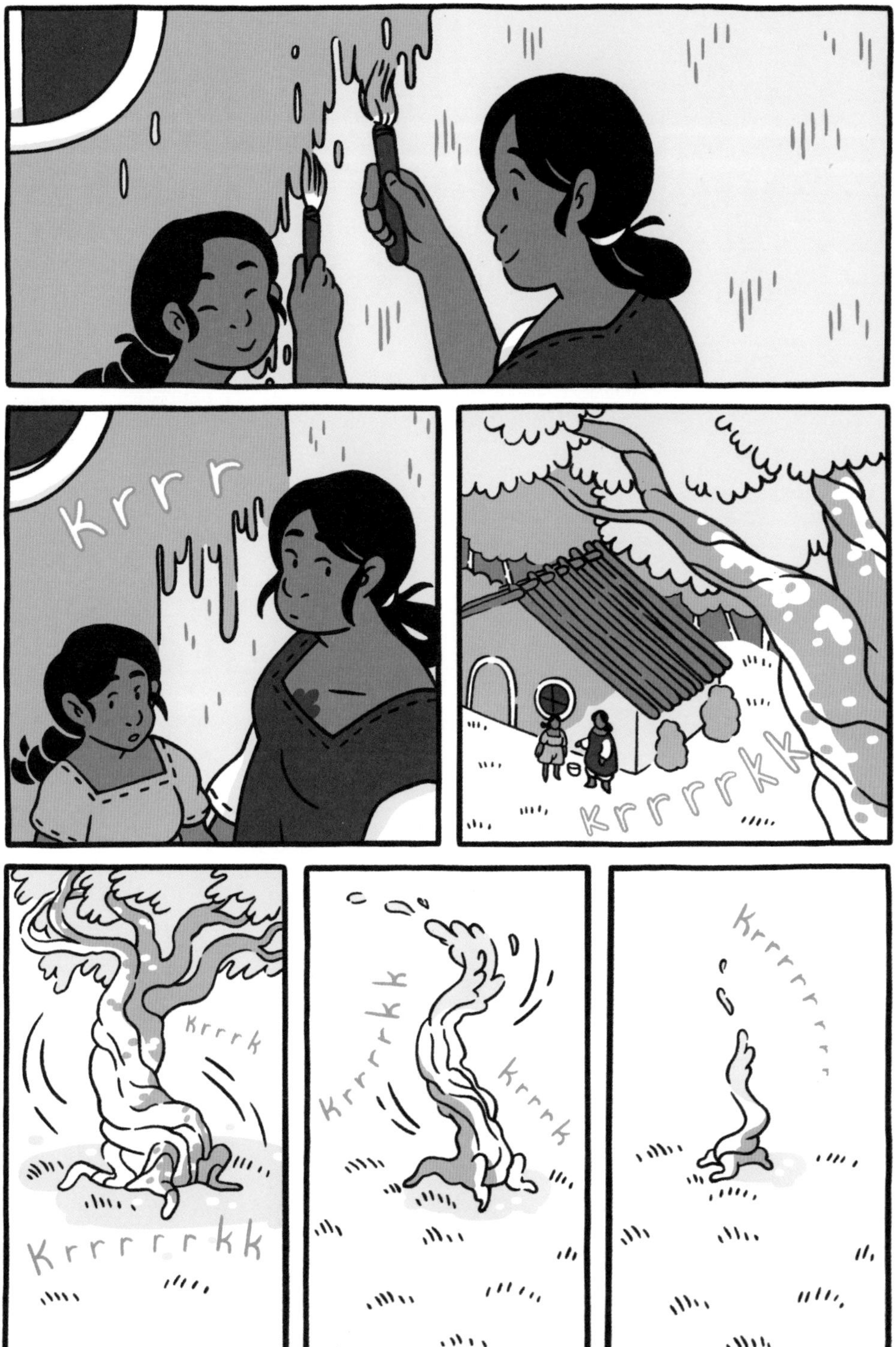
Krrr
Krrrrkk
Krrrk
Krrrrrkk
Krrrrkk
Krrrk
Krrrrrrrrr

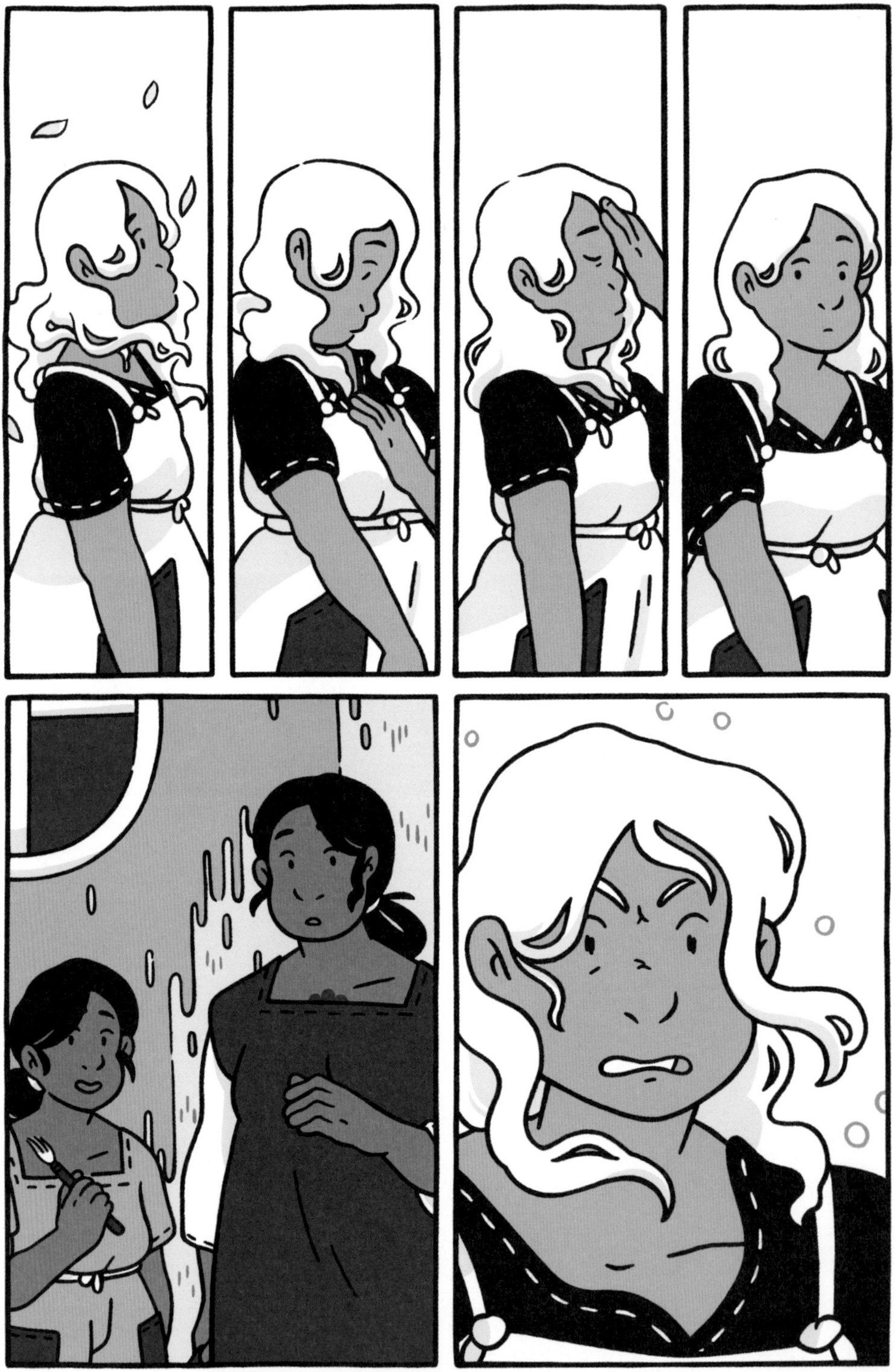

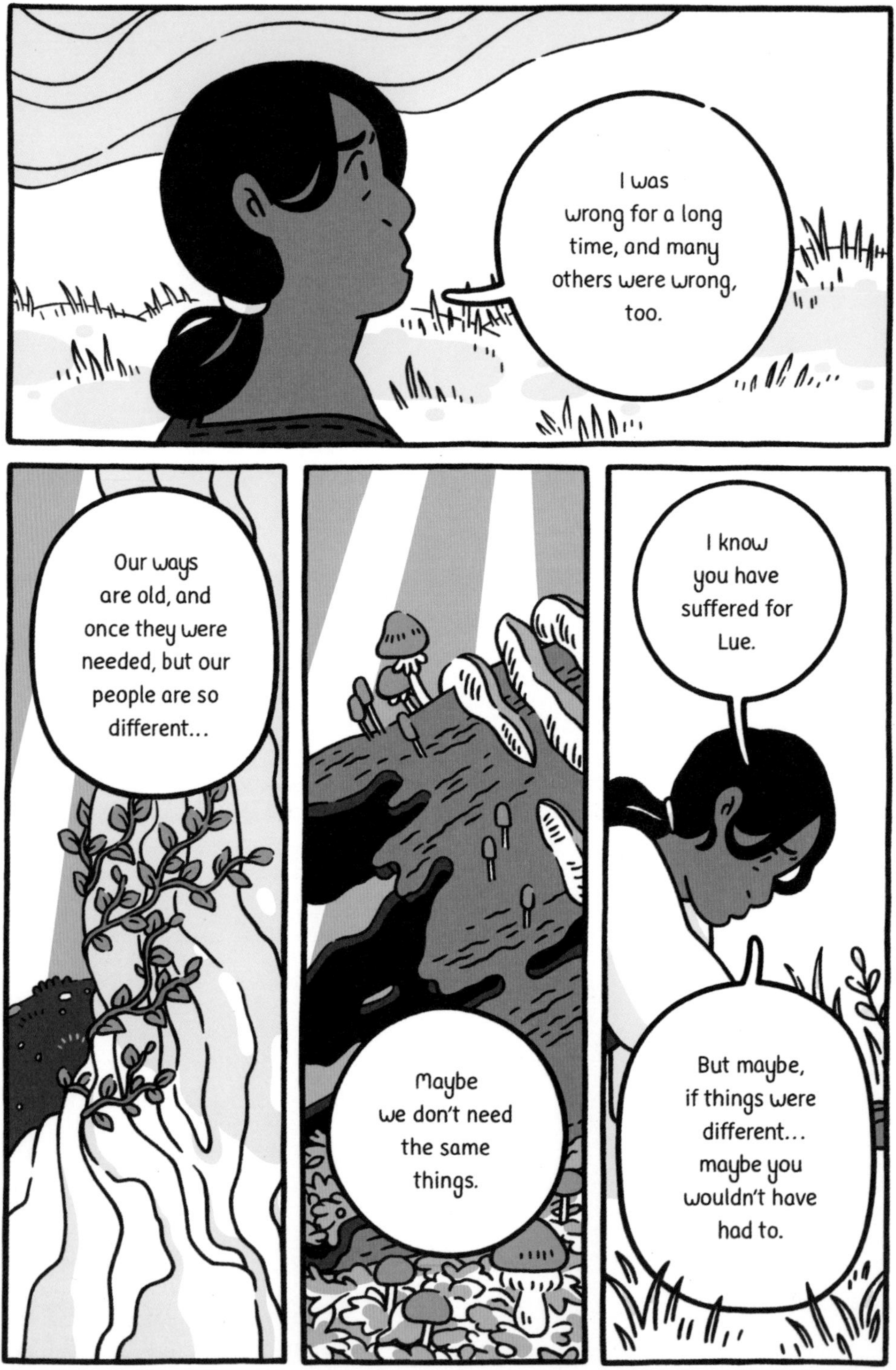
I was wrong for a long time, and many others were wrong, too.
Our ways are old, and once they were needed, but our people are so different...
Maybe we don't need the same things.
I know you have suffered for Lue.
But maybe, if things were different... maybe you wouldn't have had to.

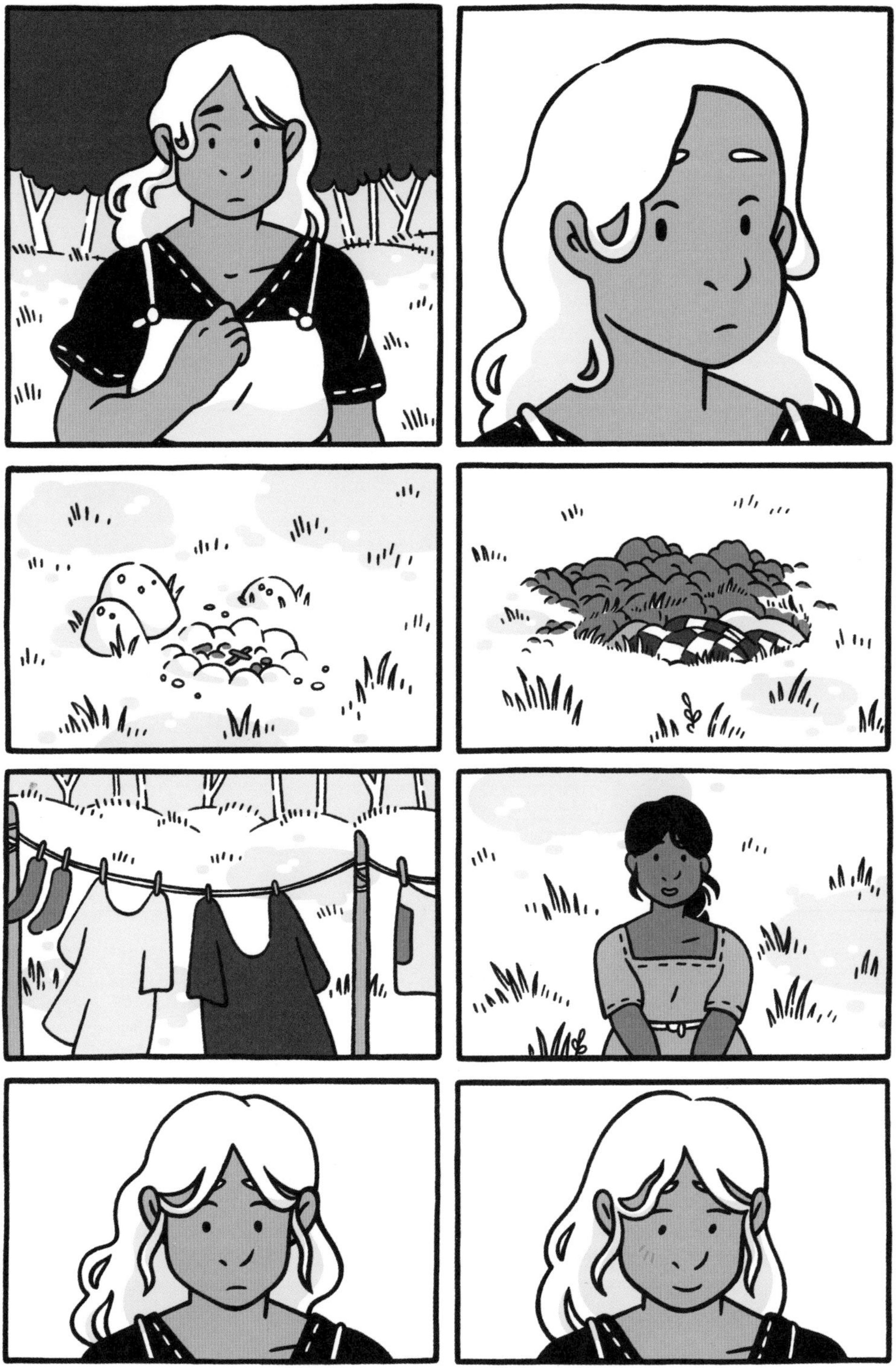

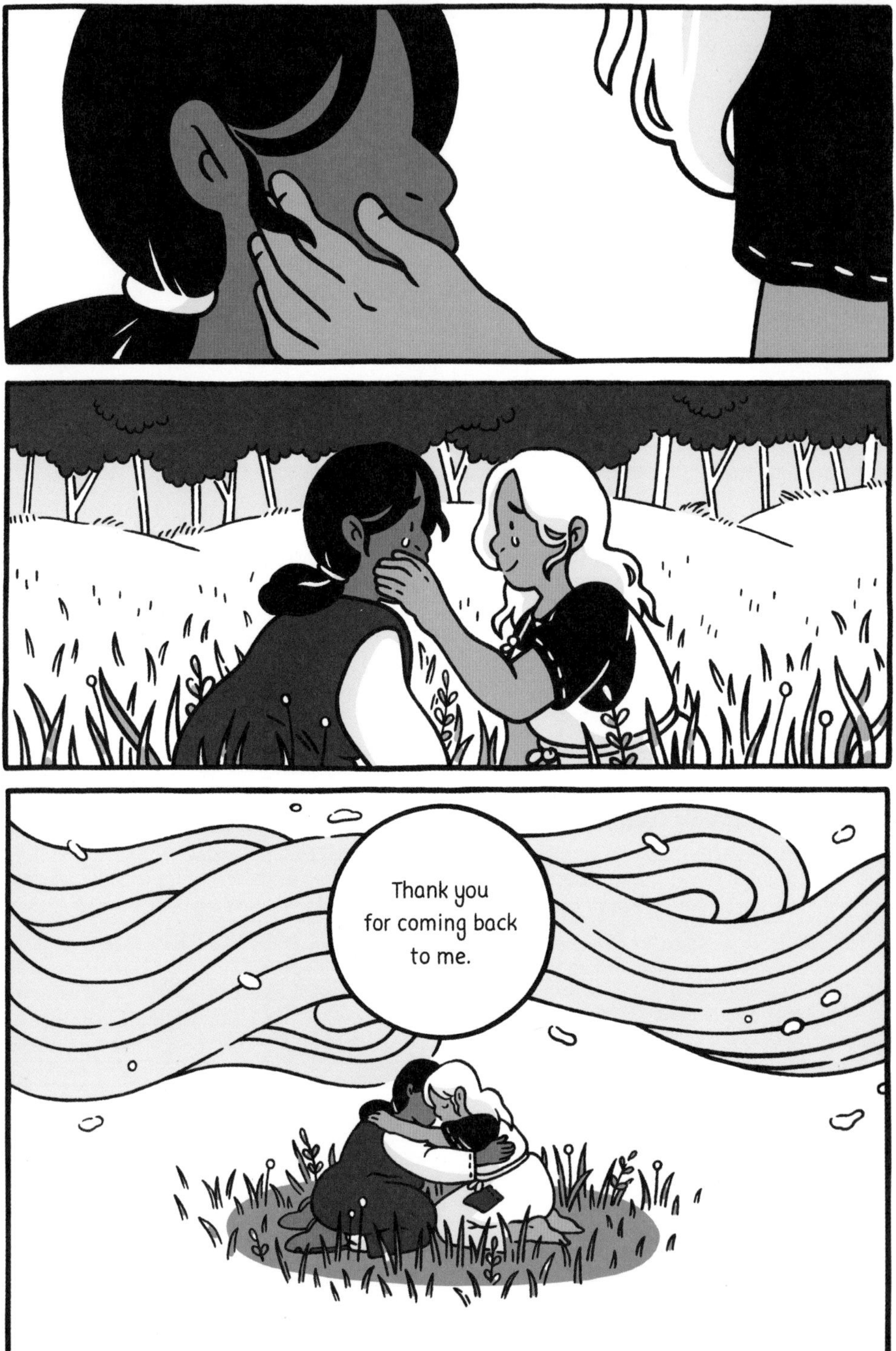
Thank you for coming back to me.

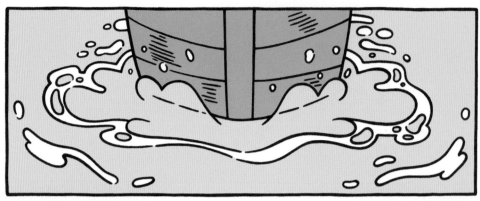

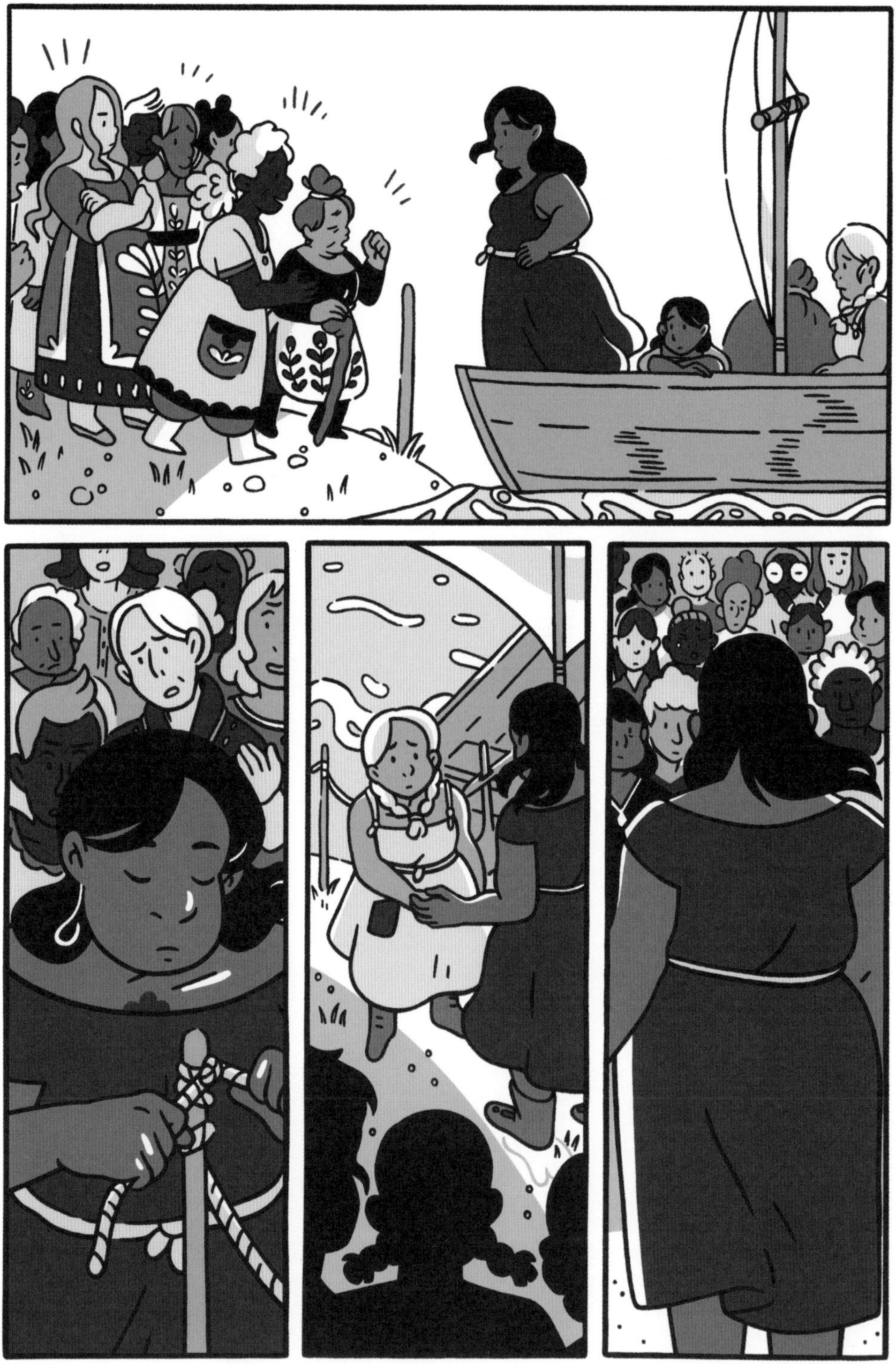

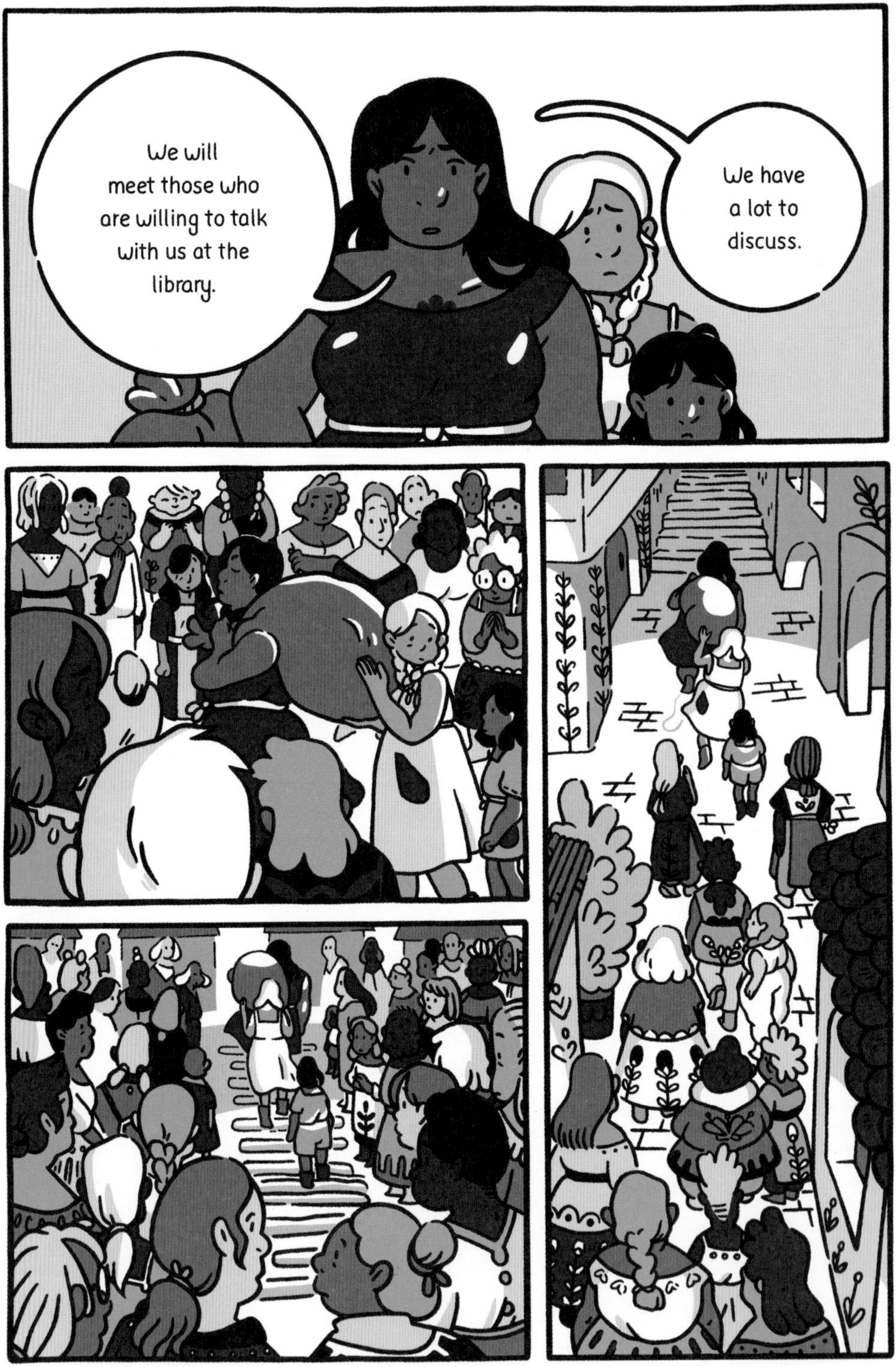
We will meet those who are willing to talk with us at the library.
We have a lot to discuss.

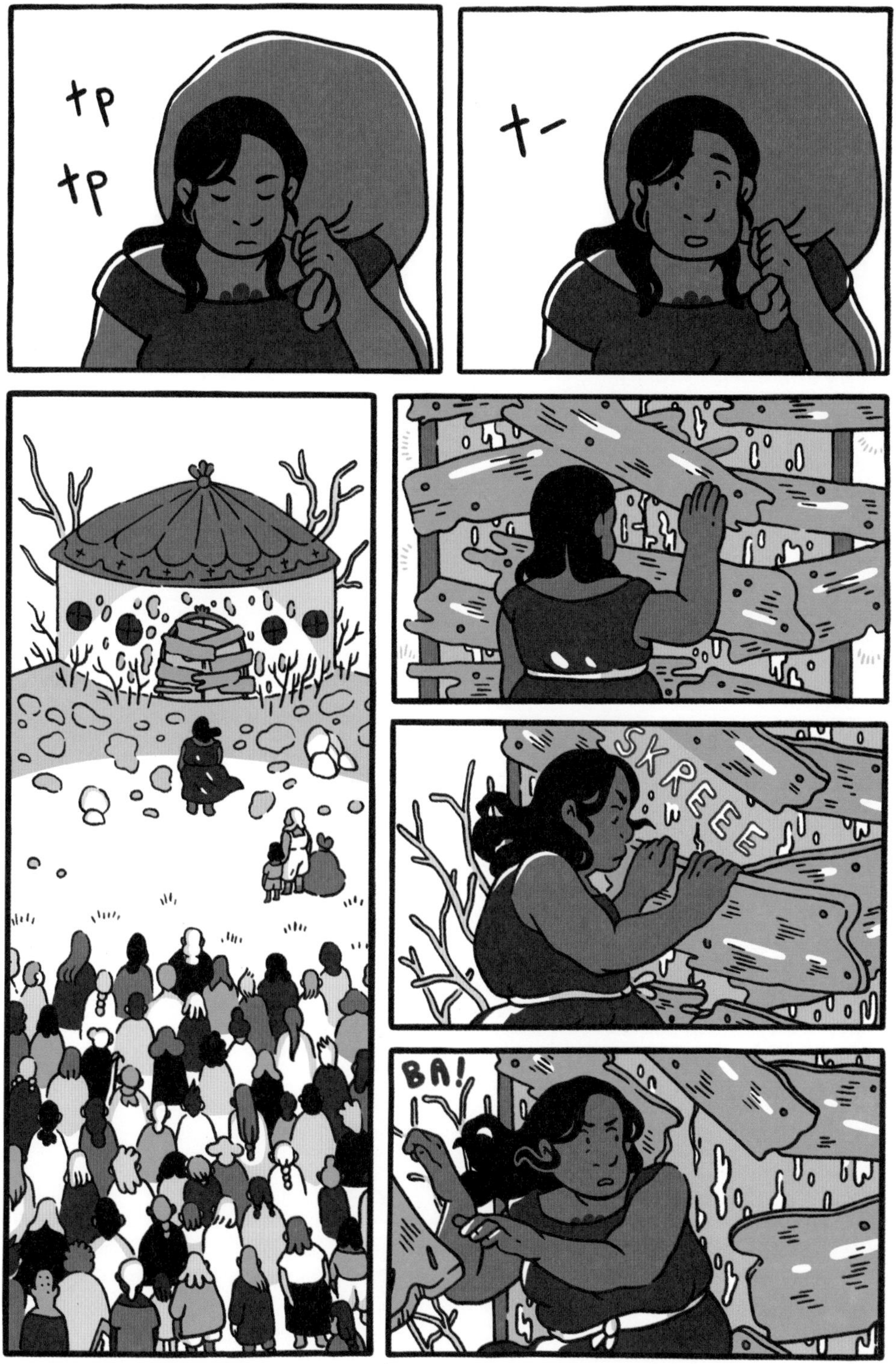
tp
tp
t-
SKREEE
BA!

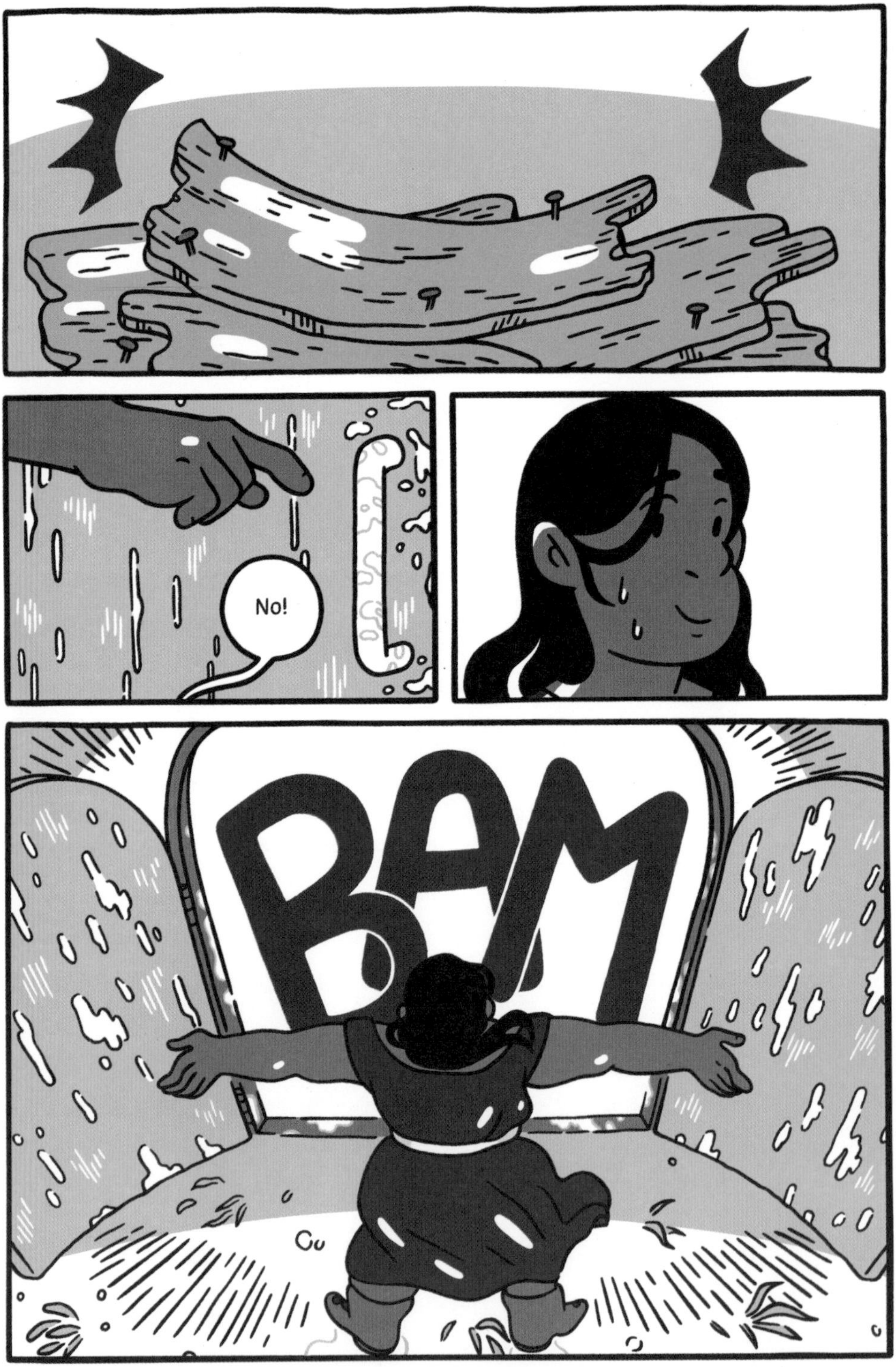
No!
BAM

The mist has stopped!

I have done as I promised.

HURRAAH!

Look! The books, the paintings!

They're all—

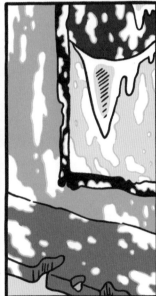

Our history, all our stories...

How will we teach our children?

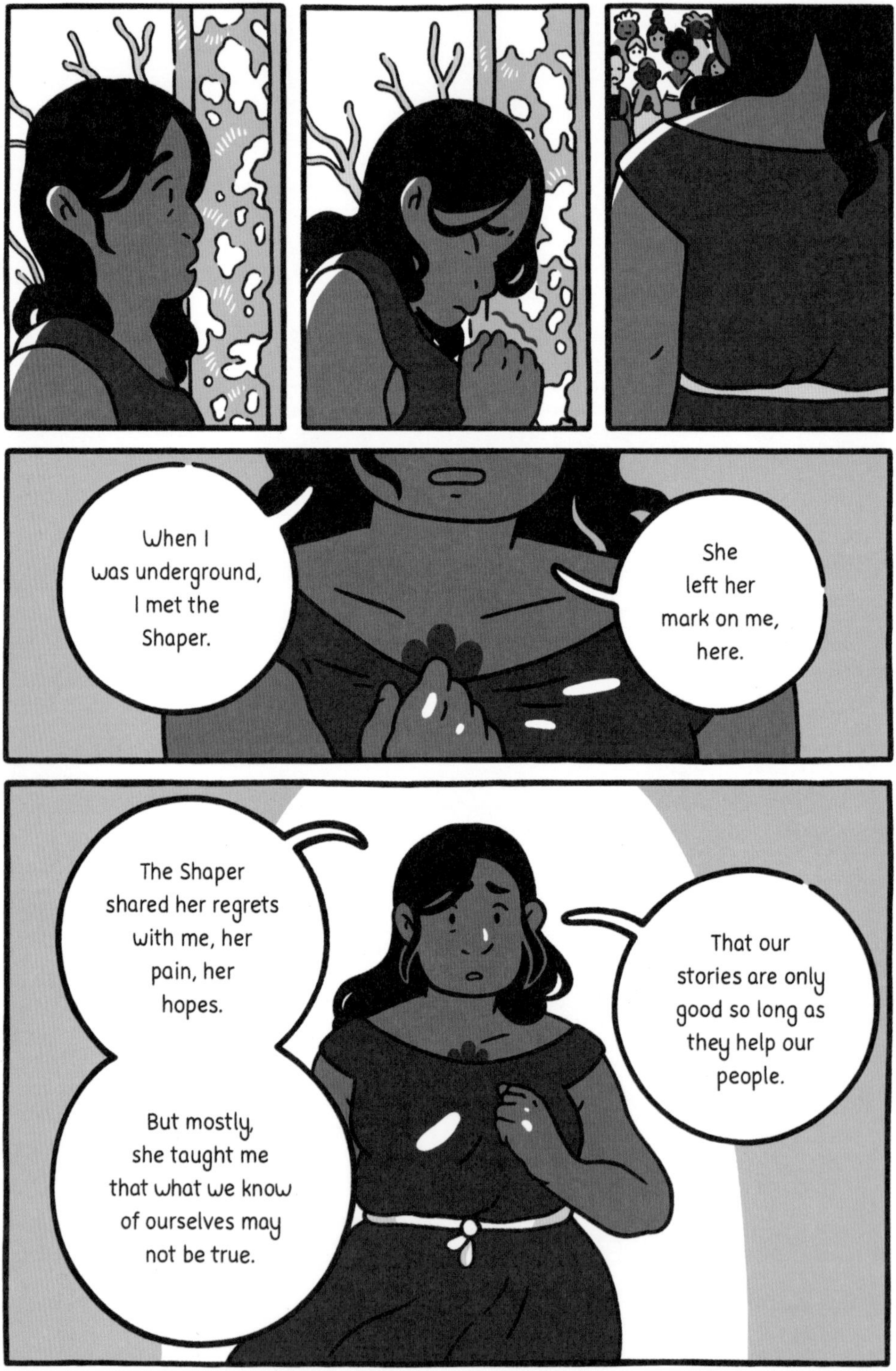
When I was underground, I met the Shaper.
She left her mark on me, here.
The Shaper shared her regrets with me, her pain, her hopes.
But mostly, she taught me that what we know of ourselves may not be true.
That our stories are only good so long as they help our people.

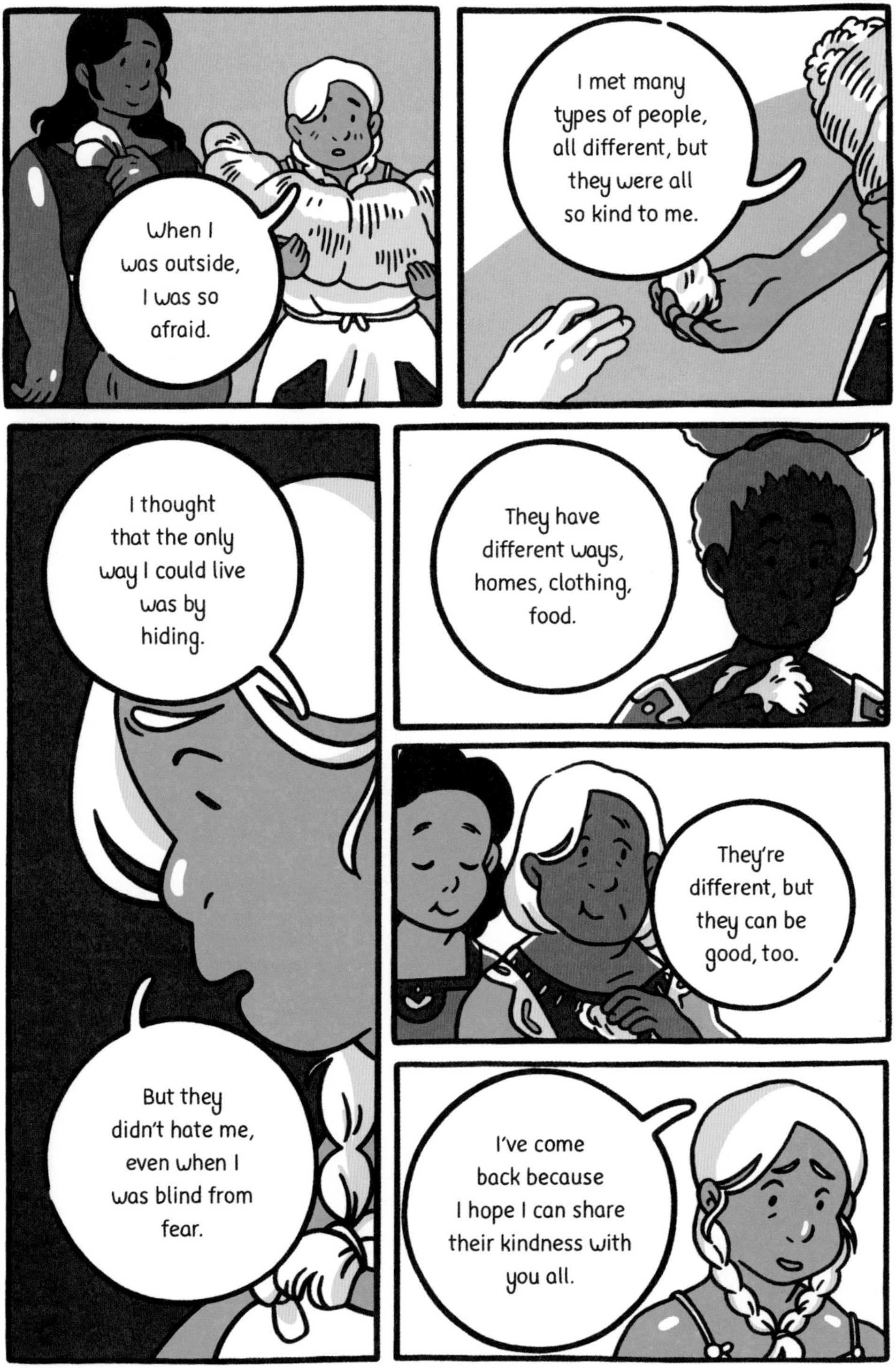
When I was outside, I was so afraid.
I met many types of people, all different, but they were all so kind to me.
I thought that the only way I could live was by hiding.
But they didn't hate me, even when I was blind from fear.
They have different ways, homes, clothing, food.
They're different, but they can be good, too.
I've come back because I hope I can share their kindness with you all.

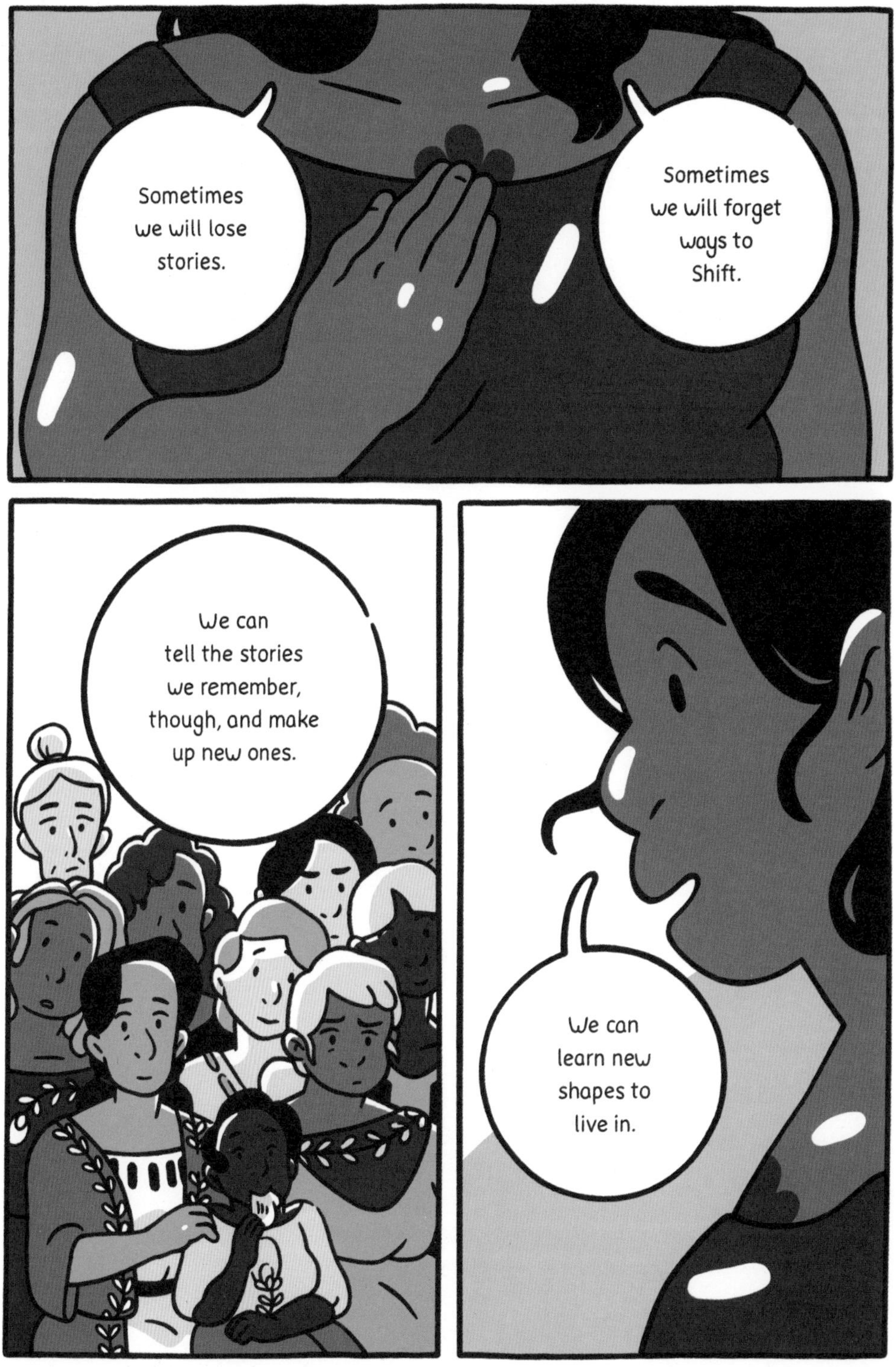
Sometimes we will lose stories.
Sometimes we will forget ways to Shift.
We can tell the stories we remember, though, and make up new ones.
We can learn new shapes to live in.

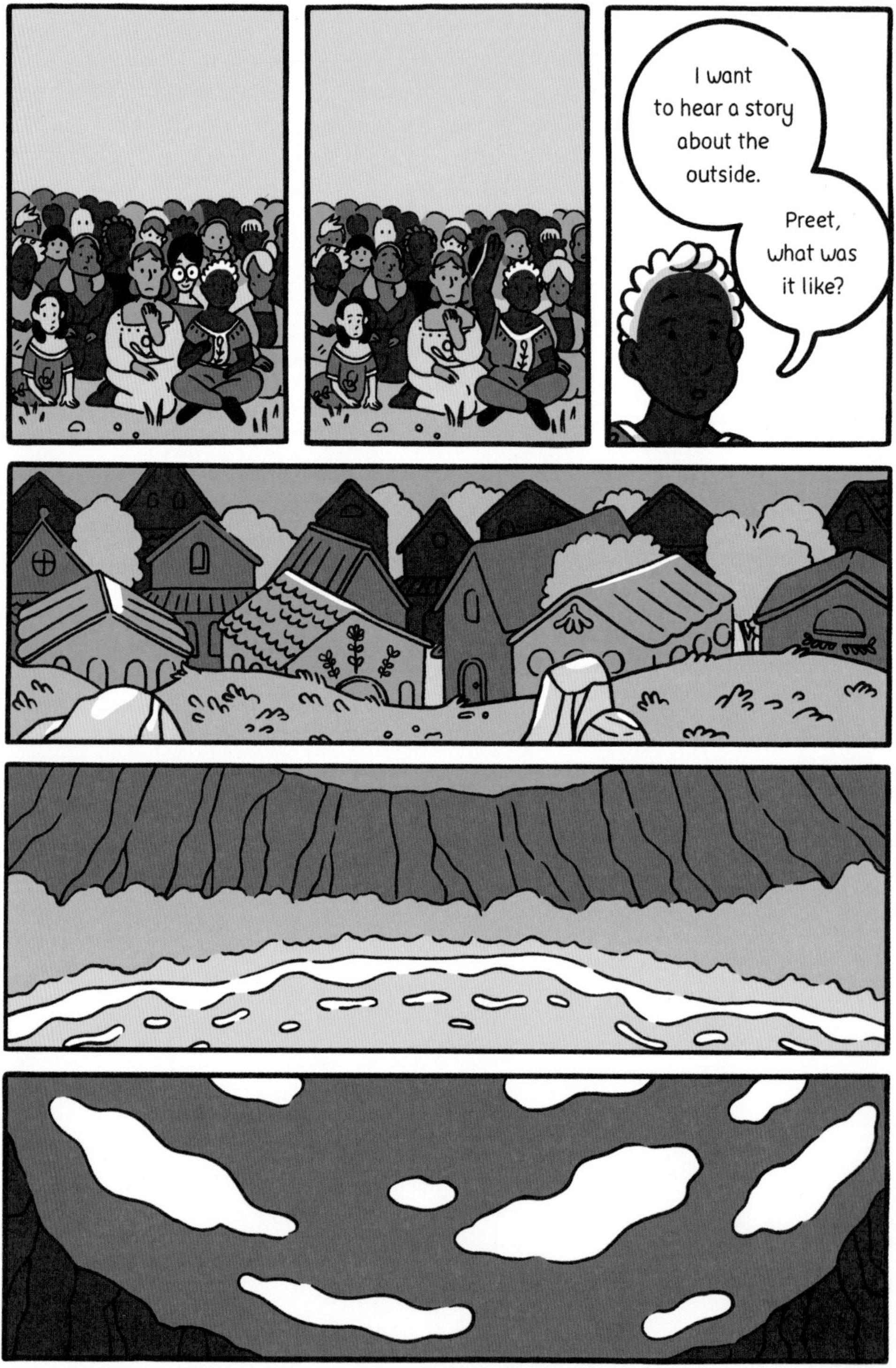
I want to hear a story about the outside.
Preet, what was it like?

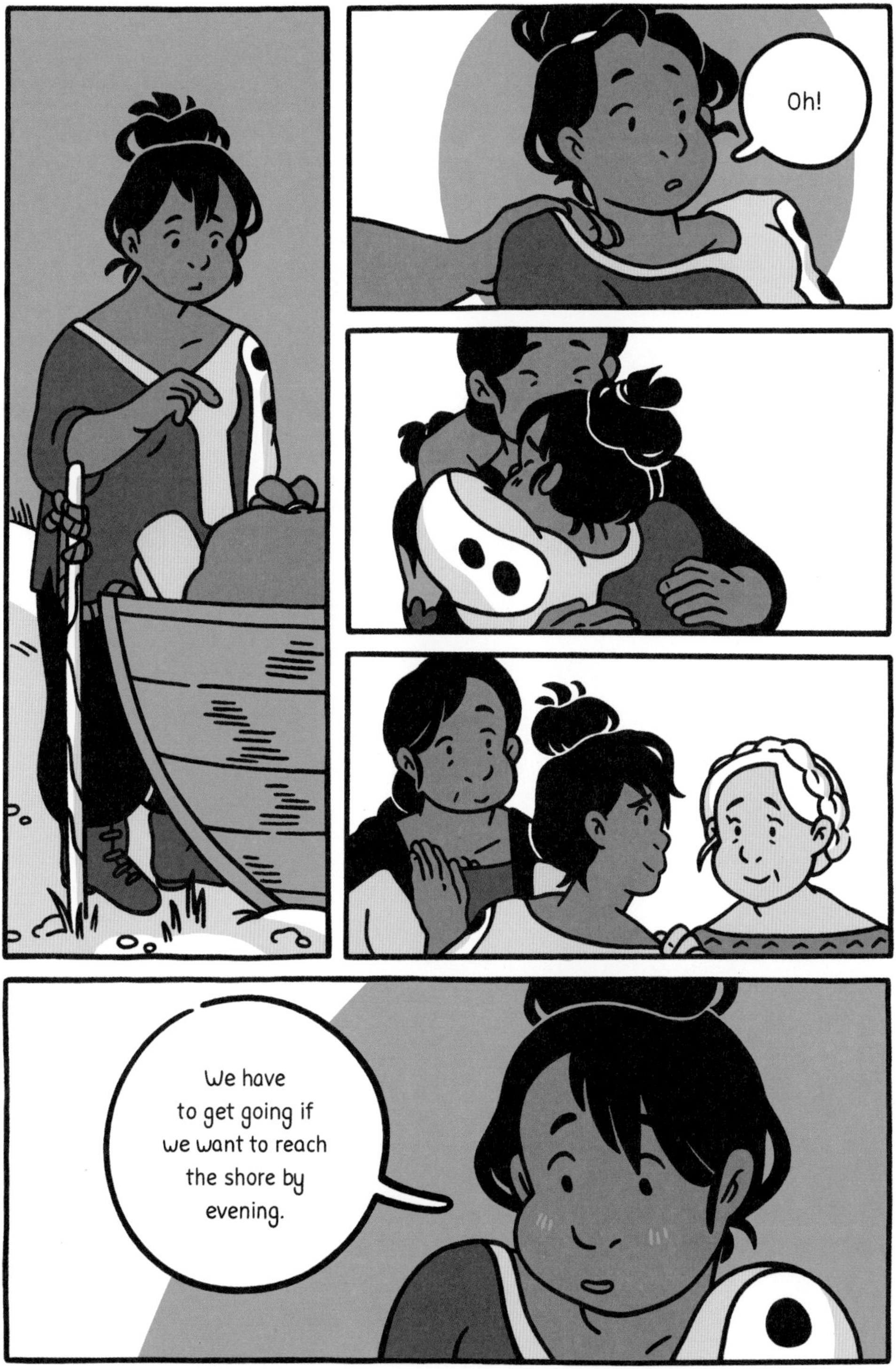
Oh!
We have to get going if we want to reach the shore by evening.

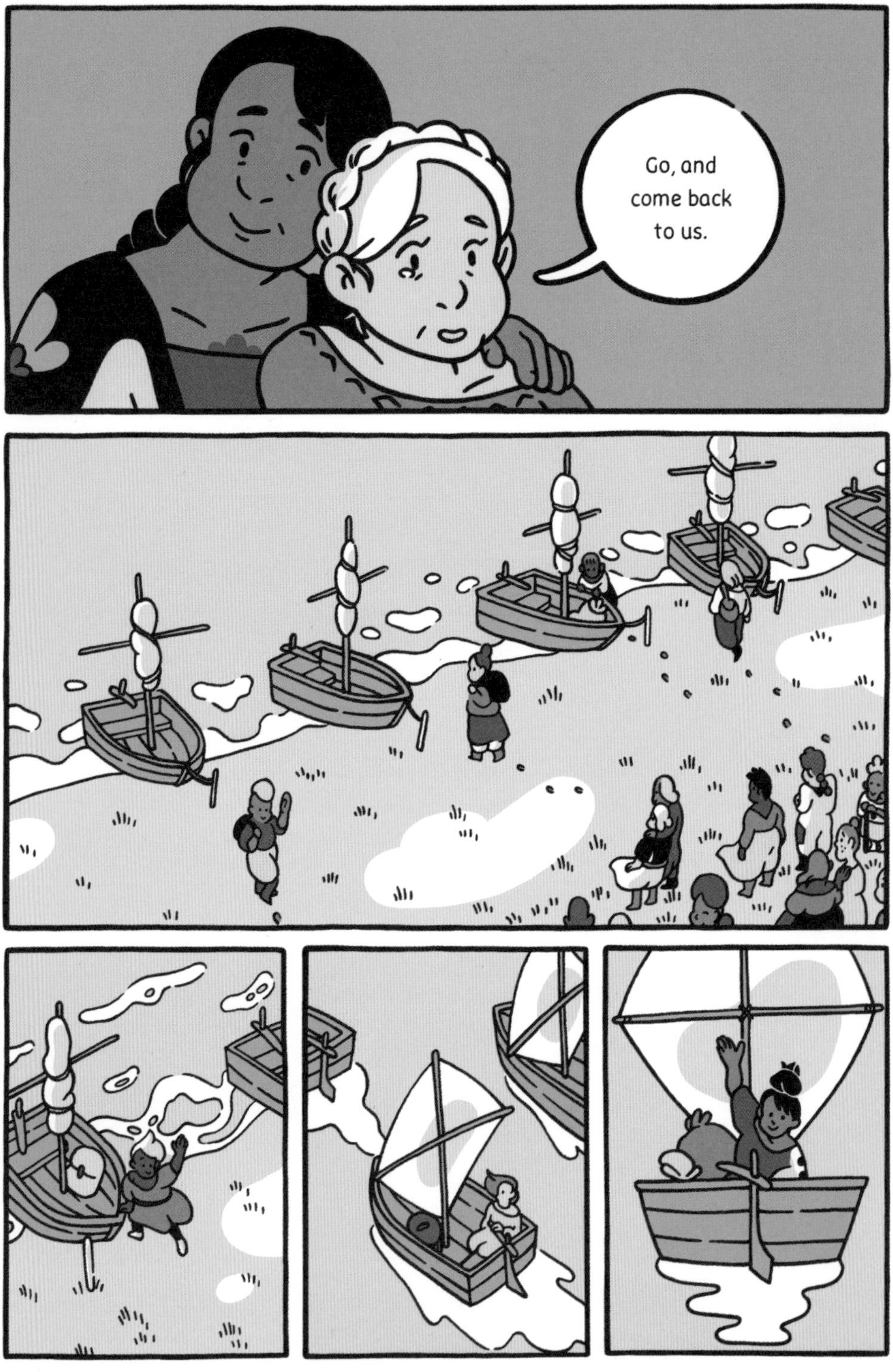
Go, and come back to us.

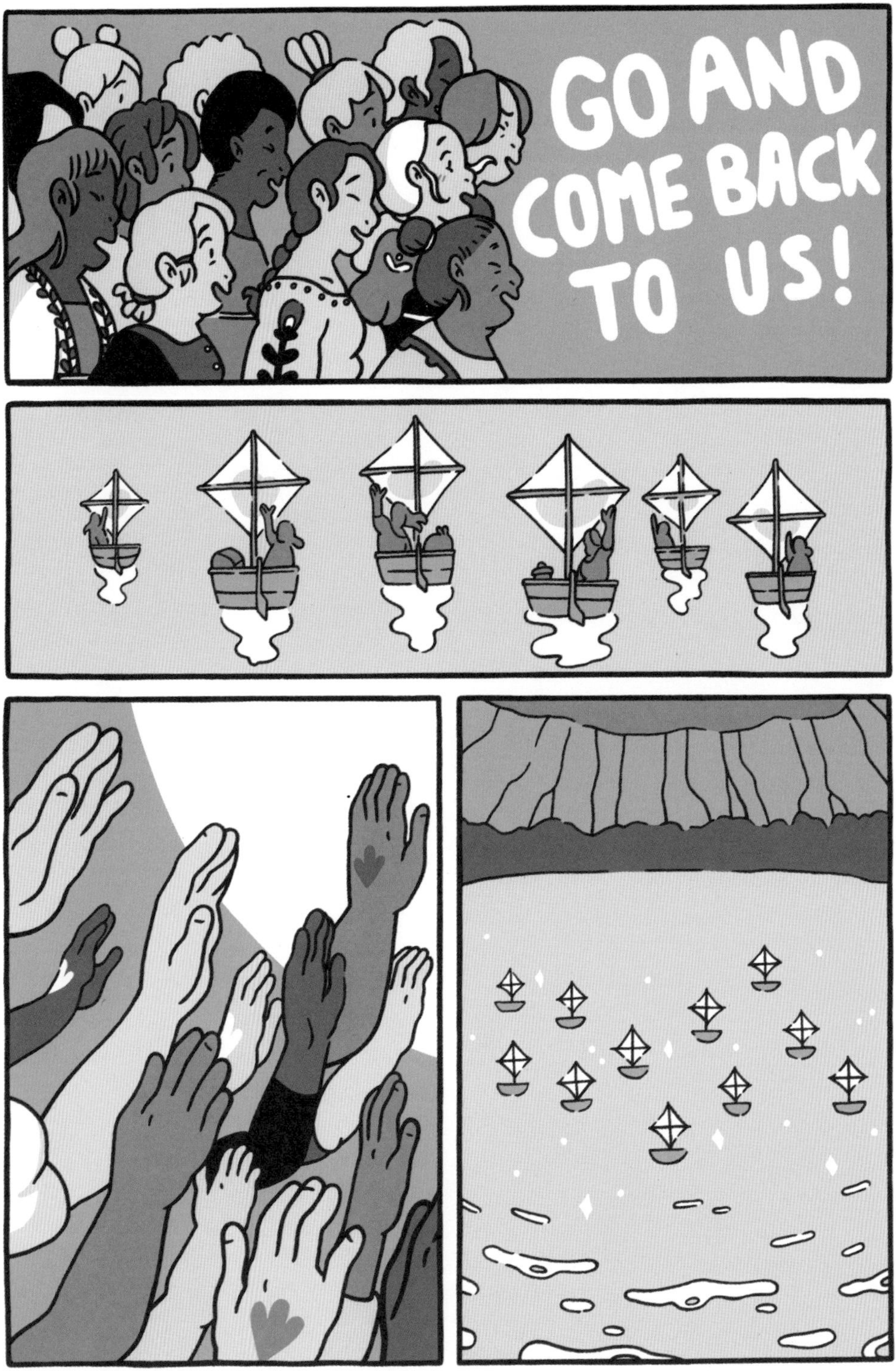
GO AND COME BACK TO US!

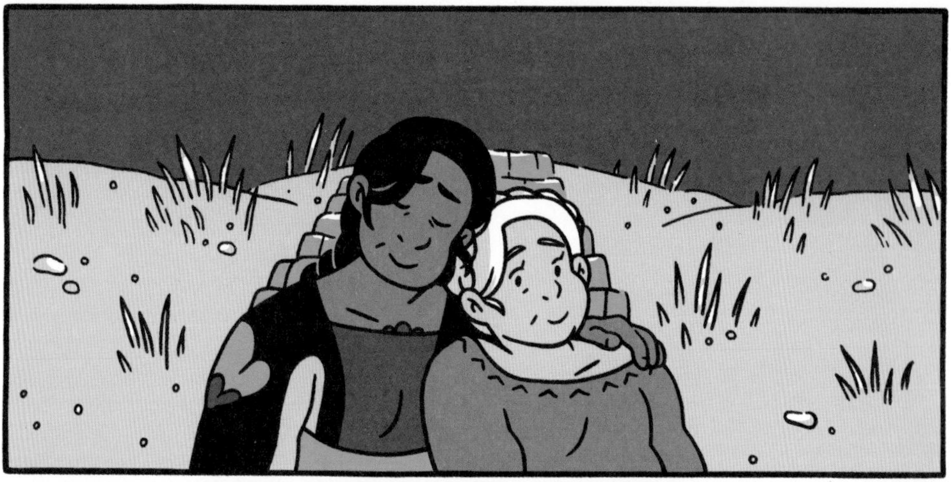

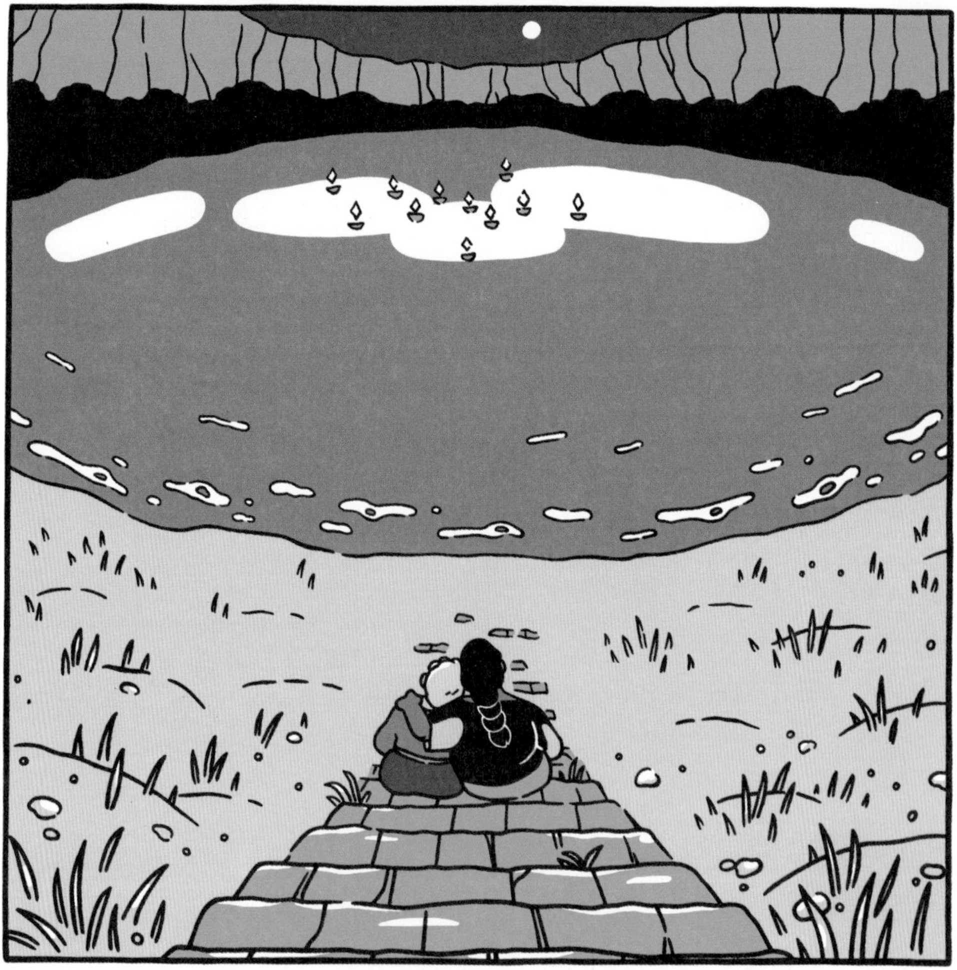